Here is a novel of time travel that goes beyond *BACK TO THE FUTURE* and *PEGGY SUE GOT MARRIED*. A strange and gripping odyssey of adventure, romance, and fascinating speculation on the meaning and nature of time, *REPLAY* may be the most unique and compelling novel you ever read . . .

REPLAY

"*REPLAY* WILL MAKE YOU WISH YOU TRULY BELIEVED THAT TIME TRAVEL IS POSSIBLE."
—*Rave Reviews*

"INTRIGUING . . . Ken Grimwood has taken a well-worn premise and breathed new life into it with superb writing, unexpected twists and careful attention to detail."
—*Atlanta Journal Constitution*

"A TRIP DOWN NOSTALGIA ROAD . . . VERY ENTERTAINING." —*Richmond Times Dispatch*

"ORIGINAL ENOUGH TO ALLOW FOR SOME INTRIGUING SPECULATION." —*Booklist*

"ENTERTAINING . . . This strange tale has a surprisingly poignant message . . . an intriguing combination of nostalgia, ironic humor and an endless list of what might have beens."
—*St. Louis Post-Dispatch*

"AN INTRIGUING FANTASY FOR ALL OF US!"
—*Best Sellers*

"GRIMWOOD HAS TRANSCENDED GENRE."
—*Publishers Weekly*

REPLAY

KEN GRIMWOOD

BERKLEY BOOKS, NEW YORK

Quotes from the *Bhagavad Gita: The Song of God* used with
permission of the Vedanta Society of Southern California, Swami
Prabhavanda and Christopher Isherwood; Vedanta Press.

This Berkley book contains the complete
text of the original hardcover edition.
It has been completely reset in a typeface
designed for easy reading and was printed
from new film.

REPLAY

A Berkley Book / published by arrangement with
Arbor House Publishing Company

PRINTING HISTORY
Arbor House edition / January 1987
Berkley edition / January 1988

ISBN: 0-425-10640-3

A BERKLEY BOOK® TM 757,375
Berkley Books are published by The Berkley Publishing Group,
200 Madison Avenue, New York, NY 10016.
The name "BERKLEY" and the "B" logo
are trademarks belonging to Berkley Publishing Corporation.

PRINTED IN THE UNITED STATES OF AMERICA

10 9 8 7 6 5 4 3 2 1

For my mother and father

≡ 1 ≡

JEFF WINSTON WAS on the phone with his wife when he died.

"We need—" she'd said, and he never heard her say just what it was they needed, because something heavy seemed to slam against his chest, crushing the breath out of him. The phone fell from his hand and cracked the glass paperweight on his desk.

Just the week before, she'd said something similar, had said, "Do you know what we need, Jeff?" and there'd been a pause—not infinite, not final, like this mortal pause, but a palpable interim nonetheless. He'd been sitting at the kitchen table, in what Linda liked to call the "breakfast nook," although it wasn't really a separate space at all, just a little formica table with two chairs placed awkwardly between the left side of the refrigerator and the front of the clothes drier. Linda had been chopping onions at the counter when she said it, and maybe the tears at the corner of her eyes were what had set him thinking, had lent her question more import than she'd intended.

"Do you know what we need, Jeff?"

And he was supposed to say, "What's that, hon?" was supposed to say it distractedly and without interest as he read Hugh Sidey's column about the presidency in *Time*. But Jeff wasn't distracted; he didn't give a damn about Sidey's ramblings. He was in fact more focused and aware than he had been in a long, long time. So he didn't say anything at all for several moments; he just stared at the false tears in Linda's eyes and thought about the things they needed, he and she.

They needed to get away, for starters, needed to get on a plane going someplace warm and lush—Jamaica, perhaps, or Barbados. They hadn't had a real vacation since that long-planned but somehow disappointing tour of Europe five years ago. Jeff didn't count their annual Florida trips to see his parents in Orlando and Linda's family in Boca Raton; those were visits to an ever-receding past, nothing more. No, what they needed was a week, a month, on some decadently foreign island: making love on endless empty beaches, and at night the sound of reggae music in the air like the smell of hot red flowers.

A decent house would be nice, too, maybe one of those stately old homes on Upper Mountain Road in Montclair that they'd driven past so many wistful Sundays. Or a place in White Plains, a twelve-room Tudor on Ridgeway Avenue near the golf courses. Not that he'd want to take up golf; it just seemed that all those lazy expanses of green, with names like Maple Moor and Westchester Hills, would make for more pleasant surroundings than did the on ramps to the Brooklyn-Queens Expressway and the glide path into LaGuardia.

They also needed a child, though Linda probably felt that lack more urgently than he. Jeff always pictured their never-born child as being eight years old, having skipped all the demands of infancy and not yet having reached the torments of puberty. A good kid, not overly cute or precocious. Boy, girl, it didn't matter; just a child, her child and his, who'd ask funny questions and sit too close to the TV set and show the spark of his or her own developing individuality.

There'd be no child, though; they'd known that was impossible for years, since Linda had gone through the ectopic pregnancy in 1975. And there wouldn't be any house in Montclair or White Plains, either; Jeff's position as news director of New York's WFYI all-news radio sounded more prestigious, more lucrative, than it actually was. Maybe he'd still make the jump to television; but at forty-three, that was growing increasingly unlikely.

We need, we need . . . to talk, he thought. To look each other straight in the eye and just say: It didn't work. None of it, not the romance or the passion or the glorious plans. It all went flat, and there's nobody to blame. That's simply the way it happened.

But of course they'd never do that. That was the main part of the failure, the fact that they seldom spoke of deeper needs, never broached the tearing sense of incompletion that stood always between them.

Linda wiped a meaningless, onion-induced tear away with the back of her hand. "Did you hear me, Jeff?"

"Yes. I heard you."

"What we need," she said, looking in his direction but not quite at him, "is a new shower curtain."

In all likelihood, that was the level of need she'd been about to express over the phone before he began to die. "—a dozen eggs," her sentence probably would have ended, or "—a box of coffee filters."

But why was he thinking all this? he wondered. He was dying, for Christ's sake; shouldn't his final thoughts be of something deeper, more philosophical? Or maybe a fast-speed replay of the highlights of his life, forty-three years on Betascan. That was what people went through when they drowned, wasn't it?

This *felt* like drowning, he thought as the expanded seconds passed: the awful pressure, the hopeless struggle for breath, the sticky wetness that soaked his body as salt sweat streamed down his forehead and stung his eyes.

Drowning. Dying. No, shit, no, that was an unreal word, applicable to flowers or pets or other people. Old people, sick people. Unlucky people.

His face dropped to the desk, right cheek pressing flat against the file folder he'd been about to study when Linda called. The crack in the paperweight was cavernous before his one open eye: a split in the world itself, a jagged mirror of the ripping agony inside him. Through the broken glass he could see the glowing red numerals on the digital clock atop his bookshelf:

1:06 PM OCT 18 88

And then there was nothing more to avoid thinking about, because the process of thought had ceased.

Jeff couldn't breathe.

Of course he couldn't breathe; he was dead.

But if he was dead, why was he aware of not being able to breathe? Or of anything, for that matter?

He turned his head away from the bunched-up blanket and breathed. Stale, damp air, full of the smell of his own perspiration.

So he hadn't died. Somehow, the realization didn't thrill him, just as his earlier assumption of death had failed to strike him with dread.

Maybe he had secretly welcomed the end of his life. Now it would merely continue as before: the dissatisfaction, the grinding loss of ambition and hope that had either caused or been caused by the failure of his marriage, he couldn't remember which anymore.

He shoved the blanket away from his face and kicked at the rumpled sheets. There was music playing somewhere in the darkened room, barely audible. An oldie: "Da Doo Ron Ron," by one of those Phil Spector girl groups.

Jeff groped for a lamp switch, thoroughly disoriented. He was either in a hospital bed recovering from what had happened in the office, or at home waking from a dream that was worse than usual. His hand found the bedside lamp, turned it on. He was in a small, messy room, clothes and books strewn on the floor and piled haphazardly on two adjacent desks and chairs. Neither a hospital nor his and Linda's bedroom, but familiar, somehow.

A naked, smiling woman stared back at him from a large photograph taped to one wall. A *Playboy* centerfold, a vintage one. The buxom brunette lay demurely on her stomach, atop an air mattress at the afterdeck of a boat, her red-and-white polka-dotted bikini tied to the railing. With her jaunty round sailor's cap, her carefully coiffed and sprayed dark hair, she bore a distinct resemblance to the young Jackie Kennedy.

The other walls, he saw, were decorated in a similarly dated, juvenile style: bullfight posters, a big blowup of a red Jaguar XK-E, an old Dave Brubeck album cover. Above one desk was a red, white, and blue banner that read, in letters made of stars and stripes, "FUCK COMMUNISM." Jeff grinned when he saw that; he'd ordered one just like it from Paul Krassner's then-shocking little rag, *The Realist*, when he was in college, when—

He sat upright abruptly, pulse sounding in his ears.

That old gooseneck lamp on the desk nearest the door had always come loose from its base whenever he moved it, he recalled. And the rug next to Martin's bed had a big blood-red stain—yes, right there—from the time Jeff had sneaked Judy Gordon upstairs and she'd started dancing around the room to the Drifters and knocked over a bottle of Chianti.

The vague confusion Jeff had felt on waking gave way to stark bewilderment. He threw off the covers, got out of bed, and walked shakily to one of the desks. His desk. He scanned the books stacked there: *Patterns of Culture, Growing Up in Samoa, Statistical Populations.* Sociology 101. Dr. . . . what? Danforth, Sanborn? In a big, musty old hall somewhere on the far side of campus, 8:00 A.M., always had breakfast after class. He picked up the Benedict book, leafed through it; several portions were heavily underlined, with margin notes in his own handwriting.

". . . WQXI pick hit of the week, from the Crystals! Now, this next one goes out to Bobby in Marietta, from Carol and Paula. Those pretty girls just want to let Bobby know, right along with the Chiffons, they think 'He's Soooo Fine' . . ."

Jeff turned off the radio and wiped a film of sweat from his forehead. He noticed uncomfortably that he had a full erection. How long had it been since he'd gotten that hard without even thinking about sex?

All right, it was time to figure this thing out. Somebody

had to be pulling an extremely elaborate joke on him, but he didn't know anyone who played practical jokes. Even if he had, how could anyone have gone to this amount of trouble? Those books with his own notes in them had been thrown away years ago, and no one could have recreated them that precisely.

There was a copy of *Newsweek* on his desk, with a cover story about the resignation of West German Chancellor Konrad Adenauer. The issue was dated May 6, 1963. Jeff stared fixedly at the numbers, hoping some rational explanation for all this would come to mind.

None did.

The door of the room swung open, and the inner knob banged against a bookcase. Just as it always had.

"Hey, what the hell are you still doing here? It's a quarter to eleven. I thought you had an American Lit test at ten."

Martin stood in the doorway, a Coke in one hand and a load of textbooks in the other. Martin Bailey, Jeff's freshman-year roommate; his closest friend through college and for several years thereafter.

Martin had committed suicide in 1981, right after his divorce and subsequent bankruptcy.

"So what're you gonna do," Martin asked, "take an F?"

Jeff looked at his long-dead friend in stunned silence: the thick black hair that had not yet begun to recede, the unlined face, the bright, adolescent eyes that had seen no pain, to speak of.

"Hey, what's the matter? You O.K., Jeff?"

"I'm . . . not feeling very well."

Martin laughed and tossed the books on his bed. "Tell me about it! Now I know why my dad warned me about mixing Scotch and bourbon. Hey, that was some honey you hit on at Manuel's last night; Judy would've killed you if she'd been there. What's her name?"

"Ahh . . ."

"Come on, you weren't that drunk. You gonna call her?"

Jeff turned away in mounting panic. There were a thousand things he wanted to say to Martin, but none of them would have made any more sense than this insane situation itself.

"What's wrong, man? You look really fucked up."

"I, uh, I need to get outside. I need some air."

Martin gave him a puzzled frown. "Yeah, I guess you do."

Jeff grabbed a pair of chinos that had been thrown carelessly on the chair at his desk, then opened the closet next to his bed and found a Madras shirt and a corduroy jacket.

"Go by the infirmary," Martin said. "Tell 'em you've got the flu. Maybe Garrett'll let you make up that test."

"Yeah, sure." Jeff dressed hurriedly, slipped on a pair of cordovan loafers. He was on the verge of hyperventilating, and he forced himself to breathe slowly.

"Don't forget about *The Birds* tonight, O.K.? Paula and Judy are gonna meet us at Dooley's at seven; we'll grab a bite first."

"Right. See you." Jeff stepped into the hallway and closed the door behind him. He found the stairs and raced down three flights, shouting back a perfunctory "Yo!" as one of the young men he passed called out his name.

The lobby was as he'd remembered it: TV room on the right, empty now but always packed for sports events and space shots; a knot of girls giggling among themselves, waiting for their boyfriends at the base of the stairs they were forbidden to ascend; Coke machines across from the bulletin boards where students posted notices seeking or selling cars, books, apartments, rides to Macon or Savannah or Florida.

Outside, the dogwood trees were in full bloom, suffusing the campus with a pink-and-white glow that seemed to reflect off the clean white marble of the stately Greco-Roman buildings. It was Emory, no question about that: the South's most studied effort to create a classically Ivy League-style university, one that the region could call its own. The planned timelessness of the architecture was disorienting; as he jogged through the quadrangle, past the library and the law building, Jeff realized it could as easily

be 1988 as 1963. There were no certain clues, not even in
the clothing and short haircuts of the students who ambled
and lounged about the grassy expanses. The youthful fashions of the eighties, aside from the postapocalyptic punk
look, were virtually indistinguishable from those of his
own early college days.

God, the times he had spent on this campus, the dreams
engendered here that had never been fulfilled . . . There
was that little bridge that led toward the church school;
how many times had he lingered there with Judy Gordon?
And over there, down by the psych building, that was
where he'd met Gail Benson for lunch almost every day
during his junior year: his first, and last, truly close pla-
tonic friendship with a woman. Why hadn't he learned
more from knowing Gail? How had he drifted so far, in so
many different ways, from the plans and aspirations born
in the reassuring calm of these green lawns, these noble
structures?

Jeff had run over a mile by the time he came to the main
campus entrance, and he expected to be out of breath, but
wasn't. He stood on the low rise below Glenn Memorial
Church, looking down at North Decatur Road and Emory
Village, the little business district that served the campus.

The row of clothing shops and bookstores looked more-
or-less familiar. One spot in particular, Horton's Drugs,
brought back a wave of memories: He could see in his
mind the magazine racks, the long white soda fountain, the
red-leather booths with individual stereo jukeboxes. He
could see Judy Gordon's fresh young face across a table in
one of those booths, could smell her clean blond hair.

He shook his head and concentrated on the scene before
him. Again, there was no way to tell for sure what year it
was; he hadn't been to Atlanta since an Associated Press
conference on Terrorism and the Media in 1983, and he
hadn't been back to the Emory campus since . . . Jesus,
probably a year or two after he'd graduated. He had no
way of knowing whether all those shops down there had
remained the same or had been replaced by high-rises,
maybe a mall.

The cars, that was one thing; now that he noticed, he

realized there wasn't a Nissan or Toyota in sight down there on the street. Nothing but older models, most of them big, gas-hungry, Detroit machines. And "older," he saw, didn't mean just early-sixties designs. There were plenty of monster-finned beasts cruising past that dated well back into the fifties, but of course there'd be as many six- and eight-year-old cars on the streets in 1963 as there were in 1988.

Still nothing conclusive, though; he was even beginning to wonder whether that brief encounter with Martin in the dorm room had been no more than an unusually realistic dream after all, one he'd woken up in the middle of. There was no questioning the fact that he was wide awake now, and in Atlanta. Maybe he'd gotten smashed trying to forget about the dreary mess his life had become, and had flown down here on some spur-of-the-moment midnight flight of nostalgia. The preponderance of old cars could easily be coincidence. Any moment now, somebody would drive past in one of those little Japanese boxes he'd grown so used to seeing everywhere.

There was a simple way to settle this once and for all. He loped down the hill toward the cab stand on Decatur Road and got into the first of the three blue-and-white taxis lined up there. The driver was young, maybe a grad student.

"Where to, fella?"

"Peachtree Plaza Hotel," Jeff told him.

"Say again?"

"The Peachtree Plaza, downtown."

"I don't think I know that one. You got an address?"

Christ, taxi drivers these days. Weren't they supposed to take some kind of test, memorize city maps and landmarks?

"You know where the Regency is, right? The Hyatt House?"

"Oh, yeah, yeah. That where you want to go?"

"Close enough."

"You got it, fella."

The driver headed south a few blocks and took a right on Ponce De Leon Avenue. Jeff reached for his hip pocket, suddenly aware that he might not have any money in these unfamiliar pants, but there was a worn brown wallet there, not his.

At least there was money inside it—two twenties, a five, and some ones—so he wouldn't have to worry about the cab fare. He'd reimburse whomever it belonged to when he returned the wallet, along with these old clothes he'd picked up from . . . where? Who?

He opened one of the small compartments of the wallet, looking for answers. He found an Emory University Student ID card in the name of Jeffrey L. Winston. A library card from Emory, also in his name. A receipt from a dry cleaner's in Decatur. A folded cocktail napkin with a girl's name, Cindy, and a phone number. A photograph of his parents standing outside the old house in Orlando, the one they'd lived in before his father had gotten so sick. A color snapshot of Judy Gordon laughing and throwing a snowball, her achingly young and jubilant face framed by a white fur collar upturned against the cold. And a Florida driver's license for Jeffrey Lamar Winston, with an expiration date of February 27, 1965.

Jeff sat alone at a table for two in the UFO-shaped Polaris bar atop the Hyatt Regency, watching the denuded Atlanta skyline rotate past him every forty-five minutes. The cab driver hadn't been ignorant, after all: The seventy-story cylinder of the Peachtree Plaza didn't exist. Gone, too, were the towers of the Omni International, the grey stone bulk of the Georgia Pacific Building, and Equitable's great black box. The most commanding structure in all of downtown Atlanta was this one, with its widely copied atrium lobby. A brief conversation with the waitress, though, had made it clear that the hotel was new and as yet unique.

The hardest moment had come when Jeff had looked into the mirror behind the bar. He'd done so purposefully, knowing full well by then what he would see, but still he was shocked to confront his own pale, lanky, eighteen-year-old reflection.

Objectively, the boy in the mirror looked somewhat more mature than that; he'd seldom had problems being served liquor at that age, as with the waitress just now, but

Jeff knew that was merely an illusion caused by his height and his deep-set eyes. To his own mind, the image in the mirror was of an untried and unscarred youth.

And that youth was himself. Not in memory, but here, now: these unlined hands with which he held his drink, these sharply focused eyes with which he saw.

"You ready for another one yet, honey?"

The waitress smiled prettily at him, lips bright red beneath her heavily mascaraed eyes and antiquated beehive hairdo. She wore a "futuristic" costume, an iridescent blue mini-dress of the sort that would be worn by young women everywhere in another two or three years.

Two or three years from *now*. The early sixties.

Jesus Christ.

He could no longer deny what had happened, couldn't hope to rationalize it away. He had been dying of a heart attack, but had survived; he had been in his office, in 1988, and now was . . . here. Atlanta, 1963.

Jeff groped without success for an explanation, something that would make even the vaguest sort of sense. He'd read a fair amount of science fiction as an adolescent, but his current situation bore no resemblance to any of the time-travel scenarios he'd ever encountered. There was no machine, no scientist, mad or otherwise; and, unlike the characters in the stories he'd read so eagerly, his own body had regenerated to its youthful state. It was as if his mind alone had made the leap across the years, obliterating his earlier consciousness to inhabit the brain of his own eighteen-year-old self.

Had he escaped death, then, or merely sidestepped it? In some alternate stream of future time was his lifeless body lying in a New York mortuary, being sliced and dissected by a pathologist's scalpel?

Maybe he was in a coma: hopelessness twisted into an imaginary new life, at the behest of a ravaged, dying brain. And yet, and yet—

"Honey?" the waitress asked. "You want me to freshen that up or not?"

"I, uh, I think I'll have a cup of coffee instead, if that's all right."

"Sure thing. Maybe an Irish coffee?"

"No, just plain. A little cream, no sugar."

The girl from the past brought his coffee, and Jeff stared out at the scattered lights of the half-built city as they came on beneath the fading sky. The sun had disappeared beyond the red-clay hills that stretched toward Alabama, toward the years of sweeping and chaotic change, of tragedy and dreams.

The steaming coffee burned his lips, and he cooled them with a sip of ice water. The world beyond those windows was no dream; it was as solid as it was innocent, as real as it was blindly optimistic.

Spring 1963.

There were so many choices to be made.

≡2≡

JEFF SPENT THE rest of the evening walking the streets of downtown Atlanta, his eyes and ears attuned to every nuance of the recreated past: "White" and "Colored" signs on public rest rooms, women wearing hats and gloves, an ad in a travel-agency window for the *Queen Mary* to Europe, a cigarette in the hand of almost every man he passed. Jeff didn't get hungry until after eleven, and then he grabbed a burger and a beer at a little joint near Five Points. He thought he vaguely remembered the nondescript bar and grill from twenty-five years ago, as someplace he and Judy had occasionally gone for an after-movie snack; but by now he was so confused, so exhausted by the unending flood of new/old sights and places, that he could no longer be sure. Each storefront, each passing stranger's face, had begun to seem disturbingly familiar, though he knew he couldn't possibly have a recollection of everything he saw. He had lost the ability to sort false memories from those that were undoubtedly real.

He desperately needed to get some sleep, to shut all this off for a little while and perhaps, against all hope, awake to the world he'd left. What he wanted most of all was an anonymous, timeless hotel room with no view of the al-

13

tered skyline, no radio or television to remind him of what
had happened; but he didn't have enough money, and of
course he had no credit cards. Short of sleeping in Pied-
mont Park, Jeff had no choice but to return to Emory, back
to the dorm room. Maybe Martin would be asleep.

He wasn't. Jeff's roommate was wide awake, sitting at
his desk, thumbing through a copy of *High Fidelity*. He
looked up coolly, put down the magazine as Jeff let himself into the room.

"So," Martin said. "Where the hell have you been?"

"Downtown. Just wandering around."

"You couldn't find time to just wander by Dooley's,
huh? Or maybe even wander by the Fox Theater? We
almost missed the first part of the goddamned movie,
waiting for you."

"I'm sorry, I . . . wasn't feeling up to it. Not tonight."

"The least you could've done was to leave me a fucking
note, or something. You didn't even call Judy, for Christ's
sake. She was going out of her mind, worrying about what
had happened to you."

"Look, I'm really wiped out. I don't much feel like
talking, O.K.?"

Martin laughed without humor. "You'd better be ready
to talk tomorrow, if you want to see Judy again. She's
gonna be pissed as all hell when she finds out you aren't
dead."

Jeff dreamed of dying, and woke to find himself still in
that college dorm room. Nothing had changed. Martin was
gone, probably to class; but it was Saturday morning, Jeff
remembered. Had there been Saturday classes? He wasn't
sure.

In any event, he was alone in the room, and he took
advantage of the privacy to poke at random through his
desk and closet. The books were all familiar: *Fail-Safe,
The Making of the President—1960, Travels with Charley.*
The record albums, in their new, unfaded, and unwarped
sleeves, conjured up a hundred multi-sensual images of the
days and nights he had spent listening to that music: Stan
Getz and Joao Gilberto, the Kingston Trio, Jimmy Wither-

spoon, dozens more, most of which he'd long since lost or worn out.

Jeff turned on the Harman-Kardon stereo his parents had given him one Christmas, put on "Desafinado," and continued to rummage through the belongings of his youth: hangers draped with cuffed h.i.s. slacks and Botany 500 sports jackets, a tennis trophy from the boarding school outside Richmond that he'd gone to before Emory, a tissue-wrapped collection of Hurricane glasses from Pat O'Brien's in New Orleans, neatly ordered stacks of *Playboy* and *Rogue*.

He found a box of letters and photographs, hauled it out, and sat on the bed to sort through the contents. There were pictures of himself as a child, snapshots of girls whose names he couldn't recall, a couple of hamming-it-up photo-booth strips . . . and a small folder full of family pictures, his mother and father and younger sister at a picnic, on a beach, around a Christmas tree.

On impulse, he dug a handful of change from his pocket, found the pay phone in the hall, and got his parents' long-forgotten old number from information in Orlando.

"Hello?" his mother said, with the distracted tone that had only increased as the years had passed.

"Mother?" he said tentatively.

"Jeff!" Her voice was muffled for a moment as she turned away from the mouthpiece. "Honey, pick up in the kitchen. It's Jeff!" Then, clear and distinct again: "Now, what's this 'Mother' business? Think you're getting too old to call me 'Mom,' is that it?"

He hadn't called his mother that since he was in his early twenties.

"How—how've you been?" he asked.

"Not the same since you left, you know that; but we're keeping busy. We went fishing off Titusville last week. Your father caught a thirty-pound pompano. I wish I could send you some of it; it's just the tenderest you've ever tasted. We've got plenty left in the freezer for you, but it won't be the same as it was fresh."

Her words brought back a rush of memories, all tenuously related: summer weekends on his uncle's boat in the

Atlantic, the sun bright on the polished deck as a dark line
of thunderheads hovered on the horizon . . . the ram-
shackle little towns of Titusville and Cocoa Beach before
the great NASA invasion . . . the big white freezer in their
garage at home full of steaks and fish, and above it shelves
of boxes stuffed with all his old comic books and Heinlein
novels . . .

"Jeff? You still there?"

"Oh, yeah, I'm sorry . . . Mom. I just forgot what I
called about for a minute, there."

"Well, honey, you know you never need a reason to—"

There was a click on the line, and he heard his father's
voice. "Well, speak of the devil! We were just talking
about you, weren't we, hon?"

"That's right," Jeff's mother said. "Not five minutes
ago, I was saying how long it'd been since you called."

Jeff had no idea whether that meant a week or a month,
and he didn't want to ask. "Hi, Dad," he said quickly. "I
hear you bagged a prize pompano."

"Hey, you should've been there." His father laughed.
"Bud didn't get a nibble all day, and the only thing Janet
came up with was a sunburn. She's still peeling—looks
like an overcooked shrimp!"

Jeff hazily remembered the names as belonging to one
of the couples his parents had been friends with, but he
couldn't put faces to them. He was struck by how vital and
full of energy his mother and father both sounded. His
father had come down with emphysema in 1982, and
seldom left the house anymore. Only with difficulty could
Jeff picture him out on the ocean, besting a powerful
deep-sea fish, the Pall Mall in the corner of his mouth
soggy with spray. In fact, Jeff thought numbly, his parents
were now almost exactly his own age—or the age he had
been this time yesterday.

"Oh," his mother said, "I ran into Barbara the other
day. She's doing just fine at Rollins, and she said to tell
you Cappy got that problem all straightened out."

Barbara, Jeff dimly recalled, was a girl he'd dated in
high school; but the name Cappy meant nothing to him
now.

"Thanks," Jeff said. "Next time you see her, tell Barbara I'm real glad to hear that."

"Are you still going out with that little Judy?" his mother asked. "That was such a darling picture you sent of her, we can't wait to meet her. How is she?"

"She's fine," he said evasively, beginning to wish he hadn't made this call.

"How's the Chevy doing?" his father interjected. "Still burning oil like it was?"

Jesus; Jeff hadn't thought about that old car in years.

"Car's O.K., Dad." That was a guess. He didn't even know where it might be parked. The smoky old beast had been a graduation present from his parents, and he'd driven it until it finally died on him during his senior year at Emory.

"How about the grades? That paper you were griping about, the one on . . . You know, the one you told us last week you were having some trouble with. What was that, anyway?"

"Last week? Yeah, the . . . history paper. I finished that. Haven't gotten the grade yet."

"No, no, it wasn't for history. You said it was some English Lit thing, what was it?"

A child's voice suddenly came on the line, babbling excitedly. Jeff realized with a jolt that the child was his sister—a woman who'd been through two divorces, who had a daughter of her own just entering high school. Hearing her nine-year-old's exuberance, Jeff was touched. His sister's voice seemed the very embodiment of lost innocence, of time turned poignantly back upon itself.

The conversation with his family had grown stifling, uncomfortably disturbing. He cut it short, promised to call again in a few days. When he hung up, his forehead was damp with chill sweat, his throat dry. He took the stairs down to the lobby, bought a Coke for a quarter, drained it in three long gulps. Someone was in the TV room, watching "Sky King."

Jeff dug in his other pocket, fished out a key ring. One of the six keys was for the dorm room, he'd used that to let himself back in last night; there were three others he didn't recognize, and two that were clearly a set of General Motors ignition and trunk keys.

He walked outside, blinked at the bright Georgia sunshine. There was a weekend feel to the campus, a distinctive lazy quietude that Jeff recognized instantly. On fraternity row, he knew, captive squads of pledges would be mopping the houses clean and hanging papier-mâché decorations for the Saturday-night round of parties; the girls in Harris Hall and the unnamed new women's dorm would be lounging about in Bermuda shorts and sandals, waiting for their afternoon dates to pick them up for a drive to Soap Creek or Stone Mountain. Off to his left, Jeff could hear the chanted cadences of the Air Force ROTC drill, being conducted without irony or protest. No one was playing Frisbee on the grass; no odor of marijuana hung in the air. The students here could not conceive of the changes the world was about to endure.

He scanned the parking lot in front of Longstreet Hall, searching for his blue-and-white '58 Chevy. It was nowhere in sight. He walked down Pierce Drive, then made a wide circle on Arkwright past Dobbs Hall and up behind the other cluster of men's dorms; the car wasn't there either.

As he walked toward Clifton Road Jeff could again hear the barked commands and rote responses from the ROTC field. The sound made something click in his mind, and he turned left over a small bridge across from the post office, then trudged up a road past the Phi Chi medical fraternity. The campus property ended there, and a block farther on he found his car. He was a freshman, so he couldn't get a parking sticker until next fall; he'd had to park off campus that first year. Even so, there was a ticket on the windshield. He should've moved the car that morning, according to the hours posted on a sign above him.

He sat behind the wheel, and the feel and smell of the car evoked a dizzying jumble of responses. He'd spent hundreds, maybe thousands, of hours in this tattered seat: at drive-in movies and restaurants with Judy, on road trips with Martin or other friends or by himself—to Chicago, Florida, once all the way to Mexico City. He had grown from adolescence to adulthood in this car, more so than in any dorm room or apartment or city. He'd made love in it, gotten drunk in it, driven it to his favorite uncle's untimely funeral, used its temperamental yet powerful V-8 engine to express anger, jubilation, depression, boredom, remorse. He'd never given the car a name, had considered the idea of doing so juvenile; but now he realized how much the machine had meant to him, how thoroughly his own identity had been meshed with the quirky personality of that old Chevy.

Jeff put the key in the ignition, started it up. The engine backfired once, then rumbled to life. He turned the car around, took a right on Clifton Road past the half-constructed bulk of the Communicable Disease Center. They'd still call it the CDC in the eighties, but by then the initials would stand for Centers for Disease Control, and the place would be world-renowned for its studies of such panic-inducing scourges of the future as Legionnaire's Disease and AIDS.

The future: hideous plagues, a revolution in sexual attitudes achieved and then reversed, triumph and tragedy in space, city streets haunted by null-eyed punks in leather and chains and spiked pink hair, death-beams in orbit around the polluted, choking earth . . . Christ, Jeff thought with a shudder, from this viewpoint his world sounded like the most nightmarish of science fiction. In many ways, the reality he'd grown used to had more in common with movies like *Blade Runner* than it did with the sunny naïveté of early 1963.

He turned on the radio: crackling, monaural AM, no FM band on the dial at all. "Our Day Will Come," Ruby and the Romantics crooned at him, and Jeff laughed aloud.

At Briarcliff Road he turned left, drove aimlessly through the shaded residential neighborhoods to the west of the campus. The street became Moreland Avenue after a ways, and he kept on driving, past Inman Park, past the Federal Penitentiary where Al Capone had served his time. The city street signs disappeared, and he was on the Macon Highway, heading south.

The radio kept him company with its unending stream of

pre-Beatle hits: "Surfin' USA," "I Will Follow Him,"
"Puff, the Magic Dragon." Jeff sang along with all of
them, pretended he was listening to an oldies station. All
he had to do was hit another button, he told himself, and
he'd hear Springsteen or Prince, maybe a jazz station
playing the latest Pat Metheny on a compact disc. Finally
the signal faded, and so did his fantasy. He could find
nothing across the dial except more of the same antiquated
music. Even the country stations had never heard of Willie
or Waylon; it was all Ernest Tubbs and Hank Williams,
not an outlaw in the pack.

Outside McDonough he passed a roadside stand selling
peaches and watermelons. He and Martin had stopped at a
stand just like that on one of their Florida drives, mainly
because of the long-legged farm girl in white shorts who'd
been selling the fruit. She'd had a big German Shepherd
with her, and after some pointless city-boy/country-girl
banter, he and Martin had bought a whole bushel basket
full of peaches from her. They hadn't even wanted the
damned things, got sick of smelling them after thirty miles
or so, and started using them for target practice on road
signs, whooping with inane glee at the "*Splat—Kerblang!*"
that resulted from a successful toss.

That had been, what, the summer of '64 or '65? A year
or two from now. As of today, he and Martin hadn't made
that trip, hadn't bought those peaches, hadn't stained and
dented half the speed-limit signs from here to Valdosta
with them. So what did that mean now? If Jeff were still in
this inexplicably reconstructed past when that June day
rolled around again, would he make the same trip, share
the same jokes with Martin, throw those same ripe peaches
at the same road signs? And if he didn't, if he chose to
stay in Atlanta that week, or if he simply drove past the
girl with the legs and the peaches . . . then what of his
memory of that episode? Where had it come from, and
what would happen to it?

In one sense he appeared to be reliving his life, replaying it like a video tape; yet it didn't seem that he was
bound by what had taken place before, not entirely. So far
as he could tell, he had arrived back at this point in his life

with every circumstance intact—enrolled at Emory, rooming with Martin, taking the same courses that he had a quarter of a century before—but in the twenty-four hours since he'd reawakened here, he'd already begun to subtly veer from the paths he had originally followed.

Standing up Judy last night—that was the biggest and most obvious change, though it wouldn't necessarily affect anything one way or the other, in the long run. They'd only dated for another six or eight months, he recalled, until sometime around next Christmas. She'd left him for an "older man," he remembered with a smile, a senior, going on to medical school at Tulane. Jeff had been hurt and depressed for a few weeks, then started going out with a string of other girls: a skinny brunette named Margaret for a while, then another dark-haired girl whose name started with a *D* or a *V*, then a blonde who could tie a knot in a cherry stem with her tongue. He hadn't met Linda, the woman he would marry, until he was out of college and working at a radio station in West Palm Beach. She'd been a student at Florida Atlantic University. They'd met on the beach at Boca Raton. . . .

Jesus, where was Linda right now? Two years younger than he, she'd still be in high school, living with her parents. He had a sudden urge to call her, maybe keep on driving south to Boca Raton and see her, meet her. . . . No, that wouldn't do at all. It would be too strange. Something like that might be dangerously far afield, might create some horrendous paradox.

Or would it? Did he really have to worry about paradoxes, the old killing-your-own-grandfather idea? That might not be an appropriate concern at all. He wasn't an outsider wandering around in this time, afraid of encountering himself at an earlier age; he actually *was* that younger self, part and parcel of the fabric of this world. Only his mind was of the future—and the future existed only in his mind.

Jeff had to pull off the road and stop for a few minutes, head in hands, as he absorbed the implications of that. He'd wondered before whether he might be hallucinating this past existence. But what if the reverse were true, what if the whole complex pattern of the next two and a half decades—everything from the fall of Saigon to New Wave rock music to personal computers—turned out to be a fiction that had somehow sprung full-blown into his head, overnight, here in the *real* world of 1963, which he had never left? That made as much sense as, maybe more than, any alternative explanation involving time travel or after-life or dimensional upheaval.

Jeff started the Chevy again, got back onto two-lane U.S. 23. Locust Grove, Jenkinsburg, Jackson . . . the dilapidated, drowsy little towns of backwoods Georgia slid past like scenes from a movie of the depression era. Maybe that was what had drawn him to make this aimless drive, he thought: the timelessness of the countryside beyond Atlanta, the total lack of clues to what year or decade it might be. Weathered barns with "Jesus Saves" painted in massive letters, the staggered highway rhymes of leftover Burma Shave signs, an old black man leading a mule . . . even the Atlanta of 1963 seemed futuristic compared to this.

At Pope's Ferry, just north of Macon, he pulled into a mom-and-pop gas station with a general store attached. No self-service pumps, no unleaded; Gulf premium for thirty-three cents a gallon, regular for twenty-seven. He told the kid outside to fill it with premium and check the oil, add two quarts if it was low.

He bought a couple of Slim Jims and a can of Pabst in the store, clawed ineffectually at the beer can for a moment or two before he realized there was no pop top.

"You must be mighty thirsty, hon." The old woman behind the counter chuckled. "Tryin' to tear that thing open with your bare hands!"

Jeff smiled sheepishly. The woman pointed to a church-key hanging on a string by the cash register, and he punched two V-shaped holes in the top of the can. The boy from the gas pumps shouted through the ratty screen door of the store: "Looks like you need about three quarts of oil, mister!"

"Fine, put in whatever it takes. And check the fan belts, too, will you?"

Jeff took a long sip of the beer, picked a magazine from

the rack. There was an article about the new pop-art craze: Lichtenstein's blowups of comic-strip panels, Oldenburg's big, floppy vinyl hamburgers. Funny, he'd thought all that happened later, '65 or '66. Had he found a discrepancy? Was this world already slightly different from the one he thought he knew?

He needed to talk to somebody. Martin would just make a big joke of it all, and his parents would worry for his sanity. Maybe that was it; maybe he should see a shrink. A doctor would at least listen, and keep the talk confidential; but an encounter like that would carry the unspoken pre-supposition of a mental problem, a desire to be "cured" of something.

No, there was really no one he could discuss this with, not openly. But he couldn't just keep avoiding everyone for fear it might come out; that would probably seem stranger than any anachronistic slip of the tongue he might make. And he was getting lonely, damn it. Even if he couldn't tell the truth, or whatever he knew of the truth, he needed the comfort of company, after all he'd been through.

"Could I have some change for the phone?" Jeff asked the woman at the cash register, handing her a five.

"Dollar's worth O.K.?"

"I want to call Atlanta."

She nodded, hit the no-sale key, and scooped some coins from the drawer. "Dollar's worth'll be plenty, hon."

≡3≡

THE GIRL AT the front desk at Harris Hall was obviously annoyed that she'd drawn Saturday-night reception duty, but was taking her weekend entertainment where she could find it, observing the rituals of her peers. She gave Jeff a coolly appraising stare when he walked in, and her voice carried a tinge of sarcastic amusement when she called upstairs to tell Judy Gordon her date was here. Maybe she knew Judy'd been stood up the night before; maybe she'd even listened in on the conversation when Jeff had called from the gas station near Macon this afternoon.

The girl's enigmatic half-smile was a little unnerving, so he took a seat on one of the uncomfortable sofas in the adjoining lounge, where a pony-tailed brunette and her date were playing "Heart and Soul" on an old Steinway near the fireplace. The girl smiled and waved at Jeff when he came into the room. He had no idea who she was, probably some friend of Judy's whom he'd long since forgotten about, but he nodded and returned her smile. Eight or nine other young men sat scattered around the airy lounge, each a respectful distance from the others. Two of them carried bunches of cut flowers, and one held a heart-shaped box of Whitman's candies. All wore stoic expres-

24

sions that did little to mask their eager but nervous anticipation: suitors at the gate of Aphrodite's temple, untested claimants to the favors of the nymphs within this fortress. Date Night, 1963.

Jeff remembered the sensation all too well. In fact, he noted wryly, his own palms were damp with tension even now.

Soprano laughter came from the stairwell, floated into the lobby. The young men straightened their ties, checked their watches, patted tufts of hair into place. Two girls found their escorts and led them through the door into the mysterious night.

It was twenty minutes before Judy emerged, her face set in what was clearly intended to be a look of frosty determination. All Jeff could see, though, was her incredible youthfulness, a vernal tenderness that went beyond the fact that she was still in her teens. Girls—women—her age in the eighties didn't look like this, he realized. They simply weren't this young, this innocent; hadn't been since the days of Janis Joplin, and certainly weren't in the aftermath of Madonna.

"So," Judy said. "I'm glad to see you could make it tonight."

Jeff pulled himself awkwardly to his feet, gave her an apologetic smile. "I'm really sorry about last night," he said. "I—wasn't feeling very well; I was in a strange mood. You wouldn't have wanted to be with me."

"You could have called," she said petulantly. Her arms were crossed under her breasts, highlighting those demure swells beneath the Peter Pan blouse. A beige cashmere sweater was slung over one arm, and she wore a Madras skirt, with low-heeled ankle-strap shoes. Jeff caught the mixed aromas of Lanvin perfume and a floral-scented shampoo, found himself entranced by the blond bangs that danced above her wide blue eyes.

"I know," he said. "I wish I had."

Her expression eased, the confrontation over before it had begun. She'd never been able to stay angry for long, Jeff recalled.

"You missed a really good movie last night," she said

without a trace of sullenness. "It starts off where this girl is buying these birds in a pet shop, and then Rod Taylor pretends like he works there, and . . ."

She went on to recount most of the plot as they walked outside and got into Jeff's Chevy. He feigned unfamiliarity with the twists and turns of the story, even though he'd recently seen the movie on one of HBO's periodic Hitchcock retrospectives. And, of course, he'd seen it when it first came out, seen it with Judy. Seen it twenty-five years ago last night, in that other version of his life.

". . . and then this guy goes to light a cigar at this gas station, but—well, I don't want to tell you anything that happens after that; it'd spoil it for you. It's a really spooky movie. I wouldn't mind going to see it again, if you want to. Or we could go see *Bye Bye Birdie*. What do you feel like?"

"I think I'd rather just sit and talk," he said. "Get a beer someplace, maybe a bite to eat?"

"Sure." She smiled. "Moe's and Joe's?"

"O.K. That's . . . on Ponce De Leon, right?"

Judy wrinkled her brow. "No, that's Manuel's. Don't tell me you forgot—take a left, right here!" She turned in her seat, gave him an odd look. "Hey, you really are acting kind of weird. Is something wrong?"

"Nothing serious. Like I told you, I've been feeling a little off kilter." He recognized the entrance of the old college hangout, parked around the corner.

Inside, it didn't look quite the way Jeff remembered it. He'd thought the bar was on the left as you went in the door, not the right; and the booths seemed different somehow, too, higher or darker or something. He led Judy toward a booth in the back, and as they approached it a man about his own age—no, he corrected himself, a man in his early forties, an *older* man—slapped Jeff's shoulder in an amiable manner.

"Jeff, how goes it? Who's your lovely young friend?"

Jeff looked blankly at the man's face: glasses, salt-and-pepper beard, wide grin. He looked vaguely familiar, but no more.

"This is Judy Gordon. Judy, ah, I'd like you to meet . . ."

"Professor Samuels," she said. "My roommate has you for Medieval Lit."

"And her name is—?"

"Paula Hawkins."

The man's grin widened further, and he nodded twice. "Excellent student. Very bright young lady, Paula. I trust my class comes recommended?"

"Oh, yes, sir," Judy said. "Paula's told me all about you."

"Then perhaps we'll be blessed with your own delightful presence in the fall."

"I can't rightly say just yet, Professor Samuels. I haven't really decided on my schedule for next year."

"Drop by my office. We'll discuss it. And you, Jeff: good job on that Chaucer paper, but I had to give you a B for incomplete citations. Watch that next time, will you?"

"Yes, sir. I'll remember."

"Good, good. See you in class." He waved them off, went back to his beer.

When they got to the booth, Judy slid in next to Jeff and started giggling.

"What's so funny?"

"Don't you know about him? Dr. Samuels?"

Jeff hadn't even been able to recall the professor's name.

"No, what about him?"

"He's a dirty old man, that's what. He chases after all the girls in his classes—the cute ones, anyway. Paula said he put his hand on her thigh one time after class—like this."

She put her girlish fingers on Jeff's leg, rubbed it, and squeezed.

"Can you imagine?" she asked in a conspiratorial tone. "He's older than my father, even. 'Drop by my office' —huh! I know what he'd want to discuss. Isn't that just the most disgusting thing you ever heard, a man his age acting like that?"

Her hand still rested on Jeff's thigh, an inch or so away from his growing erection. He looked at her innocent round eyes, her sweet red mouth, and had a sudden fantasy

of Judy going down on him right there in the booth. Dirty
old man, he thought, and laughed.

"What's so funny?" she asked.

"Nothing."

"You don't believe me about Dr. Samuels, do you?"

"I believe you. No, it's just—you, me, everything. I
had to laugh, that's all. What do you want to drink?"

"The regular."

"A triple zombie, right?"

The worried look left her face, and she laughed along
with him. "Silly; I want a glass of red wine, just like
always. Can't you remember *anything* tonight?"

Judy's lips against his were as soft as he had imagined,
had remembered. The fresh scent of her hair, the youthful
smoothness of her skin excited him to a degree he hadn't
felt since the early days with Linda, before their marriage.
The car windows were down, and Judy rested the back of
her head on the cushioned doorframe as Jeff kissed her.
Andy Williams was singing "The Days of Wine and Roses"
on the radio, and the fragrance of dogwood blossoms
mingled with the scent of Judy's soft, clean skin. They
were parked on a wooded street a mile or so away from the
campus; Judy had directed him there after they'd left the
bar.

The conversation tonight had gone better than Jeff had
expected. Basically, he'd followed Judy's lead as they
talked, let her be the one to mention names and places and
events. He'd reacted from memory or the cues he took
from her expression and tone of voice. He'd made only
one anachronistic slip: They'd been talking about students
they knew who were planning to move off campus next
year, and Jeff had said he might sublet a condo. She'd
never heard the word, but he quickly explained it away as
something new from California that he'd read about and
thought maybe they'd build in Atlanta soon.

As the evening had gone on, he'd relaxed and begun to
enjoy himself. The beers had helped, but mainly it was just
being close to Judy that had set his mind at rest for the first
time since this whole thing had started. At moments, he'd

found himself not even thinking of his future/past. He was alive; that was what mattered. Very much alive.

He brushed Judy's long blond hair back from her face, kissed her cheeks and nose and lips again. She gave a low moan of pleasure, and his fingers slid from her breast to the top buttons of her blouse. She moved his hand away, back to her covered breast. They kissed for several moments more and then her hand was on his thigh, as it had been in the booth at the bar, but moving purposefully higher, until her delicate fingers caressed and kneaded his firm penis. He stroked her nyloned calves, reached beneath her skirt to feel the soft skin above the tops of her stockings.

Judy disengaged herself from his embrace, sat up abruptly. "Give me your handkerchief," she whispered.

"What? I don't—"

She plucked the white handkerchief from his jacket pocket, where he'd tucked it automatically as he dressed in the outmoded clothes earlier tonight. Jeff reached for her again, tried to pull her toward him, but she resisted.

"Ssshh," she whispered, then smiled sweetly. "Just sit back and close your eyes."

He frowned, but did as she asked. Suddenly she was unzipping his pants and pulling his erection free with a sure, practiced move. Jeff opened his eyes in surprise, saw her staring out the window as her fingers moved on him in a constant rhythm. He stopped her hand, held it still.

"Judy—no."

She looked back at him with concern. "You don't want to tonight?"

"Not like this." He gently took her hand away, adjusted himself, and closed his pants. "I want you; I want to be with you. But not this way. We could go somewhere, find a hotel or—"

She drew back against the car door, gave him an indignant glare. "What do you mean? You know I'm not like that!"

"All I mean to say is that I want us to be together, in a loving way. I want to give you—"

"You don't have to give me a thing!" She wrinkled her

face, and Jeff was afraid she would start to cry. "I was trying to relieve you, just like we've done before, and all of a sudden you take it the wrong way, want to drag me off to some cheap hotel, treat me like a—a—prostitute!"

"Judy, for Christ's sake, it's not like that at all. Don't you understand, I want to make you happy, too?"

She took a lipstick from her purse, twisted the rearview mirror angrily so she could apply it. "I'm perfectly happy just the way we've been, thank you very much. Or at least I was, until tonight."

"Look, I'm sorry I said anything, O.K.? I just thought—"

"You can keep your thoughts to yourself, and your hands, too." She flicked on the overhead light, glanced at her thin gold watch.

"I didn't mean to upset you. We can talk about it tomorrow."

"I don't want to talk about it. I just want to go back to the dorm, right now. That is, if you can remember how to get there."

After he dropped Judy off at her dorm he found a bar on North Druid Hills Road, near the new Lenox Square shopping center. It didn't seem to be the sort of place where he was likely to encounter anyone from Emory: This was a drinkers' bar, a hangout for an older, quieter crowd seeking only an hour's escape from thoughts of mortgages and stale marriages. Jeff felt right at home, though he knew he didn't look as though he fit the clientele; the bartender even carded him, and Jeff managed to find the altered ID he'd once kept in the back of his wallet for such infrequent occasions. With a dubious grunt, the man brought Jeff a double Jack Daniel's and went off to fiddle with the horizontal hold on the black-and-white TV set above the bar.

Jeff took a long sip of his drink, stared blankly at the news: There was more trouble in Birmingham, Jimmy Hoffa had been indicted on jury-tampering charges in Nashville, Telstar II was about to be launched. Jeff thought of Martin Luther King dead in Memphis, Hoffa mysteriously gone from the face of the earth, and a skyful of communications satellites saturating the planet with MTV and re-runs of "Miami Vice." O brave new world.

The night with Judy had begun pleasantly enough, but that final scene in the car had left him depressed. He'd forgotten how artificial sex used to be. No, not forgotten; he'd never fully realized it, not when those things were happening to him for the first time. The dishonesty had all been masked by the glow of newly discovered emotion, of naive but irresistible sexual hunger. What had once seemed wondrously erotic now stood revealed in all its essential cheapness, unobscured by the distance of time: a quick hand job in the front seat of a Chevrolet, with bad music in the background.

So what the hell was he going to do now, just play along? Indulge in more heavy petting sessions with a dewy little blonde from another time who'd never heard of the pill? Go back to classes and adolescent bull sessions and spring dances as if they were all new to him? Memorize statistical tables he'd long since forgotten and had never found any use for, so he could pass Sociology 101?

Maybe he didn't have any goddamned choice, not if this phenomenal, grotesque switch in time turned out to be permanent. Maybe he really would have to go through it, all of it, again—year after painful, predictable year. This alternate reality was becoming more concrete by the moment, ever more entrenched. That other self of his was the falsehood now. He must accept the fact that he was a college freshman, eighteen years old, totally dependent on his parents and his ability to repeat successfully dozens of academic courses that now filled him with disdain and utter boredom.

The TV news was over, and a sports announcer was droning off a list of AA-league baseball scores. Jeff ordered another drink, and as the bartender brought the fresh glass Jeff's attention suddenly focused with laserlike intensity on every word from the ancient Sylvania.

". . . coming into Churchill Downs unbeaten, there are still two eastern colts that might give the California chestnut a run for the money. Trainer Woody Stephens brings Never Bend into the Derby fresh from a handsome victory in the Stepping Stone prep, and with a clean record for '63; Stephens won't go so far as to predict a victory, but . . .''

The Kentucky Derby. Why the hell not? If he really had lived through the next twenty-five years, rather than imagining them or dreaming them, one thing was clear: He had a vast store of information that could be useful in the extreme. Nothing technical—he couldn't design a computer, or anything like that—but he certainly had a working knowledge, a journalist's knowledge, of the trends and events that would influence society from now to the mid-eighties. He could make a lot of money betting on sports events and presidential elections. Assuming, of course, that he actually possessed a concrete and correct awareness of what would happen over the coming quarter century. As he'd recognized earlier, that was not necessarily a safe assumption.

''. . . 'not far off the pace.' The horse that just might set that pace is Greentree Stable's No Robbery, who holds the record, at 1:34, for the fastest mile ever run by a three-year-old in New York . . . and who won the Wood Memorial one week after setting . . .''

Shit, who had won the Derby that year? Jeff struggled to remember. The name Never Bend, unlike No Robbery, at least rang a distant bell; but that still didn't sound right.

''. . . both have an uphill battle against the team of Willie Shoemaker and the western wonder, Candy Spots. That's the combination to beat, folks; and though it looks to be an exciting Run for the Roses among these three contenders, the consensus—and it's a strong one—is that Candy Spots will wear the wreath this Saturday.''

That didn't sound right, either. What horse was it? Northern Dancer? Or maybe Kauai King? Jeff was sure those had both won Derbies; but which years?

''Say, bartender!''

''Same?''

''No, I'm O.K. for now; have you got a paper?''

''Paper?''

''A newspaper, today's, yesterday's, it doesn't matter.''

''The *Journal* or the *Constitution?*''

"Whatever. You got the sports pages?"

"Marked up a little bit. Braves coming to town next year, I've been following their averages."

"Can I take a quick look?"

"Sure thing." The bartender reached beneath the place where he kept the garnishes and produced a tightly folded sports section.

Jeff flipped past the baseball pages and found a preview of the upcoming race of races in Louisville. He scanned the list of entries: There were the favorites the announcer had mentioned, Candy Spots, Never Bend, No Robbery; then Royal Tower, Lemon Twist . . . no, no . . . Gray Pet, Devil It Is . . . never heard of either of them . . . Wild Card, Rajah Noor . . . uh-uh . . . Bonjour, On My Honor . . .

Chateaugay.

Chateaugay, at eleven-to-one odds.

He sold the Chevy to a used-car dealer on Briarcliff Road for six hundred dollars. His books, stereo, and record collection brought in another two hundred sixty dollars at a junk shop downtown. In his dorm-room desk he'd found a checkbook and savings book from a bank near campus, and he immediately withdrew all but twenty dollars from each of the two accounts; that gave him another eight hundred and thirty dollars.

Calling his parents was the hardest part. It was obvious how deeply his sudden request for an "emergency" loan worried them, and his father was clearly angered by Jeff's refusal to explain any further. Still, he came through with a couple of hundred dollars, and Jeff's mother sent another four hundred from her own savings.

Now he had to place a bet, a large one. But how? He thought briefly of going to Louisville and putting the money down right at the track; but a call to a travel agent told him what he'd already suspected, that the Derby had been sold out for weeks in advance.

There was also the problem of his age. He might look old enough to order a drink at a bar, but making a wager of this size was sure to draw close scrutiny. He needed somebody to front for him.

"A bookie? What the hell do you want to know about bookies for, kid?"

To Jeff's eyes, Frank Maddock, at twenty-two, was himself a "kid," but in this context the senior, prelaw student was an older, experienced man of the world, and obviously enjoyed playing that role to the hilt.

"I want to make a bet," Jeff said.

Maddock smiled indulgently, lit a cigarillo, and waved for another pitcher of beer.

"What on?"

"The Kentucky Derby."

"Why don't you just start a pool around your dorm? Probably get lots of guys to come in on it. Be sure to keep it quiet, though."

The senior was treating him with an affable condescension. Jeff smiled inwardly at the young man's practiced, if unearned, air of worldliness.

"The bet I want to make is fairly large."

"Yeah? Like how much?"

Manuel's was half empty on a Thursday afternoon, and no one was in earshot. "Twenty-three hundred dollars," Jeff said.

Maddock frowned. "You're talking about a hell of a lot of money there. I know Candy Spots is pretty much a sure thing, but—"

"Not Candy Spots. One of the other horses."

The older boy laughed as the waiter set a new pitcher of beer on the worn oak table. "Dream on, son. No Robbery isn't worth that kind of risk, and neither is Never Bend. Not in this race."

"It's my money, Frank. I was thinking of a seventy-thirty split on the winnings. If I'm right, you could clean up without risking·a dime."

Maddock poured them each a fresh mug, tipping the glasses to keep the foam down. "I could get in a lot of trouble over this, you know. I don't want to do anything to screw up law school. A kid like you, all that money; how do I know you wouldn't go screaming to Dean Ward if you lost it?''

Jeff shrugged. "I guess that's where your part of the gamble comes in. But I'm not that kind of guy, and I don't plan to lose.''

"Nobody ever does.''

A raucous number came up on the jukebox, Jimmy Soul doing "If You Wanna Be Happy.'' Jeff raised his voice above the music. "So, do you know a bookie or not?''

Maddock gave him a long, curious stare. "Seventy-thirty, huh?''

"That's right.''

The senior shook his head, sighed resignedly. "You got the cash on you?''

The bar on North Druid Hills Road was packed that Saturday afternoon. The commercial-laden prerace show blared from the TV set as Jeff walked in: Wilkinson Sword trumpeting its newest product, stainless-steel razor blades.

Jeff was more nervous than he would have expected. This had all seemed perfect in the planning, but what if something went wrong? As far as he'd been able to tell, the previous week's world events had duplicated the past that he recalled; still, his memory was as fallible as anyone's, and after twenty-five years he couldn't be sure that a thousand, a million, different incidents in 1963 hadn't turned out differently than they had the first time around. He'd already noticed a few minor things that seemed slightly off-kilter, and of course his own actions had been drastically altered. This race could just as easily have a new outcome.

If it did, he'd be out everything he owned, and he'd skipped midterms this week, putting his academic standing in serious jeopardy. He might not even have the option at this point of buckling down to repeat his college career. He could be out of school on his ass, broke.

With Vietnam on the horizon.

"Hey, Charlie," somebody yelled. "Another round for the house, doubles, before they leave the gate!''

There was a chorus of cheers and laughter. One of the

man's buddies said, "Spending it a little early, aren't you?"

"In the bag, man," said the generous one, "in the fucking bag!"

On the TV screen the horses were being shut into their gates, restless, hating the confinement, eager to run, as they'd been bred to do.

"Anything can happen now, Jimbo. That's what a horse race is all about."

The bartender set out the doubles the stranger had bought for everyone. Before Jeff could pick up his glass, the horses were out of the gate, Never Bend breaking away as if electrically charged, with No Robbery almost at his side. Candy Spots, with Willie Shoemaker coolly astride him, was only three lengths back at the first turn.

Chateaugay was sixth. One mile to go, ten lengths behind.

Jeff tossed back a gulp of his drink, almost choked on the near-straight whiskey.

The front-runners sped past the half-mile pole. Chateaugay hadn't gained an inch.

A smaller school, Jeff thought. Even if he flunked out of Emory, some community college would probably take him. He could work part time at a small-market radio station. His years of experience wouldn't exist on paper, but they'd count for a lot on the job.

The bar crowd yelled at the screen as if the horses and jockeys could hear them, four hundred miles away. Jeff didn't bother. Chateaugay had pulled up a bit toward the end of the backstretch, but it was as good as over; a three-horse race, just as the oddsmakers had predicted.

Shoemaker took Candy Spots in on the rail as the field turned for home, then moved him back out for the stretch. Chateaugay was in fourth place, three lengths back, and with that kind of competition ahead of him he'd never—

At the quarter pole No Robbery suddenly seemed to tire, to lose heart for the closing battle. He dropped back, and it was Never Bend and Candy Spots tearing for home, but Shoemaker wasn't getting the final spurt he needed out of the California Chestnut.

Chateaugay passed the favorite and bore down, steady and relentless, on Never Bend.

The din in the bar swelled to riotous levels. Jeff remained silent, unmoving, his hand nearly frozen, though he didn't notice, as it clutched the icy glass.

Chateaugay took the race by a length and a quarter over Never Bend, with Candy Spots relegated to a close third. No Robbery was back in the field somewhere, fifth or sixth, exhausted.

Jeff had done it. He'd won.

The other men in the bar began loudly and angrily analyzing the race they'd just seen, with most of their ire aimed at Willie Shoemaker's tactics in the last half mile. Jeff didn't hear a word they said. He was waiting for the figures to come up on the tote board.

Chateaugay paid $20.80 to win. Jeff reached reflexively for his Casio calculator watch, then laughed as he realized how long it would be before such a thing existed. He grabbed a cocktail napkin from the bar, scribbled some figures with a ballpoint.

Half of 2300 times 20.8, less Frank Maddock's 30 percent share for placing the bet . . . Jeff had won close to seventeen thousand dollars.

More importantly, the race had ended as he'd remembered it.

He was eighteen years old, and he knew everything of consequence that was going to happen in the world for the next two decades.

4

JEFF SLAPPED THE cards down one at a time, face-up, on the dark green Holiday Inn bedspread. He flicked them off the diminishing deck as fast as his fingers could move, and as he did so, Frank droned a now-familiar hypnotic chant: "Plus four, plus four, plus five, plus four, plus three, plus three, plus three, plus four, plus three, plus four, plus five—stop! Hole card's an ace."

Jeff turned the ace of diamonds over slowly, and they both grinned.

"Hot damn!" Frank chortled, slapping the bedspread and sending the cards flying. "We are a team, my man, the team to beat!"

"Want a beer?"

"Fuckin'-A told!"

Jeff uncrossed his legs, walked across the room to the cooler on the table. The curtains of the first-floor room were open, and as he pried the tops off two bottles of Coors Jeff looked with fond admiration at his new grey Studebaker Avanti by the curb, gleaming in the lights of the Tucumcari motel's parking lot.

The car had drawn curious stares and comments all the way from Atlanta, and would probably continue to do so for the rest of the drive to Las Vegas. Jeff felt totally at ease with it, even found a certain comfort in its "futuristic" design and instrumentation. The long-nosed machine, with its bobbed rear deck, would have looked attractively state-of-the-art in 1988; indeed, he seemed to recall that an independent firm had still been manufacturing limited-edition Avantis during the eighties. To him, here in 1963, the car was like a fellow voyager in time, a plush cocoon spun in the image of his own era. Nostalgic as he'd felt about the old Chevy, this machine evoked an even stronger, reverse nostalgia.

"Hey, where's that brew?"

"Comin' up."

He handed Frank the cold beer, took a long pull of his own. They'd taken off right after Maddock had graduated, at the end of May. Jeff had long since stopped going to classes, was flunking out, and no longer cared. Frank had wanted to drive the southern route, stop over in New Orleans for a few days of celebration, but Jeff had insisted they take a more direct path, skirting past Birmingham and Memphis and Little Rock. Outside the cities there were newly opened patches of interstate highway every couple of hundred miles, with speed limits of 70 or 75, and Jeff had used their smooth, broad-laned isolation to push the Avanti near its 160 mph peak.

The depression and confusion Jeff had felt after the abortive evening with Judy Gordon had been largely dissipated by the Derby win. He hadn't seen her since that night, except in passing, on campus. And he'd stopped agonizing over possible explanations for his predicament, aside from the times when he'd awake at dawn, his brain demanding answers that could not be found. Whatever the truth might be, at least he now had proof that his awareness of the future was more than just a fantasy.

So far, Jeff had managed to deflect Frank's questions about what had led him to such a spectacular win. Maddock now assumed Jeff to be a handicapping prodigy, with some secret method. That image had only been strengthened by Jeff's refusal to make a follow-up wager on the Preakness, two weeks after the Derby. He'd been sure that

Chateaugay would win two out of three of that year's Triple Crown, but he couldn't remember which of the Derby sequels the horse had lost; so, despite Frank's protests, Jeff had insisted they sit out the Preakness. Candy Spots had taken the race by three and a half lengths. Now not only was Jeff certain of victory in the upcoming Belmont Stakes, but the resurgence of Candy Spots had driven the odds back up on Chateaugay.

The betting had given Jeff a new sense of purpose, distracted him from the hopeless quagmire of metaphysics and philosophy in which the answers to his situation lay buried. If he weren't insane already, another month or so of brooding over those imponderables surely would have driven him to that point. Gambling was so clear-cut, so soothingly straightforward: win or loss, debit or credit, right or wrong. Period. No ambiguities, no second guessing; especially not when you knew the outcome in advance.

Frank had gathered up the scattered cards, was stacking and shuffling them. "Hey," he said, "let's do a double deck!"

"Sure, why not?" Jeff straddled a chair next to the bed. He took the cards, reshuffled, began to dole them out.

"Plus one, plus one, zero, plus one, zero, minus one, minus two, minus two, minus three, minus two . . ."

Jeff listened contentedly to the familiar litany, the running count of aces and tens as they were dealt. Frank had been avidly memorizing charts and tables from a new book called *Beat the Dealer*, a computer study of betting strategies in blackjack. Jeff knew from his own reading how well the card-counting method actually worked. By the mid-seventies, casinos had begun barring anyone who played with those techniques. In this era, though, the dealers and pit bosses had welcomed any sort of system players, considered them easy marks. Frank should do all right, hold his own at the very least; and if he were absorbed in the thrill of his own triumphs at the 21 tables, it might divert his attention somewhat from the more spectacular win that Jeff expected to achieve in the Belmont.

". . . minus one, zero, plus one—stop! Hole card's a ten."

Jeff showed him the jack of clubs, and they slapped five. Frank drained his beer, set the bottle on the nightstand next to half a dozen other empties. "Hey," he said. "One of those drive-ins we passed on the way into town was showing *Dr. No;* want to check it out?"

"Jesus, Frank, how many times have you seen that movie already?"

"Three or four. It gets better every time."

"Enough already; I've OD'd on James Bond."

Frank looked at him quizzically. "You what?"

"Never mind. I just don't feel like going; you take the car, the keys are on top of the TV."

"What's the matter, you in mourning for the Pope? I didn't even know you were Catholic."

Jeff laughed, reached for his shoes. "Oh, what the hell, all right. At least it's not Roger Moore."

"Who the hell is Roger Moore?"

"He'll be a saint someday."

Frank shook his head and frowned. "Are we talking about the Pope dying, or James Bond, or what? You know, buddy, sometimes I don't know *what* the fuck you're talking about."

"Neither do I, Frank; neither do I. Come on, let's go to the movies. A little escape from reality, that's what we need."

They drove straight through to Las Vegas the next day, spelling each other at the wheel of the Avanti. Jeff had never been to Nevada, and the neon-lit Strip seemed emptier, less thoroughly gaudy than he recalled from movies and television shows of the eighties. This was pre-Howard Hughes Las Vegas, he realized, before the influx of Hilton and MGM money had built the massive, "respectable" casino hotels. Those that now dominated this surreal little segment of Nevada State Road 604 were low-slung, racy legacies of the postwar gangster era: the Dunes, the Tropicana, the Sands. "Rat Pack" Vegas, straight out of old caper movies with jivey, finger-snapping soundtracks. There was still a provocative hint of evil in the hot, dry air.

They checked in at the Flamingo, put sixteen thousand dollars in cash on deposit with the hotel casino. The assistant manager, all teeth and swagger, comped them to a three-room suite and all the food and drink they wanted for the duration of their stay.

Frank spent the evening checking out the blackjack tables: number of decks used, rules on splitting and doubling down, speed and personality of the various dealers. Jeff watched along with him for a while, then grew bored and went off to wander around the casino, absorbing the bizarre ambience of the place. Everything seemed illusory here: the brightly colored chips representing enormous sums of money, the flashily dressed men and women . . . desperate facades of sexual bravado and the pretense of limitless, uncaring affluence.

Jeff went back to his room early, fell asleep watching "The Jack Paar Show." When he got up the next morning he found Frank pacing around the living room of the suite, grumbling to himself and periodically referring to a set of makeshift flash cards.

"Join me for breakfast?"

Frank shook his head. "I want to go over these one last time, and hit the tables before noon. Catch the dealers at the end of the morning shift, when they're starting to fade."

"Makes sense. Good luck; I'll probably be out by the pool. Let me know how it goes."

Jeff ate alone at a table for six in the hotel restaurant, reading the *Racing Form*. The odds were still climbing on Chateaugay for the Belmont, he noted happily; but none of the dozens of other races mentioned in the paper meant anything to him. He wolfed down a double order of scrambled eggs with a thick slice of country ham, then had a large stack of pancakes and a third glass of milk. For the last few years he'd gotten in the habit of skipping breakfast entirely, maybe grabbing a Danish and the first of many cups of coffee on his way to work; but this new, young body of his had its own appetites.

Frank had gone down to the casino by the time Jeff went back to the room to change into his bathing suit. He grabbed an oversized towel and a copy of *V*, stopped by the hotel gift shop for a bottle of Coppertone (with no PABA rating, he noted), and found himself a lounge chair by the pool.

He saw her right away: wet black hair, sculpted cheekbones. Breasts ample but firm, belly trim, legs elegant and shapely. She raised herself from the pool, smiling and shining in the desert sun, and walked toward Jeff.

"Hi," she said. "Anybody using that chair?"

Jeff shook his head, motioned an invitation for her to sit beside him. She stretched out on her back, flicked her dripping hair over the back of the canvas chaise lounge to dry.

"Can I get you something to drink?" he asked, willing his eyes not to linger too long or too obviously on her droplet-beaded body.

"No, thanks," she said, but smiled and looked straight at him, taking the edge off the refusal. "I just had a Bloody Mary, and the heat's making me a little dizzy."

"It'll do that if you're not used to it," he agreed. "Where are you from?"

"Illinois, just outside Chicago. But I've been here for a couple of months, think I might stay awhile. How about you?"

"Atlanta right now," he told her, "but I grew up in Florida."

"Oh, so I guess you've always been used to the sun, hmm?"

"Pretty much." He shrugged.

"I went to Miami a couple times. It's nice, but I wish you could gamble there."

"I grew up in Orlando."

"Where's that?" she asked.

"It's near—" He almost said "Disney World," stopped himself in time, then started to say "Cape Kennedy," though he knew that wasn't the real name of the place, even in 1988. ". . . near Cape Canaveral," he finally finished. His hesitation seemed to puzzle her, but the awkward moment passed.

"Did you ever see any of those rockets go up?" she asked.

"Sure," he said, thinking of the drive he and Linda had made to the Cape in 1969 for the launch of *Apollo 11*.

"Do you think they'll ever really get to the moon, like they say?"

"Probably." He smiled. "Oh, my name's Jeff, Jeff Winston."

She extended a slender, ringless hand, and he grasped her fingers for an instant.

"I'm Sharla Baker." She took her hand back, ran it through her straight, wet hair and down her neck. "What kind of work do you do in Atlanta?"

"Well . . . I'm still in college, actually. I'm thinking about going into journalism."

She grinned good-naturedly. "A college boy, hmm? Your momma and daddy must have plenty of money, sending you to college *and* to Las Vegas."

"No," he said, amused; she couldn't have been more than twenty-two or twenty-three herself, and he'd been automatically considering the age difference from the opposite perspective. "I paid my own way here. Won the money on the Kentucky Derby."

She raised her delicate eyebrows, impressed. "Is that so? Hey, have you got a car here?"

"Yeah, why?"

Her long, tanned arms arched lazily above her head, swelling her breasts against the nylon of the demurely styled, old-fashioned bathing suit. The effect, to Jeff, was as erotic as if she'd been wearing one of those outrageous French-cut designs of the eighties, or nothing at all.

"I just thought we might get out of the sun for a little while," she said. "Maybe take a drive over to Lake Mead. You interested?"

Sharla lived in a tidy little duplex near Paradise and Tropicana. She shared the place with a girl named Becky, who worked the 4:00 P.M.-to-midnight shift at the information booth in the airport. Sharla didn't seem to do much of anything, except hang out in the casinos at night and by the hotel pools in the afternoon.

She wasn't really a hooker, just one of those Vegas girls who liked to have a good time and weren't insulted by a little gift or a handful of chips now and then. Jeff spent most of the next four days with her, and he bought her several small presents—a silver ankle bracelet, a leather purse dyed to match her favorite dress—but she never mentioned money. They went sailing on the lake, drove up to Boulder Dam, saw Sinatra's show at the Desert Inn.

Mostly, they fucked. Frequently and memorably, at her apartment or in Jeff's suite at the Flamingo. Sharla was the first woman he'd been to bed with since this whole thing had begun, the first other than Linda since he'd gotten married. Sharla's eagerness for sex more than matched his own. She was as wanton as Judy had been coy, and Jeff reveled in the heat of her unrestrained eroticism.

Frank Maddock took occasional advantage of the outright play-for-pay girls who were a feature of every lounge and casino, but he spent most of his time at the blackjack tables. Winning. By the day of the Belmont, he'd run his own stake up another nine thousand dollars, of which he generously offered Jeff a third for having bankrolled this venture in the first place. Between them, they now had almost twenty-five thousand dollars on deposit with the hotel; and Frank was, with some reservations, willing to go along with Jeff's insistent notion that they bet it all on the one race.

When post time came that Saturday, Jeff was at the Flamingo's pool with Sharla.

"Aren't you even gonna watch it on TV?" she asked as he showed no sign of budging from his rattan mat.

"Don't have to. I know how it comes out."

"Oh, you!" She laughed, slapping his rear. "Rich college boy, think you know it all."

"I won't be rich if I'm wrong."

"That'll be the day," she said, reaching for the bottle of Coppertone.

"What? That I'm wrong, or poor?"

"Oh, silly, I don't know. Here, do the backs of my legs."

Jeff was half dozing in the sun, his hand resting on Sharla's naked thigh, when Frank came out of the hotel with a look of shock on his face. Jeff bolted to his feet when he saw his friend's expression; Christ, maybe they shouldn't have bet it all.

"What's the matter, Frank?" he asked tightly.

"All that money," Frank rasped out. "All that fucking money."

Jeff grabbed him by the shoulders. "What happened? Just tell me what happened!"

Frank's lips pulled back in a crazy half-smile. "We won," he whispered.

"How much?"

"A hundred and thirty-seven thousand dollars."

Jeff relaxed, let go of his grip on Frank's arms.

"How do you do it?" Maddock asked, staring hard into Jeff's eyes. "How the hell do you do it? Three times in a row now you've called 'em right."

"Just lucky."

"Luck, my ass. You did everything but hock the family jewels to bet on Chateaugay in the Derby. You know something you're not telling, or what?"

Sharla bit her lower lip and looked up at Jeff thoughtfully. "You did say you knew how it was gonna come out."

Jeff didn't like the turn this conversation was taking. "Hey," he said with a laugh, "next time out we'll probably lose it all."

Frank grinned again, his curiosity apparently gone. "With this kind of track record, I'll follow you anywhere, kid. When do we take the plunge again? You got any good hunches coming up?"

"Yeah," Jeff said. "I've got a hunch Sharla's roommate will call in sick from work tonight, and the four of us are gonna have one hell of a celebration. That's all I'd bet on right now."

Frank laughed and headed for the poolside bar to get a bottle of champagne, while Sharla ran to phone her girlfriend. Jeff sank back down on the mat, angry at himself for having said as much as he had and wondering how he was going to tell Frank their gambling partnership was over, at least for the summer.

He damn sure wasn't about to admit that they couldn't bet on any more races this year because he couldn't remember who'd won them.

Jeff spread a thin layer of marmalade on the hot croissant, bit off one flaky corner. From the balcony above the avenue Foch he could see both the Arc de Triomphe and the green expanse of the Bois de Boulogne, each an easy walk from the apartment.

Sharla smiled at him from across the linen-covered breakfast table. She took a large red strawberry from her plate, dipped it first in a bowl of cream and then in powdered sugar, and slowly began to suck the ripe berry, her eyes still locked with Jeff's as her lips encircled the fruit.

He set aside his copy of the *International Herald-Tribune* and watched her impromptu performance with the strawberry. The news was depressingly familiar, anyway; Kennedy had delivered his *"Ich bin ein Berliner"* speech in the divided city east of here, and in Vietnam, Buddhist monks had begun immolating themselves on street corners to protest the Diem regime.

Sharla dipped the berry back into the thick cream, held it suspended above her open mouth as she licked off the white droplets with the tip of her tongue. Her silk gown was translucent in the morning sunlight, and Jeff could see her nipples as they stiffened against the thin fabric.

He'd rented the two-bedroom apartment in the Neuilly district of Paris for the entire summer, and they had left the city only for an occasional day's excursion to Versailles or Fontainebleau. It was Sharla's first trip to Europe, and Jeff wanted to experience Paris in a different manner than he had on the whirlwind package tour he'd taken with Linda. He had certainly succeeded: Sharla's lush sensualism meshed perfectly with the romantic aura of the city. On clear days they would stroll the side streets and boulevards, stopping for lunch at whatever bistro or café might capture their interest; and when it rained, as it did often that summer, they would curl up in the comfortable apartment for long, languid days of fire and flesh, with the unseasonable hazy chill of Paris outside the windows a perfect backdrop to their passion. Jeff wrapped his fears in Sharla's sleek black hair, hid his undiminished confusion in the folds of her sweet-scented, supple body.

She looked across the table at him with an impish gleam in her eye, and devoured the plump strawberry in one carnal bite. A thin trickle of the bright red juice colored her lower lip, and she wiped it slowly away with one slender, long-nailed finger.

"I want to go dancing tonight," she announced. "I want to wear that new black dress, with nothing underneath, and go dancing with you."

Jeff let his gaze wander down her body, outlined in the white silk robe. "Nothing underneath?"

"I might wear a pair of stockings," she said in a low voice. "And we'll dance the way you taught me to."

Jeff smiled, ran his fingertips lightly across her naked thigh where the robe had fallen open. One night three weeks ago they'd been dancing at one of the new "discothèques" that had recently originated here, and Jeff had spontaneously begun to lead Sharla in the sort of sinuous, free-form dance movements that would evolve over the next decade. She'd taken to the style right away, adding several erotic flourishes of her own. The other couples, all of them doing either the Twist or the Watusi, had stepped back, one by one, to watch the ways that Jeff and Sharla moved. Then, at first tentatively but with growing enthusiasm, they'd begun to dance in a similarly unstructured, openly sexy manner.

Now he and Sharla went to New Jimmy's or Le Slow Club almost every other night, and she had started to select her dresses on the basis of how enticingly they would move across her body on a dance floor. Jeff enjoyed watching her, got a kick out of seeing the other dancers mimic her moves and, more and more, her clothing. It amused him to think that in one night out with Sharla, he might unintentionally have altered the history of popular dance forms and speeded the libidinous revolution in women's fashions that would mark the mid- and late sixties.

She took his hand, moved it between her thighs beneath the robe. His croissant and café au lait sat cooling on the breakfast table, forgotten along with the mysteries of time that had so concerned him in the spring.

"When we get home," she whispered, "I'll leave the stockings on."

"So," Frank asked, "how was Paris?"

"Very nice indeed," Jeff told him, settling into one of the commodious armchairs in the Plaza's Oak Room. "Just what I needed. What do you think of Columbia?"

His former partner shrugged, signaled for a waiter. "Looks to be as much of a grind as I'd expected. You still drink Jack Daniel's?"

"When I can find it. The French never heard of sour mash."

Frank ordered the bourbon, and another Glenlivet for himself. Faint strains of violin music drifted through the open door of the bar from the Palm Court, off the lobby of the elegant old New York hotel. Above that serene back-drop could be heard the occasional quiet clink of glass against glass and the muted ambient hum of conversation, the words themselves muffled by the room's thick drapes and plush leather.

"Not exactly the kind of joint I expected to be hanging out in, my first year of law school." Frank beamed.

"It's a step up from Moe's and Joe's," Jeff agreed.

"Is Sharla here with you?"

"She's seeing *Beyond the Fringe* tonight. I told her this would be a business talk."

"You two getting along well, I take it?"

"She's easy to be with. Fun."

Frank nodded, stirred the fresh drink the waiter had set before him. "I guess you haven't seen much more of that little girl from Emory you told me about, then."

"Judy? No, that was finished before you and I ever went to Las Vegas. She's a nice girl, sweet, but . . . naive. Very young."

"Same age as you, isn't she?"

Jeff looked at him sharply. "You playing big brother

again, Frank? Trying to tell me I'm out of my league with Sharla or something?"

"No, no, it's just—You never cease to amaze me, that's all. First time I met you, I thought you were some wet-behind-the-ears kid who had a lot to learn about horse racing, among other things; but you've shown me a thing or two, yourself. I mean, Christ, winning all that money, and tooling around in that Avanti, and taking off for Europe with a woman like Sharla . . . Sometimes you seem a lot older than you really are."

"I think now would be a real good time to change the subject," Jeff said curtly.

"Hey, look, I didn't mean to insult anyone. Sharla's quite a find; I envy you. I just feel like you've . . . I don't know, grown up faster than anybody I ever knew. No value judgment intended. Shit, I suppose you could take it as a compliment. It's just kind of strange, that's all."

Jeff willed the tension out of his shoulders, sat back with his drink. "I suppose I've got a large appetite for life," he said. "I want to do a lot of things, and I want to do them fast."

"Well, you've got a hell of a head start on the flunkies of the world. More power to you. I hope it all works out as well as it has so far."

"Thanks. I'll drink to that." They raised their glasses, silently agreed to ignore the strained moment that had passed between them.

"You mentioned that you told Sharla this would be a business meeting," Frank said.

"That's right."

Frank sipped his Scotch. "So, is it?"

"That depends." Jeff shrugged.

"On what?"

"Whether you're interested in what I have to suggest."

"After what you pulled off this summer? You think I'm not gonna listen to any other wild notions you might have?"

"This one is going to sound wilder than you imagine."

"Try me."

"The World Series. Two weeks from now."

Frank cocked one eyebrow. "Knowing you, you probably want to bet on the Dodgers."

Jeff paused. "That's right."

"Hey, let's get serious; I mean, you did one bang-up job calling the Derby and the Belmont, but come on! With Mantle and Maris back in, and the first two games here in New York? No way, man. No fucking way."

Jeff leaned forward, spoke softly but insistently. "That's how it's gonna go. A shutout, the Dodgers four straight."

Frank frowned at him strangely. "You really *are* crazy."

"No. It'll happen. One-two-three-four. We could be set for life."

"We could be back drinking at Moe's and Joe's, is what you mean."

Jeff tossed down the last of his drink, sat back, and shook his head. Frank continued to stare at him, as if looking for the source of Jeff's madness.

"Maybe a small bet," Frank allowed. "Say a couple of thousand, maybe five, if you're really stuck on this hunch."

"All of it," Jeff stated.

Frank lit a Tareyton, never taking his eyes from Jeff's face. "What is it with you, anyway? Are you determined to fail, or what? There's a limit to luck, you know."

"I'm not wrong about this one, Frank. I'm betting everything I've got left, and I'll offer you the same deal as before: my money, you place the bets, seventy-thirty split. You risk nothing if you don't want to."

"Do you know the kind of odds you'd be bucking?"

"Not exactly. Do you?"

"Not off the top of my head, but—they'd be sucker odds, because only a sucker would make a bet like that."

"Why don't you make a call, find out where we'd stand?"

"I might do that, out of curiosity."

"Go ahead. I'll wait here, order us another drink. Remember, not just a win; a Dodger sweep."

Frank was away from the table less than ten minutes.

"My bookie laughed at me," he said as he sat down and reached for the fresh Scotch. "He actually laughed at me over the phone."

"What are the odds?" Jeff asked quietly.

Frank gulped down half his drink. "A hundred to one."

"Will you handle the bets for me?"

"You're really gonna do this, aren't you? You're not just joking around."

"I'm dead serious," Jeff said.

"What makes you so goddamned sure of yourself on these things? What do you know that nobody else in the world knows?"

Jeff blinked, kept his voice steady. "I can't tell you that. All I can say is, this is far more than a hunch. It's a certainty."

"That sounds suspiciously like—"

"There's nothing illegal involved, I swear. You know they couldn't fix a Series these days, and even if they could, how the hell would I know anything about it?"

"You talk like you know plenty."

"I know this much: We can't lose this bet. We absolutely cannot lose it."

Frank looked at him intently, tossed off the rest of his Scotch, and signaled for another. "Well, shit," he muttered. "Before I met you last April I figured I'd be living on a scholarship this year."

"Meaning what?"

"Meaning I guess I'll come in with you on this fool scheme. Don't ask me why, and I'll probably blow my brains out after the first game. But just one thing."

"Name it."

"No more of this seventy-thirty crap and you putting up all the money. We both take our chances, throw in whatever we've got left from Vegas—including what I raked in at the tables—and anything we win we split down the middle. Deal?"

"Deal. Partner."

It was the October of Koufax and Drysdale.

Jeff took Sharla to Yankee Stadium for the first two games, but Frank couldn't even bring himself to watch them on television.

The Dodgers took the opener 5–2, with Koufax pitching.

Johnny Podres was on the mound the next day, and with an assist from ace reliever Ron Perranoski he held the Yankees to one run, while the Dodgers punched in four on ten hits.

The third game, in L.A., was a Drysdale classic: a 1–0 shutout, with "Big Don" putting the Yankees down one right after the other. In six of the nine innings, Drysdale came up against only the minimum three batters.

Game number four was a tight one; even Jeff, watching it in color at the Pierre in New York, started to sweat. Whitey Ford, pitching for the Yankees, was up against Koufax again, and they were both out for blood. Mickey Mantle and L.A.'s Frank Howard each slammed in homers, making it a 1–1 tie by the bottom of the seventh. Then Joe Pepitone made an error on a throw by Yankee third baseman Clete Boyer, and the Dodgers' Jim Gilliam tore into third. Willie Davis was up next, and Gilliam scored the deciding run on Davis's fly to deep center.

The Dodgers had shut out the Yankees in the World Series, the first time that had happened to the New York club since the Giants had pulled it off in 1922. It was one of the great upsets in baseball history, an event Jeff couldn't have forgotten any more than he'd be likely not to remember his own name.

At Jeff's insistence, Frank had spread their $122,000 bet among twenty-three different bookies in six cities and eleven different casinos in Las Vegas, Reno, and San Juan.

Their total winnings came to more than twelve million dollars.

5

THE BETTING WAS over; they both knew that. The word was out on him and Frank, and there wasn't a bookie or casino in the country that would accept any sizable wager from either of them.

There were, of course, other kinds of bets, under more genteel names.

". . . put the accounting section in that office there, and legal staff here across the hall. Now, down this way . . ."

Frank was obviously taking great pleasure in showing Jeff around the still only half-furnished suite of offices on the fiftieth floor of the Seagram Building. He'd selected the site, with Jeff's approval, and had taken charge of all the minutiae of organizing what needed to be done, from their original incorporation as "Future, Inc." to the hiring of secretaries and bookkeepers.

Frank had quit law school, and they'd tacitly agreed that he would oversee the day-to-day operations of the company while Jeff made the larger decisions about investments and overall corporate direction. Frank no longer questioned the validity of Jeff's recommendations, but there'd been a strange pall between the two partners since the World Series coup. They rarely socialized, but Jeff knew Frank had been drinking more than ever before. His former curiosity had been replaced with an apparent growing fear of just how much Jeff knew and how he knew it. The matter was never discussed again.

". . . through this reception area here—just wait'll you see the knockout who'll be sitting at *that* desk a couple of weeks from now—and . . . here . . . we . . . are!''

The office was expansive yet somehow cozy, impressive without being intimidating. A black Barcelona chair awaited its owner behind the large oval oak desk, which faced a well-stocked bar and a handsomely cabineted TV-stereo console. Floor-to-ceiling windows on two walls offered views of the Hudson River on one side and the towers of midtown Manhattan on the other. The several flourishing plants gave a lush feeling to every corner of the room, and the framed Pollocks offered testament to the worth of human creativity. Amusingly, and with perfect appropriateness, one block of wall space was devoted to a photographic blowup of a horse bedecked with flowers: Chateaugay, in the winner's circle after the Kentucky Derby.

"All yours, buddy," Frank said, smiling.

Jeff was touched by what his friend had done. "Frank, it's fantastic!"

" 'Course, anything you don't like, we can change right away. Designer understands it's all preliminary—you have to approve it. After all, you're the one's gotta work in here.''

"Everything's great just as it is. I'm astounded. And you can't tell me some designer came up with the idea of that picture of Chateaugay.''

"No,'' Frank admitted, "that was my suggestion. Thought you might get a kick out of it.''

"It'll give me inspiration.''

"That's what I'm counting on.'' Frank laughed. "Jesus, when I think how fast all this has happened, how—Well, you know what I mean.'' The moment of boyish glee was retracted as quickly as it had appeared. This whole experience was aging Frank: the unspoken and unanswerable

questions, the shockingly sudden and inexplicable success
. . . It was all more than he could readily deal with.

"Anyway," Frank said, looking away toward the empty
reception area, "I've got a whole pile of stuff to take care
of today. Ordered a bunch of the new office calculators
from Monroe; they should have been here two days ago.
So if you want to just settle in here a bit, get a feel for the
place . . ."

"It's all right, Frank; you go ahead. I'd very much like
to sit here and think for a while. And thanks again. You're
doing a terrific job—partner."

They shook hands, clapped each other on the shoulder
in a self-conscious gesture of camaraderie. Frank strode
away toward the near-empty offices, and Jeff eased himself into the enfolding comfort of the Barcelona chair
behind the massive desk.

It had all been so easy, easier even than he'd imagined.
The races, the inning-by-inning replays of the World Series games . . . and with the huge amount of capital
accumulated from those sure-thing bets, there was no limit
to what he could do now, with equal or greater ease.

He'd already begun studying stock prices, reviewing
what he knew of the world to come and applying that
knowledge to an extrapolation of the current market situation. He couldn't remember every dip and rise of the
economy for all those years, but he was certain he had
enough general insight to make consideration of minor
recessions and setbacks irrelevant.

Some investments were obvious: IBM, Xerox, Polaroid.
Others took a bit more thought, connecting in his mind
social changes already underway or soon to come with the
companies that would benefit from those changes. The rest
of the decade, Jeff knew, would be a time of general
prosperity, with Americans traveling widely for business
or amusement; Future, Inc. should invest heavily in hotel
and airline stocks. Similarly, Boeing Aircraft had to be in
for a long upswing, even though the much-vaunted SST
program would soon be canceled; the 727 and 747, neither
announced yet, would become the primary commercial
planes of the next twenty-five years. Other aerospace com-

panies would have their own successes and failures, and Jeff felt sure some careful research would help jog his memory as to which had been awarded the most lucrative contracts for the *Apollo* program, and, ultimately, to build the space-shuttle fleet.

He gazed down at the Hudson, thick with commerce. The Japanese auto invasion would be a long time coming, as he'd noticed on that first day, and America was near the peak of its love affair with big cars; it couldn't hurt to put a million or so into Chrysler, GM, and Ford. RCA would probably be a good short-term choice, too, since color television was about to become the standard, and it would be many years before Sony made its devastating inroads into that market.

Jeff closed his eyes, giddy from the potential of it all. The monthly financial crises he had once endured, the lifelong frustration of jobs with too much responsibility and too little pay, were now concerns not only of the past, but of a future that would never be. Who cared how this had come to pass? He was young, he was wealthy, and he would soon be immeasurably richer still. He had no wish to change any of that or even question it, much less go back to that other reality he had lived or perhaps imagined. Now he could have everything he'd ever wanted, and the time and energy to enjoy it all.

". . . whether the Republican nominee is Goldwater or Rockefeller. The Baker scandal is unlikely to have any serious effect on the president's reelection bid, although a 'dump Johnson' movement within the White House inner circle is a possibility if the investigation escalates much further. Of more immediate concern to the Kennedy staff will be—"

"Can't we watch something else?" Sharla pouted. "I don't know why you care so much about all this political stuff anyway. It's a whole year before the next election."

Jeff gave her an appeasing half-smile but didn't answer.

". . . tax cut and civil-rights bills. Unless they are enacted before Congress adjourns on December twentieth, the proposals will face an even tougher uphill battle in the spring sessions of the House and Senate, and Kennedy would be forced to begin the campaign in the shadow of continued congressional battle rather than in his hoped-for aura of dual victory.''

Sharla uncurled herself from the sofa in a silent huff, walked toward the stairs that led to the upper levels of the East Seventy-third Street town house. ''I'll be waiting for you in bed,'' she called over her shoulder, bare in the peach-colored filmy nightgown. ''That is, if you're still interested.''

''. . . despite ongoing criticism of the Bay of Pigs disaster, despite bitter problems with such disparate entities as the AFL-CIO and the steel industry, the image and the man remain inseparable for the majority of the public. His windswept youthfulness, his charming wife and devoted children, the tragedies and triumphs his family has survived, the easy grace and ready sense of humor, all—''

Jeff ran back the tape on the prototype Sony VTR that had cost him over eleven thousand dollars and was doomed to failure, a product a decade ahead of its time. The black-and-white file-footage clips of John Kennedy lit the screen a second time, so familiar and yet still heart-rending: grinning in his famous rocking-chair, scooping John-John and Caroline into his arms on an airport runway, romping with his brothers on the beach at Hyannisport. So many times Jeff had seen these brief public segments of the man's life; and always, for a quarter of a century, they had been followed by the open limousine in Dallas, the frenzied horror, the blood on Jackie's clothes and the roses in her arms. But no such images existed now. Tonight, on this tape of a news show broadcast not two hours before, there would be no photograph of Lyndon Johnson assuming the mantle of power, no funeral cortege through Washington, no Eternal Flame at the fade-out. Tonight the man of whom they spoke was alive, vital, full of plans for his own future and that of the nation.

''. . . grace and ready sense of humor, all lend at least superficial weight to the notions of a New Frontier, a fresh beginning . . . the advent, as some would have it, of a modern-day Camelot. It is this enormously positive image, rather than any solid record of first-term accomplishments, that the newly appointed Kennedy reelection team will have to work with. Sorensen, O'Donnell, Salinger, O'Brien, and Bobby Kennedy are all well aware of their candidate's strengths and weaknesses, and of the power of instant myths. You may be sure they know where to concentrate their attention in the upcoming campaign.''

The newscast switched to a shot of Charles de Gaulle visiting the Shah of Iran amid much pomp and circumstance, and Jeff turned off the machine. Kennedy alive, he thought, as he had thought so often in the past few weeks. Kennedy leading the nation toward who knew what—continued prosperity, racial harmony, an early disengagement from Vietnam?

John F. Kennedy alive. Until three weeks from now.

Unless, unless . . . what? The fantasy was irresistible, outlandish and even clichéd though it might be. But this was no television drama, no science-fiction plot; Jeff was here, in this as-yet-unshattered world of 1963, with the greatest tragedy of the era about to unfold before his too-knowing eyes. Was it possible that he might intervene, and would it be proper? He had already begun to wreak major changes in the economic realities of the time, merely by establishing the existence of Future, Inc., and the space-time continuum had not yet shown any signs of unbearable strain.

Surely, Jeff thought, there must be something he could do about the imminent assassination, short of actually confronting the killer himself in that sixth-floor room of the Texas School Book Depository on November twenty-second. A phone call to the FBI, a letter to the Secret Service? But of course no one in authority would take his warnings seriously, and even if someone did, he'd probably be arrested as a suspected conspirator.

He poured himself a drink from the wet bar by the patio entrance and considered the problem. Anyone he spoke to about it would dismiss him as a lunatic; until, that is, after the president's motorcade had passed through Dealey Plaza, had entered and so tragically departed the killing ground.

Then there'd be hell to pay, and too late to do the world a bit of good.

So what should he do, just sit back and watch the murder happen? Let history brutally repeat itself because he was afraid of appearing foolish?

Jeff looked around the tastefully appointed town house, so far superior to any residence he or Linda had ever hoped to occupy. It had taken him only six months to acquire all this, with almost no effort at all. Now he could spend a lifetime limitlessly expanding his comfort and his wealth because of what he knew; but those achievements would stick in his craw forever if he failed to act on what *else* he knew.

Something, somehow, must be done.

He flew to Dallas on the fifteenth, and stopped at the first phone booth he came to in the airport. He thumbed through the *O*'s and there it was, a listing like any other, though to his eyes the letters stood out from the page as if they had been inscribed in flames:

Oswald, Lee H. . . . . 1026 N. Beckley 555-4821

Jeff wrote down the address, then rented a plain blue Plymouth from Avis. The girl at the counter told him how to find the part of town he was looking for.

He drove past the white frame house in Oak Cliff six times. He pictured himself walking to the door, ringing the bell, speaking to the soft-voiced young Russian woman, Marina, who would answer. What would he say to her? ''Your husband is going to kill the president; you have to stop him''? What if the assassin himself came to the door? What would he do then?

Jeff drove slowly past the ordinary little house once more, thinking of the man who dwelt within it, who waited and plotted to shatter the world's complacency.

He left the neighborhood without stopping. At a K-Mart in Fort Worth he bought a cheap portable typewriter, some typing paper, and a pair of gloves. Back in his anonymous Holiday Inn room off the East Airport Expressway he put on the gloves, opened the sheaf of paper, and began composing a letter that it sickened him to write:

President John F. Kennedy
The White House
1600 Pennsylvania Avenue
Washington, D.C.

President Kennedy:

It is you who have alienated Premier Fidel Castro and the liberated peoples of Cuba. You are the oppressor, the enemy of free men throughout Latin America and the world.

If you come to Dallas I will kill you. I will shoot you in the head with a high-powered rifle, and in your spilled blood will be written JUSTICE for the freedom fighters of the Western hemisphere.

This is not an idle threat. I am well armed, and prepared to die myself if need be.

I will murder you.

VENCEREMOS!!
Lee Harvey Oswald

Jeff added Oswald's home address, drove back across town, and put the letter in a mailbox two blocks from the nondescript frame house. An hour later, and forty miles southeast of Dallas, the gloves were getting sweaty. The tightening leather numbed his hands as he pitched the typewriter off a bridge into a large lake in the middle of nowhere. It felt good to finally pull the damned gloves off, to toss them out the car window near some godforsaken town named, of all things, Gun Barrel. His hands felt freer, cleaner.

For the next four days he stayed in his room at the Holiday Inn, speaking to no one but room service and emerging only to buy the local papers. On Tuesday, the nineteenth, the *Dallas Herald* had the item he'd been waiting for, on page five: Lee Harvey Oswald had been arrested by the Secret Service for threatening the life of the president, and would be held without bail until Kennedy had completed his one-day trip to Texas at the end of the week.

Jeff got very drunk on the plane back to New York that night, but the alcohol had nothing to do with the triumph he felt, the exultant thoughts that crowded his brain: images of a world in which negotiation took the place of war in Vietnam, in which the hungry were fed, racial equality attained without bloodshed . . . a world in which John Kennedy and the hopeful spirit of humanity would not die, but would blossom and prosper upon the earth.

As his plane landed, the lights of Manhattan seemed a brilliant portent of the glorious future Jeff had just created.

At ten minutes past one on Friday afternoon, his secretary opened the door to his office without knocking. She stood there with tears streaming down her face, unable to speak. Jeff didn't have to ask what was wrong. He felt as if he had been struck in the gut by an invisible, heavy object.

Frank came in behind her, quietly told the young woman there'd be no more business conducted today; she and everyone else should go home. He took Jeff in tow, and they left the building together. People milled about Park Avenue in a general stupor. A few wept openly; some were gathered around car or transistor radios. Most just stared blankly ahead, putting one foot absentmindedly before the other in a slow, distracted gait wholly uncharacteristic of New Yorkers. It was as if an earthquake had loosened the solid concrete of Manhattan and no one was sure of stable footing. No one knew whether the streets would tremble and buckle again, or even split apart to swallow up the world. The future had arrived, in one jolting instant.

Frank and Jeff found a table at a hushed bar off Madison. On the television screen, Air Force One was leaving Dallas, the body of the president on board. In his mind's eye, Jeff saw the photograph of LBJ taking his oath of office, with a dazed Jacqueline Kennedy beside him. The bloodstained dress, the roses.

"What happens now?" Frank asked.

Jeff tore himself from his macabre reverie. "What do you mean?"

"What's next for the world? Where do we all go from here?"

Jeff shrugged. "I guess a lot depends on Johnson. What kind of president he'll make. What do you think?"

Frank shook his head. "You don't 'guess' anything, Jeff. I've never seen you make a guess. You *know* things."

Jeff looked around for a waiter; they were all watching the television, listening to a young Dan Rather recapitulate the afternoon's momentous events for the twentieth time. "I don't know what you're talking about."

"Neither do I, not exactly. But there's something that's . . . not right with you. Something odd. And I don't like it."

His partner's hands were trembling, Jeff saw; he must be in bad need of a drink.

"Frank, it's a terrible, strange day. We're all kind of in shock right now."

"You're not. Not the way I am, and everybody else. Nobody in the office even told you what had happened; it was like they didn't have to, like you knew what was coming."

"Don't be absurd." A burly police official was being interviewed on TV, describing the statewide manhunt now underway in Texas.

"What were you doing in Dallas last week?"

Jeff eyed Frank wearily. "What'd you do, check with the travel agency?"

"Yeah. What were you doing there?"

"Looking into some property for us. It's a growth market, despite what's happened there today."

"Maybe that'll change."

"I don't think so."

"You don't, huh? Why not?"

"Just a feeling I have."

"We've come a long way on these 'feelings' of yours."

"And we can go further still."

Frank sighed, ran his hand through his prematurely thinning hair. "No. Not me. I've had it. I want out."

"Jesus Christ, we've hardly even started!"

"I'm sure you'll do spectacularly well. But it's gotten too weird for me, Jeff. I don't feel comfortable working with you anymore."

"For God's sake, you don't think I had anything to do with—"

Frank held up his hand, cut him off. "I haven't said that. I don't want to know. I just want . . . out. You can hang on to the bulk of my share for working capital, pay me back out of profits over the next few years, or however long it takes. I'd recommend you turn my end of the operations over to Jim Spencer; he's a good man, knows what he's doing. And he'll follow your instructions to the letter."

"Damn it, we were in this together! All the way back to the Derby, to Emory—"

"So we were, and it's been a hell of a streak. But I'm cashing in my chips, old partner. Walking away from the table."

"To do what?"

"Finish law school, I suppose. Make some nice, conservative investments of my own; I've got enough to keep me set for life."

"Don't do this, Frank. You'd be missing out on the opportunity of a lifetime."

"Of that I have no doubt. Maybe someday I'll regret it, but right now it's what I have to do. For my own peace of mind." He stood up, extended his hand. "Good luck, and thanks for everything. It was some fun while it lasted."

They shook hands, Jeff wondering what he could have done to prevent this. Maybe nothing. Maybe it had to happen.

"I'll talk to Spencer on Monday," Frank said. "Assuming the world's still at peace and the country's functioning by then."

Jeff gave him a long, sober look. "It will be."

"Good to know. Take care, partner."

When Frank had left, Jeff moved to a stool at the bar, finally got a drink. He was on his third when CBS broke the bulletin: ". . . arrested a suspect in connection with the assassination of President Kennedy. I repeat, Dallas police have arrested a suspect in connection with the assassination of President Kennedy. The man is said to be a drifter and sometime left-wing activist named Nelson Bennett. Authorities say a telephone number found in Bennett's pocket has been traced to the Soviet Embassy in Mexico City. We'll have more on this late-breaking story as soon as . . ."

The patio of the East Side town house was bleak in the late-November chill; it was a place designed for summer, in a world where summer had been banished. The glass-topped table, the polished chrome struts of the lounge chairs, somehow made this sunless day more barren still.

Jeff pulled his thick cardigan sweater tightly closed and wondered, for the hundredth time in the past two days, just what had happened on that unstoppable day in Dallas. Who the hell was Nelson Bennett? A backup hired assassin waiting in the wings when Oswald was arrested? Or merely a fluke of chance, a random crazy, manipulated by forces far more powerful than any human conspiracy in order that the flow of reality not be disrupted?

There would be no knowing, he realized. He faced enough else beyond his comprehension in this restructured life; why should this particular element be less insoluble than all the rest? And yet it mocked him, chastened him. He had tried to use his prescience to reshape destiny in a positive way, something far surpassing the triviality of his wagers, his investment schemes—and his efforts had created no more than a minor ripple in the stream of history. A killer's name had been changed, no more.

What, he wondered, did that bode for his own future? All the hopes he had of rebuilding his life with the advantage of foreknowledge . . . were they doomed to be mere superficial changes, quantitative but not qualitative? Would his attempts at achieving genuine happiness be as inexplicably thwarted as his intervention in the Kennedy affair?

All that, too, was beyond his ken. Six weeks ago he had felt a godlike omniscience, and his potential for accomplishment had seemed without limit. Now, once more, everything was open to question. He felt a numbing sense of hopelessness worse than any he had known since boarding school, on that terrible day beside the little bridge where he'd—

"Jeff! Oh, my God, come here! They've killed Bennett, it was on the TV, I saw it happen!"

He nodded slowly, followed Sharla inside. The murder was being shown again and again, as he'd known it would be. There was Jack Ruby in his B-movie gangster's hat, appearing out of nowhere in the basement corridor of the Dallas County Jail. There was the pistol, and Nelson Bennett dying on cue, the twisted agony on his bearded face like a distorted reflection of Lee Harvey Oswald's well-documented death.

President Johnson, Jeff knew, would soon order a full investigation of the events of this bloody weekend. A special commission, headed by Chief Justice Earl Warren. Answers would be diligently sought; none would be found. Life would go on.

6

JEFF DIDN'T INVOLVE himself in much after that except making money. He was very good at making money.

Motion-picture stocks were one fairly easy pick. The mid-sixties had been a time of heavy movie attendance and the first multimillion-dollar sales of films like *The Bridge on the River Kwai* and *Cleopatra* to the networks. Jeff shied away from small electronics companies, though he knew many of them would multiply tremendously in value; he just didn't remember the names of the winners. Instead, he poured money into the conglomerates he knew had thrived through the decade on such investments: Litton, Teledyne, Ling-Temco-Vought. His selections were almost uniformly profitable from the day the stocks were purchased, and he plowed the bulk of that income back into still more shares.

It was something to do.

Sharla had enjoyed the fight, despite the fact that she'd perversely bet on Liston when Jeff told her to go with Cassius Clay. Jeff's reactions to the evening had been decidedly more mixed: not so much to the fight itself, but to the setting, the crowd. Several of the high rollers and bookies in attendance had recognized Jeff from the publicity that had spread through the gambling world after his record World Series win; even some of the men who'd had to pay off large portions of that multimillion-dollar pot gave him wide grins and "thumbs up" signs. He might have been excommunicated from their circle, but he'd become legendary within it, and was accorded all the honor due a legend of that magnitude.

In a sense, he supposed, that was what had bothered him—the gamblers' visible respect was too clear a reminder that he had begun this version of his life by pulling a massive, if unfathomable, scam on the American underworld. He would be remembered forever by them in that context, no matter what his subsequent successes in society at large. It made him want to take a long, hot shower, get rid of the implied stench of cigar smoke and dirty money.

But the problem was something more concrete, too, he thought as the limousine sped down Collins Avenue past the vulgar facades of Miami Beach's hotel row. It was, specifically, Sharla.

She had fit right in with the fight crowd, had looked perfectly at home among the other pneumatic young women in their tight, flashy dresses and excessive makeup. Face it, he thought, glancing at her in the seat beside him: She looks cheap. Expensive but cheap; like Las Vegas, like Miami Beach. From the most cursory of appraisals it was clear to anyone that Sharla was, quite simply, a machine designed for fucking. Nothing more. The very image of a Girl Not To Take Home To Mother, and he grimaced to think that he had done precisely that: They'd stopped in Orlando on their way down here for the championship bout. His family had been overwhelmed and more than a little intimidated by the extent of his sudden financial triumphs, but even that couldn't hide their contempt for Sharla, their anxious disappointment at the news that Jeff was living with her.

She leaned forward to fish a pack of cigarettes from her purse, and as she did so the black satin bodice of her dress fell slack, giving Jeff a glimpse of the creamy expanse of her generous breasts. Even now he desired her, felt a familiar urge to press his face into that flesh, slide the dress up and over her perfect legs.

He'd been with this woman for almost a year, sharing everything with her except his mind and his emotions. The thought was suddenly distasteful, her very beauty a rebuke to his sensibilities. Why had he let this go on for so long? Her initial appeal was understandable; Sharla had been a fantasy within the fantasy, a tantalizing *pièce de résistance* to go along with his restored youth. But it was an essentially empty attraction, as juvenile in its lack of substance or complexity as the bullfight posters on the walls of his college dorm room.

He watched her light the cigarette, her deceptively aristocratic face bathed in the dim red glow of the lighter. She caught him staring, raised her slender eyebrows in a look of sexual challenge and promise. Jeff looked away, out at the lights of Miami across the still, clear water.

Sharla spent the next morning shopping on Lincoln Road, and Jeff was waiting for her in the suite at the Doral when she returned. She set her packages in the foyer, moved immediately to the nearest mirror to freshen her makeup. Her short white sundress set off her glorious tan, and her high-heeled sandals made her bare brown legs look even longer and slimmer than they were. Jeff ran his thumbs along the sharp edges of the thick brown envelope in his hand, and he came very close to changing his mind.

"What are you doing inside?" she asked, reaching back to unzip the breezy cotton dress. "Let's get into our suits, grab some sun."

Jeff shook his head, motioned for her to sit in the chair across from him. She frowned, pulled the zipper closed over her tawny back, and sat where he indicated.

"What's with you?" she asked. "Why the strange mood?"

He started to speak, but had decided hours ago that words would be inappropriate. They'd never really talked anyway, about anything; verbal communication had little to do with what passed between them. He handed her the envelope.

Sharla pursed her lips as she took it, tore it open. She stared at the six neat stacks of hundred-dollar bills for several moments. "How much?" she finally asked, in a calm, controlled voice.

"Two hundred thousand."

She peered back inside the envelope, extracted the single Panagra Airlines first-class ticket to Rio. "This is for tomorrow morning," she said, inspecting it. "What about my things in New York?"

"I'll send them wherever you like."

She nodded. "I'll need to buy some more things here, before I leave."

"Whatever you want. Charge it to the room."

Sharla nodded again, put the money and the ticket back in the envelope, which she set on the table beside her. She stood up, undid the dress, and let it fall to the floor around her feet.

"What the hell," she said, unhooking her bra, "for two hundred thousand you deserve one last go."

Jeff went back to New York alone, back to his investments.

Skirts, he knew, would be getting shorter for the next few years, creating an enormous demand for patterned stockings and panty hose. Jeff bought thirty thousand shares of Hanes. All those exposed thighs had to lead somewhere; he bought heavily in the pharmaceutical houses that manufactured birth-control pills.

Eighteen months after they'd moved into the Seagram Building, Future, Inc.'s holdings had risen to a paper value of thirty-seven million dollars. Jeff repaid Frank in full, and sent a long personal letter with the final check. He never received a reply.

Not everything worked exactly as Jeff planned, of course. He wanted to acquire a major portion of Comsat when it went public, but the stock was so wildly popular that the issue was limited to fifty shares per buyer. IBM, surprisingly, remained stagnant all the way through 1965, though it took off again the following year. Fast-food chains—Jeff

chose Denny's, Kentucky Fried Chicken, and McDonald's—
went through a big slump in 1967, before skyrocketing up
an average five hundred percent one year later.

By 1968 his company's assets were into the hundreds of
millions, and he had approved an I. M. Pei design for a
sixty-story corporate-headquarters building at Park and Fifty-
third. Jeff also mandated the purchase of extensive parcels
of land in choice commercial and residential areas of
Houston, Denver, Atlanta, and Los Angeles. The company
bought close to half of the undeveloped property in L.A.'s
new Century City project, at a price of five dollars per
square foot. For his personal use, Jeff bought a three-
hundred-acre estate in Dutchess County, two hours up the
Hudson from Manhattan.

He went out with a variety of women, slept with some
of them, hated the whole meaningless process. Drinks,
dinners, plays and concerts and gallery openings . . . He
grew to despise the rigid formality of dating, missed the
easy familiarity of simply *being* with someone, sharing
friendly silences and unforced laughter. Besides, most of
the women he met were either too openly interested in his
wealth or too studiedly blasé about it. Some even hated
him for it, refused to go out with him because of it;
immense personal fortunes were anathema to many young
people in the late sixties, and on more than one occasion
Jeff was made to feel directly responsible for all the world's
ills, from starvation in the inner cities to the manufacture
of napalm.

He bided his time, focused his energies on work. June
was coming, he reminded himself constantly. June 1968;
that was when everything would change.

The twenty-fourth of June, to be precise.

Robert Kennedy was not quite three weeks dead, and
Cassius Clay, now stripped of his title and reborn as
Muhammad Ali, was appealing his conviction for draft
evasion. In Vietnam the rockets from the north had been
striking Saigon since early spring.

It had been midafternoon, Jeff recalled, on a Monday.
He'd been working nights and weekends at a Top 40

station in West Palm Beach, playing the Beatles and the Stones and Aretha Franklin and learning the essentials of broadcast journalism on his own time, selling his interviews and stories to the station and occasionally to UPI audio on a per-piece basis. He remembered the date because it was the beginning of his Monday/Tuesday "weekend," and when he returned to work that Wednesday he'd somehow managed to arrange the first big interview of his career, a long and candid telephone conversation with retiring U.S. Supreme Court Chief Justice Earl Warren. He still didn't know why Warren had consented to talk to him, a noncredentialed novice reporter from a small-time radio station in Florida; but somehow he'd managed to pull it off, and the great man's pithy ruminations on his controversial tenure had been picked up by NBC for a healthy sum. Within a month, Jeff had been doing news full time at WIOD in Miami. He was off and running; his entire adult life, such as it had been, could be traced back to that summer week.

There'd been no reason for him to choose Boca Raton; no reason not to. Some Mondays he'd drive north, to Juno Beach; on others he might head down to Delray Beach or Lighthouse Point, any of a hundred interconnected strips of sand and civilization that lined the Atlantic coast from Melbourne to South Miami Beach. But on June twenty-fourth, 1968, he'd taken a blanket and a towel and a cooler full of beer to the beach off Boca Raton, and now here he was again in that same place on that same sunny day.

And there *she* was, lying on her back in a yellow crocheted bikini, her head propped on an inflatable beach pillow, reading a hardcover copy of *Airport*. Jeff stopped ten feet away and stood looking at her youthful body, the lemony streaks in her thick brown hair. The sand was hot against his feet; the surf echoed the pounding in his brain. For a moment he almost turned and walked away, but he didn't.

"Hi," he said. "Good book?"

The girl peered up at him through her clear-rimmed, owlish sunglasses and shrugged. "Kind of trashy, but it's fun. It'd make a better movie, probably."

Or several, Jeff thought. "You seen *2001* yet?"

"Yeah, but I didn't know what it was all about, and it was kind of draggy up to the end. I liked *Petulia* better; you know, with Julie Christie?"

He nodded, tried to make his smile more natural, relaxed. "My name's Jeff. Mind if I sit with you?"

"Go right ahead. I'm Linda," said the woman who had been his wife for eighteen years.

He spread his blanket, opened the cooler, and offered her a beer. "Summer vacation?" he asked.

She shifted on one elbow, took the dewy bottle. "I go to Florida Atlantic, but my family lives right here in town. How about you?"

"I grew up in Orlando, went to Emory for a while. Living in New York now, though."

Jeff was striving for an air of nonchalance but having trouble; he couldn't keep his eyes off her face, wished she'd take off those damned sunglasses so he could see the eyes he'd known so well. His final memory of her voice reverberated in his skull, tinny and distant, a telephone voice: "We need—We need—We need—"

"I said, what do you do up there?"

"Oh, sorry, I—" he took a swig of the icy beer, tried to clear his head. "I'm in business."

"What kind?"

"Investments."

"You mean, like a stockbroker?"

"Not exactly. I have my own company. We deal with a lot of brokers. Stocks, real estate, mutual funds . . . like that."

She lowered the big round sunglasses, gave him a look of surprise. He stared into the familiar brown eyes, wanting to say so much: "It'll be different this time," or "Please, let's try it again," or even simply "I've missed you; I'd forgotten how lovely you were." He said nothing, just looked at her eyes in silent hope.

"You own the whole company?" she asked, incredulous.

"Now I do, yes. It was a partnership until a few years ago, but . . . it's all mine now."

She set her beer in the sand, scrunching the bottle back and forth until she'd dug out a space to hold it upright.

"Did you have some kind of big inheritance or something? I mean, most guys I know couldn't even get a *job* in a company like that in New York . . . or else they wouldn't want to."

"No, I built it up myself, from scratch." He laughed, starting to feel more relaxed with her, confident and proud of his achievements for the first time in years. "I won a lot of money on some bets, horse races and such, and I put it all into this company."

She regarded him skeptically. "How old are you, anyway?"

"Twenty-three." He paused a beat, realized he was talking too much about himself, hadn't expressed enough curiosity about her. She had no way of knowing he already knew everything about her, more—at this point in her life—than she knew about herself. "What about you; what are you studying?"

"Sociology. Were you a business major at Emory, or what?"

"History, but I dropped out. What year are you?"

"Senior this fall. So how big of a deal is this company of yours? I mean, have you got a lot of people working for you? Have you got an office right in Manhattan?"

"A whole building, at Park and Fifty-third. Do you know New York?"

"You have your own building, on Park Avenue. That's nice." She wasn't looking at him anymore, was drawing daisy-petal curlicues in the sand around the beer bottle. Jeff remembered a day, months before they were married, when she'd shown up unexpectedly at his door with a bunch of daisies; the sun had been behind her hair, and all of summer in her smile.

"Well, it's . . . taken a lot of effort," he said. "So, what do you plan to do when you get out of school?"

"Oh, I thought maybe I'd buy a few department stores. Start small, you know." She folded her towel, began gathering her belongings from the blanket and stuffing them into a large blue beach bag. "Maybe you could help me get a good deal on Saks Fifth Avenue, hmm?"

"Hey—hold on, please don't go. You think I'm putting you on, is that it?"

"Just forget about it," she said, cramming her book into the bag and shaking sand from the blanket.

"No, look, I'm serious. I wasn't kidding around. My company's called Future, Inc. Maybe you've even heard of—"

"Thanks for the beer. Better luck next time."

"Hey, please, let's just talk a little longer, O.K.? I feel as if I know you, as if we have a lot to share. Do you know that feeling, like you've been with someone in some previous life, or—"

"I don't believe in that kind of nonsense." She threw the folded blanket over one arm and started walking toward the highway and the rows of parked cars.

"Look, just give me a chance," Jeff said, following alongside her. "I know for a fact that if we just get to know each other we'll have a lot in common; we'll—"

She wheeled on her bare feet and glared at him over the sunglasses. "If you don't stop following me I'm going to yell for the lifeguard. Now, back off, buddy. Go pick up somebody else, all right?"

"Hello?"

"Linda?"

"It's Jeff, Jeff Winston. We met on the beach this afternoon. I—"

"How the hell did you get this number? I never even told you my last name!"

"That's not important. Listen, I'm sending you a recent issue of *Business Week*. There's an article about me in there, with a photograph. Page forty-eight. You'll see I wasn't lying."

"You have my *address*, too? What kind of stunt is this, anyway? What do you want from me?"

"I just want to get to know you, and have you get to know me. There's so much left undone between us, so many wonderful possibilities for—"

"You're crazy! I mean it; you're some kind of psycho!"

"Linda, I know this has started badly, but just give me the opportunity to explain. Give *us* the leeway to approach each other in an open, honest manner, to find—"

"I don't want to get to know you, whoever the hell you are. And I don't care if you're rich, I don't care if you're goddamn J. Paul Getty, O.K.? Just leave . . . me . . . alone!"

"I understand that you're upset. I know all this must seem very strange to you—"

"If you call this number again, or if you show up at my house, I'll call the police. Is that clear enough?"

The phone slammed loudly in Jeff's ear as she hung up.

He'd been given the chance to relive most of his life; now he'd trade it all for another shot at this one day.

The Mirassou Vineyards teemed with pickers working the slopes southeast of San Jose, great buckets of fresh green grapes atop their heads as they wound their way like harvest ants down to the crusher and the presses outside the old cellar. The hills rippled with wide-spaced rows of trellised vines, and here among the masonry buildings the oaks and elms were a splendor of October colors.

Diane had been angry at him all day, and the bucolic setting and arcane intricacies of the winery had done little to appease her. Jeff never should have taken her along with him this morning; he'd thought she might be fascinated, or at least amused, by the two young geniuses, but he was wrong.

"Hippies, that's all they were. That tall boy was *barefoot*, for God's sake, and the other one looked like a . . . a Neanderthal!"

"Their idea has a lot of potential; it doesn't matter what they looked like."

"Well, somebody ought to tell them the sixties are over, if they want to do anything with that silly idea of theirs. I just don't believe you fell for it, and gave them all that money!"

"It's my money, Diane. And I've told you before, the business decisions are all mine, too."

He couldn't really blame her for the way she'd reacted; without benefit of foresight, the two young men and their garageful of secondhand electronic components would indeed seem unlikely candidates for a spot on the Fortune 500. But within five years that garage in Cupertino, California would be famous, and Steve Jobs and Steve Wozniak would prove to be the soundest investment of 1976. Jeff had given them half a million dollars, insisted they follow the advice of a retired young marketing executive from Intel they had recently met, and told them to make whatever they wanted as long as they continued to call it "Apple." He had let them keep forty-nine percent of the new enterprise.

"Who in the world would want a computer in their house? And what makes you think those scruffy boys really know how to make one, anyway?"

"Let's drop it, all right?"

Diane went into one of her petulant silences, and Jeff knew the matter wouldn't really be dropped, not even if she remained silent about it from now on.

He'd married her a year ago, out of convenience if nothing else, soon after he'd turned thirty. She'd been a twenty-three-year-old socialite from Boston, heiress to one of the country's oldest and largest insurance firms; attractive in a reedy sort of way, and able to handle herself quite well in any gathering where the individual net worths of the participants exceeded seven figures. She and Jeff got along as well as could be expected for two people who had little in common other than their familiarity with money. Now Diane was seven months pregnant, and Jeff had hopes that the child might bring out the best in her, forge a deeper bond between them.

The young blond woman in the tailored navy suit led them inside the main winery building, to the tasting room in one front corner. Diamond-shaped racks of bottled wine lined the walls, broken by softly lit recesses in which photographs of the vineyards were displayed, along with cut flowers and standing bottles of the Mirassou product. Jeff and Diane stood at the rosewood bar in the center of the room, accepted ritual sips of Chardonnay.

Linda had, apparently, meant everything she'd said after that disastrous meeting on the beach seven years ago. His letters to her had been returned unopened, and the gifts he'd sent were all refused. After a few months he had finally stopped attempting to contact her, though he added her name to the list of "Personal/Priority" subjects to be kept track of by the clipping service to which he subscribed. That was how he'd learned, in May of 1970, that Linda had married a Houston architect, a widower with two young children. Jeff wished her happiness, but couldn't help feeling abandoned . . . by someone who had never known him, as far as she was concerned.

Again he had sought solace in his work. His most recent coup had been the sale, at enormous profit, of his oil fields in Venezuela and Abu Dhabi, and their immediate replacement with similar properties in Alaska and Texas, plus the contracts for a dozen offshore drilling rigs. All deals completed, of course, just before the OPEC sword had fallen.

The women whose company he sought had all been similar, in most respects, to Diane: attractive, well-groomed companions, versed in all the most rarefied of social skills, accomplished, and, on occasion, enthusiastic in bed. Daughters of fortune, a sisterhood of what passed for the American *beau monde*. Women who knew the ground rules, had understood from birth the boundaries of and obligations attendant upon the holders of great wealth. They were his peers now; they constituted the pool from which he should in all rationality select a mate. His choice of Diane among them had been almost random. She fit the appropriate criteria. If something greater were eventually to grow of their pairing, well and good . . . and if not, then at least he had not come to the marriage with unrealistically high expectations.

Jeff cleansed his palate with a bit of cheese and sampled a semisweet Fleuri Blanc. Diane abstained this time, patted her swollen belly by way of explanation.

Maybe the child would make a difference, after all. You never knew.

*   *   *

The plump orange cat skittered across the hardwood floor in a headlong broken-field run good enough to match the best performance of O. J. Simpson. His prey, a shiny yellow satin ribbon, had suffered crippling damage and would soon be shredded if the cat had his way with it.

"Gretchen!" Jeff called. "Did you know Chumley's tearing up one of your yellow ribbons?"

"It's O.K., Daddy," his daughter answered from the far corner of the large sitting room, near the window overlooking the Hudson. "Ken's home now, and Chumley and I are helping to celebrate."

"When did he get home? Isn't he still in the hospital in Germany?"

"Oh, no, Daddy; he told the doctors he wasn't sick and he had to get home right away. So Barbie sent him a ticket for the Concorde, and he got home before *anybody* else, and as soon as he walked in the door she cooked him six blueberry muffins and four hot dogs."

Jeff laughed aloud, and Gretchen shot him the most withering look her wide-eyed five-year-old's face could muster. "They don't have hot dogs in Iran," she explained. "Or blueberry muffins, either."

"I guess not," Jeff said, keeping his expression carefully somber. "I suppose he'd be hungry for American food by now, huh?"

" 'Course he would. Barbie knows how to make him happy."

The cat darted back in the other direction, batting the tattered ribbon between his paws, then settled on his side in a patch of sunlight to gloat over his conquest, kicking at it in sporadic bursts with his hind legs. Gretchen went back to her own games, absorbed in the alternate reality of the elaborate dollhouse that Jeff had spent more than a year building and expanding to her specifications. The miniature trees in its green felt front yard were now festooned with bright yellow ribbons, and for the past week she'd been following news reports of the end of the hostage crisis with a depth of interest most children invested only in the Saturday-morning cartoon shows. At first Jeff had been concerned about her fascination with the events in Tehran, had wanted to protect her from the potentially traumatizing effects of watching all those rabid mobs chanting "Death to the U.S."; but he'd known the episode would have a peaceful, upbeat conclusion, so he chose to respect his daughter's precocious grasp of the world and to trust in her emotional resilience.

He loved her to a degree he had not thought possible, found himself simultaneously wanting to shield her from all darkness and share with her all light. Gretchen's arrival had done nothing to cement his marriage to Diane, who, if anything, seemed to resent the constraints on her life that the child represented. But no matter, Gretchen herself was source and object of all the deep affection he could encompass or imagine.

Jeff watched as she took another ribbon from one of the dollhouse trees, taunted fat old Chumley with it. The cat was tired, didn't want to play anymore; it put a soft paw entreatingly on Gretchen's cheek, and she buried her face in its furry golden belly, nuzzling the animal to full contentment. Jeff could hear its purr from across the room, mingled with his daughter's gentle laughter.

The sun slanted higher through the tall bay windows, fell in brilliant striated beams upon the polished floor where Gretchen snuggled with the cat. This house, this tranquil, wooded place in Dutchess County, was good for her; its serenity was balm for any human soul, young or old, innocent or troubled.

Jeff thought of his old roommate, Martin Bailey. He'd called Martin soon after Gretchen was born, reestablished the contact that had somehow, in this life, been broken for so many years. Jeff hadn't been able to talk him out of what would prove to be a particularly disastrous marriage, one that had originally led the man to suicide; but he'd made sure Martin had a secure position with Future, Inc., and some excellent stock tips now and then. His friend was divorced again, miserably so, but at least he was alive, and solvent.

Jeff seldom thought of Linda these days, or of his old existence. It was that first life that seemed a dream now; reality was the emotional stalemate with Diane, the blissfulness of being with his daughter, Gretchen, and the mixed blessings of his ever-growing wealth and power. Reality was knowledge and all that it had brought him— good and ill.

The image on the screen was one of pure organic motion: liquid rippling smoothly through curved chambers, expansion and contraction alternating in a perfect, lazy rhythm.

". . . no apparent blockage of either ventricle, as you can see. And, of course, the Holter EKG showed no evidence of tachycardia during the twenty-four hours that you wore it."

"So what exactly does all that boil down to?" Jeff asked.

The cardiologist turned off the video-cassette machine that had been displaying the ultrasonic depiction of Jeff's heart, and smiled.

"What it means is that your heart is in as close to perfect condition as any forty-three-year-old American male could hope it to be. So are your lungs, according to the X rays and the pulmonary-function tests."

"Then my life expectancy—"

"Keep yourself in this kind of shape, and you'll probably make it to a hundred. Still going to the gym, I take it?"

"Three times a week." Jeff had profited from his anticipation of the late-seventies fitness craze in more ways than one. He not only owned Adidas and Nautilus and the Holiday Health Spa chain; he'd made full use of all their equipment for over a decade.

"Well, don't stop," the doctor said. "I only wish all my patients took such good care of themselves."

Jeff made small talk for a few more minutes, but his mind was elsewhere: It was on himself at exactly this age, in this same year, yet more than twenty years ago. Himself as a sedentary, overstressed, and slightly overweight executive, clutching his chest and pitching face-forward on his desk as the world went blank.

Not this time. This time he'd be fine.

*   *   *

Jeff preferred the comfort of the back room at La Grenouille, but Diane considered even lunch an occasion at which seeing and being seen was of prime importance. So they always ate in the front room, crowded and noisy though it invariably was.

Jeff savored his poached salmon with tarragon, basil, and mild-vinegar sauce, doing his best to ignore both Diane's present sulk and the conversations from the tables pressed tightly on either side of them. One couple was discussing marriage, the other divorce. Jeff and Diane's luncheon talk was somewhere in the middle.

"You do want her to be accepted at Sarah Lawrence, don't you?" Diane snapped between bites of bay scallops *à la nage*.

"She's thirteen years old." Jeff sighed. "The admissions office at Sarah Lawrence doesn't give a damn what she does at that age."

"I was at Concord Academy when I was eleven."

"That's because your *parents* didn't give a damn what you did at that age."

She set down her fork, glared at him. "My upbringing is no concern of yours."

"But Gretchen's is."

"Then you should want her to have the best possible education, from the beginning."

One waiter cleared their empty plates away as another approached with the dessert wagon. Jeff took advantage of the interruption to lose himself in the multiple reflections from the restaurant's many mirrors: the fir-green walls, the crimson banquettes, the splendid floral bouquets that looked freshly cut from a Cezanne landscape.

He knew Diane was less concerned for Gretchen's education than for her own freedom from daily responsibility. Jeff saw his daughter little enough as it was, and he couldn't bear the thought of her living two hundred miles from home.

Diane picked crossly at her raspberries in Grand Marnier sauce. "I suppose you think it's all right for her to continue associating with all those little urchins she keeps dragging home from public school."

"For Christ's sake, her school is in Rhinebeck, not the South Bronx. It's a wonderful environment for her to grow up in."

"So is Concord. As I know from personal experience."

Jeff dug into his Peach Charlotte, unable to say what was really on his mind: that he had no intention of seeing Gretchen mature into a clone of her mother. The brittle sophistication, the world-be-damned attitude, great wealth seen as a birthright, something to be assumed and utterly relied upon. Jeff had acquired his own riches by a stroke of supranormal good fortune and by force of will. Now he wanted to protect his daughter from money's potentially corrupting influence as much as he wanted her to reap its benefits.

"We'll discuss it another time," he told Diane.

"We have to let them know by next Thursday."

"Then we'll discuss it Wednesday."

That put her into a serious pout, one he knew she could resolve only by a concentrated, almost vicious, splurge at Bergdorf's and Saks.

He patted his jacket pocket, took out two foil-wrapped tablets of Gelusil. His heart might be in excellent shape, but this life he'd created for himself was playing hell with his digestion.

Gretchen's slender young fingers moved gracefully over the keyboard, yielding the poignant strains of Beethoven's "Für Elise." The fat orange cat named Chumley slept sprawled beside her on the piano bench, too old now to frolic with the reckless abandon he once had shown, content merely to be close to her, soothed by the gentle music.

Jeff watched his daughter's face as she played, her smooth, pale skin surrounded by the dark curls of her hair. There was an intensity to her expression, but it was not caused, he knew, by concentration on the notes or tempo of the piece. Her natural gift for music was such that she needed never struggle to memorize or drill herself on the basics of a composition once she'd played it through the first time. Rather, the look in her eyes was one of transport, of a melding with the wistful melody of the deceptively simple little bagatelle.

She rendered the coda of chords and double notes over a repeated-note pedal point with expert legato, and when she was done she sat silent for several moments, returning from the place the music had taken her. Then she grinned with delight, her eyes those of a playful girl again.

"Isn't that pretty?" Gretchen asked ingenuously, referring only to the beauty of the music itself.

"Yes," Jeff said. "Almost as pretty as the pianist."

"Oh, Daddy, cut it out." She blushed, swung herself coltishly from the bench. "I'm gonna have a sandwich. You want one?"

"No, thanks, honey. I think I'll wait till dinner. Your mother should be back from the city any time now; when she gets home, tell her I took a walk down by the river, O.K.?"

"O.K.," Gretchen called, scampering toward the kitchen. Chumley woke, yawned, and followed her at his own ambling pace.

Jeff stepped outside, walked along the path through the trees. In autumn the corridor of elms was like a half-mile shaft of enveloping flame. Emerging from it, Jeff saw first the broad meadow descending gently toward the Hudson, then the steeper drop a hundred yards to the left where a rocky chain of waterfalls cascaded in the chill. The dramatic entrance to this place never failed to give him a thrill of awe, that such beauty could exist; and of pride, that it was his possession.

He stood now at the crest of the sloping green, contemplating the vista. Two small boats moved quietly down the river beneath the blaze of fall colors on the far side. A trio of young boys ambled along the opposite bank, idly tossing stones into the coursing water. At the top of a rise above them was a stately home, less grand than Jeff's but still imposing.

In another three months the river would be frozen solid, a great white highway stretching south toward the city and north toward the Adirondacks. The trees would be bereft of leaves, but seldom barren: Snow would lace their branches, and some days even the smallest twigs would be encased in a cylinder of ice, glittering by the millions in the winter sunlight.

This was the land, the very county, that Currier and Ives had mythologized as the American ideal; they'd even sketched this precise view. Standing here, it was easy to believe that all he'd done had been worthwhile. Standing here, or holding Gretchen in his arms, embracing the child he and Linda had once yearned for but could never have.

No, he wouldn't send his daughter to Concord. This was her home. This was where she belonged until she was old enough to make her own decisions about leaving it. When that day came, he'd support whatever choices she might make, but until then—

Something unseen stabbed his chest, something more painful and powerful than he had ever felt before . . . except once.

He crumpled to his knees, struggling to remember what day it was, what time it was. His staring eyes took in the autumn scene, the valley that had, an instant before, seemed the very emblem of hope regained and possibilities unbounded. Then he fell on his side, facing away from the river.

Jeff Winston gazed helplessly at the orange-red tunnel of elms that had led him to this meadow of promise and fulfillment, and then he died.

7

HE WAS SURROUNDED by darkness, and by screams. A pair of hands clutched at his right arm, fingernails stabbing through the fabric of his sleeve.

Jeff saw before him an image of Hell: weeping children, shrieking and stumbling as they ran, unable to escape the black, winged creatures that swooped and pecked at the children's faces, mouths, eyes . . .

Then an icily perfect blond woman pulled two of the little girls into an automobile, safe from the onslaught. He was watching a movie, Jeff realized; a Hitchcock movie, *The Birds*.

The pressure on his arm subsided along with the scene's intensity, and he turned his head to see Judy Gordon smiling a girlish, embarrassed smile. On his left, Judy's friend Paula snuggled into the protective curve of young Martin Bailey's arm.

1963. It had all begun again.

"How come you're so quiet tonight, honey?" Judy asked him in the back seat of Martin's Corvair as they rode to Moe's and Joe's after the movie. "You don't think I was silly to get so scared, do you?"

"No. No, not at all."

She intertwined her fingers with his, leaned her head against his shoulder. "O.K., just so you don't think I'm a ninny." Her hair was fresh and clean, and she'd dabbed a few drops of Lanvin on her slim, pale neck. Her sweet scent was exactly as it had been on that awkward night in Jeff's car, twenty-five years ago . . . and before that, almost half a century ago, on this same night.

Everything he'd accomplished had been erased: his financial empire, the home in Dutchess County . . . but most devastating of all, he had lost his child. Gretchen, with her gangly almost-woman manner and her intelligent, loving eyes, had been rendered nonexistent. Dead, or worse. In this reality she had simply never been.

For the first time in his long, broken life he fully understood Lear's lament over Cordelia:

> . . . thoul't come no more,
> Never, never, never, never, never.

"What's that, honey? D'you say something?"

"No," he whispered, pulling the girl to his chest. "I was just thinking out loud."

"Mmmm. Penny for your thoughts."

Precious innocence, he thought; blessed sweet unawareness of the wounds a demented universe can inflict.

"I was thinking how much it means to me to have you here. How much I need to hold you."

His old boarding school outside Richmond, like the Emory campus, remained unchanged. Some aspects of the place seemed slightly askew from his memories of it: The buildings looked smaller; the dining commons was closer to the lake than he recalled. He'd come to expect that sort of minor discontinuity, had long ago decided it was due to faulty recollection rather than to any concrete change in the nature of things. This time, nearly fifty years of fading recollection had passed since he'd last been here. A full adult lifetime, though split in two, and now begun again.

"College treating you all right?" Mrs. Braden asked.

"Not too bad. Just felt like getting away for a couple of days—thought I'd come up and see the old school."

The plump little librarian chuckled maternally. "It hasn't even been a year since you graduated, Jeff; nostalgia setting in that soon?"

"I guess so." He smiled. "It seems a lot longer."

"Wait until it's been ten years, or twenty; then you'll see how distant all this can seem. I wonder if you'll still want to come back and visit us then."

"I'm sure I will."

"I do hope so. It's good to know how the boys turn out, how all of you deal with the world out there. And I think you'll do just fine."

"Thank you, ma'am. I'm working at it."

She glanced at her watch, looked distractedly toward the front door of the library. "Well, I'm supposed to meet a group of next year's new students at three, give them the twenty-five-cent tour; you be sure and look up Dr. Armbruster before you go, won't you?"

"I'll be sure to."

"And next time, come by the house; we'll have a glass of sherry and reminisce about the old days."

Jeff bade her good bye, made his way through the stacks and out a side exit. He hadn't intended to talk to any of the faculty or staff, but had known when he'd driven up here that a chance meeting or two would be inevitable. All in all, he thought he'd handled himself pretty well with Mrs. Braden, but he was relieved that the conversation had been brief. He'd grown confident about handling such encounters at Emory now, but here they would be much more difficult to deal with; his memory of the place, the people, was so distant.

He ambled down a path behind the library, into the secluded Virginia woods that surrounded the campus where he'd grown from adolescence to young manhood. Something had drawn him here, something stronger, more compelling than mere nostalgia. Christ, by now he'd had far too much fulfilled nostalgia thrust upon him to seek out any more.

Perhaps it was the fact that this was the last significant

living environment of his life that he had *not* replayed, and that still existed as he remembered it. He'd already been back to his childhood home in Orlando, had twice returned to Emory. And the places he had originally lived after college, where he'd been a young bachelor and later married to Linda, contained no part of him in this life or the one he'd most recently been through. Here, though, he was remembered; he had put his own small stamp of personality upon this school, just as it had, in this existence as well as the others, had its greater effects on him. Maybe he simply needed to touch base here, to confirm his own being and remind himself of a time when reality was stable and nonrepetitive.

Jeff pushed back the overhanging branch of an elm that was drooping over the path, and without warning he saw the bridge that had haunted him with guilt and shame for all this time.

He stood there in shock, staring at the scene that had troubled five decades of his dreams. It was just a little wooden footbridge across a creek, a simple structure not more than ten feet long, but Jeff could barely control the panic that rose in his chest at the sight of it. He'd had no idea this was where the path was leading.

He let go the elm branch, walked slowly toward the diminutive bridge, with its hand-sawn planks and lovingly crafted three-foot guardrail. It had been rebuilt, of course; he'd always assumed that. Still, he'd never come back to this spot again while he was in school, not since that day.

He sat down on the creek bank next to the bridge, ran his hand along the weathered wood. On the other side of the stream a squirrel nibbled on an acorn that it held between its paws, and regarded him with a placid but wary eye.

Jeff hadn't really been a shy boy, that first year here at school; quiet, and serious about his studies, but by no means timid. He'd made several friends quickly, and joined in the boisterous dormitory horseplay: shaving-cream battles, draping another student's room with toilet paper, that kind of thing. As far as girls went, he'd had as much, and as little, experience as might be expected at fifteen, in that more innocent year. There'd been one steady girlfriend his last year in junior high, but as yet no one special among the high-school girls who came in from Richmond on weekends for the dances here on campus; that fondly recalled encounter, with a girl named Barbara, would have to wait until he was sixteen.

That first year, though, he fell in love. Thoroughly, mind-numbingly in love with his French teacher, a woman in her mid-twenties named Deirdre Rendell. He wasn't alone in his obsession; roughly eighty percent of the boys on the all-male campus were in love with the willowy brunette, whose husband taught American History. Each night at dinner, there would be a mad scramble for the six student seats at the Rendells' table in the dining commons; Jeff managed to grab himself a place there two or three nights a week.

He was convinced she felt a special something for him, more than just the bright warmth she displayed to the other boys; he was positive he perceived a special glow, a flame, in her eyes when she spoke to him. Once, in class, she had stood behind his chair and slowly, casually massaged his neck as she led the students in reciting Baudelaire. That had been a moment of high erotic intensity for him, and he'd basked in the envious glares of his classmates. For a while he'd even stopped masturbating over the *Playboy* centerfolds, had reserved his sexual fantasies for Deirdre, as he thought of her privately, for Deirdre alone.

By the end of November it became obvious that Mrs. Rendell was pregnant. Jeff did his best to ignore what that implied about the health of her relationship with her husband, and focused instead on the fresh beauty that impending motherhood brought to her face.

She took her maternity leave in the winter, and another teacher took over her classes until she was able to return. The baby was born in mid-February. Mrs. Rendell was back at the couple's table in the dining commons by April, her breasts gorgeously swollen with milk. She kept the infant in a portable bassinet when she didn't have it in her arms; and her husband doted on her constantly from the seat next to her. Between the two of them, they captured almost every moment of her cherished attention; Jeff could no longer imagine he read secret endearments in the rare smiles she bestowed on him.

The Rendells lived in a house off-campus, on the other side of the woods behind the library. On sunny days, Mrs. Rendell liked to walk to and from school, through the peaceful stand of elms and birches. There was a well-worn footpath that led that way, though it was broken by a small creek. In the fall, she'd been able to ford the narrow rivulet easily; but now, pushing the baby in its perambulator, the stream presented a serious obstacle.

Her husband labored for six weeks, building the little bridge. He cut the lumber to size on the band saw in the school's shop, planed the wood to smoothness, made the joists and crossbeams of the tiny span twice as sturdy as they needed to be. The night of the day it was completed, Mrs. Rendell kissed him right at the table in the dining commons, kissed him long and lovingly. She'd never done anything like that in front of any of the boys before. Jeff stared at his uneaten food, his stomach tight and cold.

The next day he walked into the woods to be alone, to sort out the awful feelings that overwhelmed him; but something seemed to snap inside when he came across the bridge.

His mind was blank with unaccustomed rage when he picked up the first large rock from the creek bed, hurled it with all his strength at the wooden guardrail.

Again and again he heaved rocks, the heaviest ones he could find and lift. The buttresses were the hardest parts to crush; they'd been built to last, but under Jeff's furious assault the beams finally gave way, collapsed into the creek along with the splintered remains of the rest of the bridge.

When it was done, Jeff stood staring at the sodden wreckage, his breath coming in great gulps of exhaustion and anguish. Then he glanced up, and saw Mrs. Rendell standing in the path on the other side of the stream. The face that he'd adored for so many months was an expressionless mask as she looked at him. Their eyes locked for several seconds, and then Jeff bolted.

He assumed he'd be expelled; but nothing was ever said about the incident. Jeff never sat at the Rendells' table again. He avoided seeing either of them as much as he was able. She remained unfailingly polite, even pleasant, to him in class, and at the end of the year he received an A in French.

He tossed a pebble into the lazy creek, watched it bounce off a rock and plop into the water. Destroying the bridge had been a vile, unforgivable act. Yet Mrs. Rendell had forgiven him, protected him, had even had the good sense not to shame him further by expressing her forgiveness in words. She must have understood the lonely, mindless fury that had led him to such an extreme, must have recognized that in his childlike way he had seen her love for her husband and baby as betrayal of the deepest sort.

And it had been, in Jeff's crush-distorted view of things. It had been his introductory encounter with the death of hope.

Now he knew what had drawn him back here to the school, to this quiet clearing in the woods of his youth. He must again face that emptiness of infinite loss, but this time on a more complex level. This time he knew he could not crack beneath the weight of the intolerable. There were no more bridges to destroy; he must learn to go forward, and to build, despite the torment of his daughter's death, of knowing what could never be.

At a quarter to eleven on a Friday night, at least twenty couples embraced in the shadows outside Harris Hall: arms around each other, faces pressed together for a last few minutes of fevered contact before the young women would be called into the dorm by their vigilant housemother. Jeff and Judy shared a stone bench away from the huddling pairs. She was upset.

"It's that Frank Maddock, isn't it? It was all his idea; I know it was."

Jeff shook his head. "I told you, I suggested it to him."

Judy wasn't listening. "You shouldn't hang around with him. I knew something like this would happen. He thinks he's so cool, thinks he's Mr. Sophistication. Can't you see through that act of his?''

"Honey, it's not his fault. The whole thing was my idea, and it'll work out fine. Just wait'll tomorrow, you'll see.''

"Oh, what do you know about it?'' A chilly night breeze came up, and she took her hand from his to pull her rabbit jacket closed. "You're not even old enough to go make the bets yourself; you have to get him to do it.''

"I know enough,'' Jeff said, smiling.

"Sure, enough to throw all your money away. Enough to sell your car. I still can't believe that—you actually sold your car to bet on a horse race.''

"I'll buy another one tomorrow afternoon. You can come with me, help me pick it out. What would you like, a Jaguar, a Corvette?''

"Don't talk foolish, Jeff. You know, I used to think I knew you pretty well, but this . . .''

The wind picked up a fallen dogwood blossom and dropped it in her hair. He reached to retrieve the flower, and the motion became a caress. She softened at his touch, and he gently ran the white petals along her cheek, pressed them lightly to her lips and then to his.

"Oh, honey,'' she whispered, moving closer to him, "I don't mean to be a scold. It's just that this has got me so worried for you, I can't—''

"Hush,'' he said, holding her face in both his hands. "There's nothing to worry about, I promise.''

"But you don't know—''

He quieted her with a kiss that lasted until a woman's harsh voice interrupted them, calling, "Curfew in five minutes!''

Girls hurried past them as he walked her to the brightly lit front door of the dorm. "So,'' he said, "do you want to go car-shopping with me tomorrow?''

"Oh, Jeff.'' She sighed. "I've got a term paper to finish tomorrow afternoon, but if you come by around seven I'll buy you a burger at Dooley's. And don't get too depressed when you lose; at least it'll be a good lesson.''

"Yes, ma'am." He grinned. "I'll be sure and take notes."

A red-jacketed valet parked the Jaguar for them at the Coach and Six. Jeff slipped the wine steward a twenty, and nobody asked for Judy's ID when he ordered them a magnum of Moët et Chandon.

"To Chateaugay," Jeff toasted when the champagne was poured.

Judy hesitated, holding her glass in midair. "I'd rather just drink to tonight," she said.

They clinked glasses, sipped the wine. Judy looked wonderful tonight, in a dark blue low-cut gown she'd bought for the spring formal: halfway between a girl playing dress-up and a vibrantly sexy woman. He had been too quick to dismiss her before, had been seeking a woman whose experience would match his own. But of course that was an impossible goal. Now he basked with delight in the warm honesty of her ingenuousness, so different from Sharla's cheap eroticism or Diane's cold, sophisticated manner. Such innocence deserved to be nurtured, not denied.

The fare at the Coach and Six was standard upscale American, nothing adventurous on the menu, but Judy seemed impressed, was obviously taking pains to stay on her best adult behavior. Jeff ordered lobster for her, prime rib for himself. She watched to see which forks he used for the salad and the appetizer, and he loved her for her open artlessness.

After dinner, over Drambuie, Jeff handed her the little blue Claude S. Bennett jeweler's box. She opened it, and stared at the perfect two-carat diamond ring for several moments before she started to cry.

"I can't," she murmured, closing the box carefully and setting it down on his side of the table. "I just can't."

"I thought you said you loved me."

"I do," she said. "Oh, damn, damn, damn."

"Then what's wrong? We could wait a year or two if you think we're too young, but I'd like to make our plans official right now."

She dried her eyes with a napkin, smearing what little

makeup she wore. Jeff wanted to kiss the streaks away, wanted to bathe her with his mouth as a cat would a kitten.

"Paula says you haven't been to class in weeks," she told him. "She says you might even flunk out."

Jeff beamed, took her hand. "Is that all? Honey, it doesn't matter. I'm quitting school anyway. I just won seventeen thousand dollars, and by October I can make . . . Look, it's nothing to be concerned about. We'll have plenty of money; I'll always see to that."

"How?" she asked bitterly. "Gambling? Is that how we'd live?"

"Investments," he told her. "Perfectly legitimate business investments, in big companies like IBM and Xerox and—"

"Be realistic, Jeff. You got real lucky on one horse race, and now all of a sudden you think you can strike it rich in the stock market. Well, what if the stocks go down? What if there's a depression or something?"

"There won't be," he said quietly.

"You don't know that. My daddy says—"

"I don't care what your daddy says. There isn't going to be any—"

She set her napkin down, pushed her chair back from the table. "Well, I do care what my parents say. And I hate to even think how they'd react if I told them I was getting married to an eighteen-year-old boy who's dropped out of school to be a gambler."

Jeff could think of nothing to say. She was right, of course. He must seem an irresponsible fool to her. It had been a terrible mistake to tell her what he was doing.

He slipped the ring back in his jacket pocket. "I'll hold on to this for now," he said. "And maybe I'll reconsider about school."

Her eyes went moist again, their vivid blue shimmering through the layer of tears. "Please do, Jeff. I don't want to lose you, not because of some craziness like this."

He squeezed her hand. "You'll wear that ring someday," he said. "You'll be proud of it, and proud of me."

They were married at the First Baptist Church in Rockwood,

Tennessee in June of 1968, the week after Jeff received his
M.B.A. Just four days before the date he'd met Linda—
twice, with such drastically different outcomes—in those
other lives. Rockwood was Judy's hometown, and the
reception her parents threw afterward was a big, informal
barbecue at their summer place on nearby Watts Bar Lake.
Jeff noticed that his father's cough was getting worse, but
still he wouldn't listen to his son's entreaties that he stop
chain-smoking Pall Malls. He wouldn't quit until the emphysema was diagnosed, years from now. Jeff's mother
was happier than she'd been at his weddings to Linda and
Diane, though of course she had no memory of either
occasion. His sister, a shy fifteen-year-old with braces on
her teeth, had taken to Judy right away.

The Gordon family, likewise, had welcomed Jeff into
the fold wholeheartedly. He had transformed himself into
the very image of a perfect catch: twenty-three, good
education, industrious, responsible. A nice little nest egg
already set aside and a conservative but steadily building
portfolio of stocks in his and Judy's names.

It hadn't been easy. The five years of school were tough
enough, forcing himself back into the long-abandoned reg-
imen of studies and term papers and exams; but the hardest
part had been contriving not to get rich. The last time he'd
been this age he'd been a financial *wunderkind,* the major
partner in a powerful conglomerate. Such a sudden infu-
sion of massive wealth would have thrown Judy off balance, would have created significant problems between
them. So he'd passed up the Belmont and World Series
bets entirely, and had painstakingly avoided the many
high-yield investments with which he could easily have
made another multimillion-dollar fortune.

He and Frank Maddock had drifted apart soon after the
Kentucky Derby this time. His unknowing one-time partner at the pinnacle of corporate success had finished Columbia Law School and was now a junior attorney with a
firm in Pittsburgh.

Jeff and Judy assumed the mortgage on a pleasant little
fake-colonial house on Cheshire Bridge Road in Atlanta,
and Jeff rented a four-room office in a building near Five

Points that he'd once owned. Five days a week he put on a suit and tie, drove downtown, bid his secretary and associates good morning, locked himself in his office, and read. Sophocles, Shakespeare, Proust, Faulkner . . . all the works he'd meant to absorb before but had never had the time to read.

At the end of the day he'd dash off a few memos to his partners, recommending perhaps that they not risk investing in an unproven company like Sony, but should keep their gradually growing principal in something safe, such as AT&T. Jeff steered the small company carefully away from any sources of sudden wealth, made sure he and his associates remained comfortably but unspectacularly entrenched in the upper middle class. His partners frequently followed his advice; when they didn't, the losses tended to balance out the gains, so the net effect remained as Jeff intended.

At night he and Judy would cuddle in the den to watch "Laugh-In" or "The Name of the Game" together, then maybe play a game of Scrabble before they went to bed. On warm weekends they'd go sailing on Lake Lanier, or play tennis and hike the nature trails at Callaway Gardens.

Life was quiet, ordered, sublimely normal. Jeff was thoroughly content. Not ecstatic—there was none of the sense of absolute enchantment he had felt in watching his daughter, Gretchen, grow up at the estate in Dutchess County—but he was happy, and at peace. For the first time, his long, chaotic life was defined by its utter simplicity and lack of turmoil.

Jeff dug his toes into the sand, raised himself to his elbows, and shaded his eyes from the sun with one hand. Judy was asleep on the blanket beside him, curled fingers still holding her place in a copy of *Jaws*. He gently kissed her half-open mouth.

"Want some Piña Colada?" Jeff asked as she stretched herself awake. "We've still got half a thermos left."

"Mmm. Just want to lie here like this. For about twenty years."

"Better turn over every six months or so, then."

She twisted her head to look at the back of her right shoulder, saw it was getting red. She rolled faceup, close to him, and he kissed her again; longer this time, and deeper.

A few yards down the beach another couple had a radio playing, and Jeff broke the kiss as the music ended and a Jamaican-accented announcer began reading about John Dean's testimony that day in the Watergate hearings.

"Love you," Judy said.

"Love you," he answered, touching the tip of her sun-pink nose. And he did, Lord God how he did.

Jeff allowed himself six weeks of vacation every year, in keeping with his pretense of a regular work schedule. The arbitrarily imposed limitation made the time seem all the sweeter. Last year they'd bicycled through Scotland, and this summer they planned to take a hot-air balloon tour of the French wine country. At this moment, though, he could think of no place he'd rather be than here in Ocho Rios, with the woman who had brought sanity and delight to his disjointed life.

"Necklace for the pretty missy, mon? Nice cochina necklace?"

The little Jamaican boy was no older than eight or nine. His arms were draped with dozens of delicate shell necklaces and bracelets, and a cloth pouch tied at his waist bulged with earrings made from the same colorful shells.

"How much for . . . that one, there?"

"Eight shilling."

"Make it one pound six, and I'll take it."

The boy raised his eyebrows, confused. "Hey, you crazy, mon? You s'pose go lower, not higher."

"Two pounds, then."

"I'm not gonna argue with you, mon. You got it." The child hurriedly took the necklace from his arm, handed it to Judy. "You wan' buy any more, I got plenty. Ever'body on the beach know me, my name Renard, O.K.?"

"O.K., Renard. Nice doing business with you." Jeff handed him two one-pound notes, and the boy scampered away down the beach, grinning.

Judy slipped the necklace on, shook her head in mock

dismay. "Shame on you," she said, "taking advantage of a child that way."

"Could have been worse." Jeff smiled. "Another minute or so and I might have bargained him up to four or five pounds."

She looked down to rearrange the necklace, and when her eyes met his again there was sadness in them. "You're so good around children," she said. "That's my only regret, that we've never—"

Jeff placed his fingers lightly on her lips. "You're my baby girl. All I need."

He could never tell her, never even let her guess, about the vasectomy he'd had in 1966, soon after they'd started making love. Never again would he give life to a human being, as he had to Gretchen, only to see her entire existence negated. To everyone but Jeff, she did not even live in memory; and on the unthinkable chance that he might be doomed to repeat his life yet again, he refused to leave in that sort of absolute limbo someone he'd not only loved, but had created.

"Jeff . . . I've been thinking."

He looked back at Judy, tried to keep the pain and guilt from showing. "About what?"

"We could—don't answer right away; give yourself time to consider it—we could adopt."

He didn't say anything for several seconds, just looked at her. Saw the love in her face, saw the need for even more of an outlet through which to express that love.

It wouldn't be as if the children were his own, he thought. Even if he grew to love them, he wouldn't be responsible for their having come into being. They already existed, had been born, whoever they might be. The worst could happen, and they'd still exist, though with a different life in store for them.

"Yes," he told her. "Yes, I'd like that very much."

The put-in was at a place called Earl's Ford, at the southern edge of the great Appalachian forests, near the spot where North and South Carolina met the upper tip of Georgia. There were six rafts in all: black, ungainly-looking things, inflated at the base camp and hauled with difficulty to the edge of the Chattooga River. Jeff, Judy, and the children shared one raft with a jolly, gray-haired woman and a guide who looked to be of college age, his face and arms brown from the sun.

As the raft slid into the clear, leisurely-flowing water, Jeff reached to cinch April's life vest tighter around the child's thin frame. Dwayne saw the paternal motion and tightened his own vest, a look of manly determination in his young eyes.

April was a charming little blond-haired girl who'd been severely abused by her natural parents; her brother was an intense, very bright child whose mother and father had died in an automobile accident. The children's names weren't necessarily what Jeff or Judy would have chosen to call them, but they'd been six and four years old when they were adopted, and it seemed best not to further disturb either one's sense of self by changing their given names.

"Daddy, look! A deer!" April pointed at the far bank of the river, her face agleam with excitement. The animal stared back at them complacently, poised to run if need be, but unwilling to interrupt its feeding simply for having seen these strange apparitions.

Soon the wooded banks on either side began to rise, become a rocky gorge. As the canyon deepened, the river's speed increased, and before long the flotilla of rafts had entered the first set of rapids. The children whooped with pleasure as the craft bucked and swayed in the downward current.

Jeff looked at Judy after they had cleared the white water and were again drifting smoothly downstream. He was gratified to see that her earlier anxiety had been replaced with an exhilaration matching that of the children. She'd been worried about taking them on this outing, but Jeff hadn't wanted the children to be deprived of anything so joyfully inspiring.

The expedition pulled ashore at a small island, and Judy spread out the lunch she'd packed in a watertight chest. Jeff munched on a chicken leg and sipped his cold beer, watching April and Dwayne explore the triangular wedge of land. The children's curiosity and imagination never ceased to fascinate him; through their eyes, he had come to appreciate this tired world anew. When he and Judy had decided to adopt them, he'd bought some Apple and Atari stock at the right time; not much, just enough to edge the family's income up a couple of notches. They'd bought a larger house, on West Paces Ferry Road; it had a huge backyard, with a shallow fishpond and three big oak trees. Perfect for the children.

The rafts got underway again, breached another, larger set of rapids a mile or so downriver. The current was moving much more swiftly now, even in the blue-water segments of the journey; but Jeff could see that his wife had lost her fear of the river, was caught up in the beauty and the thrill of it. She held his hand tightly as they shot through the torrent of Bull Sluice Falls, and then it was over, the water calm again and the sun retreating behind the pines.

April and Dwayne were manifestly sad to see the bus that stood waiting to take them back to Atlanta, but Jeff knew their adventures, like the summer, had scarcely begun. He'd soon be taking his family on an unhurried, two-month drive through France and Italy; next year he planned a trip for them to Japan and the newly accessible vastness of China.

Jeff wanted them to see it all, experience every bit of glory and wonder the world had to offer. Still, he had a secret fear that all these memories, along with all the love he had given them, would soon be obliterated by a force he could understand no better than they.

After three days his chest had begun to itch something fierce where the electrodes were taped, but he wouldn't allow the EKG to be unhooked, not for a minute.

The nurses were full of contempt for him; Jeff knew that. They laughed about him when they thought they were out of earshot, resented having to cater to a perfectly healthy hypochondriac who was taking up valuable bed space.

His physician felt more or less the same way, had said

so openly. Still, Jeff had demanded, had been vehement. Finally, after making a sizable donation to the hospital's building fund, he'd gotten himself admitted for the week.

The third week of October 1988. If it was going to happen, this would be the time.

"Hi, honey; how you feeling?" Judy wore a rust-colored fall outfit; her hair was piled loosely atop her head.

"Itching. Otherwise fine."

She smiled with a slyness uncharacteristic of her still-innocent face. "Anything I can scratch?"

Jeff laughed. "I wish. Think we're gonna have to wait another few days, though, till I get unwired."

"Well," she said, holding up a pair of shopping bags, one from the Oxford Book Store and another from Turtle Records. "Here's some stuff to keep you occupied in the meantime."

She'd brought him the latest Travis McGee and Dick Francis mysteries (tastes he had acquired this time around), plus a new biography of André Malraux and a history of the Cunard shipping line. For all she'd never learned about him, Judy certainly understood the eclectic nature of his interests. The other bag contained a dozen jewel-boxed compact discs, ranging from Bach and Vivaldi to a digital transfer of "Sergeant Pepper." She slid one of the shiny discs into the portable CD player at his bedside, and the exquisite strains of Pachelbel's "Canon in D" filled the hospital room.

"Judy—" His voice broke. He cleared his throat and started again. "I just want you to know . . . how very much I have always loved you."

She answered in measured tones, but couldn't hide the look of alarm in her eyes. "We'll always love each other, I hope. For a long, long time to come."

"As long as possible."

Judy frowned, started to speak, but he shushed her. She leaned over the bed to kiss him, and her hand was trembling as it found his.

"Come home soon," she whispered against his face. "We haven't even started yet."

*   *   *

It happened a little over an hour after Judy had left the room to get lunch in the hospital cafeteria. Jeff was glad she wasn't there to see it.

Even through his pain he could see the astonishment on the nurse's face as the EKG went berserk; but she behaved with complete professionalism, didn't delay calling the Code Blue for an instant. Within seconds Jeff was surrounded by a full medical team, shouting instructions and status reports as they worked over him:

"Epi, one cc!"

"Bicarb two amps? Gimme three-sixty joules!

"Stand back . . ." WHUMP!

"V-tach! Blood pressure eighty palpable; two hundred watt seconds, lidocaine seventy-five milligrams IV, stat!"

"Take a look—V-Fib."

"Repeat epi and bicarb, defib at three-sixty; stand back . . ." WHUMP!

On and on, their voices fading with the light. Jeff tried to scream in anger because it wasn't fair; he'd been totally prepared this time. But he couldn't scream, he couldn't even cry, he couldn't do a goddamned thing but die again.

And wake again, in the back seat of Martin Bailey's Corvair with Judy beside him. Judy at eighteen, Judy in 1963 before they ever fell in love and married and built their lives together.

"Stop the car!"

"Hang on, buddy," Martin said. "We're almost back to the girls' dorm. We'll—"

"I said stop the car! Stop it now!"

Shaking his head in bewilderment, Martin pulled the car to a halt on Kilgo Circle, behind the history building. Judy put her hand on Jeff's arm, trying to calm him, but he jerked away from her and shoved the car door open.

"Jesus, what the hell are you doing?" Martin yelled, but Jeff was out of the car and running, running hard in whatever direction it was; it didn't matter.

Nothing mattered.

He raced through the quadrangle, past the chemistry and psych buildings, his strong young heart pounding in his chest as if it had not betrayed him minutes ago and twenty-five years in the future. His legs carried him past the biology building, across the corner of Pierce and Arkwright drives. He finally stumbled and fell to his knees in the middle of the soccer field, looking up at the stars through blurry eyes.

"Fuck you!" He screamed at the impassive sky, screamed with all the force and despair he'd been unable to express from that terminal hospital bed. "Fuck you! Why . . . are . . . you . . . DOING THIS TO ME!"

8

JEFF JUST DIDN'T much give a shit after that. He'd done all he could, achieved everything a man could ever hope to—materially, romantically, paternally—and still it came to nothing, still he was left alone and powerless, with empty hands and heart. Back to the beginning; yet why begin at all, if his best efforts would inevitably prove futile?

He couldn't bring himself to see Judy again. This sweet-faced adolescent girl was not the woman he had loved, but merely a blank slate with the potential to become that woman. It would be pointless, even masochistic, to repeat by rote that process of mutual becoming, when he knew too well the emotional and spiritual death to which it all would lead.

He went back to that anonymous bar he'd found so long ago on North Druid Hills Road, and started drinking. When the time came, he again went through the charade of convincing Frank Maddock to place the bet on the Kentucky Derby. As soon as the money came in he flew to Las Vegas, alone.

After three days of wandering the hotels and casinos he finally found her, sitting at a dollar-minimum blackjack table at the Sands. Same black hair, same perfect body, even the same red dress he'd once ripped in a moment of shared impatient lust on the living-room sofa of her little duplex.

"Hi," he said. "My name's Jeff Winston."

She smiled her familiar seductive smile. "Sharla Baker."

"Right. How'd you like to go to Paris?"

Sharla gave him a bemused stare. "Mind if I finish this hand first?"

"There's a plane to New York in three hours. It makes a direct connection with Air France. That gives you time to pack."

She took a hit on sixteen, busted.

"Are you for real, or what?" she asked.

"I'm for real. You ready to go?"

Sharla shrugged, scooped the few chips she had left into her purse. "Sure. Why not?"

"Exactly," Jeff said. "Why not?"

The sweetly harsh scent of a hundred smoldering Gauloises and Gitanes cigarettes hung in the air of the club like a rancid fog. Through the haze, Jeff could see Sharla dancing alone in a corner, eyes closed, drunk. She seemed to drink more this time around than he'd remembered; or maybe it was just that she was keeping pace with him, and he was drinking more now than he ever had. At least the liquor made him gregarious; there were half a dozen people at his table tonight, most of them ostensibly "students" of one sort or another, but all more interested in the city's neverending night life than in their books.

"You have these clubs in U.S., *hein?*" Jean-Claude asked.

Jeff shook his head. The Caveau de la Huchette was a Parisian jazz cavern in the classic mold, a rock-walled dungeon full of music as smoky and pungent as the cigarettes everyone here seemed to exist on. Unlike the newer discothèques, it was a style that would never catch on in the States.

Mireille, Jean-Claude's petite red-haired girlfriend, gave a wry and lazy smile. *"C'est dommage,"* she said. "The blacks, no one likes them in their home country, so they must come here for to play their music.''

Jeff made a noncommittal gesture, poured himself another glass of red wine. America's present racial troubles were a major topic of conversation in France right now, but he had no interest in getting involved in that discussion. Nothing serious, nothing that would make him think or remember, held any interest for him now.

"You must to visit *l'Afrique*," Mireille said. "There is much of beauty there, much to understand."

She and Jean-Claude had recently returned from a month in Morocco. Jeff kindly didn't mention France's recent debacle in Algeria.

"*Attention, attention, s'il vous plaît!*" The owner of the club stood on its tiny stage, leaning close to the microphone. "*Mesdames et messieurs, copains et copines . . . Le Caveau de la Huchette a le plaisir extraordinaire de vous présenter le* blues hot . . . *avec le maître du* blues, *personne d'autre que—Monsieur Sidney . . . Bechet!*"

There was wild applause as the old expatriate musician took the stage, clarinet in hand. He kicked things off with a rouser, "Blues in the Cave," and followed that with a soulfully sexy version of "Frankie and Johnny." Sharla continued her solo dance in the corner, her body undulating with the visceral thrust of the music. Jeff emptied the wine bottle, signaled for another.

The old blues man grinned and nodded as the second number ended and the young crowd roared its appreciation of his alien art form. "Mercy, mercy, mercy!" Bechet exclaimed. "*Mon français n'est pas très bon,*" he said with a thick black-American accent, "so I just gots to say in my own way that I can tell y'all knows the blues. You heah me?"

At least half the audience understood enough English to answer enthusiastically. "*Mais oui!*" they cheered. "*Bien sûr!*" Jeff gulped his fresh glass of wine, waited for the music to carry him away again, to wipe out all the memories.

"Well, all right!" Bechet said from the stage, wiping the mouthpiece of his clarinet. "Now, this next one is really what the blues is most about. You see, there's some blues for folks ain't never had a thing, and that's a sad blues . . . but the saddest kind of blues is for them that's had everything they ever wanted and has lost it, and knows it won't come back no more. Ain't no sufferin' in this world worse than that; and that's the blues we call 'I Had It But It's All Gone Now.' ''

The music began, deep-throated sounds of evanescence and regret in a minor key. Irresistible, unendurable. Jeff slumped in his chair, trying to blot out the sound of it. He reached for his glass, spilled the wine.

"Something?" Mireille said, touching his shoulder.

Jeff tried to answer, couldn't.

"Allons-y," she said, pulling him to his feet in the smoke-filled nightclub. "We go outside, to breathe some air."

A light drizzle was falling as they stepped out onto the rue de la Huchette. Jeff raised his face to the cool rain, let it trickle across his forehead. Mireille reached up, put a slender hand on his cheek.

"Music can hurt," she said softly.

"Mm."

"No good. Better to . . . *comment dit-on 'oublier'?*"

" 'Forget.' "

"Oui, c'est ça. Better to forget."

"Yeah."

"For a while."

"For a while," he agreed, and they set off toward the boul'Mich to find a taxi.

Back in the living room of Jeff's apartment on the avenue Foch, Mireille filled a small pipe with crumbly brown hashish and an equal measure of opium. She sat beside him on an Oriental rug, lit the potent mixture, and passed the pipe to him. He inhaled deeply, relit it when it went out.

Jeff had smoked a joint now and then, mainly in his first existence, but he'd never felt such a deep rush of blissful calm as this. It was, as Malraux had described the opium experience, "like being carried away on great motionless

wings''; yet the hashish kept his mind active and open,
kept him from drifting off entirely into dreams.

Mireille lay back on the carpet, her green silk dress
rising to her thighs. The rain against the window beat an
insistent cadence, and she lolled her head in a rhythmic
circle to the sound, her lustrous russet hair falling now
across her face, now upon her naked shoulders. Jeff stroked
her calf, then her inner thigh, and she made a soft murmur
of acquiescence and desire. He leaned forward, undid the
front of her dress, slid the smooth fabric away from her
girlish breasts.

There on the floor they used each other's bodies
wordlessly, almost furiously. When they were done, Mireille
filled another pipe with the opiated hash, and they smoked
it in the bedroom. This time they came together languor-
ously beneath the downfilled blanket, their legs and arms
entwining with newly familiar ease; and later, as the bells
of Saint-Honoré d'Eylau called early Mass, Mireille climbed
atop him once again, her slim hips riding his in playful joy.

Sharla let herself back into the apartment with the drab
dawn. ''Morning,'' she said as she opened the bedroom door,
looking spent. ''You guys want coffee?''

Mireille sat up in bed, shaking her tousled hair. ''With
perhaps a little Cognac?''

Sharla pulled off her wrinkled dress, fished in the closet
for a robe. ''That sounds good,'' she said. ''Same for you,
Jeff?''

He blinked, rubbed the drug haze from his eyes. ''Yeah,
I guess.''

Mireille got up and padded casually to the bathroom for
a shower. When Sharla came back with the breakfast tray,
the little redhead was sitting on the edge of the bed, still
nude, drying her hair. As they sipped their coffee laced
with brandy, the two women talked pleasantly about a new
lingerie shop on the rue de Rivoli.

A little after nine Mireille said she had to go home and
change; she was meeting another friend for brunch, and
didn't want to show up at the café wearing last night's
silk. She kissed Jeff goodbye, gave Sharla a quick hug,
and was gone.

As soon as Mireille had left, Sharla cleared the coffee cups from the bed, pulled back the sheets, and moved her warm tongue down Jeff's belly. He was limp when she took him in her mouth, but soon grew hard again.

Jeff never asked where Sharla had been all night; it didn't really matter.

The Mediterranean lapped gently against the pebbly beach, its quiet waves a whisper of eternity, of changelessness. The scent of a fresh pot of bouillabaise drifted from one of the cafés nearby. Jeff was getting hungry; as soon as the girls finished swimming, he'd suggest lunch.

The weather had broken for a week or so in early July, and they'd taken Le Mistral south with Jean-Claude and Mireille and the rest of the crowd. They'd all been drunk by the time the train got to Toulon, where the eight of them boisterously crammed themselves into two taxis for the forty-three-mile ride to St.-Tropez.

The little fishing village had undergone a major up-heaval in the past six years, since Vadim and Bardot had discovered and popularized it as a youthful alternative to the more sedate, old-money Côte d'Azur resorts of Antibes and Menton; but, lively as it already was, the town was still free of the suffocating hordes of tourists who would make it all but unlivable in the decades to come.

A shadow crossed Jeff's half-closed eyes, and he was pressed to the sand by a pair of smooth female thighs, someone sitting on his rump. Sharla? Mireille? Then the woman's naked breasts brushed his back, caressing, nipples stiff from the sea breeze.

"Chicca?" he guessed, lifting one hand up toward the girl's hair to feel how long it was, how thick. She shook her head away, giggled.

"T'es fou," the girl teased, clamping his thighs more tightly with her own and pressing her breasts flush against him: smaller than Sharla's, fuller than Chicca's.

"Couldn't be Mireille," he said, reaching back to pat her taut little ass. "Much too fat."

Mireille let forth a stream of curses in French, and punctuated them by lifting the waistband of his brief trunks and emptying a cup of iced lemonade inside. He rolled her off him with a yelp and pinned her on her back in the sand, arms struggling playfully against his grip.

"*Sadique.*" She grinned. Jeff freed one hand long enough to shake the ice out of his trunks, and she grasped his cock through the thin cloth. "See?" she said. "You love it."

He wanted to take her there and then, her hair loose and wild, her breasts and belly glistening in the sunlight, the slight swell of her crotch outlined through the white bikini bottom. She slid her fingers down the front of his trunks, squeezed him harder. He drew a sharp breath.

"People around," he said, voice strained.

Mireille shrugged, her hand working steadily on his penis. He glanced up at the crowded beach, saw Sharla walking toward them, her own bare breasts swaying, her arm around Jean-Claude's waist.

"Mireille," he whispered urgently.

She ground her sandy hips against his, kneaded him harder, faster. He couldn't stop it now. He shut his eyes and moaned, and there were lips touching his own, a tongue probing his mouth, one set of nipples against his chest and another pressed to his shoulder, hair and breasts and mouths and hands . . . He came, with Sharla kissing him as Mireille brought him to orgasm; or was it the other way around? And what was the difference, after all?

"Everybody work up an appetite, *hein?*" Jean-Claude said, laughing.

Jeff told Mireille that evening, in the garden of the hotel, after they'd all shared several pipes of opiated hash and Sharla had wandered up to one of the rooms with Jean-Claude and Chicca and another couple. The drugs helped to loosen his tongue, and the secret that had burned within him for so many years now burst forth of its own accord; Mireille just happened to be there when it did.

"I've lived this life before," he said, staring at the late-setting sun through the pine trees of the Résidence de la Pinède.

Mireille crossed her bare legs in a lotus position, her white cotton dress billowing on the grass around her.

"Déjà vu." She smiled. "Me, too, sometimes I feel that way."

Jeff shook his head, frowned. "I mean literally. I mean— not this exact life, here with you and Sharla and everything, but . . ."

And it spilled out, all of it, a tumble of words and memories he'd hidden for so long: the heart attack in his office, that first morning in the dorm room back at Emory, the fortunes made and lost, his wives, his children, the dying, and dying, and dying yet again.

Mireille listened without a word. The lowering sun backlit her hair, turning it the color of flame, and left her face in deepening shadow. At long last his voice trailed off, defeated by the incredibility of what he had tried to tell her.

It was dark by then, and Mireille's face was impossible to read. Did she think he was mad, or recounting an opium dream? Her silence began to erode the cathartic relief he had felt in telling her.

"Mireille? I didn't mean to shock you; I—"

She rose to her knees, put her slender arms around his neck. The tight curls of her copper hair pressed softly against his cheek.

"Many lives," she whispered. "Many pains."

He held her slim young body tightly, breathed long and deep of the crisp, pine-scented air. Scattered laughter drifted toward them through the trees, and then the clear, sweet, buoyant sounds of the latest Sylvie Vartan record.

"Viens," Mireille said, standing up and taking Jeff's hand. "Let's go join the party. *La vie nous attend."*

They all went back to Paris in August, when the rains started again. Mireille never said anything more to Jeff about what he'd told her that evening in the garden at St.-Tropez; she must have attributed it all to the hash, and that was just as well. Nor did Jeff and Sharla talk openly about the group sex and the drugs that were now part of the normal routine of their lives. Those things had happened; they kept on happening. There was no reason to discuss them as long as everybody was having a good time.

One of the new couples who periodically drifted in and out of the scene introduced them to a *partouze* in the rue le Chatelier, a few blocks north of what would continue to be called Place de l'Etoile until De Gaulle died in 1970. The *partouze,* one of several that had flourished in the city since the twenties, was a well-run, sumptuously appointed establishment: glass-encased antique-doll collection in the parlor, thick maroon carpet to match the walls, which were hung with *fin de siècle* prints . . . and three uniformed maids to serve the thirty or forty naked couples who wandered and frolicked through the place's two floors of well-equipped, very large bedrooms.

The St.-Tropez crowd began frequenting the *partouze* every weekend. One night Jeff and Sharla had a threesome with a coltish American starlet new to Paris, who would soon be known more for her radical feminism than for her acting; another night, Mireille and Sharla and Chicca held an impromptu contest to see which of them could be first to have sex with twenty men at one party. Sharla won.

Jeff was amazed at how quickly this unceasing roundelay of casual public sex with beautiful strangers had grown to seem perfectly normal; he was struck by the fact that such activities could go on without the slightest fear of those plagues from his own time, herpes and AIDS. That carefree sense of safety gave the decadent proceedings a retrospective air of innocence—naked children at play in the Garden before the Fall. He wondered what had happened to the *partouzes,* and their counterparts in America and the rest of Europe, in the eighties. If they'd survived at all, they must be rife with disease-inspired paranoia and guilt.

The eighties: a decade of loss, of broken hopes, of death. All of which would come again, he knew, and far too soon.

≡9≡

THEY'D BEEN IN London less than a month when he met the girl who offered him the LSD; met her as she was coming out of the Chelsea Drugstore, in fact. They had a good laugh about that as he chatted her up over Campari and soda. Jeff said he'd gone down to get his prescription filled and gotten *exactly* what he wanted. She thought that was funny, though of course she didn't catch the reference; the Stones wouldn't record that song for another year.

Her name was Sylvia, she confided to him, but everybody called her Sylla, "like the singer, Cilla Black, y'know?" Her mum and dad lived in Brighton (she made a face), but she was sharing a flat in South Kensington with two other birds, and had a job at Granny Takes a Trip, where she could get all her clothes at half price—like the blue vinyl mini-skirt and the yellow patterned stockings she was wearing now.

"We've got just the closest gear there, y'know; lots closer than Countdown or Top Gear. Cathy McGowan shops there all the time, and Jean Shrimpton was in just yesterday."

Jeff smiled and nodded, tuning out her mindless patter. It wasn't her he was interested in, it was the drug; he had

114

been for a long time, and hated to admit he'd always been afraid to try it. This girl seemed casual enough about it, hadn't suffered any apparent ill effects (assuming she'd been born this vapid). He'd picked her up out of habit more than anything else, commenting on the new Animals album she had under her arm, and within five minutes she'd asked him if he wanted to drop some acid. Well, what the hell? Why not?

Back in the town house on Sloane Terrace, Sharla was asleep in bed with some guy she'd met last night at Dolly's. Jeff closed the bedroom door, put on a Marianne Faithfull record at low volume in the living room, asked Sylla if she wanted another drink.

"Not if we're gonna do the acid," she said. "They don't mix well, y'know?"

Jeff shrugged, poured himself another Scotch anyway. He needed the alcohol to relax, to ease his nervousness over taking the psychedelic. What could it hurt?

"That your wife in the other room?" Sylla asked.

"No. Just a friend."

"She gonna mind me being here?"

Jeff shook his head and laughed. "Not a bit."

Sylla grinned, tossed her straight brown hair out of her eyes. "I never . . . did it, y'know, with another bird around. Except my flat-mates, of course, and that's just 'cause we don't have that much room."

"Well, she's *my* flat-mate, and it's O.K. There's another bedroom downstairs. Would you feel more comfortable in there?"

She rummaged in the yellow vinyl purse whose material matched her skirt, its color her stockings. "Let's do the acid first, wait for it to come on. Then we can go downstairs."

Jeff took the little purple-stained square of blotter paper she handed him, washed it down with the last of the whiskey. Sylla wanted some orange juice with hers, so he fetched a container from the fridge.

"How long does it take before you feel the effect?" he asked.

"Depends. D'you eat lunch today?"

"No."

" 'Bout half an hour, then," she said. "More or less."

It was less. Within twenty minutes the walls had turned to rubber, had begun to recede and approach. Jeff waited for the visions he had expected to appear, but none did; instead, everything around him just seemed slightly twisted, indefinably askew, and sort of sparkly.

"Y'feel it, luv?" she asked.

"It's . . . not what I'd thought it would be like." His words came out distinctly but felt thick in his mouth. Sylla's face was changing, flowing like hot wax; her lipstick and rouge now seemed obscenely garish, layers of red paint covering her flesh.

"Fab, though, innit?"

Jeff closed his eyes and, yes, there were patterns there, circles within circles, interconnected by a complex, shimmering latticework. Wheels, mandalas: symbols of eternal cycles, of illusory change that merely led back to where the change had begun and would begin again . . .

"Feel my stocking; feel that." Sylla placed his hand on her thigh, and the yellow patterned panty hose became a landscape of textures and ridges, lit by an alien sun; that sun, too, a part of the endless cycles of being, the—

Sylla giggled, pressed his hand between her legs. "Take me downstairs now, O.K.? Wait'll you see what *this* feels like on acid."

He complied, though he wanted only to lie back and give his mind up to these recurring waves of quietude and acceptance. In the small bedroom downstairs Sylla undressed him, ran her red-tipped fingers over his body, leaving a trail of cool fire wherever they touched. She stepped out of her mini-skirt and stockings, pulled her thin blouse over her head, drew his mouth to her right nipple. He sucked it with more curiosity than desire, like an infant suddenly aware of its place in the chain of existence, an omniscient child seeing its own birth, death, rebirth.

Sylla guided him inside her, and he grew hard automatically. Her wet inner flesh was like something ancient, something protohuman; receptive yin to his vital yang, together the creators of these endlessly regenerating cycles, these—

Jeff opened his eyes and the girl's face changed shape again. It had become Gretchen's face. He was fucking Gretchen, fucking his daughter: she to whom he had given life, yet who had never been.

He withdrew from her with instant revulsion.

"Awwrr!" the girl cried in frustration and reached for his limp penis, stroking it. "C'mon, luv, c'mon!"

The waves within his mind no longer soothed; they battered his emotions with a vicious impact. Cycles, wheels . . . within that universal chain there was no place for him, no pattern that would fit his mutant existence out of time.

The girl parted her blood-red lips and bent to suck him. He pushed her face away toward the pulsing wall, tried to shut out what he had seen in her.

"Mind if we join the party?" Sharla stood in the open doorway, naked. Behind her was a skinny young man with long, straggly hair and a pitted face. Sylla frowned uncertainly at the newcomers, then relaxed and let fall the sheet she had pulled up to cover her breasts.

"Might's well," Sylla said. "Acid didn't seem to agree with your mate, here."

"Acid?" the young man said excitedly. "You got some with you?"

Sylla nodded, reached for the purse she'd brought downstairs.

"Here, give us a couple hits, willya?" he said. Then, to Sharla: "You ever fuck on acid? It's tremendous!"

They were on the bed, all of them, Sharla stroking Sylla's hair, Gretchen's hair—or was it Linda doing that? —and then the stranger became Martin Bailey, blood from the self-inflicted gunshot wound to his head spewing across the sheets, soaking the naked bodies of Jeff's wife and daughter, they were dead all of them dead except for him and he couldn't die no matter how many times he died. He was the wheel; he was the cycle.

Sharla tapped her foot impatiently as they waited in the first class lounge at San Francisco International. Her face was ghostly pale, after the latest mode, framed in the sleek straightness of her black hair. Her eyebrows were bleached to near-invisibility, her lipstick like a streak of chalk. The crazily zebra-patterned op-art print dress and white tights she wore completed the utter lack of color.

"How much longer now?" she asked curtly.

Jeff glanced at his watch. "Should be boarding any minute."

"And then how long till we get there?"

"It's a four-and-a-half hour flight." He sighed. "We've been through this before."

"I don't know why we're doing this, anyway. I thought you were sick of the goddamned tropics. That's exactly what you said before we left Brazil. Why do we have to go to Hawaii all of a sudden?"

"I want some quiet time in the sun, nobody else around for a change. I want some time to think, O.K.? And we've been through this before, too."

She shot him a cynical look. "Yeah, well, you just think you've been through *everything* before, don't you?"

He stared back at her, incredulous. "What do you mean by that?"

"All that crap about living your life over again, all that reincarnation shit or whatever."

Jeff turned in the uncomfortable seat, grasped her tightly by the wrist. "Where did you hear anything like that? I never—"

"Let go of me," she said, shaking her hand loose from his. "Jesus Christ, you can't get it up for one little dolly bird, you freak out on acid, and all of a sudden you want to run away, you start grabbing at me—"

"Shut up, Sharla. Just tell me what you heard, and where."

"Mireille told me all about it last year. Said you tried to lay some kind of mystical trip on her, told her you'd died and come back again. What a crock!"

The revelation struck Jeff with almost physical force. Of all the people he had known in any of his lives, there'd been some sense of empathy and understanding in Mireille alone that had led him to share his secret with her. He'd thought she wouldn't make judgments about what he told her, would keep it as private as it must be kept. . . .

"Why—" His voice cracked. "Why did she tell you?"

" 'Cause she thought it was funny. We all did; everybody we knew in Paris was laughing behind your back for months."

He put his head in his hands, trying to absorb the implication of what she was telling him. "I trusted Mireille," he said softly.

Sharla snorted with derision. "Right, your special little girlfriend, uh-huh. I made it with her first, you know; who do you think told her to go hop in bed with you, get you out of that stupid moody funk you were in half the time? I was getting sick of you. I just wanted to have a good time and get laid. Mireille would have fucked a goddamn monkey if Jean-Claude and I told her to, so we did. Weren't you the lucky one?"

A woman's disembodied voice called their flight. Jeff made his way to the gate in a stupor of disbelief, Sharla beside him, a tight, satisfied smile on her face. They found their seats on the right side of the still-new Boeing 707, just behind the wing. Neither spoke as they stowed their carry-on luggage and fastened their seat belts. A stewardess came by, offering candy and gum; Jeff mutely declined. Sharla took a piece of orange hard candy, sucked at it with relish.

"Good morning, ladies and gentlemen, and welcome aboard Pan American World Airways Flight 843 from San Francisco to Honolulu. Your pilot today is Captain Charles Kimes, and with him in the cockpit are First Officer Fred Miller, Second Officer Max Webb, and Flight Engineer Fitch Robertson. We'll be flying at an altitude of approximately . . ."

Jeff stared out the window at the drab gray tarmac rolling slowly past.

In truth, he had no one to blame but himself. He had set the tone for this heedless, sybaritic replay when he'd gone to Las Vegas with the express purpose of seeking out Sharla.

". . . be serving lunch about thirty minutes after

we take off. Please observe the 'No Smoking' and the 'Fasten Seat Belts' signs when they are lit, and for your comfort . . .''

What should he feel now, he wondered—anger, defeat? Neither emotion would do him any good; the damage had been done. Obviously, no one—not even Mireille—had believed what he'd told her in St.-Tropez. At least the deception that she and Sharla had perpetrated didn't present any threat to him; all it really did was leave him more alone than before.

The jet sped down the runway, lifted gracefully. He glanced toward the front of the cabin. No movie screen, of course; TWA still had exclusive rights to in-flight motion pictures. Too bad. He would have welcomed the distraction.

Jeff looked out the window as the jet climbed over the busy Bayshore Freeway. He should have brought along a book. Tom Wolfe's *Kandy-Colored Tangerine Flake Streamline Baby* had just been published; he wouldn't have minded rereading—

The big plane shuddered heavily, rocked by a dull explosion. As Jeff watched in horror, the right outboard engine tore loose from its mounting and ripped a jagged hole in the wing as it fell away toward the city beneath them. Kerosene spurted from the wing-tip tank, then burst into a curling white flame that spat shards of molten metal.

"Look, the wing is on fire!" someone behind him shouted. The cabin filled with screams and the wails of children.

The outer third of the burning wing fell off, and the plane yawed crazily to the right. Jeff saw homes nestled in the pass between the hills, then the blue water of the Pacific, not more than a thousand feet below.

Sharla clutched at his left hand. He squeezed hers back, rancor and regret forgotten in the face of this appalling moment.

Only two years into this wasted replay, he thought with dread; would he return from a death so early, so violent? For all he'd cursed his repeated lives, he desperately wished now for life to continue.

The plane shook again, dipped further toward the right.

The Golden Gate Bridge came into view, its towers shockingly close.

"We're going to hit it," Sharla whispered urgently. "We're going to hit the bridge!"

"No," Jeff rasped out. "We're still more or less level. We haven't dropped much since the engine went. We'll miss the bridge, anyway."

"This is Captain Kimes," a studiedly calm voice said. "We have a minor problem, ladies and gentlemen. . . . Well, maybe it's not so minor."

They were limping back over land now, back toward the hills and high rises of San Francisco.

"We're gonna try to—We're gonna head for Travis Air Force Base—that's about forty miles—because they've got a nice, long runway there we can use, longer than anything at San Francisco International. I'm gonna be pretty busy up here, so just settle down and I'll put Second Officer Webb on to tell you what you need to know about the landing."

"He doesn't think we can make it," Sharla wailed. "We're going to crash, I know we are!"

"Keep quiet," Jeff told her. "Those kids across the aisle can hear you."

"This is Second Officer Max Webb," said the new voice from the tinny speakers. "We'll be making an emergency landing at Travis in about ten minutes, so . . ."

Sharla began to whimper, and Jeff held her hand more tightly.

". . . If we use the chutes, please stay calm. Remember, you will sit down to go out the chute. Don't panic. When we do land, and if it is a rough landing—which is a possibility—please lean forward in your seats. You grab your ankles and stay down, or put your arms under your knees. Move as far forward as you possibly can. Do not move until we tell you what we're going to do . . ."

The plane was losing altitude fast. As they approached the broad expanse of the military base, Jeff could see fire equipment and ambulances lining the longest of the crisscrossing, empty runways.

They began a long, looping circle, just a few hundred

feet above the Air Force barracks and hangars. Jeff heard the wheels emerge in jerky fits and starts from the plane's undercarriage. The crew must be cranking them down manually, he thought. The explosion had probably wrecked the hydraulic system.

Sharla was mumbling something beside him; it sounded like she was praying. Jeff took a last look out the window and saw a whirlwind kicking up dust at the near end of the runway they were aiming for. That could mean trouble; with the damage the plane had already sustained, a last-minute spate of turbulence might—Well, there was no point thinking about it. He pulled his hand away from Sharla's, helped her get into a fetal position, then curled his own head between his knees, clutching his ankles.

The remaining engines gave a sudden burst of power, and the plane heaved to the left, then lurched back on course. Pilot must have been trying to avoid that whirlwind, must have—

The wheels touched, screeched against the tarmac, seemed to hold. For several agonizing seconds they raced along the runway. Then the engines roared again and they were slowing, stopping . . . they had landed.

The passengers burst into applause. Then the stewardesses threw open the emergency exits and everyone scrambled to slide down the escape chutes. The crippled plane reeked of jet fuel, and when he was outside Jeff could see the clear, flammable liquid pouring from cracks in the broken right wing. He pulled Sharla along with him and they ran from the plane.

Three hundred yards away they collapsed, exhausted, on a grassy strip between two runways. Military fire engines were dousing the 7O7 with white foam, and all around them people milled about in a state of shock.

"Oh, Jeff," Sharla cried, putting her arms around his neck and her face against his shoulder. "Oh my God, I was so scared up there. I thought—I thought—"

He pried her arms loose, pushed her away, and stood up. The stark black-and-white makeup she wore was streaked with tears, her op-art dress stained from the escape chute, the smoke, the grass.

Jeff looked around, spotted one building off to the left that seemed to be a center of activity, a hive of returning ambulances and asbestos-suited emergency personnel. He started walking in that direction, leaving Sharla where she lay weeping on the ground.

"Jeff!" she screamed after him. "You can't leave me, not now! Not after that!"

Why not? he thought, started to say it aloud, then just kept on walking.

≡10≡

JEFF FINISHED HIS eggs and bacon as the sun was coming up, scrubbed the dishes, and left the pan to soak. Usually he took a cup of coffee on the little porch of the steep-roofed white house, but this morning he was running late, and there was much to do.

He pulled a down jacket over his flannel shirt and stepped outside. Third week of May, but the air still had a bite to it; last frost of the year had come night before last. He nodded his respects to the rock pile where old man Smyth was buried, and strode over to one of the newly furrowed corn fields, all staked out and ready for planting. Smyth had worked this land alone, too, after he'd home-steaded it in the 1880s. Had fallen ill after some sort of accident, Jeff had been told, and nobody'd found his body for weeks. People who'd bought the place in the tax auction afterward had never planted a thing; hadn't even kept the land, not once they'd found the small fortune in gold coins that Smyth had hidden in the Dutch oven. The old man had had some secrets of his own, it seemed.

Jeff dug the toe of his boot into the thick black topsoil where he'd be planting the first corn of the season this afternoon, the Sugar and Gold early variety. Good vol-

canic California soil it was, rich in minerals. He had
nothing but contempt for the family that, so long ago, had
let it lie fallow, had taken Sylvester Smyth's gold and
departed The Cove in search of unearned joys and com-
forts. Land like this demanded to be tilled, and the fresh
food it would yield in return held far greater value than
any coins. That was the contract, the bargain struck between man and earth ten thousand years ago in Mesopota-
mia. To abandon good land, Jeff believed, was to break an
ancient and almost holy bond.

He walked on past the plot where the asparagus would
soon be coming up; he'd get at least another two years out
of that original planting, and it was time now for the first
of the plants' twice-yearly feedings. The late spring frosts
didn't seem to bother them at all; Jeff thought it made the
stalks crisper. He knelt beside the spring that ran through
his property, scooped a double handful of the icy mountain
water to his mouth. As he drank, a pair of German brown
trout swam past. If he finished planting the corn and
feeding the asparagus before nightfall, he decided, he'd
bring a rod down and catch some dinner.

The sun continued to climb the sky, lighting the tips of
the pines on the humped rise of Hogback Mountain to the
southwest. Jeff followed the meandering uphill path of the
spring, pausing every twenty feet or so to clean it of
accumulated debris, opening the clogged collection boxes
and pipes on which his crops depended for irrigation.

He'd bought the place nine years ago, a few weeks after
the near-disaster on the plane to Honolulu. He hadn't seen
Sharla since that day beside the smoky runway. Hadn't
seen much of anybody since that summer, truth to tell.

His closest full-time neighbor was at Turtle Pond, three
miles east along an old wagon road. Only way into or out
of Jeff's place was by way of a switchback road that was
often washed away. From November through January the
snows and rains and mud made the passage over Marble
Creek all but impossible; he'd learned to stockpile well for
the winter.

Rest of the year he kept to himself almost as much.
Every week or so he'd drive into the little town of Mont-

gomery Creek, buy some things at the store there or get his pickup serviced at the two-pump Shell station. He'd quit drinking, by and large, but if the harvest was a good one he might celebrate with a beer and dinner at the Forked Horn or the Hillcrest Lodge. An amiable family, the Mazzinis, owned the Forked Horn, and the wife, Eleanor, ran a branch of the Shasta County library out of their big, rambling house in town. Jeff would chat with one or the other of them sometimes, about this and that. Their son Joe was a couple of years younger than Jeff, and his intelligent curiosity about the outside world seemed to know no bounds. Yet none of the family ever pried; they never dug too deeply into why Jeff had sought such an isolated life for himself. Joe had helped him set up a shortwave rig out at The Cove, and the radio had become Jeff's only contact with civilization, aside from his occasional talks with the Mazzinis.

This little corner of northern California was populated mostly by lumberjacks and Indians, neither of whom Jeff had any contact with. A smattering of hippies and other back-to-the-land types had come in shortly after he'd moved here, but most of them hadn't stayed long. Working the land was harder than they'd expected, and it took more than marijuana crops to keep a place going.

The worst part of these years, he supposed, was the celibacy, though not for the reasons he would have imagined. He'd damn near OD'd on sex for the sake of sex during his time with Sharla and Mireille.

It had seemed, for a while, that he could live perfectly well without sexual contact, and he'd been surprised at how easy it was to kill that part of himself. But he'd soon discovered, much to his unpleasant surprise, just how strong was his need for simple human touch. The loss of that tore at him daily, troubled him both waking and sleeping. Sometimes he would dream of a woman simply touching his cheek, or of himself holding her head against his chest. The woman in these dreams might be Judy or Linda, even Sharla; more often she was faceless, an abstraction of femininity.

Always, he would awake from those dreams with an

overpowering sadness and the familiar knowledge that this deprivation could not be alleviated without the risk of further betrayal and the eventual certainty of absolute erasure. Both pains were too extreme to face again. Better, it seemed, just to let his soul die slowly, bit by lonely bit.

His back was starting to ache from all the stooping he'd done to clear the irrigation system, so he sat down beside the spring. Far to the north, beyond the Flatwoods and halfway to Oregon, the astonishing white cone of Mount Shasta dominated the horizon like the sleeping god the Indians around here had once supposed it to be.

He took a chew of beef jerky, washed it down with another cold sip of spring water. This new home of his was right on the spine of the volatile Cascade range, dead center between Mount Lassen and Mount Shasta. North of there were the ruins of the massive prehistoric volcano that had collapsed to form Crater Lake, and then came Mount Hood, and on up into Washington State, Mount St. Helen's rumbled quietly . . . for the moment. It would explode with deadly fury seven years from now, just as it had done three times before; an event that Jeff, and Jeff alone, recalled.

He was in the grip of forces that could destroy a mountain, then put it back together and destroy it again, over and over and over, like a child playing in the sand. What use was there in even attempting to comprehend something like that? If he ever did come to understand it, even partially, the knowledge might be more than one human brain could accept and still allow him to retain some measure of sanity.

Jeff folded the rest of the beef jerky in its cellophane wrapper, stuck it back in his pocket. The sun was high overhead now; time to start planting this year's rows of corn. He made his way back down the hill, following the spring, never once raising his eyes to gaze again on the snowy heights of the distant mountain.

"How 'bout peat moss? You stocked O.K.?"

"I could do with another couple hundred pounds," Jeff said. "And I'll need another forty gallons of Sevin."

The storekeeper clucked in sympathy, added the insecticide to the order. "Yeah, them corn earworms is something else this season, ain't they? Old Charlie Reynolds up at Buckeye has done lost three acres to 'em already."

Jeff nodded, grunted as politely as he could remember how. These twice-yearly major supply runs down to Redding were his only contact with total strangers.

"What do you think about the Arabs, and these here gasoline lines?" the man queried. "Never thought I'd see the day."

"I figure it'll get better," Jeff said. "Let me have one of those big boxes of beef jerky, too; the spicy kind."

"Never thought I'd see the day. You ask me, Nixon ought to be droppin' a bomb on them Arabs, 'stead of going over to talk to 'em. As if he didn't already have troubles enough of his own right back here."

Jeff idly scanned the posters and notices tacked up behind the supply store's cash register, hoping the man would soon realize he didn't want to get drawn into a political conversation. The sheriff, Jeff read, was auctioning off somebody's foreclosed property in Burney; the local hippie holdouts were throwing a big dance at Iron Canyon; lots of cars and pickups were for sale. . . . Now, there was an odd one. It really looked out of place: a blue-black poster of the night sky, with a phosphorescent wave breaking in space above a half-full moon. Thin gold letters at the bottom spelled one word: *Starsea*.

"What's that all about?" Jeff asked, pointing at the poster.

The storekeeper turned to look, then gazed back at Jeff with a disbelieving frown. "Boy, how far back in the woods you been? You ain't seen *Starsea?*"

"What is it?"

"Hell, it's a movie. Last movie I saw before that was, I think, *The Sound of Music,* but no way could I miss this one. Kids dragged me and the wife down to Sacramento to see it three, four months ago. Seen it twice since then, and we'll probably go again now it's opened in Redding. Never seen nothing like it, I tell you."

"Popular movie, is it?"

"Popular?" The man laughed. "Biggest damn movie ever, they say. I hear tell it's done made a hundred million dollars, and still goin' strong. Never thought I'd see the day."

That was impossible; no movie would make that much money until *Jaws,* more than a year from now. Jeff had never even heard of anything called *Starsea,* certainly not in 1974. The big movies this year, he recalled, were *Chinatown* and the sequel to *The Godfather.*

"What's it about?"

"If you don't know, I wouldn't want to spoil it for you. It's playing up at the Cascade; you ought to see it before you drive back. Worth the delay, I tell you."

Jeff felt a spark of curiosity, something he hadn't experienced for years.

The storekeeper thumbed through a copy of the *Redding Record-Searchlight.* On the front page, Kissinger was embracing Yitzhak Rabin. "Here it is, next show's at . . . 3:20." The man glanced at the big clock on the back wall of the store. "I can hold your order here for you if you like. You could see the show and still get home before dark."

Jeff smiled. "You get a kickback from the theater or something?"

"I told you, I don't usually care for movies, but this one here's something special. Go ahead, I'll have your stuff all boxed and ready to load when you get back."

The line for *Starsea* stretched more than a block, on a Tuesday afternoon in Redding. Jeff shook his head in amazement, bought a ticket, and joined the waiting crowd. They were of all ages, from wide-eyed six-year-olds to taciturn couples in their seventies wearing worn overalls. From the hushed conversations around him, Jeff gathered that many had already seen the movie more than once. Their attitude was almost as if they were coming together for a shared religious experience, worshipers quietly but joyously approaching a beloved shrine.

The movie was everything the storekeeper had claimed, and far more. Even to Jeff's eyes it was years ahead of its time in theme, look, special effects; like an undersea version of Kubrick's *2001: A Space Odyssey*, yet with the warmth and humanity of Truffaut at his best.

The film began with an elegiac illumination of the ancient bond between humans and dolphins, then extended that mythic connection to include a philosophical race of extraterrestrials who had long ago established contact with the intelligent mammals of earth's oceans. That race, according to the plot, had appointed the Cetaceans as benevolent caretakers of humanity until such time as mankind was ready to be welcomed to the galactic family. But near the end of the twentieth century, the dolphins learned that the mentors of Cygnus IV, whose return had been awaited for millenia, had been destroyed by an interstellar catastrophe. The dolphins then made their true nature and their great history known to humanity, in a moment of simultaneous exhilaration and deep mourning. For the first time, this planet became genuinely whole, a linked community of minds on land and undersea . . . yet more alone in the bleakness of space than ever, with earth's unmet benefactors having vanished for eternity.

The movie expertly conveyed, with sophistication and a rare cinematic depth of insight, the unbearable irony of ultimate hopes lost even as they are realized. Jeff found himself moved to tears of poignant rapture along with the rest of the audience, his years of self-imposed exile and detachment shattered in the space of two hours.

And it was new, all of it. Jeff couldn't possibly have remained unaware of an artistic achievement this magnificent, this successful in every sense, had it appeared within either of his previous replays.

He read the list of credits with almost as much astonishment as the film itself had generated: Directed by Steven Spielberg . . . Written and Produced by Pamela Phillips . . . Creative Consultant and Special Effects Supervisor, George Lucas.

How could all this be? Spielberg's first big movie, *Jaws*, hadn't even begun shooting yet, and it would be two years before Lucas turned the industry on its ear with *Star*

Wars. But most puzzling, most intriguing, of all—Who the hell was Pamela Phillips?

"I don't care what it takes, Alan, except time. I want that appointment set up, and I want it next week."

"Mr. Winston, it's just not that easy. Those people down there have their own little hierarchy, and right now this woman's pretty much at the top of it. Half the writers and producers in Hollywood are trying to get in to—"

"I'm not looking to sell her anything, Alan. I'm a businessman, not a moviemaker."

There was a long silence on the other end of the line. Jeff knew what the broker must be thinking. It had been nine years since he'd spoken directly to his client. What kind of businessman did that make him? Jeff Winston was a hermit, a recluse who'd shown up at the brokerage house in San Francisco only once, in 1965, to deposit a lump sum of cash with them. He lived in the woods and occasionally sent a cryptic message directing that they buy large amounts of some obscure or ill-advised stock in his name. And yet, and yet . . .

"What's the current value of my holdings, Alan?"

"Sir, I don't have that information right here at my fingertips. Yours is a very complex and highly diversified account; it would take me several days to—"

"Ballpark figure."

"Well, keeping in mind the possible fluctuations of—"

"I said I want a rough estimate, off the top of your head. Now."

The man gave a sigh of resignation. "Approximately sixty-five million, plus or minus five million or so. You understand, I don't keep—"

"Yes, I understand. I just want to make sure *you* understand what we're talking about here. We are talking about someone with a great deal of money to invest and someone else who's in a business that absolutely depends on fresh input of capital. Does that make sense to you?"

"Certainly, sir. But remember that Miss Phillips's company is awash in new capital right now from the proceeds of her film. That may not be her highest priority at the moment.''

"I'm sure she'll recognize the long-term value of my interest. If not, take a different approach; don't you have somebody there with contacts in the film industry?''

"Well . . . I believe Harvey Greenspan, in our Los Angeles office, has a number of clients who are connected with the studios.''

"Then have him call in some favors, use whatever connections he's got.''

There was a polite rap on the door of Jeff's hotel suite.

"Bellman, sir. The man from Brooks Brothers is here for the fitting.''

"I have to go, Alan,'' Jeff said into the phone. "You can reach me at the Fairmont when you've got this arranged.''

"I'll do what I can, Mr. Winston.''

"Do it soon. I'd hate to have to take my account elsewhere, after all these years.''

The offices of Starsea Productions, Inc. were located in a two-story white stucco building south of Pico, in a nondescript commercial area between MGM and Twentieth Century Fox. The reception area was done in blue and white, with a billboard-sized poster for the movie behind the reception desk. An eclectic mix of abstract art and undersea photographs decorated the other walls, and on the large, Spanish-tile coffee table were displayed half a dozen books reflecting the themes of the film: *Intelligent Life in the Universe, The Mind of the Dolphin, Programming and Metaprogramming in the Human Biocomputer*. . . . Jeff flipped through a collection of color plates of Jupiter from the first *Pioneer* mission and waited.

"Mr. Winston?'' The cheery little brunette receptionist smiled professionally at him. "Miss Phillips will see you now.''

He followed her down a long corridor, past half a dozen open office doors. Everyone he saw was on the telephone.

Pamela Phillips's spacious office had the same blue-and-white color scheme as the reception area, but there were no movie memorabilia on the walls, no Pollock prints or photographs of dolphins. Here there was one visual motif, repeated in a dozen variations: mandalas, wheels, circles.

"Good morning, Mr. Winston. Would you care for some coffee or juice?"

"I'm fine, thanks."

"That'll be all, then, Natalie. Thank you."

Jeff studied the woman he had waited a month to see. She was tall, probably five ten; wide mouth, round face, very little makeup; straight, fine blond hair in a modified Dutch-boy cut. Jeff was glad he'd outfitted himself at Brooks Brothers; Pamela Phillips was dressed for business, in a well-tailored gray suit and high-necked maroon blouse with matching low-heeled shoes. No jewelry, except for a small gold lapel pin in a design of concentric circles.

"Have a seat, Mr. Winston. I understand you wished to discuss Starsea Productions as an investment opportunity?"

Right to the point, no dillydallying or amiable warm-up chatter. Like a mid-eighties corporate woman, in 1974.

"Yes, that's right. I find myself with some excess capital to—"

"Let me make it clear from the outset, Mr.—"

"Jeff, please."

She ignored his attempt at first-name familiarity, went right on with what she'd been saying. "My firm is privately financed and wholly self-supporting. I granted you this appointment out of courtesy to a friend, but if you want to invest in the motion-picture industry I'm afraid you've come to the wrong place. If you'd like, my attorney could draw up a list of some other production houses that might—"

"It's Starsea that interests me, not the business in general."

"If the company ever goes public, I'll see that your broker receives an offering. Until then . . ." She was rising from behind her desk, hand extended, ready to dismiss him.

"Aren't you even curious about my interest?"

"Not particularly, Mr. Winston. Since the film opened in December, it's generated a great deal of interest in many quarters. My own energies are devoted to other projects at this point.'' She extended her hand again. "So if you don't mind, I have a busy schedule. . . ."

The woman was making this more difficult than he'd expected; he had no choice but to plunge ahead. "What about *Star Wars?*" he asked. "Will your company have a hand in that?"

Her green eyes narrowed. "Rumors of upcoming films float around this town constantly, Mr. Winston. If I were you, I wouldn't listen to everything I hear around the pool at the Bel-Air.''

Might as well go all the way, Jeff thought. "And *Close Encounters?*" he asked. "I'm not sure whether Spielberg would even want to make that now—what do you think? It might seem like kind of a lame follow-up to *Starsea.*"

The anger hadn't left her eyes, but now it was joined by something else. She sat back down, stared at him cautiously. "Where did you ever hear that title?"

He returned her steady gaze, sidestepped the question. "Now, *E.T.,*" he said conversationally, "that's a different matter entirely. I don't see any conflict between the two. Same thing with *Raiders of the Lost Ark,* of course. Completely unrelated movie. First sequel to that one was lousy, though. Maybe you can talk to him about it.''

He had her full attention now. Her fingers nervously stroked her throat, and her face had lost all hint of any emotion but astonishment.

"Who are you?" Pamela Phillips asked in a low voice. "Who the hell are you?"

"Funny." Jeff smiled. "I've been wondering the same thing about you.''

≡11≡

PAMELA'S HOUSE IN Topanga Canyon was as isolated and difficult to reach as any home so close to a major city could possibly be, set in the middle of a five-acre plot that had gone wild with vegetation: jacarandas, lemon trees, grape vines, blackberry bushes . . . all in an undisciplined tangle of unchecked growth.

"You ought to trim back some of that," Jeff said as they wound their way toward the house in her Land Rover. She handled the four-wheel-drive vehicle with easy confidence, unaware or uncaring of how incongruous she looked in it, with her smart gray skirt and lacquered fingernails. She'd put her tailored jacket on the back seat and kicked off her shoes to better operate the clutch but otherwise still looked as if she belonged in the boardroom of an insurance company, not driving down a dirt road off an untamed canyon.

"That's the way it grows." She shrugged. "If I wanted a formal garden, I'd live in Beverly Hills."

"You've got a lot of good fruit going to waste, though."

"I get all the fruit I need at the Farmer's Market."

He let the matter drop. She could do whatever she wanted with her land, though it galled Jeff to see such lushness gone to seed. He still didn't know much about her. After tersely verifying what he'd suspected, that she was a replayer too, she'd insisted on hearing his own story from the beginning, and had frequently interrupted to grill him for more details. He'd left out a lot, of course, particularly some of the episodes with Sharla, and he'd yet to hear anything about her own experiences. Clearly, though, she was a person of many contradictions. Which made perfect sense; so was he. How could either of them be anything else?

The house was plainly but comfortably furnished, with an oakbeamed ceiling and a big picture window on one side that looked over the messy jungle of her property to the ocean far below. As in her office, the walls were hung with framed mandalas of many types: Navajo, Mayan, East Indian. Near the window was a large desk stacked with books and notebooks, and in the center of it sat a bulky, greenish-gray device that incorporated a video screen, a keyboard, and a printer. He frowned quizzically at it. What was she doing with a home computer this early? There was no—

"It's not a computer," Pamela said. "Wang 1200 word processor, one of the first. No disk drive, just cassettes, but it still beats a typewriter. Want a beer?"

"Sure." He was still a bit startled by her quick recognition of what he'd been thinking as he looked at the machine. It was going to take some time to get used to the idea that, after all these decades, he was in the presence of someone who actually shared his extraordinary frame of reference.

"Refrigerator's through there," she said, pointing. "Get me one, too, while I get out of this costume." She walked toward the back of the house, shoes in hand. Jeff found the kitchen, opened two bottles of Beck's.

He surveyed her shelves of books and records as he waited for her to change. She didn't seem to read much fiction or listen to a lot of popular music. The books were mostly biography, science, and the business side of the film industry; her records were weighted toward Bach, Handel, and Vivaldi.

Pamela came back into the living room wearing faded

jeans and a baggy USC sweat shirt, took the beer from him, and plopped down in an overstuffed recliner. "That thing you told me about the plane, the one that almost crashed; that was stupid, you know."

"What do you mean?"

"At the end of my second cycle, when I realized I might go through it again, I memorized a list of every plane crash since 1963. Hotel fires, too, and railway accidents, earthquakes . . . all the major disasters."

"I've thought of doing the same thing."

"You should have already. Anyway, what happened next? What have you been doing since then?"

"Isn't this all a bit one-sided? I'm just as curious about you, you know."

"Wrap up your story; then we'll get to mine."

He settled himself on a sofa across from her and tried to explain his voluntary exile of the last nine years: his ascetic sense of union with things that grew in the earth, his fascination with their eternal symmetry in time—living entities that withered so they might flower, blossoms and green fruits that sprang recurrently to life from the previous year's shriveled vines.

She nodded thoughtfully, concentrating on one of her intricate mandalas. "Have you read the Hindus?" she asked. "The *Rig-Veda,* the *Upanishads?*"

"Only the *Bhagavad-Gita.* A long, long time ago."

" 'You and I, Arujna,' " she quoted easily, " 'have lived many lives. I remember them all: You do not remember.' " Her eyes lit with intensity. "Sometimes I think *our* experience is what they were really talking about: not reincarnation over a linear time scale, but little chunks of the entire world's history occasionally repeated over and over again . . . until we realize what's happening and are able to restore the normal flow."

"But we have been aware of it, and it keeps on happening."

"Maybe it continues until everyone has the knowledge," she said quietly.

"I don't think so; we both knew immediately, and it

seems you either recognize it or you don't. Everybody else just keeps going through the same patterns."

"Except the people whose lives we touch. We can introduce change."

Jeff smiled cynically. "So you and I are the prophets, the saviors?"

She looked out at the ocean. "Perhaps we are."

He sat upright, stared at her. "Wait a minute; that's not what this movie of yours is all about, is it, setting people up for . . . ? You're not planning to—"

"I'm not sure what I'm planning, not yet. Everything's changed, now that you've shown up. I wasn't expecting that."

"What do you want to do, start some kind of damned cult? Don't you know what a disaster—"

"I don't know anything!" she snapped. "I'm as confused as you are, and I just want to make some sense of my life. Do you want to just give up, not even try to figure out what it means? Well, go ahead! Go back to your goddamned farm and vegetate, but don't tell me how I'm supposed to deal with all this, O.K.?"

"I was only offering my advice. Can you think of anybody else qualified to do that, given the circumstances?"

She scowled at him, her anger not yet cooled. "We can talk about it later. Now, do you want to hear my story or not?"

Jeff sank back into the soft cushions, eyed her warily. "Of course I do," he said in a level tone. There was no telling what might set her off. Well, he could understand what she must have been through; he could make allowances.

She nodded once, brusquely. "I'll get us another beer."

Pamela Phillips, Jeff learned, had been born in Westport, Connecticut in 1949, daughter of a successful real-estate broker. She'd had a normal childhood, the usual illnesses, the ordinary joys and traumas of adolescence. She'd studied art at Bard College in the late sixties, smoked a lot of dope, marched on Washington, slept around as much as the other young women of her generation. True to form, she'd "gone straight" not long after Nixon resigned; she'd married a lawyer, moved to New Rochelle. Had two children, a boy and a girl. Her reading habits veered toward romance novels, she painted as a hobby when she got the chance, did some charity work now and then. She'd fretted about not having a career, sneaked an occasional joint when the kids were in bed, did aerobics to keep her figure in shape.

She'd died of a heart attack when she was thirty-nine. In October 1988.

"What day?" Jeff asked.

"The eighteenth. Same day it happened to you, but at 1:15."

"Nine minutes later." He grinned. "You've seen the future. More of it than I have."

That almost brought a smile to her lips. "It was a dull nine minutes," she said. "Except for dying."

"Where were you when you woke up?"

"In the rec room of my parents' house. The television was on, a rerun of 'My Little Margie.' I was fourteen."

"Jesus, what did you—Were they home?"

"My mother was out shopping. My father was still at work. I spent an hour walking around the house in a daze, looking at the clothes in my closet, flipping through the diary that I'd lost when I went to college . . . looking at myself in the mirror. I couldn't stop crying. I still thought I was dead, and this was some bizarre way God had of giving me one last glimpse of my time on earth. I was terrified of the front door; I really believed that if I walked through it I'd be in Heaven, or Hell, or Limbo, or whatever."

"You were Catholic?"

"No, my mind was just swirling with all these vague images and fears. Oblivion, that's a better word; that was what I really expected to find when I went outside. Mist, nothingness . . . just death. Then my mother came home, walked in through that door I was so frightened of. I thought she was some kind of disguised apparition come to drag me off to doom, and I started screaming.

"It took her a long time to quiet me down. She called the family doctor, he came over, gave me an injection—

Demerol, probably—and I passed out. When I woke up again my father was there, standing over the bed, looking very worried, and I guess that was when I first began to realize I wasn't really dead. He didn't want me to get up, but I went running downstairs and opened the front door, walked out in the yard in my nightgown . . . and of course everything was perfectly normal. The neighborhood was just the way I'd remembered it. The dog from next door came bounding over and started licking my hand, and for some reason that set me off crying again.

"I stayed home from school for the next week, lay around my room pretending to be sick, and just thought. . . . Tried at first to figure out what had happened, but it didn't take me long to decide that was a hopeless task. Then, as the days went on and nothing changed, I started trying to figure out what I was going to do.

"Remember, I didn't have the options you did; I was only fourteen, still living at home, still in junior high school. I couldn't bet on any horse races or move to Paris. I was stuck."

"That must have been horrible," Jeff said sympathetically.

"It was, but somehow I managed. I had no choice. I became . . . I forced myself to become a young girl again, tried to forget everything I'd been through in my first life: college, marriage . . . children."

She paused, looked down at the floor. Jeff thought of Gretchen, and reached out to put his hand on Pamela's shoulder. She shrank from his touch, and he withdrew the gesture.

"Anyway," she went on, "after a few weeks—a couple of months—that first existence seemed to recede in my mind, as if it had been a long dream. I went back to school, started learning everything all over again, as if I'd never studied any of it before. I became very shy, bookish; totally unlike the way I'd been the first time. Never went out on dates, stopped hanging around with the crowd of kids I'd known. I couldn't stand having these memories, or visions, of the adults my friends would become in the years ahead. I wanted to blank all that out, pretend to myself that I didn't have that kind of awareness.''

"Did you ever . . . tell anyone?''

She took a sip of beer, nodded. "Right after the screaming episode when I first came back, my parents sent me to a psychiatrist. After a few sessions I thought I could trust her, so I started trying to explain what I'd been through. She'd smile and make little encouraging sounds and act very understanding, but I knew she thought it was all a fantasy. Of course that's what I wanted to believe, too . . . so that's what it became. Until I told her about the Kennedy thing a week before it happened.

"That unnerved her completely. She got very angry and refused to see me any more. She couldn't deal with the fact that I'd described the assassination in such detail, that this 'fantasy' of mine had suddenly become a reality in the most awful, devastating way imaginable.''

Pamela looked at Jeff for a moment, silent. "It scared me, too,'' she went on. "Not just that I'd known he was going to be shot, but because I was so sure that Lee Harvey Oswald was the one who'd done it. I'd never heard of this Nelson Bennett person—of course, I had no idea you'd gone to Dallas and interfered the way you did—and after that my whole sense of reality changed. It was as if one minute I seemed to know everything about the future, and then all of a sudden I knew absolutely nothing. I was in a different world, with different rules. *Anything* might happen—my parents might die, there could be a nuclear war . . . or, at the simplest level, I could become an entirely different person than the one I'd been, or maybe imagined myself to have been.

"I went to Columbia instead of Bard, majored in biology, then went on to med school. It was tough going. I'd never cared much for science before; my whole training had been in art the first time around. But, by the same token, that made it far more interesting, because I wasn't just repeating something I'd studied before. I was learning an entire new field, a new world, to go with my new existence.

"I didn't have much time for socializing, but during my

residency at Columbia Presbyterian I met a young orthopedist who . . . well, he didn't really remind me of my first
husband, but he had a similar intensity, the same sort of
drive. Only this time it was something we had in common,
a shared devotion to medicine. Before, I'd hardly even
known what my husband did every day, and he'd just
assumed I wouldn't care about it, so he never discussed his
legal work with me. But with David—that was the
orthopedist—it was just the opposite. We could talk about
everything.''

Jeff gave her an inquisitive look. ''You don't mean—''

''No, no; I never told him what had happened to me. He
would've thought I was insane. I was still trying to put it
out of my own mind. I wanted to bury all those memories
and pretend they'd never happened.

''David and I got married as soon as I'd finished my
residency. He was from Chicago, and we moved back
there; he went into private practice, and I worked in the
intensive care unit at Children's Memorial Hospital. After
having lost my own children irretrievably—well, you know
what that's like—I kept putting off having another, but in
the meantime I had a whole hospital full of surrogate sons
and daughters, and they needed me so desperately, they
. . . Anyway, it was an extremely rewarding career. I was
doing exactly the sort of thing I'd dreamed of when I was
a frustrated housewife in New Rochelle: using my mind,
making a positive difference in the world, saving lives.
. . .'' Her voice trailed off. She cleared her throat and
closed her eyes.

''And then you died,'' Jeff said gently.

''Yes. I died, again. And was fourteen years old again,
and totally helpless to change a goddamned thing.''

He wanted to tell her how thoroughly he understood,
that he knew the deepest hurt had been her knowledge that
the sick and dying children she had tended were then
destined to go through their suffering once more, her
efforts to help them having been obliterated; but no words
were needed. The pain was all there on her face, and he
was the only person on earth who could comprehend the
depth of her loss.

"Why don't we take a break," Jeff suggested, "get a bite to eat someplace? You can tell me the rest of your story after dinner."

"All right," she said, grateful for the interruption. "I can fix us something here."

"You don't have to do that. Let's just go to one of those little seafood places we passed down on the Pacific Coast Highway."

"I don't mind cooking, really—"

Jeff shook his head. "I insist. Dinner's on me."

"Well . . . I'll have to change again."

"Jeans are fine. Just put on a pair of shoes, if you feel like going formal."

For the first time since he'd met her, Pamela smiled.

They ate at a secluded table on an outside deck, overlooking the surf. When they'd finished and were sipping coffee with Grand Marnier, the moon rose above the Pacific. Its reflection in the tall glass windows at the back of the restaurant seemed to meld the white orb with the blackness of the ocean.

"Look," Jeff said, indicating the illusion. "It's just like—"

"—the poster for *Starsea*. I know. Where do you think I got the idea for the artwork?"

"Great minds." Jeff smiled, raising his liqueur glass in a toast. Pamela hesitated, then lifted her own glass, clinked it briefly against his.

"Did you really like the movie?" she asked. "Or was that just a ploy to find out who I was?"

"You don't need to ask that question," he said sincerely. "You know how good the film is. I was as moved by it as anyone, though I'm sure no one else was so shocked to see it appear."

"Now you know how I felt that first time, when somebody I'd never heard of killed President Kennedy. What do you think that meant? Why did the assassination still happen, after what you did to prevent it?"

Jeff shrugged. "Two possibilities. One, maybe there really was a massive conspiracy to murder Kennedy, and

Oswald was a minor, expendable figure. Whoever planned it had Bennett waiting in the wings in case something went wrong, and probably more backups besides. Everything was thoroughly arranged in advance, right down to having Jack Ruby kill whoever took the fall. Eliminating Oswald from the picture was no more than a trivial inconvenience for the people who were behind it all. Kennedy would have died no matter what I did, because they were just too strongly organized for anyone or anything to stop them, whoever they were.

"That's one possibility. The other is less specific, but it has much deeper implications for you and me, and it's the one I tend to believe."

"And that is?"

"That it's impossible for us to use our foreknowledge to effect *any* major change in history. There are limits to what we can do; I don't know what those limits are, or how they're imposed, but I think they're there."

"But you created an international conglomerate. You owned major companies that had never before been linked. . . ."

"None of that really affected the overall course of things," Jeff said. "The companies existed as they always had, turning out the same products, employing the same people. All I did was rechannel the flow of profits a bit, in my direction. The changes in my own life were extreme, but in the larger scheme of things, what I did was insignificant. Outside the financial community, most people—you included—didn't even know I existed."

Pamela twisted her napkin pensively. "What about *Starsea,* though? Half the population of the planet knows about that. I've introduced a new concept, a new way for humanity to view itself in relation to the universe."

"Arthur Knight in *Variety,* right?"

She blushed, raised her hand to hide it.

"I looked up all the reviews before I came to see you. It's a wonderful movie, I grant you that, but it's still essentially a piece of entertainment, nothing more."

Her eyes flashed moonlight back at him, beams of anger and hurt pride. "It could be much more. It could be the beginning of—'' She stopped, composed herself. ''Never mind. I don't share your pessimism about our capabilities; let's leave it at that. Now, do you want to hear about my second . . . 'replay'—that's what you call the cycles, isn't it?''

''That's how I've come to think of them. It's as good a name as any other. Do you feel like continuing?''

''You've told me your experiences. I might as well bring you up to date on mine.''

''And then?''

''I don't know,'' she said. ''We seem to have very different attitudes about this.''

''But there's no one else we can discuss it with, is there?''

''Just let me finish what I was telling you, all right?'' She'd shredded the paper napkin into strips, which she now crumpled and piled into the ashtray.

''Go ahead,'' Jeff told her. ''Want another drink? Or another napkin?''

She looked at him sharply, searching for sarcasm in his face. She found none, nodded once. Jeff made a circular motion with his hand in the air, signaling the waitress for another round of Grand Marnier.

''The second time I died,'' Pamela began, ''I was more infuriated than anything else. As soon as I came to, in my parents' house, fourteen years old again, I knew exactly *what* was happening, if not why. And I just wanted to smash something. I wanted to scream with rage, not fear. The way you said you felt on your third . . . replay. It all seemed such a waste: medical school, the hospital, all the children I had treated . . . pointless, all of it.

''I became extremely rebellious, vicious, even, with my family. I'd spent more years as an adult than my mother and father put together, had been married twice, had a career as a physician. And here I was legally a child, with no rights or options whatsoever. I stole some money from my parents, ran away from home. But it was dreadful— nobody would rent me an apartment, I couldn't get a job . . . There's nothing a girl that age can do on her own, other than go on the streets, and I wasn't about to put myself through *that* kind of hell. So I crawled back to Westport, devastated, incredibly alone. Went back to school, despising every moment of it, flunking half my classes because I just couldn't stand to memorize the same damned algebra formulas for the third time.

"They sent me to the psychiatrist I'd seen before, the one who'd gotten so upset when I knew about the Kennedy assassination. This time I didn't tell her anything real about myself. I'd studied most of the standard texts on child development and psychology myself by then, so I just fed her the answers I knew would make me come across as a mildly screwed-up adolescent 'going through a phase,' well within the normal range."

She paused while the waitress set down their drinks, waited until the girl was well away from the table before she resumed her narrative.

"To keep at least some of my sanity intact, I went back to my first love, painting. My parents bought me whatever materials I asked for, and I asked for the works. But they were proud of my art; it was the one thing I was doing that they could recognize as constructive. Never mind that I was sneaking gin from their liquor cabinet, staying out half the night with guys in their twenties, and being put on academic probation every semester. They'd just about given up trying to control me. They could see there was something too strong and willful behind my misbehavior for them to cope with. But I had my talent; it was quite real, and I worked at it as hard as I had worked at being a doctor. They couldn't ignore that; no one could.

"I dropped out of high school when I was seventeen, and my parents found an art institute in Boston that was willing to take me on the basis of my portfolio, despite my terrible record in school. There I blossomed; I could finally start living as an adult again. I shared a loft with one of the older girls from the school, started dating my composition instructor, painted day and night. My work was full of bizarre, sometimes brutal images: maimed children falling down a black vortex, photorealistic close-ups of ants crawling out of surgical incisions . . . strong stuff, as unschoolgirlish as you could imagine. Nobody knew what to make of me.

"I had my first show in New York when I was twenty. That's where I met Dustin. He bought two of my canvases, and then, after the gallery closed, we went out for a drink. He told me he'd—"

"Dustin?" Jeff interrupted.

"Dustin Hoffman."

"The actor?"

"Yes. Anyway, he liked my paintings, and I'd always been impressed with his work—*Midnight Cowboy* had just come out that year, and I had to keep reminding myself not to say anything to him about *Kramer vs. Kramer* or *Tootsie*. We hit it off right away. We started seeing each other whenever he was in New York. We got married a year later."

Jeff couldn't hide his amused surprise. "You married Dustin Hoffman?"

"In one version of his life, yes," she said with a trace of annoyance. "He's a very nice man, very bright. Now, of course, he knows me only as a writer and producer; he has no idea we spent seven years together. I ran into him at a party just last month. It's strange, seeing such a complete lack of recognition in someone you've been that intimate with, shared that much time with.

"Anyway, it was a good marriage, by and large; we respected each other, supported our separate goals. . . . I continued to paint, had some modest success with it. My best-known work was a triptych called *Echoes of Selves Past and Future*. It was—"

"My God, yes! I saw that at the Whitney, on a trip to New York with my third wife, Judy! She liked it all right, but she couldn't understand why I was so thoroughly taken with it. Hell, I bought a print of it, had it framed over the desk in my den! *That's* where I'd heard your name before."

"Well, that was my last major work. Somehow I just . . . dried up after that, I don't know. There was so much I wanted to express, but I either didn't dare to or I couldn't capture it all on canvas any longer. I don't know whether my art failed me or the other way around, but I essentially stopped painting around 1975. That was the same year Dustin and I separated. No major blowup; it was just over, and we both knew it. Like my painting.

"I guess it had something to do with the fact that I was halfway through that replay, and knew that everything I was achieving would be wiped out again in a few years. So I just became a sort of butterfly, roaming around the world and hanging out with people like Roman Polanski and Lauren Hutton and Sam Shepard. With them, there was a sense of . . . transient community, a network of interesting friendships that never grew too close and could be stopped or started again at any time, depending on your mood and what country you were in at the time. It didn't really matter."

" 'Nothing matters,' " Jeff said. "I've felt that way myself, more than once."

"It's a depressing way to live," Pamela said. "You have an illusion of freedom and openness, but after a while everything just blurs together. People, cities, ideas, faces . . . they're all part of some shifting reality that never comes into any clear focus and never leads anywhere."

"I know what you mean," Jeff said, thinking of the years of random, transitory sex he and Sharla had gone through together. "It seems appropriate to our circumstances—but only in theory. The reality doesn't work out too well."

"No. Anyway, I drifted like that for several years, and when the time came I rented a quiet, isolated little house on Majorca. I was there alone for a month, just waiting to die. And I promised myself . . . I decided, during that month, that next time, *this* time, things would be different. That I had to make an impact on the world, change things."

Jeff looked at her skeptically. "You did that when you were a doctor. And when the next replay began, the children you had treated were doomed to go through their pain all over again. Nothing had changed."

She shook her head impatiently. "That's a false analogy. In the hospital, I was doing patchwork repairs on a few individuals. Purely physical work, and limited in scope. It was well intentioned, but meaningless.''

"And now you want to save the whole world's collective soul, is that it?"

"I want to awaken humanity to what's taking place. I want to teach them to be aware of these cycles, just as you and I are conscious of them. That's the only way we—any of us, all of us—can ever break out of the pattern, don't you see?"

"No." Jeff sighed. "I don't see. What makes you think people can be *taught* to carry over that awareness from one replay to the next? You and I have been through this thing three times now, and we've known from the beginning that it was happening to us. Nobody had to tell us."

"I believe we were meant to lead the others. At least I believe that about myself; I never expected you to show up. Can't you understand what an important task we've been entrusted with?"

"By whom, or what? God? This whole experience has made me agree even more with Camus: If there is a God, I despise him."

"Call it God, call it the Atman, call it whatever you like. You know the *Gita:*

> The recollected mind is awake
> In the knowledge of the Atman
> Which is dark night to the ignorant:
> The ignorant are awake in their sense-life
> Which they think is daylight:
> To the seer it is darkness.

"We can illuminate that darkness," she said with unexpected fervor. "We can—"

"Look, let's drop the spiritual stuff for a minute. Finish your story. What have you done during this replay? How did you manage to get that movie made?"

Pamela shrugged. "It wasn't difficult, not when I was putting up most of the money myself. I bided my time in school, making plans. Motion pictures were obviously the most effective way to communicate my ideas to a mass audience, and I was already familiar with the industry through Dustin and all the people I'd known the last time through. So when I was eighteen I started making some of the same investments you've talked about: IBM, the mutual funds, Polaroid . . . You know what the market was like in the sixties. It was hard to lose money even if you were buying blindly, and for someone with any knowledge of the future it was easy to parlay a few thousand dollars into several million in three or four years.

"I'm proud of the screenplay I did, but I'd had many, many years to think about it. After I'd written it and formed my production company, it was just a matter of hiring the right people. I knew who they all were and what their strengths would be. It all fell together exactly the way I'd planned it."

"And now—"

"Now it's time to move on to the next step. It's time to alter the consciousness of the world, and I can do it." She leaned forward, looked at him intently. "*We* can do it . . . if you'll join me."

≡12≡

"... APPARENT MURDER-SUICIDE. Initial reports indicate a scene of awesome mass carnage, bodies strewn everywhere about the settlement, the corpses of infants still in their dead mothers' arms. A few of the victims had been shot to death, but most seem to have taken their own lives, in a macabre ritual unlike any—"

Jeff reached for the frequency dial of the shortwave set, tuned it away from the BBC news broadcast until he found a jazz program.

The coffeepot began to burble. He poured himself a mug, added a dash of Myers's Rum for extra warmth. There'd been a fresh snowfall last night, six inches or more; one windblown drift already covered the lower half of the kitchen window. He really should shovel it away this afternoon, he thought. And it was time to get out to the storage shed, split another batch of cedar kindling, and haul some more white oak firewood up to the back porch. But he didn't feel like doing any of that, not right now, at least.

Maybe he was still vulnerable to the general malaise that always gripped the world the week of the Jonestown horror, despite his having heard the loathsome tale revealed

151

afresh three times before. Whatever it was, all he wanted
to do today was sit by the crackling wood stove and read.
He was halfway through the second volume of Hannah
Arendt's *The Life of the Mind,* and was planning to reread
A Distant Mirror: The Calamitous Fourteenth Century
next. Both had been published just this year, but he'd first
read the Tuchman book over twenty years ago, the summer he took Judy and the children across Soviet Asia on
the Trans-Siberian Express. Just looking at the cover of the
volume brought back memories of the vast steppes, the
infinity of silver birches outside Novosibirsk, and little
April's fascination with the ancient yellow samovar in the
corridor of their railway car. The conductress had kept the
samovar steaming with chunks of slow-burning peat, had
served up endless glasses of hot tea from it on the six-
thousand-mile journey from Moscow to Khabarovsk, north
of Manchuria. The metal holders for the glasses had been
engraved with images of cosmonauts and *Sputniks.* At the
end of the trip the conductress had given April a pair of
them to take home with her. Jeff remembered seeing his
adopted daughter curled up before the fireplace in the
house on West Paces Ferry Road in Atlanta, sipping a
glass of hot milk in one of those holders, just a week
before he'd died. . . .

He cleared his throat, blinked away the memories. Maybe
it would be best if he did do some chores today, kept
himself physically occupied instead of just sitting in the
cabin and thinking. There'd be enough of those kind of
days ahead, anyway, what with winter—

Jeff cocked his ear, thought he heard an engine. No,
couldn't be. Nobody'd be fool enough to head out this way
until spring, not unless Jeff had put out an emergency call
on the shortwave. But there it was again, by God, a whine
and a roar, louder, sounded as if it were headed right down
his road.

He pulled on a down parka and a wool cap, stepped
outside. Was there some trouble over at the Mazzinis'
place? Somebody sick or hurt, a fire, maybe?

A glimmer of recognition flashed in his mind as the
mud-spattered Land Rover made a hard left through his

open gate; then he saw the driver's straight blond hair, and he knew.

"'Morning," Pamela Phillips said, swinging a booted foot onto the running board of the rugged four-wheel-drive vehicle. "Hell of a driveway you've got."

"Don't usually get much traffic."

"I'm not surprised," she said, hopping down from the cab. "Looks like one poor guy's car hit a land mine back there, a long time ago."

"They tell me that was a man named Hector, George Hector. He had a portable still installed on that Model T during prohibition, kept moving it from place to place so he wouldn't get caught. It blew up one night."

"What about Hector? Did he blow up with it?"

"He wasn't hurt, apparently. Had to build another still, but he gave up on the portability idea. At least, that's what they say."

"So much for innovative thinking, hmm?" She took a deep breath of the clean, cold mountain air, let it out slowly, looking at him. "Well. How have you been?"

"Not too bad. Yourself?"

"Pretty busy since I saw you last. That was . . . Jesus, three and a half years ago." She rubbed her hands briskly together. "Hey, is there anyplace around here a lady could get warm?"

"Sorry; come on in, I've got some coffee. You took me by surprise, that's all."

She followed him into the cabin, pulled off her jacket, and took a chair by the stove as he poured the coffee. He held up the bottle of Myers's with a questioning look, and Pamela nodded. He splashed a dollop of the rich gold liquid into her mug, handed it to her. She sipped the mixture, mimed approval with her mouth and eyebrows.

"How'd you find me?" he asked, settling into the chair across from her.

"Well, you told me the place was near Redding; my lawyer spoke to your broker in San Francisco, and he was kind enough to narrow it down a little more. When I got up here I asked around in town; took awhile before I found anybody who was willing to give me directions, though."

"They have a deep respect for privacy around here."

"So I gathered."

"A lot of people don't like having somebody drive up on their land without warning. Especially if it's a stranger."

"I'm not a stranger to you."

"Damn near," Jeff said. "I thought that was pretty much how we left it in Los Angeles."

She sighed, absentmindedly stroked the sheepskin collar of the faded denim jacket that she'd folded across her lap. "As much as we had in common, we were coming from opposite directions. We got pretty pissed off at each other, there at the end."

"Yeah, you could put it that way. Or you could say you were just too damned obstinate to see past your own obsessions, to—"

"Hey!" she snapped, setting the coffee mug down sharply next to the shortwave radio. "Don't make this any harder for me than it is already, O.K.? I drove six hundred miles to see you. Now just hear me out."

"All right. Go ahead."

"Look, I know you're surprised to see me today. But try to imagine how surprised I was when *you* showed up. You'd seen *Starsea*. You'd had time to speculate about me, and had come to the obvious conclusions. You knew I was probably a replayer, too, but I had no idea there was anybody else like me out there. I thought I'd found the only possible explanation for what was happening to me—to the world. I believed I was doing the right thing."

"Well, I still don't know. Maybe I was, maybe I wasn't; it's a moot point now."

"Why?"

"Could I have another splash of rum in this? And maybe some more coffee?"

"Sure." He freshened both their mugs, sat back to listen.

"I'd already begun working on the screenplay for my next film when you came to L.A.; we had the shooting script ready by October.

"Naturally, budget wasn't a problem. I signed Peter Weir to direct; he hadn't made *The Last Wave* yet, so everybody thought I was crazy to use him." She smiled wryly, leaned forward with her long hands wrapped around the steaming mug. "The special-effects team I put together was interesting. First I hired John Whitney. By then he'd already done all the groundwork in computer-generated images, and a lot of his short films had focused on mandalas; I wanted that to be the central image in the film. I gave him free rein, set him up with one of the very first prototypes of the Cray supercomputer.

"Then I got hold of Douglas Trumbull, who'd done the special effects for *2001*. I nudged him in the direction of inventing Showscan a few years earlier than he would have. We shot the whole film in that process, even though—"

"Wait a minute," Jeff interrupted, "what's 'Showscan'?"

Pamela gave him a look of surprise, which contained a touch of wounded pride. "You haven't seen *Continuum?*"

He shrugged apologetically. "It never showed in Redding."

"No; in this area, it played only in San Francisco and Sacramento. We had to specially adapt all the theaters."

"Why?"

"The Showscan process produces incredibly realistic images on a movie screen, but to get that effect you need special projection equipment. You know the basic principle of how motion pictures work, right? Twenty-four frames, twenty-four still pictures a second . . . As one image begins to fade on the retina, the next appears, creating an impression of fluid, unbroken movement. Persistence of vision, it's called. Actually, there are forty-eight frames a second, because each of the images is repeated once, to help fool the eye. But of course it's not really the eye that's being tricked, it's the brain. Even though we think we're seeing uninterrupted motion on the screen, at some deeper, unconscious level we're aware of the stops and starts. That's one of the reasons video tape has a sharper, 'realer' look than film; it's recorded at thirty frames per second, so there are fewer gaps.

"Well, Showscan takes that process a step further. It's shot at a full sixty frames a second, with no redundant frames. Trumbull used EEGs to monitor the brain waves of people watching film shot and projected at various rates, and that's where the responses peaked. It appears that the visual cortex is programmed to perceive reality at that particular speed, in sixty bursts of visual input each second. So Showscan is like a direct conduit to the brain. It's not 3-D; the effect is more subtle than that. The images seem to strike deep chords of recognition; they somehow resonate with authenticity.

"So, anyway, we shot the whole movie in Showscan, including all the computer-generated mandalas and Mandelbrot sets and other effects that the Whitneys and their team came up with. We filmed most of it at Pinewood Studios in London. The actors were all talented unknowns, mainly from the Royal Academy of Dramatic Art. I didn't want any star's ego or presence to overshadow the theme of the film, its . . . message."

She finished her coffee, stared at the bottom of the heavy brown mug. "*Continuum* opened on June eleventh, worldwide. And it was a total failure."

Jeff frowned. "How do you mean that?"

"Just the way I said it. The movie flopped. It did good business for about a month, and then fell off to nothing. The critics hated it. So did the audiences. Word of mouth was even worse than the reviews, and they were bad enough. 'Leftover sixties mysticism' pretty much summed up the general reaction. 'Muddled,' 'incoherent,' and 'pretentious' were thrown in there a lot, too. The only reason most people went to see it at all was for the novelty value of the Showscan process and for the computer graphics. Those went over well, but they were just about the only things anybody liked about the film."

There was a long, awkward silence. "I'm sorry," Jeff said finally.

Pamela laughed bitterly. "Funny, isn't it? You refused to have anything more to do with me because you were concerned about the potentially dangerous impact this film might have, the global changes it might set in motion . . . and the world ended up ignoring it, treating it like a stale joke."

"What went wrong?" he asked with gentleness.

"Part of it was the timing: the 'Me Generation,' discos, cocaine, all that. Nobody wanted any more lectures about the oneness of the universe and the eternal chain of being. They'd had enough of that in the sixties; now all they wanted to do was party. But it was mainly my fault. The critics were right. It was a bad movie. It was too abstract, too esoteric; there was no plot, there were no real characters, no one for an audience to identify with. It was purely a philosophical exercise, a self-indulgent 'message picture,' with no meat to it. People stayed away in droves, and I can't blame them."

"You're being kind of hard on yourself, aren't you?"

She turned her empty mug around in her hands, kept her eyes down. "Just facing facts. It was a painful lesson to learn, but I've grown to accept it. Both of us have had to accept a lot. Had to lose a lot."

"I know how much it meant to you, how much you believed in what you were doing. I respect that, even if I disagreed with your methods."

She looked at him, her green eyes softer than he'd ever seen them. "Thank you. That means a lot to me."

Jeff stood up, took his parka from the hook by the door. "Get your coat on," he told her. "I want to show you something."

They stood in fresh snow at the top of the hill where he'd been clearing out the irrigation system the week before he first saw *Starsea*. The Pit River was clogged with ice now, not salmon, and the trees on Buck Mountain were heavy with their burden of white. In the distance, the majestic conic symmetry of Mount Shasta rose up to meet the clear November sky.

"I used to dream about that mountain," Jeff told her. "Dream it had something of great import to tell me, an explanation for all I'd been through."

"It looks . . . unreal," she murmured. "Sacred, even. I can understand a vision like that coming to dominate your dreams."

"The Indians around here did consider it holy. Not just

because it's a volcano; some of the other Cascade peaks have been more active, made more of an immediate impact on the environment. But none of them ever had the same allure Shasta did.''

"And still does," Pamela whispered, staring at the silent mountain. "There's a . . . power there. I can feel it."

Jeff nodded, his eyes fixed, like hers, on the far-off stately slopes. "There's a cult—white, not Indian—that still worships the mountain. They think it has something to do with Jesus, with resurrection. Others believe there are aliens, or some ancient offshoot race of humans, living in the magma tunnels beneath it. Strange, crazy stuff; Mount Shasta seems to inspire that kind of thinking, somehow."

The wind gusted colder, and Pamela shivered. Reflexively, Jeff put his arm around her shoulders, drew her to his warmth.

"At one time or another," he said, "I've imagined just about every possible explanation, no matter how bizarre, for what's been happening to me—to us. Time warps, black holes, God gone berserk . . . I mentioned the people who think Mount Shasta is populated by aliens; well, I once had myself convinced this was all some sort of experiment being conducted by an extraterrestrial race. The same idea must have occurred to you once or twice; I could see elements of it in *Starsea*. And maybe that's the truth—maybe we're the sentient rats who have to find our way out of this maze. Or maybe there's a nuclear holocaust at the end of 1988, and the collective psychic will of all the men and women who have ever lived has chosen this way to keep it from spelling an absolute end to humanity. I don't know.

"And that's the point: I *can't* know, and I've finally grown to accept my inability to understand it, or to change it."

"That doesn't mean you can't keep wondering," she said, her face close to his.

"Of course not, and I do. I wonder about it constantly. But I'm no longer consumed by that quest for answers, haven't been for a long time. Our dilemma, extraordinary though it is, is essentially no different than that faced by everyone who's ever walked this earth: We're here, and we don't know why. We can philosophize all we want, pursue the key to that secret along a thousand different paths, and we'll never be any closer to unlocking it.

"We've been granted an incomparable gift, Pamela; a gift of life, of awareness and potential greater than anyone has ever known before. Why can't we just accept it for what it is?"

"Someone—Plato, I think—once said, 'The unexamined life is not worth living.' "

"True. But a life too closely scrutinized will lead to madness, if not suicide."

She looked down at their footprints in the otherwise-pristine snow. "Or simply failure," she said quietly.

"You haven't failed. You made an attempt to draw the world together, and in the process you've created magnificent works of art. The effort, the creation—those acts stand on their own."

"Until I die again, perhaps. Until the next replay. Then it all vanishes."

Jeff shook his head, his arm tightly around her shoulders. "Only the products of your work will disappear. The struggle, the devotion you put into your endeavors . . . That's where the value truly lies, and will remain: within you."

Her eyes filled with tears. "So much loss, though, so much pain; the children . . ."

"All life includes loss. It's taken me many, many years to learn to deal with that, and I don't expect I'll ever be fully resigned to it. But that doesn't mean we have to turn away from the world, or stop striving for the best that we can do and be. We owe that much to ourselves, at least, and we deserve whatever measure of good may come of it."

He kissed her tear-streaked cheeks, then kissed her lightly on the lips. To the west, a pair of hawks circled slowly in the sky above Devil's Canyon.

"Have you ever been soaring?" Jeff asked.

"You mean in a sailplane, a glider? No. No, I never have."

He put both arms around her waist, hugged her close. "We will," he whispered into the softness of her tawny hair. "We'll soar together."

Past Revelstoke, the train sped alongside great, somber glaciers as it began its climb into the Rockies. Thick forests of red cedar and hemlock covered the surrounding hillsides, and around one bend a field of heather trapped between two glaciers suddenly came into view. The pink and purple flowers rippled, shimmered in the soft spring breeze, their ephemeral beauty a quiet rebuke to the impassive walls of ice enclosing them.

There was a certain erotic quality about the flowers, Jeff thought: Their fragile, wind-blown caress against the unyielding glacier, their vibrant color so like a woman's lips, or . . .

He smiled at Pamela in the seat beside him, rested his hand on her bare knee and let his fingers slide beneath the hem of her skirt. Her cheeks flushed as he tenderly stroked her inner thigh; she glanced around the dome car to see if anyone was looking at them, but the eyes of the other passengers remained fixed on the passing spectacle outside the train.

Jeff's hand moved higher, touched moist silk. Pamela let out a tiny groan as he gently pressed her cleft, and she arched back against the leather seat. He slowly pulled his hand away, letting the tips of his fingers trail lightly down her leg.

"Want to take a walk?" he asked, and she nodded. He took her hand, led her out of the observation car and toward the rear of the train. Between the club car and the diner they paused, maintaining a precarious balance together as they stood and kissed on the swaying metal platform. The wind whipping through the open window was at least fifteen degrees cooler than when they'd left Vancouver that morning, and Pamela shivered in his arms.

Their sleeping car was empty; everyone else, it seemed, had left to seek the panoramic vistas of the dome car or the diner. Once inside their double roommette, Jeff lowered one of the foldaway beds and Pamela reached to draw the windowshade closed. He stopped her, pulled her to him.

"Let's let the scenery inspire us," he said.

She resisted, teasing. "If we leave it open, we'll be part of the scenery ourselves."

"Nobody to watch us except a few birds and deer. I want to see you in the sunlight."

Pamela stepped back from him. Framed against the changing backdrop of snow-fed rivers and sheer glacial cliffs, she undid her blouse, slipped it off her arms. She plucked at the belt of her skirt, and the garment fell softly to the floor.

"Why aren't you looking at the scenery?" she asked with a smile.

"I am."

She slid off the rest, stood nude before the rugged wilderness rushing past outside. Jeff's eager gaze swept her body as he undressed, and then he moved to her, was joined with her, was pressing her urgently into the soft chair beside the open window as the afternoon sun flickered across their faces and the rumbling wheels on the tracks below rocked them with a steady rhythm.

The train took four days and nights to reach Montreal, and a week later they rode it back west again.

"What about the Middle Ages?" Pamela asked. "Imagine what that would have been like, the dreadful sameness of it, over and over."

"The Middle Ages weren't quite as totally dreary as most people assume. I still think a major war, and the years leading up to it, would have been far worse; picture always coming back to Germany in 1939."

"At least you could have left, gone to the U.S. and known you'd be safe."

"Not if you were Jewish. What if you were already in Auschwitz, say?"

It was their favorite topic this month: what the experience of replaying would have been like for someone in another historical period, how best to have dealt with a vastly different set of repeated world events and circumstances than those they knew so well.

Once the floodgates of conversation had been opened between them, it seemed there was no end of things to talk about: speculations, plans, memories . . . They had gone back over their own varied lives in detail, expanding on the brief personal histories they'd recounted to each other during that first wary meeting in Los Angeles in 1974. Jeff had told her all about the empty madness of his time with Sharla, the healing grace of his years alone in Montgomery Creek. She, in turn, had imparted a vivid sense of the dedication she had given to her medical career, her frustration at knowing she could never again put all that training to full use, and the subsequent creative exhilaration of making *Starsea*.

A tall, bearded young black man roller-skated past them, deftly weaving his way along the crowded East Fifty-ninth Street sidewalk toward the entrance to Central Park. Giorgio Moroder's pulsating arrangement of Blondie's "Call Me" blared from the big Panasonic radio he balanced on his shoulder, drowning out Pamela's reply to Jeff's hypothetical question about reliving the hell of Auschwitz.

They'd been in New York for six weeks, after more than a year of alternating their time between Jeff's cabin in northern California and Pamela's place in Topanga Canyon. Now that they were together, the isolation of the two retreats suited them even more. There was so much to catch up on, so many intensely private thoughts and emotions to be shared. But they hadn't withdrawn from the world, not totally. Jeff had begun dabbling in venture capital, backing small companies and products that apparently had been unable to obtain adequate funding in previous replays and whose success or failure he had no way of projecting. One desk-top toy, a Lucite cube with small magnets performing a slow-motion ballet in a suspension of clear viscous fluid, had already caught on in a big way, had been the Christmas 1979 version of the Pet Rock. He hadn't been as lucky, so far, with a holographic video system that had been proposed by two cinematographer friends of Pamela's. There were continual technical problems with the camera, and maybe the idea had always failed for those reasons. It didn't matter, though; the uncertainty of these schemes, their very unpredictability, was precisely what appealed to him.

For her part, Pamela had launched herself back into moviemaking with a new sense of fun and freedom. No longer bound by her self-imposed mission to elevate humanity to new levels of consciousness and being, she had written a lightly poignant romantic comedy about mismatched, mistimed love affairs. A young unknown, Darryl Hannah, had been cast as the female lead, and Pamela had insisted on granting directorial responsibilities to a TV comic actor, Rob Reiner. As always, her associates were aghast at her selection of such untested talent, but as producer and sole financer of the project, she retained final say in those matters. She and Jeff had come to New York so that she could oversee preproduction and location scouting for the new film. Shooting would begin in a few days, the second week of June.

They turned right and walked north on Fifth Avenue, resuming their discussion of historical fantasies.

"Think what Da Vinci might have achieved if he'd had our opportunity," Pamela said musingly. "The statues, the paintings he might have done in different lives."

"Assume he did; maybe the world continued on a different time line for each of his existences, and has for each of ours. In one version of twentieth-century reality he might have been remembered more for his inventions than for his art, if he'd had the time to rework and refine them. In another he might have retreated into his thoughts and left absolutely nothing of note behind. In the same way, there may be one future that will remember you for *Starsea*, and another in which Future, Inc. has continued as a major corporate presence."

" '*Has* continued'?" She frowned. "Don't you mean 'will continue'?"

"No," Jeff said. "If the flow of time is continuous—uninterrupted as far as the rest of the world is concerned, ignoring this loop you and I keep experiencing, and branching out from each version of the loop into new lines of reality depending on the changes we put into motion each time around—then history should have progressed twenty-five years for each replay we've been through.''

She pursed her lips, thinking for a moment. ''If that's true, though, the individual time lines would be staggered. Each branch would have continued on its path from 1988, when we died, but the preceding one would be twenty-five years ahead of it.''

''That's right. So in the world of our most recent replay, the one in which you married Dustin Hoffman and I was living in Atlanta, it's been only seventeen years since we died. The year is 2005; most of the people we knew would still be alive.

''But starting from our first replay, the life in which you were a doctor in Chicago and I built my conglomerate, forty-two years have passed. It would be the year 2029; my daughter Gretchen would be over fifty, probably with grown children of her own.''

Jeff grew silent, sobered by the thought of his only true child still alive, yet objectively a decade older than he himself had ever been.

Pamela finished the projection for him. ''And on the time line of our original lives, sixty-seven years would have gone by. The world we grew up in would be into the second half of the twenty-first century. My own children . . . they'd be in their seventies. My God.''

Their game of speculation had turned more serious, more troubling than either of them had expected it to. Absorbed in their separate quiet reflections, they almost didn't notice the smartly dressed blond woman in her late thirties and the teenaged boy who stood with her outside the Sherry-Netherland Hotel, waiting as the doorman hailed a taxi.

The woman crinkled her eyes with mild curiosity as Jeff and Pamela walked past. Something about the expression suddenly registered in his busy mind.

''Judy?'' he said tentatively, stopping beneath the hotel's awning.

The woman stepped back a pace. ''I'm afraid I don't

recall—no, wait," she said, "you were at Emory, weren't you? Emory University, in Atlanta?"

"Yes," Jeff said softly, "I was. We were there together."

"You know, I thought you looked familiar just now. I could have sworn . . ." She blushed, just the way she always had. Perhaps she'd suddenly remembered a night in the backseat of the old Chevy, or on a bench outside Harris Hall before curfew; but Jeff could see she was having trouble coming up with his name, and he spoke quickly to spare her the embarrassment.

"I'm Jeff Winston," he said. "We used to go to the movies now and then, or out for a beer at Moe's and Joe's."

"Well, of course, Jeff, I remember you. How have you been?"

"Fine. Just fine. Pamela, this is . . . someone I used to know in college. Judy Gordon. Judy, my friend Pamela Phillips."

Judy's eyes widened, and for a moment she almost looked eighteen again. "The movie director?"

"Producer," Pamela said, smiling pleasantly. She knew exactly who Judy was and how much this woman had meant to Jeff, in another replay.

"My goodness, isn't that something? Sean, how about that?" Judy asked the gangly young boy who stood beside her. "This is an old schoolmate of mine, Jeff Winston, and his friend here is Pamela Phillips, the movie producer. This is my son, Sean."

"I'm so pleased to meet you, Miss Phillips," the boy said with unexpected enthusiasm. "I just want to say . . . well, to tell you how much *Starsea* meant to me. That movie changed my life."

"You know, he's not joking." Judy beamed. "He was twelve years old when he first saw it, and he must have gone back to see it a dozen times. After that, all he could talk about was dolphins, and how to communicate with them. It wasn't just a passing interest, either. Sean's going to college in the fall, to the University of California at San Diego, and he's going to major in—You tell them, honey."

"Marine biology. With a double minor in linguistics

and computer science. I hope to work with Dr. Lilly someday, on interspecies communication. And if I ever do, I'll have you to thank for it, Miss Phillips. You don't know how much that means to me, but, well, maybe you do. I hope so.''

A tall man with graying temples came out of the hotel, followed by a bellman wheeling a cart of luggage. Judy introduced her husband to Jeff and Pamela, explained that the family was just ending a vacation in New York. Did Jeff or Pamela ever get down to Atlanta? If they did, be sure to stop by; the name was Christiansen now, here's the address and phone number. What was the new movie going to be called? They'd be sure to look for it and tell all their friends.

The cab pulled away, and Jeff and Pamela locked arms, held firmly to each other. They smiled as they walked on up Fifth Avenue to the Pierre, but in their eyes was a recognition of mutual sorrow, for all the worlds they once had known and now would know no more.

Jeff poured himself another glass of Montecillo, watched the lowering sun highlight the steep, rocky coastline to the west. Below the slope where the villa perched, and past another hill green with almond groves and olive trees, he could see the fishing boats returning to the red-roofed village of Puerto de Andraitx. A shift in the still-warm October breeze suddenly brought the scent of the Mediterranean through the open window, and it mingled with the robust aroma of simmering paella from the kitchen behind him.

"More wine?" he called.

Pamela leaned through the kitchen doorway, a large wooden spoon in one hand. She shook her head. "Cook stays sober," she said. "At least until dinner's on the table."

"Sure you don't want some help?"

"Mmm . . . you could slice some pimientos, if you want to. Everything else is just about ready."

Jeff ambled into the kitchen, began cutting the sweet red peppers into thin strips. Pamela dipped her spoon into the shallow iron pan, held out a taste of the paella for him to sample. He sipped the rich red broth, chewed a tender bite of *calamari*.

"Too much saffron in the rice?" she asked.

"Perfect as is."

She smiled with satisfaction, motioned for him to get the plates. He did, though it was difficult for them both to maneuver in the cramped kitchen. The little hillside house was a "villa" in rental agents' terms only; it was much smaller and plainer than the grandiose appellation implied. But then, Pamela had taken the temporary residence with one simple purpose in mind. Jeff tried to think about that as little as possible, but it was hard to ignore.

She saw the look in his eyes, touched her fingertips lightly to his cheek. "Come on," she said, "time to eat."

He held the plates as she ladled up the steaming paella, then topped the rich seafood stew with green peas and the pimiento strips he'd cut. They took their dinner back to the table by the window in the front room. Pamela lit candles and put on a Laurindo Almeida tape, "Concierto de Aranjuez," as Jeff poured them each a fresh glass of wine. They ate in silence, watching the lights come on in the fishing village far below.

When they were finished, Jeff cleared the dishes while Pamela set out a platter of *manchego* cheese with sliced melon. He picked halfheartedly at the dessert, sipped from a snifter of Soberano brandy, and tried again, unsuccessfully, to avoid thinking about why they were here on Majorca.

"I'll be leaving in the morning," he said at last. "No need to drive me; I can get a boat back to Palma, take a cab to the airport."

She reached across the table, took his hand. "You know I wish you would stay."

"I know. I just don't want to . . . put you through it."

Pamela squeezed his hand. "I could deal with it. I could be there for you, be with you . . . And yet, if it were going to be me first, I wouldn't want you to see it happen. So I understand how you feel. I respect that."

He cleared his throat, glanced around the earth-hued

room. In the dim glow of the candlelight, he couldn't help but reflect, it seemed exactly what it was: a place for dying. The very place where she *had* died, a quarter of a century ago, and would die again not two weeks hence, soon after his own heart had once more failed.

"Where will you go?" she asked softly.

"Montgomery Creek, I suppose. I think you have the right idea about choosing an isolated place to . . . let it happen. A special place."

She smiled, a warm, open smile of tenderness and recollected joy. "Remember that day I first showed up at your cabin? God, I was so scared."

"Scared?" Jeff said, smiling now himself. "Of what?"

"Of you, I guess. What you might say to me, how you'd react. You'd been so angry at me the last time I saw you, in Los Angeles; I thought you still might be."

He put both hands on hers. "It wasn't so much that I was angry at you; I was just concerned about the possible consequences of what you were doing."

"I know that now. But at the time . . . When you came into my office at Starsea, out of the blue, I didn't know how the hell to react. I don't think I even realized quite how lonely, how desperate, I'd become. I just assumed, by then, that I'd never meet anyone else like me, not even anyone who would believe what I'd been through, let alone someone who'd shared the experience. You'd withdrawn into the land, to your mountains and your crops . . . while I'd put up emotional barriers of a different sort: outward-focused ones, a very public form of solitude. Trying to save the world was my way of hiding from my own needs. That was a hard thing to admit—to you, or to myself."

"I'm glad you had that courage. It taught me I didn't have to hide from my own feelings or my fears."

Pamela looked long and deeply at him, tenderness in her eyes and on her face. "We've soared, all right, haven't we? We really have."

"Yes," he whispered, returning the gaze. "And we will again, soon. Hold on to that. Don't forget it."

*   *   *

Jeff stood at the stern of the boat, watching the village and the hills behind it recede into the distance. He watched until he could no longer discern the figure of Pamela on the wooden dock. Then he lifted his eyes to the red-and-white speck that was her little villa and watched until that, too, had blurred into invisibility.

The wind off the open sea stung his eyes, and he moved into the enclosed section of the passenger ferry, bought a beer, and took a seat alone, away from the scattering of off-season French and German tourists.

It wasn't really over, he forcibly reminded himself, just as he'd told Pamela to do. Only this replay, that was all that was ending; they'd be together again very soon, could make a fresh start of everything. But God, how he hated to leave behind this particular reality, this life in which he and she had come to know and love each other. They'd come so far, done so much; he was as proud of Pamela's achievements in film as if they'd been his own. How heartrending to think of entering a world where *Starsea,* and the enormously successful string of touching, all-too-human comedies and dramas she had made in the years since, never had existed and never would.

He clung tenaciously to the concept of time lines that they'd discussed in New York, years before. Somewhere, he was sure, there would be a branch of reality in which her artistic legacy lived on, would continue to move and enlighten audiences for generations to come. Perhaps Judy's son, Sean, really would find a way for the dual intelligent species of earth's oceans and its land masses to communicate with one another; if he did, that supreme gift of shared planetary wisdom would have sprung directly from Pamela's vision.

It was a hope worth harboring, a dream to cherish; but now they would have to concentrate on new hopes, new dreams, another life as yet unlived.

Jeff reached into his jacket pocket, took out the small, flat package she had handed him as he boarded the boat. He removed the tissue wrapping carefully, and his throat tightened with emotion when he saw what she had given him.

It was a painting, a precisely done miniature, of Mount Shasta as it appeared from the hill on his property; and in the serene sky above the mountain, two figures swooped and soared on brilliantly feathered wings: Jeff and Pamela, like mythological creatures come to life, in eternal exultant flight together toward a destiny never before encompassed in reality or myth.

He stared at the tiny work of art and love for several moments, then rewrapped it and put it back into his pocket. He closed his eyes, listened to the churning of the boat as it cut through the waves of the Bahia de Palma, and settled quietly into the first leg of his journey home to die.

≡13≡

A DULL GRAY early-morning light filtered through the louvered window and the blue-green drapes. As Jeff opened his eyes he saw a sleek, seal-point Siamese cat peacefully asleep at the foot of the king-sized bed. It raised its head as he stirred. The cat yawned once, then issued an annoyed and clearly interrogative "Rowwr?"

Jeff sat up, turned on the bedside lamp, and scanned the room: stereo console and TV against the far wall, flanked by shelves of model airplanes and rockets; bookcase on the right-hand wall; uncluttered dresser below the windows to his left. Everything neat, ordered, well-kept.

Oh, shit, he thought; he was in his boyhood room at his parents' house in Orlando. Something had gone wrong, dreadfully wrong. Why wasn't he in the dorm room at Emory? Good God, what if he had come back as a *child* this time? He threw back the covers, looked down at himself. No, he had pubic hair, even had a morning erection; he rubbed his chin, felt stubble. At least he wasn't prepubescent.

He leaped out of bed, hurried to the adjoining bathroom. The cat followed, hoping for an early breakfast as long as they were going to be getting up at this hour. Jeff flicked on the light, stared in the mirror: His appearance seemed to match the way he'd always looked at eighteen. Then what the hell was he doing at home?

He pulled on a pair of faded jeans and a T-shirt, slipped his sockless feet into some old sneakers. The clock by his bed put the time at almost a quarter to seven. Maybe his mother would be up; she always liked to have a quiet cup of coffee before starting her day.

He rubbed the cat's neck. Shah, of course, who'd gotten run over during Jeff's junior year; he'd have to tell the family to keep him inside. The regal animal strutted alongside him as Jeff walked down the hall, through the terazzo-floored Florida room, and into the kitchen. His mother was there, reading the *Orlando Sentinel* and sipping her coffee.

"Well, goodness gracious," she said, raising her eyebrows. "What's the night owl doing up with the robins?"

"I couldn't sleep, Mom. Got a lot to take care of today." He wanted to ask what day it was, what year it was, but didn't dare.

"What's so important that it rouses you at the crack of dawn? I've been trying to do that for years, and never succeeded. Must have to do with a girl, is that it?"

"Sort of. Could I have part of the paper, please? Maybe the front page, if you're done with it?"

"You can have the whole thing, honey. I'm about to start breakfast anyway. Want some French toast? Or eggs and sausages?"

He started to say, "Nothing," then realized how hungry he was. "Uh, eggs and sausages would be great, Mom. And maybe some grits?"

She gave him a mock-insulted frown. "Now, when have I ever made you breakfast without grits? They paste your ribs together, you know that."

Jeff grinned at his mother's old, breakfast-table joke, and she set to preparing the meal as he picked up the newspaper.

The main headline stories were about civil rights clashes in Savannah and a total eclipse of the sun in the northeastern U.S. It was mid-July 1963. Summer vacation; that was why he was here in Orlando. But Christ, it was three full months later than it should have been! Pamela must be frantic, wondering why he hadn't contacted her yet.

He ate his breakfast hurriedly, ignoring his mother's admonitions to slow down. Glancing at the kitchen clock, he saw it was just after seven; his father and sister would be getting up any minute. He didn't want to get embroiled in a family discussion of what he knew he had to do.

"Mom . . ."

"Mm-hmm?" she said distractedly, getting more eggs ready for the later risers.

"Listen, I'm gonna have to go out of town for a few days."

"What? Where to? Are you going down to Miami to see Martin?"

"No, I have to, uh, go up north a ways."

She eyed him suspiciously. "What does that mean, 'up north a ways'? Are you going back to Atlanta so early?"

"I have to go to Connecticut. But I don't want to talk about it to Dad, and I need some extra cash for the trip. I'll pay you back real soon."

"What in the world is in Connecticut? Or I should say, who in the world? Is it some girl from school?"

"Yes," he lied. "It's a girl from Emory; her family lives in Westport. They invited me up to stay for a week or so."

"Which girl is this? I don't remember your mentioning anybody from Connecticut. I thought you were still going out with that cute little girl from Tennessee, Judy."

"Not anymore," Jeff said. "We broke up right before finals."

His mother looked concerned. "You never told me; is that why you haven't been eating right since you've been home?"

"No, Mom, I'm fine. It's no big deal; we just broke up, that's all. Now I really like this girl in Westport, and I need to go see her. So can you help me out?"

"Won't she be back in school in September? Can't you wait till then to see her again?"

"I'd really like to see her now. And I've never been to New England. She said we might drive up to Boston. Her and her folks,'' he added quickly, remembering the mores of the time and his mother's own sense of propriety.

"Well, I don't know . . .''

"Please, Mom. It would mean a lot to me. This is really important.''

She shook her head in exasperation. "At your age, everything is important; everything has to happen right *now*. Your father was counting on that fishing trip next week. You know how much—''

"We'll go fishing when I get back. Look, I have to go up there one way or the other; I just wanted to let you know where I was going to be, and it would be a big help if you could lend me a little extra money. If you don't want to, then—''

"Well, you're old enough to be in college, so you're old enough to go wherever you please. I just worry about you, that's all. It's what mothers are for . . . besides lending money.'' She winked, and opened her purse.

Jeff threw some clothes in a suitcase, put the two hundred dollars his mother had given him into a pair of rolled-up socks. He was out of the house before his father or sister got up.

The old Chevy was parked in the curved driveway, behind his father's big Buick Electra and his mother's Pontiac. The car gave a familiar cough when Jeff started it up, then came rumbling to life.

He pulled out of the suburban development where his parents lived, skirted Little Lake Conway, and sat for a moment with the engine idling when he came to the intersection of Hoffner Road and Orange Avenue. Had the Beeline Expressway to the Cape been built yet? He couldn't remember. If it had, that'd be a straighter shot to I-95 north. There hadn't been anything in the paper about a launch this morning, so the traffic around Cocoa and Titusville shouldn't be too bad; but if the expressway hadn't been built yet, he'd find himself stuck for too long on a pitted old two-lane road. He decided to play it safe, go on into town, and take I-4 up to Daytona.

Jeff drove through the sleepy little city, still untouched

by the Disney boom to come and only just beginning to feel the spillover development of the NASA presence forty miles away. He picked up I-95 sooner than he'd expected, tuned the radio to WAPE in Jacksonville: "Little" Stevie Wonder doing "Fingertips, Part II," then Marvin Gaye belting out "Pride and Joy."

Three months. How the hell could he have lost three months this time? What did it mean? Well, there was no use worrying about it now; it was beyond his control. Pamela would be upset, with good reason, but at least he'd see her soon. Concentrate on that, he told himself as he sped north through the long stretches of pine woods and scrub brush.

He made Savannah by noon; there was a brief gap in the interstate there, slowing his progress, and the streets of the gracious old city were incongruously lined with scowling, helmeted police. Jeff made his way past the barricades cautiously, aware of the demonstrations and subsequent racist violence that had broken out here this week. It was sad to see that all begin yet again, but there was nothing he could do other than avoid the bloody confrontations.

He stopped for a quick sandwich a little after three, at a Howard Johnson's outside Florence, South Carolina. The flatlands of Florida and coastal Georgia were behind him now, and he drove through rural hill country, keeping the speedometer of the powerful old V-8 a notch above the posted 70 mile-per-hour speed limit.

It was dark when he drove past the turnoff to his boarding school in Virginia, where he'd made that unplanned pilgrimage so many years ago to see the little bridge that had become to him the very icon of loss and futility. He could see the lights of the Rendells' house from the highway; his pretty young former teacher and object of his onetime adulation would be preparing dinner for her husband, and for the child whose birth had sparked Jeff's adolescent jealous rage. Love your family well, he wished her silently as he sped past the peaceful home on its scenic ridge; there's enough pain in the world as it is.

He had a late meal of fried chicken and sweet potatoes at a truck stop north of Richmond, bought a thermos, and had the waitress fill it with black coffee. The Beltway took him around Washington, and he made it to Baltimore just after midnight. At Wilmington, Delaware, he switched from I-95 to the Jersey Turnpike, avoiding whatever predawn traffic there might be through Philadelphia and Trenton. As the night wore on he marveled again, as he always did at the beginning of each replay, at his own youthful stamina; in his thirties and forties, he'd have needed to break this drive up into at least two days, and even that pace would have been exhausting.

The George Washington Bridge was all but deserted at 4:00 A.M., and Jeff kept the radio jacked up to full volume as Cousin Brucie whooped and wailed along with the Essex on "Easier Said than Done." Driving through New Rochelle on the New England Thruway, images of a Pamela he had never known filled his mind: She had lived here in her first existence, raised a family . . . died here, assuming it was the end of her life, unaware that her many lives had just begun.

What had death been like for her this time, he wondered, there on Majorca? Calmer, he hoped, more accepting, as it had been for him at the cabin near Montgomery Creek, knowing that this time they'd have each other to come back to. But he didn't want to dwell on the thought of her agony, however short-lived. That part was over, for now, and they had a limitless future together to look forward to.

The first light of day was beginning to tinge the eastern sky as Jeff reached Westport. He located the address of Pamela's family in a phone book at a Shell station. It was much too early in the morning for him to show up at her house yet. He found a twenty-four-hour coffee shop, forced himself to go through the *New York Times* from front page to last, just to kill time. Things were still tense in Savannah, he read; Ralph Ginzburg was appealing his obscenity conviction for publishing *Eros* magazine, and controversy was growing over the Supreme Court's recent ruling against compulsory school prayer.

Jeff looked at his watch: 7:25. Would 8:00 A.M. be too

early? The family, ought to be up by then, maybe having breakfast. Should he interrupt them while they were eating? What difference did it make, he thought? Pamela would introduce him as a friend; and they'd invite him to join them. He dawdled nervously over his coffee until twenty to eight, then asked the coffee-shop cashier for directions to the address he'd written down.

The Phillipses' house was a two-story neo-colonial on a shaded, upper-middle-class street. Nothing to differentiate it from a thousand other homes in a thousand other towns across the country; only Jeff knew of the miraculous event that had taken place there.

He rang the doorbell, tucking his T-shirt into his jeans. It suddenly occurred to him that he should have changed; he should have at least found a rest room where he could shave—

"Yes?"

The woman bore a startling resemblance to Pamela; only the hairstyle was different, a moderate bouffant instead of the straight, Dutch-boy cut Jeff had grown so fond of. She was about the same age Pamela had been when he'd seen her last, and the impression was unsettling.

"Is, uh, Pamela Phillips home, ma'am?"

The woman frowned, pursing her lips slightly in the same expression of mild consternation Jeff had seen so frequently on Pamela's face. "She's not up yet. Are you a friend of hers from school?"

"Not exactly from school, but I do—"

"Who is it, Beth?" came a man's voice from inside the house. "Is it the man about the air conditioning?"

"No, dear, it's a friend of Pam's."

Jeff shifted his feet uneasily. "I'm sorry to disturb you this early in the morning, but it really is important that I speak to Pamela."

"I don't even know if she's awake yet."

"If I could just come inside and wait—I don't want to put you to any inconvenience, but . . ."

"Well . . . Why don't you come on in and have a seat, for a minute at least?" Jeff stepped into a small foyer, followed her into a comfortably furnished living room, where a man in a gray pinstriped suit stood before a mirror, adjusting his tie.

"If that fellow does show up this morning," the man was saying, "tell him the thermostat is—" He stopped as he caught sight of Jeff in the mirror. "You're a friend of Pam's?" he asked, turning to face Jeff.

"Yes, sir."

"Is she expecting you?"

"I . . . believe so."

"What do you mean, you 'believe so'? Isn't this a bit early to pop in on someone unannounced?"

"Now, David . . ." his wife cautioned.

"She is expecting me," Jeff said.

"Well, this is the first I've heard about it. Beth, did Pam say anything to you last night about someone coming over this morning?"

"Not that I recall, dear. But I'm sure—"

"What's your name, young man?"

"Jeff Winston, sir."

"I don't remember Pam's mentioning anyone by that name. Do you, Beth?"

"David, don't be so rude to the boy. Would you like some cinnamon toast, Jeff? I just made some, and a fresh pot of coffee, too."

"No, ma'am, thank you very much, but I've had breakfast."

"Where do you know our daughter from?" Pamela's father asked.

From Los Angeles, Jeff thought, giddy with lack of sleep and too many cups of coffee and a thousand miles of highway. I know her from Montgomery Creek, he wanted to say; from New York, and Majorca.

"I said, where did you meet Pam? You look a little old to be one of her classmates."

"We . . . met through a mutual friend. At the tennis club." That ought to sound plausible; she'd told him she'd played tennis since she was twelve.

"And who might that be? I think we know most of Pam's friends, and—"

"Daddy! Did I leave my Green Stamp book in your car?
It was almost full, and now I can't find—"

She stood at the top of the stairs, all gangly teenaged
arms and legs in a pair of white Bermuda shorts and a
yellow polo shirt, her fine blond hair pulled into two little
ponytails, one over each ear.

"Could you come down here, Pam?" her father said.
"There's someone here to see you."

Pamela walked slowly down the stairs, looking at Jeff.
He wanted to run to her, take her in his arms, and kiss
away all the torment that he knew she'd been through; but
there'd be time enough for that. He grinned, and she
smiled back at him.

"Do you know this young man, Pam?"

Her eyes were full of youth and promise as they met
Jeff's loving gaze.

"No," she said. "I don't think so."

"He says he met you at the tennis club."

She shook her head. "I think I'd remember if I had. Do
you know Dennis Whitmire?" she asked Jeff innocently.

"Majorca," Jeff said in a voice hoarse with strain.
"The painting, the mountain . . ."

"I'm sorry?"

"I think you'd better be on your way, whoever you
are," her father cut in.

"Pamela. Oh, Jesus, Pamela . . ."

The man took Jeff's arm firmly, ushered him toward the
door. "Look, fella," he said in a quiet but commanding
tone, "I don't know what your game is, but I don't want
to see you around here again. I don't want you bothering
my daughter, not here at the house, not at school, not at
the tennis club. Nowhere. Got that?"

"Sir, this has all been a misunderstanding, and I apologize for the trouble. But Pamela does know me; she—"

"Anyone who knows my daughter calls her 'Pam,' not
'Pamela.' And let me remind you that she is fourteen years
old, is that clear? Do you get my drift? Because I don't
want you claiming there's been any 'misunderstanding'
about the fact that you are harassing a minor."

"I don't want to bother anyone. I just—"

"Then get the hell out of my house before I call the police."

"Sir, Pamela will remember who I am soon. If I could just leave a number where she can get in touch with me—"

"You're not leaving anything except this house. Now."

"It's unfortunate we had to meet this way, Mr. Phillips. I'd really like us to be able to get along in the future, and I hope—"

Pamela's father shoved him roughly onto the outside steps, and the door slammed in his face. Jeff could hear raised voices through the window to the living room: Pamela crying in confusion, her mother pleading for calm, her father's strident tones alternately protective and accusatory.

Jeff walked back to his car, sat in the driver's seat, and rested his weary, jangled head on the steering wheel. After a while he started the engine, and headed south.

Dear Pamela,

I'm sorry if I confused you yesterday, or upset your parents. Someday soon, I hope you'll understand. When that time comes, you can contact me through my family in Orlando, Florida. Their number is 555-9561. They'll know where I can be reached.

Please don't lose this letter; hide it somewhere safe. You'll know when you need it.

With fondest regards,
Jeff Winston

July and August were a sinkhole of torpid inertia, the dank heat of Florida's "dog days," broken only by the violent thunderstorms that appeared almost every afternoon. Jeff went fishing with his father, taught his sister how to drive; but most of the time he spent in his room, watching reruns of "The Defenders" and "The Dick Van Dyke Show." Waiting for the telephone to ring.

His mother fretted over his inactivity, his sudden loss of

interest in friends and girls and midnight cruising at the local drive-ins. Jeff wanted to leave, to escape the oppressive parental concern and the stultifying boredom of Orlando, but there was no place he could go. The freedom of movement he'd grown so used to was severely limited by his lack of funds: The Derby and the Belmont had already been run, and he had no other immediate source of income.

Summer ended, with no word from Pamela. Jeff went back to Atlanta, ostensibly to begin his sophomore year at Emory. He registered for a full course load, just so he could be assigned space in one of the dormitories, but he never bothered to attend any of the classes. He ignored the threatening letters from the dean's office, bided his time until October.

Frank Maddock had graduated the previous June, and was now at Columbia, beginning law school without ever having met his erstwhile partner. Jeff found another rakish gambler in the senior class who was willing to place the World Series bet for him. Only for a flat fee, though; nobody wanted a percentage, no matter how generous, of such a patently foolish wager. Jeff bet a little under two thousand dollars, won a hundred and eighty-five thousand. At least he wouldn't have to worry about money again for a while.

He moved to Boston, took an apartment on Beacon Hill. History moved through its familiar paces: Diem was overthrown in Saigon; John Kennedy was murdered yet again. The Vatican Council de-Latinized the Catholic Mass, and the Beatles arrived to lighten the hearts of America.

Jeff called the Phillipses' house in March, the week Jack Ruby was convicted and sentenced to death for the killing of Lee Harvey Oswald; no one had ever heard of Nelson Bennett. Pamela's mother answered the phone.

"Hello, may I speak with . . . Pam, please?"

"May I tell her who's calling?"

"This is Alan Cochran, a friend of hers from school."

"Just a minute, let me see if she's busy."

Jeff nervously coiled and uncoiled the telephone cord as he waited for Pamela to come on the line. He'd dredged the false name out of his memory, as someone Pamela had once mentioned having dated in high school; but had she even met the boy at this point? He had no way of knowing.

"Alan? Hi, what's up?"

"Pam, please don't hang up; this isn't Alan, but I need to talk to you."

"Who is it, then?" There was more intrigue than annoyance in her kittenish voice.

"It's Jeff Winston. I came by your house one morning last summer, and—"

"Yeah, I remember. My dad said I'm not supposed to talk to you, ever."

"I can understand that he might feel that way. You don't have to tell him I called. I just . . . wondered if you'd started to remember anything yet."

"What do you mean? Like remember what?"

"Oh, maybe about Los Angeles."

"Yeah, sure."

"You do?"

"Sure, my folks and I went to Disneyland when I was twelve. How come I wouldn't remember that?"

"I was thinking more along the lines of something else. A movie, maybe, one called *Starsea?* Does that sound at all familiar?"

"I don't think I ever saw that one. Hey, you're pretty weird, you know that? How come you want to talk to me, anyway?"

"I just like you, Pamela. That's all. Do you mind if I call you that?"

"Everybody else calls me Pam. And besides, I shouldn't even be talking to you. I better hang up now."

"Pamela—"

"What?"

"Do you still have that letter I sent you?"

"I threw it away. If my dad had found it, he'd've had a fit."

"That's O.K. I'm not in Florida anymore; I'm living in Boston now. I know you don't want to write my number down, but I'm listed with information. If you ever feel like getting in touch with me—"

"What makes you think I'd want to do that? Boy, you really *are* weird."

"I guess so. Don't forget, though, you can call me any time, day or night."

"I'm gonna hang up now. I don't think you ought to call me anymore."

"I won't. But I hope I'll hear from you soon."

" 'Bye." She sounded wistful, her youthful curiosity piqued by this persistent young man with his peculiar questions. But curiosity meant nothing, Jeff thought sadly as he told her goodbye; he remained a stranger to her.

The clerk at the Harvard Coop rang up the sale, gave Jeff his change and the copy of *Candy* he'd just bought. Outside, the square teemed with students preparing to begin the new school year. A purposefully scruffy lot, Jeff noted; and as he glanced toward the University Theater, where *A Hard Day's Night* was playing, he saw one bearded young man discreetly hawking five-dollar matchboxes of marijuana. It had already been a year and a half since Leary and Alpert were dismissed from Harvard and had set up their short-lived "International Federation for Internal Freedom" across the river, on Emerson Place. The sixties as they'd be remembered were arriving earlier in Cambridge than they had at Emory. Even so, the transformation of eras wasn't quite complete yet; only one lone protestor stood in Harvard Square, quietly distributing leaflets decrying the growing American presence in Vietnam. At a table set up near the newsstand kiosk, a pair of students offered buttons reading "Stop Goldwater" and "LBJ 64." Their disillusionment wouldn't be long in coming.

Jeff went down the steps of the MTA station, entered one of the trolleylike old subway cars. Past Kenmore Square, the train came aboveground, crossed the Charles on Longfellow Bridge. To his right, Jeff could see workers on scaffolding putting the final touches on the new Prudential Center; the John Hancock Tower, with its ill-fated, popping windows, was still a long way in the future.

What would he do with that future now, he wondered, with the long and empty years he faced, again alone? It had been over a year since he'd begun this fourth replay of his life, and all the hopefulness with which he had once anticipated sharing this cycle with someone he fully loved, someone whose experience and understanding matched his own, had disappeared. Pamela remained an unfamiliar child, ignorant of who and what she—they—had previously been.

Perhaps some of her notions of eastern religion had been correct, in a manner unfathomable to either of them. Maybe she had attained complete enlightenment in her last existence, and her soul or essence or whatever had gone on to some form of Nirvana. Where, then, did that leave the innocent young girl who now lived in Westport? Was that person merely a shell of a body, now devoid of all spirit; a simulacrum of the real Pamela Phillips, moving through this lifetime without purpose? Maybe her, or its, purpose could be likened to an animated prop in a play or movie, a soulless robot. The unthinkable outside force that had set these replays in motion might be using the false Pamela solely to maintain the illusion that the world continued in its normal, original patterns, with its multibillion-person cast intact.

But for whose benefit? Who was the audience that was supposed to be fooled? Jeff? He had thought he was the first, and, until he met Pamela, the only, person this had ever happened to; perhaps, though, he'd been the last, or at least among the last, to become aware of the endless repetition. Pamela had theorized that these years would continue to reduplicate themselves until everyone on earth recognized what was going on. Could it instead be that the realization was intended to happen on a piecemeal basis, one individual at a time rather than a sudden planetary awareness? And as each person saw the truth, had he or she then begun the climb to escape the infinite recurrence of what had once been thought to be reality?

That meant all of human history, past and future, might be nothing but a sham: false implanted memories and records, deceptive hopes for a world to come. The creation of the human species, its cultures and technology and annals prechosen and already set in place by some unseen power, may have occurred in 1963 . . . and mankind's total span on this earth might stretch no more forward in subjective time than 1988, or soon thereafter. This rhythmic loop might encompass the totality of the human experience, and recognition of that fact could be the hallmark of an individual's having reached the zenith of awareness.

Which would mean that Jeff, and everyone else, had been unknowingly replaying for eons, literally since the beginning of time; and this might be his final cycle, as the previous one had been Pamela's. The rest of the population, then, existed either in a state of preconsciousness or as rote, mechanical figures whose real souls and minds had outgrown those bodies, as had Pamela. And there was no way to tell which of the people he encountered were still "sleeping," as it were, and which had already gone on to another level of being, leaving their living, breathing likenesses behind as part of the vast stage set that was earth.

It was too much to absorb at once. Even assuming it was true, he still had at least the twenty-five remaining years of this replay in which to grapple with the idea. For now he had to begin deciding how he was going to deal with those years on a day-to-day basis, having lost the only consummate companion he had ever known.

Jeff got off the train at the next stop, walked down Charles Street past the flower shops and coffeehouses. The nasal whine of a folk singer drifted from the open door of the Turk's Head, and a sign outside the Loft promised jug-band music on weekends. Up Chestnut Street the staid old homes, many of them now converted to apartments, presented a facade of urbane serenity.

What should he do? Go back to Montgomery Creek, spend the rest of this life—perhaps his final one—contemplating the incomprehensibility of the universe? Maybe he should make one last, albeit ultimately futile, attempt at improving humanity's lot: reestablish Future, Inc. as a philanthropic foundation, pour all those hundreds of millions into Ethiopia, or India.

He climbed the steps to his second-floor apartment, his mind swimming against the tide of a thousand competing thoughts and unlikely options. If he simply gave up, committed suicide, what then? Would he—

One corner of the yellow envelope protruded into the hallway where it had been slipped beneath his door. He picked up the telegram, ripped it open:

> BEEN CALLING ALL DAY. WHERE HAVE YOU BEEN? I'M BACK. I'M BACK. I'M BACK. GET HERE RIGHT AWAY. I LOVE YOU.
>
> PAMELA

It was after eleven o'clock that night when he pulled up in front of the house in Westport. He'd tried to get a flight from Logan to Bridgeport, but there'd been nothing leaving immediately. It was quicker to drive, he decided, and he made the brief trip in record time.

Pamela's father answered the door, and Jeff could see right away that this wasn't going to be easy.

"I want you to know that I'm allowing this meeting only because my wife insisted that I do so," the man began without preamble. "And even she was persuaded only because of Pam's threats to leave home if we didn't let her talk to you."

"I'm sorry this has become such an issue, Mr. Phillips," Jeff said with all the sincerity he could muster. "As I told you last year, I never intended to cause any problems in your family; it's all been an unfortunate misunderstanding."

"Whatever it is, it will not be repeated. I've spoken to my lawyer, and he says we can get a restraining order issued before the end of the week. That means you'll be arrested if you come anywhere near my daughter again before she turns eighteen; so whatever you have to say to her, you'd better get it said tonight. Is that understood?"

Jeff sighed, tried to peer through the half-open door. "Could I just see Pamela now, sir? I won't cause any problems, but I've waited a long time to talk to her."

"Come inside. She's in the living room. You have one hour."

Pamela's mother had obviously been crying; her eyes

were rimmed with red and haunted with defeat. Her fifteen-year-old daughter, sitting beside her on the sofa, was by contrast totally composed, though the girl's wide grin told Jeff she was fighting to restrain the jubilant relief she at last felt. The ponytails were gone; she'd brushed her hair into an approximation of the style she'd worn as an adult. She wore a cashmere sweater with a beige wool skirt, stockings, heels, and light, expertly applied makeup. The change in her since the last time he'd seen her went far deeper than her physical appearance, however; in her alert, knowing eyes Jeff could see instantly that this was in fact the woman he had loved and lived with for a decade.

"Hi, there," he said, returning her broad smile. "Want to go soaring?"

She laughed, a rich, throaty laugh full of mature irony and sophistication. "Mother, Father," she said, "this is my dear friend Jeff Winston. I believe you've met before."

"How is it that you've suddenly decided you know this . . . man, after all?" Her father had also noted the drastic change in Pamela's voice and demeanor, Jeff could see, and was greatly displeased by her inexplicable overnight growth to adulthood.

"I suppose my memory must have had some gaps in it last year. Now, you promised me we could have an hour alone together. Do you mind if we get started on that, please?"

"Don't try to leave the house." Her father scowled, addressing the two of them. "Don't even leave the living room."

Mrs. Phillips rose reluctantly from her place beside her daughter. "Your father and I will be in the den if you need us, Pam."

"Thanks, Mother. Everything is fine, I promise you."

Her parents left the room, and Jeff took her in his arms, hugging her as tightly as he could without crushing the breath out of her. "My God," he rasped in her ear, "where have you been? What happened?"

"I don't know," she said, pulling back to look at him. "I died in the house on Majorca just when I expected to, on the eighteenth. I only started replaying this morning; I was dumbfounded when I discovered what year it was.''

"I showed up late, too," Jeff said, "but only by about three months. I've been waiting for you for over a year."

She touched his face, gave him a look of tender sympathy. "I know," she said. "My mother and father told me what happened that summer."

"You don't remember, then? No, of course you wouldn't."

She shook her head sadly. "My only memories of that time are from my original existence, and the replays since. From my perspective, I last saw you just twelve days ago, on the dock at Puerto de Andraitx."

"The miniature," he said with a warm smile. "It was perfect. I wish I could have kept it."

"I'm sure you have," she said quietly. "Where it counts most."

Jeff nodded, hugged her again. "So . . . how did you find me in Boston?"

"I called your parents. They seemed to know who I was—vaguely, at least."

"I told them I knew a girl at school who was from Connecticut, when I first came up here."

"God, Jeff, it must have been awful when I didn't recognize you."

"It was. But now that you're back, I'm kind of grateful to have had a glimpse of what you were really like at fourteen."

She grinned. "I bet I thought you were cute, whoever you were. Actually, I'm kind of surprised I didn't lie, and tell my parents I did know you."

"I phoned you last March. You said you thought I was 'weird' . . . but you did sound kind of interested."

"I'm sure I was."

"Pam?" her father called from the hallway. "Everything all right in there?"

"No problem at all," she answered.

"You've got another forty-five minutes," he reminded her, and went back toward the rear rooms of the house.

"This *is* going to be a problem," Jeff said with a worried frown. "You're legally a minor; your father was talking about seeking a restraining order to prevent me from seeing you."

"I know," she said ruefully. "That's partly my fault. There was a hell of a scene here this afternoon, after I told them I was expecting a call or a visit from you. I had no idea they'd ever heard of you before; my father went through the roof when I brought your name up, and I'm afraid I didn't react too well in return. They never heard language like that out of me at this age, except in my second replay, when I turned rebellious. And of course, they don't remember that."

"Do you think he's serious about keeping us apart? He could really make things difficult if he chooses to."

"Unfortunately, he means what he says. We may have a rough time of it for a while."

"We could . . . run away together."

Pamela laughed dryly. "No. I tried that route once, remember? It didn't work out then, and it won't now."

"Except that I have money now, and access to as much more as we need. It's not as if we'd be out on the streets."

"But I'm still underage; don't forget that. You'd be in a lot of trouble if they caught us."

Jeff managed a grin. "Jailbait. I kind of like that idea."

"I just bet you do," she taunted. "But it's no joke, particularly not in this era. The 'Summer of Love' is still three years away; in 1964, they took that kind of thing very, very seriously."

"You're right," he agreed dejectedly. "So what the hell are we going to do?"

"We're just going to have to wait for a little while. I'll be sixteen in a few months; maybe by then they'll at least let us date, if I butter them up and play the role of the obedient daughter for now."

"Christ . . . I've already waited a year and a half to be with you."

"I don't know what else we can do," she said with compassion. "I don't like the prospect any better than you do, but I don't think we have any other choice right now."

"No," he admitted. "We don't."

"What are you going to do in the meantime?"

"I guess I'll go back to Boston; it's a nice city, not too far from here, and I'm more or less settled in there. Probably work on building up our nest egg, so we don't have to bother with making money once we're able to be together. Can I at least call you? Write you?"

"Not here, I don't think, not yet. I'll get a post-office box so we can write, and I'll call you as often as I can. From outside the house, after school."

"Jesus. You're really going back to high school again?"

"I have to." She shrugged. "I can put up with it. I've done it so many times before, I think I know every answer to every test."

"I'm going to miss you. . . . You know that."

She kissed him, long and passionately. "So will I, love; so will I. But the wait will be more than worth it."

≡14≡

PAMELA ADJUSTED THE tassel on her mortarboard, looked out into the crowded auditorium, and spotted Jeff, sitting alongside her parents. Her mother beamed with happy pride. Pamela caught Jeff's eye, winked, and got a wry smile in return. They were both aware of the comic irony in this ceremony: She, a woman who had been a practicing physician, a successful artist, and a celebrated motion-picture producer, was at last being awarded her high-school diploma. For the third time.

It had required considerable tenacity, and she was glad Jeff had understood how tedious the past three years had been for her. He'd had his own experience of reentering the academic world, at the college level, during his second replay; but going through high school again, this many times, was a unique subcircle of Hell.

Her perseverance had paid off, though, as she'd known it would. Her family had relented somewhat when she turned sixteen, a well-behaved A student who exhibited no interest in going out with the boys in her supposed peer group, and she was allowed to see Jeff two nights a week. He took an apartment in Bridgeport for their weekend use, and was scrupulously punctual about having her back at her parents' home by midnight every Friday and Saturday night. As far as her mother and father were concerned, the young couple saw a lot of movies; and if there were ever any question of that, they could easily recite the plots of such films as *Morgan!*, *Georgy Girl*, or *A Man for All Seasons*, having seen them all at least twice in the years past.

The arrangement had been kind of fun, in an odd way, once the negative parental pressure had begun to ease. There'd been a delicious erotic tension arising out of the limitations on their time together and the necessary furtiveness of their passion. They'd loved each other with their fresh young bodies as if they had never been intimate before, never given or received such libidinous delight with each other—or indeed with anyone.

If her parents had ever suspected anything about her sexual involvement with Jeff—and they must have, certainly by now—they'd been admirably silent about it. Their initial cautious tolerance of Jeff had soon given way to acceptance, then approval, and eventually an outright fondness. The four-year chasm of age that had loomed so disturbingly in her parents' eyes when he was eighteen and she fourteen had become a thoroughly conventional discrepancy by the time they were twenty-two and eighteen. Besides, in this era of LSD and promiscuous nonconformity, her mother and father were obviously relieved that she had developed a stable relationship with such a clean-cut, well-mannered, and prosperous young man.

The last of the diplomas was handed out, and the fledgling graduates who surrounded her raced from the stage with boisterous cheers. Pamela made her way calmly toward where Jeff waited with her parents.

"Oh, Pam," her mother said, "you looked so lovely up there! You just put all the rest of them to shame."

"Congratulations, honey," her father said, embracing her.

"I have to turn in the cap and the gown," Pamela told Jeff. "Then we can get going."

"Do you really have to leave so soon?" her mother

asked, chagrined. "You could stay for dinner, get an early start in the morning."

"Jeff's family is expecting us Thursday evening, Mom; we really ought to get as far as Washington tonight. Here, hold this," she said to Jeff, handing him the scrolled diploma. "I'll be right back."

In the girls' locker room she took off the black cotton robe, changed into a blue skirt and white blouse. A few of the other girls shyly congratulated her, and she them, but she was subtly excluded from their general camaraderie, the excited talk of boyfriends and summer plans and the various colleges they'd be going to in the fall. These girls had been her friends in her original existence; she'd fully shared in all their shenanigans and banter and tentative first steps to womanhood. But this time, as when she'd repeated her high-school years at the beginning of her first replay, there was a gulf between them that the girls somehow recognized, incapable though they were of understanding what it was. Pamela had kept her distance from them, ignored the social aspects of adolescence, had done what she had to do to fulfill her promise to her parents that she would finish school before leaving home to be with Jeff. Now that day had come, and she hoped the awkwardness of her departure could be kept to a minimum.

She finished changing, went back into the gradually emptying auditorium to rejoin her parents and the man with whom she would share the remainder of this life.

"So," her father was saying to Jeff, "you really do think I ought to hang on to those quarters, do you?"

"Yes, sir," Jeff replied. "As a long-term investment, most definitely. I'd say in ten to twelve years you'll see a very healthy return on it."

Her father's question had been designed to ease the tension, Pamela recognized, and she was grateful. The exchange reaffirmed that he had come to personally respect Jeff as an astute, creative investor and that he was aware his daughter would be well taken care of. Jeff himself had purchased several thousand dollars' worth of the phased-out ninety-percent-silver dimes and quarters before the coins disappeared, and had recommended that her father do the same. It was a logical, conservative-seeming financial move that would not startle her father by skyrocketing with suspicious swiftness or trouble him by appearing too obscurely risky. It would certainly pay off in its time, however; specifically, in January of 1980, when the Hunt brothers' illegal secret manipulations of the silver market would drive the price of the precious metal up to fifty dollars an ounce. Jeff had told Pamela he would contact her father that month, make sure he unloaded the coins before the precipitous crash that would soon follow.

"Will you be staying in Orlando long, darling?" her mother asked.

"Just a few days," Pamela said. "Then we're going to drive down to the Keys, maybe rent a boat for a couple of weeks."

"Have you decided yet where you'll be going when . . . the summer's over?"

That was still a sore point between them; even though her parents knew that she and Jeff would lack for nothing materially, they lamented her refusal to go on to college.

"No, Mom. We might get a place in New York; we're just not sure yet."

"It's not too late to register at NYU; you know they gave you an automatic acceptance on your National Merit scores."

"I'll think about it. Is everything in the car, Jeff?"

"All packed, gassed up, and ready to go."

Pamela hugged her mother and father, couldn't stop the tears that came to her eyes. They'd only wanted what was best for her, hadn't known their loving guidance and discipline had been long since unnecessary; she couldn't fault them for that. But now, at last, she and Jeff were truly free: free to be themselves, to strike out into this familiar world as the independent adults—and more—that they had always been beneath their deceptively juvenile exteriors. It was an auspicious day, after all they had been through.

She pulled herself out of the water with one graceful move, climbed the short ladder at the stern of the boat, and caught the towel Jeff tossed to her as she hoisted herself aboard.

"Beer?" he asked, reaching into the cooler.

"Sure," Pamela said, wrapping the big blue towel around her naked body and giving her hair a vigorous shake.

Jeff opened two bottles of Dos Equis, handed her one, and sprawled into a canvas deck chair. "Good swim." He grinned.

"Mmm," she agreed contentedly, pressing the icy bottle to her face. "That water's almost like a Jacuzzi."

"Gulf Stream. Warm current carries all the way across the Atlantic from here. We're sitting right on top of the heating vent that keeps Europe from having another Ice Age."

Pamela raised her face to the sun, closed her eyes, and inhaled the fresh salt air. A sudden sound roused her from her reverie, and she looked up to see a great white heron swoop elegantly above the boat, its long legs and tapered bill extended in aerodynamic symmetry as it dived toward the shoreline of the nameless key off which they'd anchored that morning.

"God." She sighed. "I don't ever want to leave this spot."

Jeff smiled, raised his bottle of Dos Equis in a silent toast of concurrence.

Pamela walked to the side of the boat, leaned against the railing, and stared into the sparkling blue-green sea from which she had just emerged. In the distance, to the west, the tranquil water churned with the playful antics of a passing school of dolphins. She watched them for several moments, then turned to Jeff.

"There's something we've been avoiding," she said. "Something we've needed to discuss, and haven't."

"What's that?"

"Why it took me so long to start replaying this time. Why I lost a year and a half. We've ignored all that for too long."

It was true. They'd never discussed the troublesome deviation from the cyclical pattern that had grown so familiar to each of them. Jeff had seemed so grateful just to have her back again, and she'd put her own worries in the back of her mind as she concentrated on the laborious task of finishing school and the delicate diplomacy of convincing her parents to accept her need to be with him.

"Why bring it up now?" he asked, a frown creasing his sun-browned forehead.

She shrugged. "We have to, sooner or later."

His eyes met hers, imploring. "But we don't have to be concerned about it for another twenty years. Can't we just enjoy ourselves until then? Savor the present?"

"We'd never be able to ignore it," she said gently, "not completely. You know that."

"What makes you think we can figure out why it happened, any more than we can decipher anything else about the replays? I thought we'd settled that."

"I don't necessarily mean *why* it happened, or how; but I've been considering it, and I think it may be part of an overall pattern, not just some one-time abberation."

"How so? I know I came back three months later than usual myself this time, but that's never happened before, to either of us."

"I'm not so sure; never to that extent, certainly, but there's been a . . . a skew developing in the replays, almost from the very start. Now it's simply begun to accelerate."

"A skew?"

She nodded. "Think about it. At the beginning of your second replay you weren't in your dorm room; you were at a movie theater, with Judy."

"It was the same day, though."

"Yes, but . . . what, eight or nine hours later? And the first time I came back it was early afternoon, but the next time was in the middle of the night. I'd say about twelve hours later."

Jeff grew thoughtful. "The third time—the last time I started replaying before this, when I was in Martin's car with Judy . . ."

"Yes?" she prodded.

"I just assumed it was that same night, that we were coming home from having seen *The Birds*. I was so upset about the loss of my daughter, Gretchen, that I wasn't really paying that much attention to anything around me. I just got drunk and stayed drunk for a couple of days. But the Kentucky Derby seemed to come up a lot faster that time. I got my bet in through Frank Maddock only the day before it was run. As shaken as I was, I still remember being relieved that at least I hadn't blown that opportunity. I thought I'd lost track of time because of the binge, but I could have started the replay late, by two or three days. I might have been returning home from a completely different evening with Judy.''

Pamela nodded. ''I wasn't focusing on the calendar that time, either,'' she told him. ''But I do remember that both my parents were home when I started replaying that morning, so it must have been a weekend; and the previous one had started on a Tuesday, the last day of April. So the skew was probably up to four days, maybe five.''

''How could it jump from a matter of a few days to—months? Over a year, in your case?''

''Maybe it's a geometric progression. If we knew the exact time differences between each of our replays, I think we could figure it out, possibly even project what the skew will be . . . next time.''

The thought of death, and yet another, possibly longer, separation cast a sudden pall of silence between them. The herons on the remote beach beyond the breakers stalked back and forth on their spindly legs, lonely and aloof. The school of dolphins to the west had moved on, leaving the sea once more untroubled.

''It's too late for that, though, isn't it?'' Jeff said. It was more a statement than a question. ''We'll never be able to reconstruct those divergences exactly. We weren't paying any attention to them then.''

''We had no reason to be. It was all too new, and the skew was so minor. We each had a lot more on our minds than that.''

''Then it's pointless to speculate. If there is a geometric progression and it's escalated from hours to days to months, then any rough estimate we might be able to come up with could be off by years.''

Pamela gave him a long, steady look. "Maybe someone else was making more careful note of the skew."

"What do you mean, 'somebody else'?"

"You and I discovered each other almost by accident, because you happened to respond to *Starsea* as something new and you were able to arrange a meeting with me. But there could be other replayers, many of them; we've never made a concerted effort to track them down."

"What makes you think they exist?"

"I don't know that they do, but then, I never expected to encounter you. If there are two of us, there could just as easily be more."

"Don't you think we would have heard of them by now?"

"Not necessarily. My films were extremely well publicized, and your interference in the Kennedy assassination the first time around caused quite a conspicuous ripple. Other than that, though, how much of a noticeable impact has either of us had on society? Even the existence of your company, Future, Inc., probably wasn't that well known outside the financial community. I know I wasn't aware of it when I was busy with med school and then my work in the children's hospital in Chicago. There may have been all sorts of other minor, localized changes—due to other replayers—that we simply haven't noticed."

Jeff pondered that for a moment. "I've often wondered about that, of course. I was just always too wrapped up in my own experiences to do anything about it—until I saw *Starsea* and then found you."

"Maybe it's time we did do something about it. Something more simple, and more direct, than I was trying to accomplish when you first met me. If there are others out there, we could all learn a lot. We'd have a great deal to share among us."

"True," Jeff said, smiling. "But right now the only person I want to share anything with is you. We've waited a long time to be together like this again."

"Long enough." She smiled back, undoing the blue terry-cloth towel and letting it drop to the sun-drenched wooden deck.

*   *   *

They placed the small display ad in the *New York Times*, *Post*, and *Daily News;* the *Los Angeles Times* and *Herald-Examiner; Le Monde, L'Express,* and *Paris-Match; Asahi Shimbun* and *Yomiyuri Shimbun;* the *London Times, Evening Standard,* and *Sun; O Estado de São Paulo* and *Jornal do Brasil.* Taking into account their own specialized areas of interest during various replays, the ad also began appearing regularly in the *Journal of the American Medical Association, Lancet,* and *Le Concours Médical;* the *Wall Street Journal,* the *Financial Times,* and *Le Nouvel Economiste; Daily Variety* and *Cahiers du Cinéma; Playboy, Penthouse, Mayfair,* and *Lui.*

In all, more than two hundred newspapers and magazines worldwide carried the superficially innocuous announcement, which would be utterly meaningless except to those unknown, and possibly nonexistent, few for whom it was intended:

Do you remember Watergate? Lady Di? The shuttle disaster? The Ayatollah? *Rocky? Flashdance?*
If so, you're not alone. Contact P.O. Box 1988, New York, N.Y. 10001

"Here's another one with a dollar bill enclosed," Jeff said, tossing the envelope aside. "Why the hell do so many of them think we're selling something?"

Pamela shrugged. "Most people are."

"What's even worse are the ones who think we're running some sort of contest. This could get to be a problem, you know."

"How so?"

"With the postal authorities, unless we're careful. We're going to have to come up with a form letter explaining that the ad isn't any sort of come-on, and send it to all these people. Especially the ones who've mailed us money. We have to make sure it's all returned. We don't need any complaints."

"But we haven't offered anyone anything," Pamela protested.

"Even so," Jeff said, "how would you like to try explaining to a postal inspector in 1967 what 'Watergate' means?"

"I suppose you're right." She opened another envelope, scanned the letter, and laughed. "Listen to this one," she said.

" 'Please send me more information on your memory-training course. I don't remember any of the things you mentioned in your ad.' "

Jeff chuckled along with her, glad she could still keep a sense of humor about all this. He knew how much the search meant to her: The time skew of her replay starting dates was obviously much more advanced than his, and if it was proceeding along a curve that had taken it from four or five days' delay all the way to eighteen months in one jump, the duration of her next repeated life might be severely truncated. They'd never discussed it but were both aware of the possibility that she might even not come back at all.

In the past four months, they'd received hundreds of replies to the ad, most of which assumed it was a contest or a sales pitch for anything from magazine subscriptions to the Rosicrucians. A few were tantalizingly ambiguous, but on follow-up investigation had proven worthless. The most promising, yet maddening, of them all had been a one-line message postmarked Sydney, Australia, with no signature or return address: "Not this time," it read. "Wait."

Jeff had begun to despair of the whole endeavor. It had made sense to try, and he felt they'd done it in the best way possible, but it hadn't produced the results they'd hoped. Maybe there really weren't any other replayers out there, or if they did exist, they had elected not to respond. More than ever before, though, Jeff now believed he and Pamela were alone in this, and would remain so.

He opened another envelope from the day's stack, ready to dump it with the other worthless, confused replies; but the first line stopped him, and he read the rest of the brief letter in stunned amazement.

Dear Whoever,

You forgot to mention Chappaquiddick. That's coming up again pretty soon now. And what about the Tylenol scare, or the Soviets shooting down the Korean 747? Everybody remembers those.

Any time you want to talk, head on out this way. We can reminisce about the good old days to come.

Stuart McCowan
382 Strathmore Drive
Crossfield, Wisconsin

Jeff stared at the signature, checked the address against the postmark. They matched. "Pamela . . ." he said quietly.

"Hmm?" She glanced up from the envelope she was about to tear open. "Another funny one?"

Jeff looked at the pretty, smiling face that he had known and loved so strangely out of sequence: first in maturity, and now in youth. He felt a vague foreboding, as if the closeness they had shared were about to be invaded, their mutual uniqueness shattered by a stranger. They had found what they'd been seeking, but now he wasn't at all certain they ever should have begun the quest.

"Read this," he said, and handed her the letter.

A light snow began to fall from the iron-drab sky as they drove into Crossfield, about thirty-five miles south of Madison. In the passenger seat of the big Plymouth Fury Pamela tensely ripped a Kleenex into thin strips of tissue, wadding them one by one and depositing them in the dashboard ashtray. Jeff hadn't seen her display that nervous habit since the night at the restaurant in Malibu when they'd first met, nineteen years ago and five years in the future.

"Do you still think there'll be just the one man?" she asked, looking out at the barren winter skeletons of the birch trees that lined the streets of the little town.

"Probably," Jeff said, peering through the snow at the black-and-gray street signs. "I don't think that reference to 'everybody' remembering the Tylenol killings and the Korean plane meant anything. I'm sure he was referring to people in general, after the incidents have happened, not some group of replayers he's gathered together."

Pamela finished shredding the Kleenex, reached for another. "I don't know whether I hope that's true or the other way around," she said in a perplexed tone. "In a way, it would be such an incredible relief to find a whole network of people who understand what we've been through. Yet I'm not sure if I'm ready to deal with . . . that much accumulated pain of such a familiar sort. Or to hear all the things they may have learned about replaying."

"I thought that was the whole point."

"It's just a little frightening, that's all, now that we're so close to it. I wish this Stuart McCowan had been listed with information; I'd feel a lot more comfortable if we'd been able to call him, get a better idea of who he is than from just that note. I hate showing up cold like this."

"I'm sure he's expecting us. Obviously, we weren't about to turn down his invitation, not after the effort we went through to find him."

"There's Strathmore," Pamela said, pointing to a street that wound up a hill to the left. Jeff had already passed the intersection; he made a U, turned onto the broad, deserted street.

Number 382 was an isolated three-story Victorian home on the other side of the hill. An estate, actually, with spacious, well-kept grounds behind the rough-hewn flagstone walls. Pamela began to tear at another Kleenex as they drove through the imposing gate, but Jeff stopped her fitful hand with his and gave her a warm smile of encouragement.

They parked under the wide portico, grateful for the shelter from the steadily increasing snowfall. An ornate brass knocker was mounted on the front door of the house, but Jeff found the doorbell and pressed that instead.

A matronly woman in a severe brown dress with a white

bib collar answered the door. "Can I help you?" she asked.

"Is Mr. McCowan in, please?"

The woman frowned above her pince-nez bifocals. "Mr. . . ."

"McCowan. Stuart McCowan. Doesn't he live here?"

"Oh, dear me, *Stuart*. Of course. Do you have an appointment?"

"No, but I believe he's expecting us; if you'll just tell him it's his friends from New York, I'm sure—"

"Friends?" Her frown deepened. "You're friends of Stuart's?"

"Yes, from New York."

The woman seemed flustered. "I'm afraid . . . Why don't you come in out of the cold, have a seat for a moment? I'll be right back."

Jeff and Pamela sat together on an overstuffed, high-backed settee in the musty entrance hall as the woman disappeared down a hallway.

"There *is* more than one of them," Pamela whispered. "He doesn't even own this house, apparently. The maid only knew him by his first name. It's some kind of commune, some—"

A tall, gray-haired man in a tweed suit emerged from the hallway, with the plump woman in the pince-nez glasses behind him. "You say you're friends of Stuart McCowan's?" he asked.

"We're, ah . . . We've been in correspondence with him," Jeff said, standing.

"And who initiated this correspondence?"

"Look, we're here at Mr. McCowan's express invitation. We've come all the way from New York to see him, so if you could just let him know—"

"What was the nature of your correspondence with Stuart?"

"I don't see that that's any of your business. Why don't you ask him?"

"Everything that concerns Stuart is my business. He is in my care."

Jeff and Pamela exchanged a quick look. "What do you mean, in your care? Are you a doctor? Is he ill?"

"Quite seriously. Why are you interested in his case? Are you journalists? I will not tolerate any invasion of my patients' privacy, and if you're from some newspaper or magazine, I suggest you leave immediately."

"No, neither of us is a reporter." Jeff handed the man one of the business cards that identified him as a venture-capital consultant, and introduced Pamela as his associate.

The wary tension in the man's face eased, and he gave an apologetic smile. "I'm so sorry, Mr. Winston; if I'd known it was a business matter . . . I'm Dr. Joel Pfeiffer. Please understand that I was only trying to protect Stuart's interests. This is a very exclusive, very discreet facility, and any—"

"This isn't Stuart McCowan's home, then? This is some sort of hospital?"

"A treatment center, yes."

"Is it his heart? Are you a cardiologist?"

The doctor frowned. "You're not familiar with his background?"

"No, we're not. Our connection with him is strictly . . . business-oriented. Investment matters."

Pfeiffer nodded understandingly. "Whatever his other problems, Stuart retains a tremendous sense of the market. I encourage his ongoing involvement in financial affairs. Of course, all his profits go into a trust now, but perhaps someday, if he continues to make progress . . ."

"Dr. Pfeiffer, are you saying—Is this a mental hospital?"

"Not a hospital. A private psychiatric unit, yes."

Christ, Jeff thought. So that's it; McCowan said too much to the wrong people at some point, and they've committed him. Jeff glanced at Pamela, saw that she, too, had understood immediately. They'd both recognized the risk that too open an admission of their experiences might lead to an outsider's assumption that they were insane; now here was living proof of that danger.

The doctor misunderstood their interchange. "I hope you won't hold Stuart's problems against him," he said with concern. "I assure you, his financial judgement has been impeccable throughout all this."

"That won't be an issue," Jeff told him. "We understand it must have been . . . difficult for him, but we're well aware of the sound management he's continued to apply to his portfolio." The lie seemed to ease Pfeiffer's worry. Jeff guessed that the McCowan trust was responsible for a large share of the operating costs of this place, perhaps even its initial endowment.

"Could we see him now?" Pamela asked. "If we'd known the circumstances in advance, naturally we would have arranged an appointment through you, but considering we've already come all this distance . . ."

"Of course," Dr. Pfeiffer assured her. "We have no set visiting hours here; you can see him right away. Marie," he said, turning to the gray-haired woman behind him, "could you have Stuart brought down to the sitting room, please?"

A pretty young woman in a lacy yellow dress sat in a window alcove of the room Dr. Pfeiffer showed them to. She was watching the snowfall, but turned expectantly as they walked in.

"Hello," the girl said. "Are you here to see me?"

"They're here to see Stuart, Melinda," the doctor told her gently.

"That's all right," she said with a cheerful smile. "Somebody's coming to see me on Wednesday, aren't they?"

"Yes, your sister will be here Wednesday."

"I could bring Stuart's guests some tea and cake, though, couldn't I?"

"If they'd like some, certainly."

Melinda descended from her white-backdropped perch. "Would you care for some tea and cake?" she asked politely.

"Yes, thank you," Pamela said. "That would be very thoughtful."

"I'll go get it, then. The tea is in the kitchen and the cake is in my room. My mother made it. Will you wait?"

"Of course, Melinda. We'll be right here."

She went out a side door of the room, and they could hear her rushing footsteps on the stairs. Jeff and Pamela examined their surroundings: comfortable leather chairs arranged in a semicircle around the brick fireplace, where two logs burned brightly; muted blue wallpaper dotted with a subtle fleur-de-lis pattern; a Tiffany lamp hanging in the opposite corner of the room, above a mahogany table where someone had half-completed a jigsaw puzzle of a monarch butterfly. Plush, dark blue drapes were opened to reveal a snowy hilltop vista.

"This is quite nice," Jeff said. "It doesn't look at all like—"

"Like what it is?" The doctor smiled. "No, we try to maintain as normal, and as pleasant, an environment as possible. No bars on the windows, as you can see; none of the staff members wear uniforms. I believe the atmosphere speeds the recovery process and makes the transition back to everyday life much easier when a patient is ready to go home."

"What about Stuart? Do you think he'll be ready to leave here soon?"

Pfeiffer pursed his lips, looked out the window at the steady snow. "He's made excellent progress since his transfer here. I have high hopes for Stuart. There are complications, naturally, a number of legal hurdles to be—"

A slight, sallow-faced man in his early thirties came into the room, followed by a muscular young man in jeans and a gray wool sweater. The paler man wore blue slacks, well-polished Italian loafers, and an open-necked white dress shirt. His hair had begun to recede and was thinning somewhat on top.

"Stuart," the doctor said expansively. "You have unexpected visitors. Business associates, I believe, from New York. Jeff Winston, Pamela Phillips; Stuart McCowan."

The prematurely balding man smiled pleasantly, extended his hand. "At last," he said, gripping first Jeff's hand, then Pamela's. "I've waited a long time for this moment."

"I know how you feel," Jeff responded quietly.

"Well," Dr. Pfeiffer said, "I'll leave you to your meeting. I'm afraid Mike, here, will have to stay. It's a stipulation imposed on us by the court; I have no choice in the matter. But he won't be in your way. You can speak as privately as you wish."

The burly attendant nodded, took a seat at the table beneath the Tiffany lamp, and began working on the jigsaw puzzle as the doctor left the room.

"Have a seat," Stuart said, indicating the chairs by the fireplace.

"God," Jeff said with immediate sympathy, "how awful this must be for you."

Stuart frowned. "It's not so bad. Much, much better than some of the other places."

"I don't mean the place itself, I mean the fact that this has happened to you at all. We'll do everything we can to get you out of here as soon as possible. I have an excellent attorney in New York; I'll see to it that he's on a plane out here tomorrow morning. He can straighten this out, I know."

"I appreciate your concern. It'll take awhile, though."

"How did you—"

"Tea and cake," Melinda announced brightly, coming through the door with a silver tray.

"Thank you, Melinda," Stuart said. "That's very sweet of you. I'd like you to meet some friends of mine, Jeff and Pamela. They're from my own time, from the 1980s."

"Oh," the girl said happily, "Stuart's told me all about the future. About Patty Hearst and the SLA, and what happened in Cambodia, and—"

"Let's not talk about all that now," Jeff interrupted her, glancing over his shoulder at the attendant, who sat obliviously engrossed in the jigsaw puzzle. "Thanks for the refreshments. Here, I'll take the tray."

"If you want any more, I'll be in the front room. It was nice to meet you; can we talk about the future later?"

"Maybe," Jeff said tersely. The girl smiled and left the room. "Jesus, Stuart," Jeff said when she had gone. "You shouldn't have done that. You shouldn't have confided in her at all, let alone told her about us. How's that going to look if she says anything to anybody?''

''No one really pays any attention to what we say in here. Hey, Mike,'' he called, and the attendant looked over. ''Know who's going to win the World Series three years running, starting in 1972? Oakland.''

The attendant nodded blankly, went back to his puzzle.

''See what I mean?'' Stuart grinned. ''They don't even listen. When the A's start winning, he won't remember I ever told him they would.''

''I still don't think it's a good idea. It could make our efforts to get you out of here much more difficult.''

The pale man shrugged. ''That's neither here nor there.'' He turned to Pamela. ''You made *Starsea,* didn't you?''

''Yes,'' she said with a smile. ''It's nice to know someone remembers it.''

''Very, very well. I almost wrote you a letter after I saw that; I knew right away you must be a repeater, and the movie validated a lot of things I'd learned myself. It renewed my sense of purpose.''

''Thank you. You mention the things you've learned. I wondered—have you . . . experienced the skew? The accelerating start dates of the replays, or repeats, as you think of them?''

''Yes,'' Stuart said. ''This last one was almost a year late.''

''Mine was a year and a half; Jeff's was only three months. We've been thinking that, if we could plot an exact curve between the various starting times, we might be able to predict . . . how much time we'll lose on the next cycle. But it would have to be very precise. Have you kept track of—''

''No, I haven't been able to.''

''If we all three compared notes, maybe it would jog your memory; we could at least start to narrow it down.''

He shook his head. ''It wouldn't work. The first three times I began repeating, I was unconscious. In a coma.''

''What?''

''I had a car accident in 1963—You did start coming

back in 1963, didn't you?'' he asked, looking from Pamela
to Jeff and back again.

"Yes," Jeff assured him. "Early May."

"Right. Well, that April I'd been in an accident, totaled
my car. I was in a coma for eight weeks, and every time
I'd wake up, I'd be repeating. I thought the coma had
something to do with it, until this time. So I don't know
whether my—what did you call it? The difference in the
start dates?"

"The skew."

"I don't know whether my skew the first three times
was a matter of hours or days or weeks. Or if there was
any at all." The disappointment in Pamela's face was
evident, even to McCowan. "I'm sorry," he said. "I wish
I could be of more help."

"It's not your fault," she said. "I'm sure that must
have been terrible for you, coming to in a hospital that
way, and now—"

"It's all part of the performance; I accept it."

" 'Performance'? I don't understand."

Stuart frowned quizzically at her. "You have been in
touch with the ship, haven't you?"

"I don't know what you mean. What ship?"

"The Antarean ship. Come on, you did *Starsea*. I'm a
repeater, too; you don't have to play ignorant with me."

"We honestly don't know what you're talking about," Jeff
told him. "Are you saying you've been in touch with the
. . . people, or beings, who are responsible for all this?
That they're extraterrestrials?"

"Of course. My God, I just assumed . . . Then you
haven't been performing the appeasement?" His already
wan face went whiter still.

Jeff and Pamela looked at each other, and at him, in
confusion. They'd both considered the possibility that an
alien intelligence might somehow be involved in the replays, but had never received the slightest indication that
this was in fact the case.

"I'm afraid you're going to have to explain all this from
the beginning," Jeff said.

McCowan glanced at the still-impassive young man,

who remained hunched over the jigsaw puzzle in the far corner of the room. He moved his chair closer to Jeff and Pamela, spoke in subdued tones.

"The repeating, or replaying—they don't care anything about that," he said, jerking his head to indicate the attendant. "It's the appeasement that gets them upset." He sighed, looked searchingly into Jeff's eyes. "You really need to hear the whole story? From the start?"

≡15≡

"I GREW UP in Cincinnati," Stuart McCowan told them. "My father was a construction worker, but he was an alcoholic, so he wasn't always able to find work. Then, when I was fifteen, he got drunk on a job and let a cable slip. He lost a leg, and after that the only money we had coming in was from my mother—she did piecework for a company that made police uniforms—and what I could pick up in tips as a bag boy at Kroger's.

"My father always got after me about being so skinny and not very strong physically; he was a big, powerful man himself, had forearms half again as thick as Mike's, there. After he lost the leg everything got even worse between us. He couldn't stand the fact that, puny as I was, I was at least whole. I had to carry things for him sometimes, when he couldn't manage both an armload of packages and his crutches. He hated that. He really got to despise me after a while, and the drinking got worse . . .

"I left home when I was eighteen; that was in 1954. Went west, out to Seattle. I wasn't very strong, but my eyes and my hands were steady. I managed to find work at Boeing, learned to machine-tool some of the lighter aircraft parts, trim tabs and such. I met a girl out there, got married, had a couple of kids. It wasn't so bad.

"Then I had my accident in the spring of '63, the one I told you about. I'd been drinking a little myself, not like my dad used to, but a few beers on the way home from work, and a shot or two once I got home, you know . . . and I was drunk when I hit that tree. Didn't come to for eight weeks, and nothing was ever really the same after that. The concussion had screwed up my hand-eye coordination, so I couldn't hack it at work anymore. It seemed like everything was happening to me just the way it had to my dad. I started drinking more, and yelling at my wife and kids. . . . Finally she just packed up and moved out, took the children with her.

"I lost the house not long after that; the bank foreclosed. I went back out on the road, started drifting, drinking. Did that for almost twenty-five years. One of 'the homeless,' as they call it in the eighties. But I always knew what I was—just a bum, a wino. I died in an alley in Detroit; didn't even know how old I was then. I figured it out later, though; I was fifty-two.

"And then I woke up, back in that same hospital bed, coming out of my coma. Like I'd just dreamed all those bad years, and for the longest time I believed I actually had—I didn't remember much of them, anyway. But I remembered enough, and pretty soon I could tell something really strange was going on."

McCowan looked at Jeff with a sudden sparkle in those eyes that had gone weary with telling the story of his first life. "You a baseball fan?" he asked. "Did you bet on the Series that year?"

Jeff grinned back at him. "I sure did."

"How much?"

"A lot. I'd bet on Chateaugay in the Kentucky Derby and the Belmont first, ran up a good stake."

"How much did you bet?" Stuart persisted.

"I had a partner then—not another replayer, just somebody I knew from school—and between us, we bet almost a hundred and a quarter."

"K?"

Jeff nodded, and McCowan let out a long, low whistle. "You hit the big time early," Stuart said. "Me, all I could scrape up was a couple hundred bucks, and my wife damn near left home early when she found out—but not after I got back twenty thousand; she wasn't going anyplace then.

"So I kept on betting—just the big things, the obvious ones—heavyweight championships, Super Bowls, presidential elections, all the things that even a lifelong drunk couldn't have forgotten how they came out. I stopped drinking, gave it up for good. Never have had so much as a beer since, not in all the repeats I've been through.

"We moved into a big house in Alderwood Manor, up in Snohomish County, north of Seattle. Bought a nice boat, kept it in the Shilshole Bay Marina; used to cruise up and down Puget Sound every summer, sometimes over to Victoria, B.C. Life of Riley, you know how it is. And then—then I started hearing from them."

"From . . . ?" Jeff left the question hanging.

McCowan leaned forward in his chair, lowered his voice. "From the Antareans, the ones that are doing this."

"How did . . . they get in touch with you?" Pamela asked tentatively.

"Through the television set, at first. Usually during the news. That's how I came to find out it was all a performance."

Jeff was growing increasingly edgy. "What was a performance?"

"Everything, all the stuff on the news. And the Antareans liked it so much, they just kept running it over and over again."

"What was it that they liked?" Pamela asked, frowning.

"The gory stuff, the shooting and killing, all that. Vietnam; Richard Speck, who did those nurses in in Chicago; the Manson thing; Jonestown . . . and the terrorists—Jesus, yes, they really get off on the terrorists: Lod Airport, all the IRA bombings, the truck bomb at Marine headquarters in Beirut, on and on. They can't get enough of it."

Jeff and Pamela exchanged a quick look, a brief nod. "Why?" Jeff asked McCowan. "Why do the extraterrestrials like violence here on earth so much?"

"Because they've grown weak themselves. They're the first to admit it. For all their power, controlling space and time, they're *weak!*" He slammed a thin fist down hard on the table, rattling the saucers and cups. Mike, the hefty attendant, looked over with raised eyebrows for a moment, but Jeff waved an O.K. signal, and the man went back to his jigsaw puzzle.

"None of them ever dies anymore," Stuart went on impassionedly, "and they've lost the killing genes, so there's no more war or murder where they come from. But the animal part of their brains still needs all that, at least vicariously. That's where we come in.

"We're their entertainment, like television or movies. And this segment of the twentieth century is the best part, the most randomly bloody time of them all, so they keep playing it again and again. But the only people who know all this are the performers, the ones on stage: the repeaters. Manson is one of us, I know; I can see it in his eyes, and the Antareans have told me. Lee Harvey Oswald, too, and Nelson Bennett that time he got to Kennedy first. Oh, there's a lot of us now."

Jeff kept his voice as calm, as kind, as possible when he spoke again. "But what about you and me and Pamela?" he asked, looking to evoke some remnant of rationality in the man. "We haven't done all those terrible things; so why are we replaying, or repeating?"

"I've done my share of appeasement," McCowan stated proudly. "Nobody can accuse me of slacking off there."

Jeff felt suddenly ill, and didn't want to ask the next question, the one that had to be asked. " . . . You've used that word before: 'appeasement.' What do you mean by it?"

"Why, it's our duty. All of us repeaters, we have to keep the Antareans from getting bored. Or else they'll shut it all off, and then the world will be over. We have to appease them, entertain them, so they'll keep watching."

"And—how have you done that yourself? Appeased them?"

"I always start off with the little girl in Tacoma. I do her with a knife. That one's easy, and I never get caught.

Then I move on, do a couple of hookers in Portland, maybe Vancouver . . . never too many close to home, but I travel a lot. Overseas, sometimes, but mostly I do them here in the states: hitchhikers in Texas, street kids in L.A. and San Francisco . . . Don't think I'll try Wisconsin again; I got caught here pretty early this time. But I'll be out in four or five years. They always say I'm crazy, and I end up in one of these places, but I've gotten real good at fooling doctors and parole boards. I always get out eventually, and then I can go back to performing the appeasement.''

Pamela leaned against the doorframe of the car, sobbing, as they drove through the swirling snow.

"It's my fault!" she cried, the tears flowing unchecked down her face. "He said it was *Starsea* that—that gave him 'a sense of purpose.' With everything I'd hoped to accomplish through that film, all I ended up doing was encouraging a mass murderer!"

Jeff kept his hands tight on the wheel of the rented Plymouth, negotiating the icy road. "It wasn't just the movie. He'd started killing long before that, from the very first replay. He was insane to begin with; I don't know if it was that accident he had, or the shock of replaying, or a combination of the two. Maybe a lot of different factors; there's no way to tell. But for God's sake, don't blame yourself for what he's done.''

"He killed a little girl! He keeps *on* killing her, stabbing her, every time!"

"I know. But it's not your fault, understand?"

"I don't care whose fault it is. We've got to stop him."

"How?" Jeff asked, squinting to see the road through the enveloping sheets of snow.

"Make sure he never gets out this time. Get to him next time before he starts killing.''

"If they decide he's 'cured,' they're going to release him no matter what we say. Why should the doctors, or the courts, listen to us? Do we tell them we're replayers, just like McCowan, only we're sane and he isn't? You know how far that would get us.''

"Then next time . . .''

"We go to the police in Seattle, or Tacoma, and tell them this solid citizen, with his expensive suburban house and his yacht, is about to start roaming the country, murdering people at random. It wouldn't work, Pamela; you know it wouldn't."

"But we've got to do *something!*" she pleaded.

"What should we do? Kill him? I couldn't do that; neither could you."

She wept quietly, her eyes closed against the deathly whiteness of the winter storm. "We can't just sit back and let it happen," she whispered at last.

Jeff cautiously turned left onto the highway heading back toward Madison. "I'm afraid we have to," he said. "We have to just accept it."

"How can you accept something like that!" she snapped. "Innocent people dying, being murdered by this maniac, when we know in advance that he's going to do it!"

"We've always accepted it, from the very beginning: Manson, Berkowitz, Gacey, Buono and Bianchi . . . that sort of aimless savagery is part of this time period. We've become inured to it. I don't even remember half the names of all the serial killers who'll crop up over the next twenty years, do you?"

Pamela was silent, her eyes red from crying, her teeth tightly clenched.

"We haven't tried to intervene in all those other murders, have we?" Jeff asked. "It's never even occurred to us to do so, except that first time when I tried to stop the Kennedy assassination, and that was something of a very different order. We—not just you and me, but everyone in this society—we live with brutality, with haphazard death. We almost ignore it, except when it seems to threaten us directly. Worse, some people even find it entertaining, a vicarious thrill. That's eighty percent, at least, of what the news business is all about: supplying America with its daily fix of tragedy, of other people's blood and torment.

"*We* are the 'Antareans' of Stuart McCowan's demented fantasies. He and all the other subhuman butchers out there are indeed performers on a stage, but the gore-hungry audience is right here, not somewhere in outer space. And there's nothing you or I can ever do to change that or to stem even the smallest trickle of that blood tide. We simply do what we've always done and always will: accept it, put it out of our minds as best we can, and go on with the rest of life. Get used to it, just as we do with all the other hopeless, inescapable pain."

The ad continued to draw responses, though none bore fruit. In 1970, they cut back on the number of publications in which it appeared; by the middle of the decade it was being printed only once a month, in fewer than a dozen of the largest-circulation newspapers and magazines.

Their apartment on Bank Street, in the west Village, came to be dominated by rows of filing cabinets. Jeff and Pamela saved even the most vaguely promising replies to the ad, along with clippings from the voluminous stacks of periodicals they pored over daily in search of potential anachronisms that might indicate the handiwork of another replayer somewhere in the world. It was frequently hard to be certain, one way or the other, about whether some minor event or product or artwork had or had not existed in the previous replays; they had never before focused so intently on such minutiae. Many times they contacted inventors or entrepreneurs whose indifferently publicized creations were unfamiliar to them; without exception, the apparent leads proved false.

In March of 1979, Jeff and Pamela found this story in the *Chicago Tribune:*

WISCONSIN KILLER FREED; "SANE," SAY DOCS

Crossfield, Wisc. (AP) Admitted mass murderer Stuart McCowan, declared not guilty by reason of insanity in the 1966 slayings of four young college women at a sorority house in Madison, was released today from the private mental institution where he had been held for the past twelve years. Dr. Joel Pfeiffer, director of the Crossfield Home, said McCowan "is fully recovered from his patterns of delusion, and presents no threat to society at this point."

McCowan was accused in the mutilation-killings of the four coeds after a witness identified his car as the one seen leaving the parking lot of the Kappa Gamma sorority house in the early morning hours of February 6th, 1966, the day the bodies were discovered. Wisconsin State Police apprehended McCowan later that same day, outside the town of Chippewa Falls. They found a blood-stained ice pick, hacksaw, and other implements of torture in the trunk of his automobile.

McCowan freely admitted having murdered the young women, and claimed to have been instructed to do so by extraterrestrial beings. He further claimed to believe that he had been reincarnated a number of times and had carried out other killings in each of his "previous lives."

He was named as a suspect in similar multiple slayings in Minnesota and Idaho in 1964 and 1965, but his connection to those crimes was never established. On May 11, 1966, McCowan was judged incompetent to stand trial and was committed to the Wisconsin State Hospital for the Criminally Insane. He was transferred at his own expense to the Crossfield Home in March 1967.

Pamela pulled the rubber tubing tighter around Jeff's arm, showed him which vein to hit and how to slide the hypodermic needle in with the bevel upward and the slender shaft parallel and lateral to the vein.

"What about psychological addiction, though?" he asked. "I know our bodies will be free of it when we come back, but won't we still crave the sensation?"

She shook her head as she watched him make the practice injection, the harmless saline solution flowing smoothly into the bulging blue vein in the crook of his elbow. "Not if we only use it a couple of times," she said. "Wait until the morning of the eighteenth; just do enough to keep you sedated. Then double the dosage to the amount I showed you and inject that a few minutes before one o'clock. You should be unconscious by the time . . . cardiac arrest occurs."

Jeff emptied the syringe into his arm, waited a beat before he withdrew the needle. He tossed the hypodermic into the wastebasket, swabbed the injection site with a wad of cotton soaked in alcohol. Two matching leather kits lay on the coffee table; each contained a supply of fresh sterile needles and syringes, a coiled length of rubber tubing, a small bottle of alcohol, a box of cotton wads, and four glass vials filled with pharmaceutical-quality heroin. It hadn't been difficult to obtain the drug and the equipment with which to use it; Jeff's stockbroker had recommended a reliable cocaine dealer, and the dealer was equally well stocked for the growing upper-middle-class heroin trade.

Jeff stared at the expensively tooled death kits, looked up at Pamela's face. There was a delicate tracery of fine lines across her forehead. The last time he'd known her at this age, the tiny wrinkles had been at the corners of her mouth and eyes; her forehead had been as smooth as when she was a girl. The difference between a lifetime of happiness and one of almost unrelieved anxiety was etched into the patterns of her skin.

"We didn't do a very good job of it, did we?" he said glumly.

She tried to smile, faltered, gave it up. "No. I guess we didn't."

"Next time . . ." he began, and his voice trailed off. Pamela reached out to him, and they squeezed each other's hand.

"Next time," she said, "we'll pay more attention to our own needs, day to day."

He nodded. "We kind of lost control this time, just let it slip away."

"I got carried away with the search for other replayers. It was kind of you to indulge me so, but—"

"I wanted to succeed in that as much as you did," he interrupted, bringing her hand to his lips. "It was something we had to do; it's no one's fault it turned out the way it did."

"I suppose not . . . but looking back, those years seem so stagnant, so passive. We seldom even left New York, for fear of missing the contact we kept waiting for."

Jeff pulled her to him, put his arms around her. "Next time we take charge again," he promised. "We'll be the ones who make things happen—for us."

They rocked together gently on the sofa, neither saying what was most deeply on their minds: that they had no way of knowing how long it would be before Pamela would rejoin him after this new death . . . or even if the next replay would enable them to be together again at all.

The heroin sleep was interrupted with shocking abruptness. Jeff found himself surrounded on all sides by cascading sheets of white-hot flame, a cylindrical Niagara of milky fire at whose core he was inexplicably suspended. At the same time, his ears were assaulted by the blaring trumpets and exaggerated harmonies of a mariachi band performing, at excruciating volume, "Feliz Navidad."

Jeff had no memory of having died this time, no recollection of the agony he had always felt with each stopping of his heart. The drug had served its anesthetic purpose, but it allowed him no easy transition from that dullard slumber to this startling and unknown environment. The new young body he now inhabited again had not a trace of the narcotic in its system, and he was forced to come fully awake without a moment's groggy respite.

The encircling fire-fall, and the music, besieged his battered senses, held him in a terrifying limbo of disorientation. There was no light in this place, save from that burning cataract around him, but against its brilliant phosphorescence he now perceived the silhouettes of other people: sitting, standing, dancing. He himself was seated, at a small table; there was an icy drink in his shaking hand. He sipped it, tasted the salty bite of a margarita.

"Damn!" someone shouted in his ear, above the clamor of the music. "Isn't that a sight? Wonder what it looks like from outside."

Jeff set the drink down, turned to see who had spoken. In the white glow of the down-rushing flames he could make out the sharp-boned features of Martin Bailey, his roommate from Emory. He looked around again, his eyes growing accustomed to the bizarrely incandescent lighting from all sides of the large room. It was a bar or nightclub; laughing couples sat at dozens of other small tables, the mariachi band next to the dance floor was costumed in outrageous finery, and brightly colored *piñatas* in the shape of donkeys and bulls hung from the ceiling.

Mexico City. Christmas vacation, 1964; he'd driven down here with Martin that year, on a spur-of-the-moment trip. Desert roads with mangy cattle roaming in the two-lane highway, mountain passes of blind curves, with Pemex gasoline trucks passing the Chevy in the cottony fog. A whorehouse in the Zona Rosa, the long climb up the stone steps of the Pyramid of the Sun.

The tumbling radiance outside the windows of this place was a fireworks show, he realized, streams of liquid pyrotechnics pouring from the roof of the hotel atop which the nightclub perched. Martin was right; it must be spectacular from the streets below. The hotel would look like a fiery needle, blazing thirty or forty stories up into the city's nighttime sky.

What was this, Christmas Eve, New Year's? Those were the nights for this sort of display in Mexico. Whichever, it was the end of '64, beginning of '65. He'd lost another fourteen months on this replay; as much, now, as Pamela had on her last one. God knows what that might mean for her this time, and for them.

Martin grinned, gave him an exuberant, friendly punch on the shoulder. Yeah, they'd had a good time on this trip, Jeff remembered. Nothing had gone sour; it didn't seem then as if anything ever could go wrong in either of their lives. Good times today, good times ahead—that was how they'd seen it. At least Jeff had managed to prevent his old friend's suicide each replay, whatever his own circumstances. Even though he couldn't stop Martin from marrying badly and no longer had a multinational corporation where he could offer his old roommate a lifetime position, he'd always helped Martin avert eventual bankruptcy by setting him up with some excellent stocks early on.

Which raised the subject of what Jeff was going to do for immediate cash himself; his old standby, the '63 World Series, was in the record books by now, and there weren't

many other bets even approaching the short-term profit-
ability of that one. The pro football season was already
over, and they wouldn't start playing Super Bowls for
another two years. If this were New Year's Eve, he might
or might not have time to arrange a bet from Mexico City
on Illinois over Washington in the Rose Bowl tomorrow. It
was possible that he'd have to be satisfied for the time
being with what he could eke out of the basketball schedule now underway, but he'd never be able to get any
decent odds on the Boston Celtics, not in their eighth
straight NBA championship season.

The fire-fall outside the windows trickled to a sputtering
halt, and the dim lights of the nightclub came back up as
the band broke into "Cielito Lindo." Martin was checking
out a svelte blonde a couple of tables over, and he raised
an eyebrow to ask if Jeff had any interest in her red-haired
friend. The girls were tourists from the Netherlands, Jeff
recalled; he and Martin wouldn't score, but they'd spend—
had spent—a pleasant enough evening drinking and dancing with the Dutch girls. Sure, he shrugged to Martin; why
not?

As far as the money problem went, well, money didn't
matter that much to him anyway, not at this point. All he
needed was enough to keep him going for . . . however
long it took until Pamela showed up. From here on out, it
was just a waiting game.

Pam was stoned; she was flat-out wrecked. This was really
some killer weed Peter and Ellen had come up with, the
best she'd smoked since the stuff that guy had given her at
the Electric Circus last month, and that had probably
seemed better than it actually was because of all the strobes
and the music and the fire eaters on the dance floor and
everything. The music was great right now, too, she thought
as Clapton started that dynamite riff going into "Sunshine
of Your Love"; she just wished the little portable stereo
could play it louder, that was all.

She curled her bare feet up under her thighs, leaned
back against the big Peter Max poster that covered the wall
behind her bed, and got into the back cover of the "Dis-

raeli Gears" album. That eye was really something, with the flowers growing right out of its lashes, and the names of the songs just barely visible over the white part and the iris . . . and, God, there was another eye. The more you looked it seemed like there was nothing but eyes; that was all you noticed. Even the flowers looked like they had eyes, slanted, like a cat's eyes, or an Oriental's. . . .

"Hey, check this out!" Peter called. She glanced up; he and Ellen were watching Lawrence Welk with the sound turned down. Pam stared at the black-and-white scene of old couples dancing, a polka or something, and sure enough, it looked just like they were moving in time to the record. Then the picture switched to Welk waving his little baton up and down, and she started laughing; Welk was keeping right to the beat, as if the old fart were conducting Cream on "Dance the Night Away."

"Come on, you guys, let's go down the road," Ellen insisted, bored with the television. "Everybody's gonna be there tonight." She'd been trying to get them motivated to get out of the room and make the trek to Adolph's for the past hour. She was right: It would be a good night at the college bar; there was a lot to celebrate. Earlier in the week, Eugene McCarthy had damn near beat Johnson in the New Hampshire primary, and just today, Bobby Kennedy had announced that he'd changed his mind, he was going to run for the Democratic nomination after all.

Pam put on her boots, grabbed a thick wool scarf and her old navy surplus pea jacket from the hook on the door. Ellen took her time negotiating the circular staircase leading down to the lobby; she'd started tripping off on the old mansion-turned-dorm's being Tara, from *Gone With the Wind*. By the time they got outside, Peter had joined in the game. He wandered off into the adjoining formal garden and started declaiming lines real and imagined from the movie in a heavy mock-southern accent. But the March night was too biting to keep up the playful stoned pretense for long, and soon the three of them were crunching through the snow toward the warmly inviting wooden building at the edge of campus, across from the Annandale post office.

Adolph's was packed with the usual Saturday-night crowd. Everybody who hadn't gone to New York for the weekend ended up here sooner or later; it was the only bar within walking distance of the school, and the only one on this side of the Hudson where the shaggy, unconventionally dressed Bard students could relax and feel totally welcome. There was a serious town-gown conflict in the generally conservative region north of Poughkeepsie; the permanent residents, young and old, despised the flamboyant nonconformity of the Bard students' appearance and behavior, and told tales—many of them truer than they could ever imagine, Pam thought with amusement—of rampant drug use and sexual promiscuity on campus.

Sometimes the young townie guys would come into Adolph's, drunk, trying to pick up "hippie chicks." There weren't any townies in evidence tonight, Pam noted with relief, except for that one weird guy who'd been hanging around campus all year, but he seemed O.K. He was a loner and very quiet; he'd never given anybody any trouble. Sometimes she felt as if he were watching her, not quite following her around or anything, but purposely showing up a couple of times a week in some place where she'd probably be: the library, the gallery at the art department, here . . . He'd never bothered her, though, never even spoke to her. Sometimes he'd smile and nod, and she'd kind of smile back a little, just enough to acknowledge that they recognized each other. Yeah, he was O.K.; he'd even be attractive if he let his hair grow.

Sly and the Family Stone were on the jukebox, "Dance to the Music," and the dance floor in the front room was packed. Pam and Ellen and Peter squirmed their way through the crowd, looking for a place to sit.

Pam was still stoned. They'd smoked another joint on the walk down from campus, and the colorfully raucous scene in the bar suddenly struck her as a painting, or a series of paintings. To highlight a twirling fringed vest here, a swirl of long black hair there, the faces and the bodies and the music and noise . . . yes, she'd like to try to capture on canvas the *sound* of this pleasantly familiar place, translate it visually, the way that synesthetic transformation so often happened in her mind when she was this stoned. She looked around the bar, picking out people and details of scenes, and her eyes focused on that strange guy she was always running into.

"Hey," she said, nudging Ellen, "you know who I'd like to paint?"

"Who?"

"That guy over there."

Ellen looked in the direction Pam had discreetly indicated. "Which one? You don't mean that straight guy, do you? The townie?"

"Yeah, him. There's something about his eyes; they're . . . I don't know, it's like they're ancient or something, like he's way older than he really is, and has seen so much. . . ."

"Sure," Ellen said with pointed sarcasm. "He's probably some ex-Marine, and he's seen lots of dead babies and women he shot in Vietnam."

"You talking about the Tet offensive again?" Peter asked.

"No, Pam's got the hots for some townie."

"Kinky." Peter laughed.

Pam blushed angrily. "I never said any such thing. I just said he had interesting eyes and I'd like to paint them."

"Dock of the Bay" came on the jukebox, and most of the dancers found their way back to their tables. Pam wondered who had played the mournfully contemplative Otis Redding tune, such an ironic self-epitaph of the singer, who had died before the record was released. Maybe it was that guy with the strange eyes. It seemed like the kind of music he might be into.

"Wastin' tiiime . . ." Peter sang along with the record, then grinned mischievously. He took off his watch, dropped it into the half-full pitcher of beer with a theatrical flourish. "We drown time!" he declared, and raised his glass, clinked it against the others'.

"I hear Bobby's a head," Ellen commented, apropos of nothing, when they had drunk the toast. "Gets his grass from the same dealer who supplies the Stones when they're over here.''

They were on one of Peter's favorite topics now. ''They say R.J. Reynolds has secretly . . . what's the word, patented? All the good brand names.''

''Trademarked.''

''Right, right, trademarked. 'Acapulco Gold,' 'Panama Red' . . . the cigarette people have got all the good names, just in case.''

Pam listened to the familiar rumors, nodded with interest. ''I wonder what the packs would look like, and the ads.''

''Paisley cartons,'' Ellen said with a smile.

''Get Hendrix to do the TV commercials.'' Peter put in.

They started cracking up, getting into one of those endless communal stoned laughing jags that Pam loved so much. She was laughing so hard the tears were coming to her eyes, she was getting giddy, hyperventilating, she—

Where the hell was she this time, Pamela wondered, and why was she so dizzy? She blinked away an inexplicable film of tears, took in the new environment. Jesus Christ, it was Adolph's.

''Pam?'' Ellen asked, suddenly noticing that her friend had stopped laughing. ''You O.K.?''

''I'm fine,'' Pamela said, taking a long, slow breath.

''You're not freaking out or anything?''

''No.'' She closed her eyes, tried to concentrate, but her mind wouldn't stay still; it kept drifting. The music was extremely loud, and this place, even her clothes, reeked of—She was stoned, she realized. Usually had been when she went to Adolph's, ''down the road,'' they used to call it, ease on down, ease on down . . .

''Have another beer,'' Peter said, concern in his voice. ''You look weird; you sure you're all right?''

''I'm positive.'' She hadn't become friends with Peter and Ellen until after winter field period of her freshman year. Peter had graduated, and Ellen had dropped out and moved to London with him, when Pamela was a sophomore; that meant this had to be 1968 or 1969.

A new record started playing on the jukebox, Linda

Ronstadt singing "Different Drum." No, Pamela thought, not just Linda Ronstadt, the Stone Poneys. Keep it all straight, she told herself, reacclimate slowly, don't let the marijuana in your brain make this more difficult than it already is. Don't try to make any decisions or even talk too much right now. Wait'll you come down, wait until—

There he was, my God, sitting not twenty feet away, looking right at her. Pamela gaped in disbelief at the incongruous, impossibly wonderful sight of Jeff Winston sitting quietly amid the youthful din of her old college hangout. She saw him register the change in her eyes, and he smiled a warm, slow smile of welcome and assurance.

"Hey, Pam?" Ellen said. "How come you're crying? Listen, maybe we better go back to the dorm."

Pamela shook her head, put a reassuring hand on her friend's arm. Then she stood from the table and walked across the room, across the years, into Jeff's waiting embrace.

"Tattooed lady." Jeff chuckled, kissing the pink rose on her inner thigh. "I don't remember that being there before."

"It's not a tattoo, it's a decal. They wash off."

"Do they lick off?" he asked, looking up at her with a wicked gleam.

She smiled. "You're welcome to try."

"Maybe later," he said, sliding up to prop himself beside her on the pillows. "I kind of enjoy you as a flower child."

"You would," she said, and poked him in the ribs. "Pour us some more champagne."

He reached for the bottle of Mumm's on the bedside table, refilled their glasses.

"How did you know when I'd start replaying?" Pamela asked.

"I didn't. I've been watching you for months; I rented the house here in Rhinebeck at the beginning of the school year, and I've been waiting ever since. It was frustrating, and I was starting to get impatient; but the time here helped me come to terms with some old memories. I used to live just up the river, in one of the old estates, when I was with Diane . . . and my daughter Gretchen. I always thought I'd never be able to come back here, but you gave me a reason to, and I'm glad I did. Besides which, I enjoyed seeing you the way you really were in this time, originally.''

She grimaced. "I was a college hippie. Leather fringe and tie dye. I hope you never listened to me talking to my friends; I probably said 'far out' a lot.''

Jeff kissed the tip of her nose. "You were cute. *Are* cute," he corrected, brushing her long, straight hair away from her face. "But I couldn't help imagining all these kids fifteen years from now, wearing three-piece suits and driving BMW's to the office.''

"Not all of them," she said. "Bard turned out a lot of writers, actors, musicians . . . and," she added with a rueful grin, "my husband and I didn't have a BMW; we drove an Audi and a Mazda.''

"Point granted." He smiled, and took a sip of champagne. They lay together contentedly, but Jeff could see the gravity beneath her cheerful expression.

"Seventeen months," he said.

"What?"

"I lost seventeen months this time. That's what you were wondering, wasn't it?''

"I'd been wanting to ask," she conceded. "I couldn't help but wonder. My skew is up to . . . This is March, you said? '68?"

Jeff nodded. "Three and a half years.''

"Counting from last time. It's five years off from the first few replays. Jesus. Next time I could—''

He put a finger to her lips. "We were going to concentrate on *this* time, remember?''

"Of course I do," she said, snuggling closer to him beneath the covers.

"And I've been thinking about that," he told her. "I've had awhile to consider it, and I think I've come up with a plan, of sorts.''

She pulled her head back, looked at him with an interested frown. "What do you mean?"

"Well, first I thought about approaching the scientific

community with all this—the National Science Foundation, some private research organization . . . whatever group might seem most appropriate, maybe the physics department at Princeton or MIT, somebody doing research on the nature of time.''

''They'd never believe us.''

''Exactly. That's been the stumbling block all along. And yet we've done our part to maintain that obstacle, by remaining so secretive each time.''

''We've had to be discreet. People would think we were insane. Look at Stuart McCowan; he—''

''McCowan *is* insane—he's a killer. But it's no crime to make predictions of events; nobody would lock us up for doing that. And once the things we predict have actually happened, we'll have proven our knowledge of the future. They'd have to listen to us. They'd know something real— unexplained, but real—was going on.''

''How would we get in the front door to begin with, though?'' Pamela objected. ''No one at a place like MIT would even bother looking at any list of predictions we gave them. They'd lump us in with the UFO fanatics and the psychics the minute we told them what we had in mind.''

''That's just the point. We don't approach them; they come to us.''

''Why should—You're not making sense,'' Pamela said, shaking her head in confusion.

''We go public,'' Jeff explained.

≡16≡

THIS TIME THERE was no need for the global-saturation coverage they had employed with their previous ad, the small one with which they had hoped to attract the attention only of other replayers. Also, both the ambiguity and anonymity of that first notice were unnecessary for their present purpose. The *New York Times* refused to carry the one-time-only, full-page ad, but it ran in the *New York Daily News*, the *Chicago Tribune*, and the *Los Angeles Times*.

DURING THE NEXT TWELVE MONTHS:

The U.S. nuclear submarine *Scorpion* will be lost at sea in late May.

A major tragedy will disrupt the American presidential campaign in June.

The assassin of Martin Luther King, Jr., will be arrested outside the United States.

Chief Justice Earl Warren will resign on June 26th, and will be succeeded by Justice Abe Fortas.

The Soviet Union will lead a Warsaw Pact invasion of Czechoslovakia on August 21st.

Fifteen thousand people will be killed in an earthquake in Iran on the first of September.

An unmanned Soviet spacecraft will circle the moon and be recovered in the Indian Ocean on September 22nd.

In October, there will be military coups in both Peru and Panama.

Richard Nixon will narrowly defeat Hubert Humphrey for the presidency.

Three American astronauts will orbit the moon and return safely to earth during Christmas week.

In January 1969, there will be an unsuccessful assassination attempt against Soviet leader Leonid Brezhnev.

A massive oil spill will contaminate the beaches of Southern California in February.

French President Charles de Gaulle will resign at the end of next April.

We will have no further comment to make on these statements until May 1, 1969. We will meet with the news media on that date, at a location to be announced one year from today.

> Jeff Winston & Pamela Phillips
> New York, N.Y., April 19, 1968

Every seat of the large conference room they had rented at the New York Hilton was occupied, and those who could not find a chair milled impatiently in the aisles or at the sides of the room, trying to keep their feet from becoming entangled in the snaking microphone and television cables.

At 3:00 P.M. precisely, Jeff and Pamela came into the room and stood together on the speaker's platform. She smiled nervously as the blinding lights for the TV cameras came on, and Jeff gave her hand an encouraging, unseen squeeze. From the moment they'd walked in, the room was a hubbub of shouted questions, the reporters all vying at once for their attention. Jeff called several times for silence, finally got the level of noise down to a dim roar.

"We'll answer all your questions," he told the assembled journalists, "but let's establish some kind of order here. Why don't we take the back row first, one question per person, left to right. Then we'll move to the next row, in the same order."

"What about the people who don't have seats?" cried one of the men at the side of the room.

"Latecomers take their turns last, left side of the room first, back to front. Now," Jeff said, pointing, "we'll take the first question from the lady in the blue dress. No need to identify yourselves; just ask anything you like."

The woman stood, pen and pad in hand. "The most obvious: How were you able to make such accurate predictions about such a wide range of events? Are you claiming to have psychic powers?"

Jeff took a deep breath, spoke as calmly as possible. "One question at a time, please, but I'll answer both of those this once. No, we do not pretend to be psychic, as that term is commonly understood. Both Miss Phillips and I have been the beneficiaries—or the victims—of a recurring phenomenon that we initially found as difficult to believe as you undoubtedly will today. In brief, we are each reliving our own lives, or certain portions of them. We both died—will die—in October 1988 and have returned to life and subsequently died again, several times over."

The noise that had greeted them as they entered the room was nothing compared to the pandemonium that ensued at this statement, and the overall derisive tone of the cacophony was unmistakable. One television crew shut off its lights and began packing away its equipment, and several reporters stalked out of the room in an insulted huff, but there were many others eager to take the vacated seats. Jeff signaled for quiet again, pointed to the next journalist in line for a question.

"This one's obvious, too," the portly, scowling man said. "How the hell do you expect any of us to believe that crap?"

Jeff maintained his composure, smiled reassuringly at Pamela and calmly addressed the scornful crowd. "I told you before that what we have to say will seem barely credible. I can only point to the complete validity of the 'predictions' we published a year ago—which were already memories, to us—and ask that you reserve judgment until you've heard us out."

"Are you going to make any more predictions today?" asked the next reporter.

"Yes," Jeff said, and the uproar threatened to begin anew. "But only after we've answered all your other questions and feel that we've told everything we need to tell."

It took them almost an hour to give the essential, sketchy outline of their lives: who they'd been originally, what they'd done of note in each of their replays, how they came to know each other, the troubling fact of the accelerating skew. As previously agreed, they left out a great deal about their personal lives, as well as anything they felt might be dangerous or unwise to reveal. But then came the question they'd known would be raised and still hadn't decided how to handle: "Do you know of anyone else who's . . . replaying, as you call it?" asked a cynical voice in the third row.

Pamela glanced at Jeff, then spoke up emphatically before he had a chance to answer. "Yes," she said. "A man named Stuart McCowan, in Seattle, Washington."

There was a momentary pause as a hundred pens scratched the name on a hundred note pads. Jeff gave Pamela a warning frown, which she ignored.

"As far as we know, he's the only other one," she went on. "We spent most of one replay searching for others, but McCowan is the only one we ever verified. Let me tell you, though, that he has some ideas about all this with which we strongly disagree; that's why he's not here with us today. But I think you might find it very interesting to interview him, even keep close track of everything he does, to see how he deals with this situation that the three of us find ourselves in. He's an unusual man, to say the least."

She looked back at Jeff, and he complimented her with a pleased smile. She'd said nothing libelous or incriminating about McCowan but had made sure his background would be thoroughly investigated and his every public move watched from now on. He'd kill no more, not this time.

"What do you expect to get out of all this?" asked another reporter. "Is this some kind of moneymaking scheme you're launching, some sort of cult?"

"Absolutely not," Jeff said firmly. "We can make all the money we need or want through ordinary investment channels, and I would like each of your stories to include our specific request that *no one* send us money, not in any amount, not for any purpose. We will return all such gifts. The only thing we're seeking is information, a possible explanation of what we're going through and how it will all end. We would like the scientific establishment—particularly physicists and cosmologists—to be aware of the reality of what's happening to us and to contact us directly with any opinions they might have. That's our sole purpose in making this phenomenal situation a matter of public record. We've never revealed ourselves before and wouldn't have now, but for the very real concerns we've outlined."

The room buzzed with skepticism. Everybody was selling something, as Pamela had once pointed out; it was difficult for this collection of hardened journalists to accept the fact that Jeff and Pamela weren't pulling a scam of one sort or another, despite the couple's apparent sincerity and the irrefutable evidence of their inconceivably accurate foreknowledge.

"Then what do you intend to do, if you're not trying to capitalize on these claims?" someone else asked.

"It depends on what we find out as a result of having announced ourselves this way," Jeff replied. "For the time being, we're just going to wait and see what happens when you make our story known. Now, are there any further questions? If not, I have here a number of copies of our newest set of . . . predictions, as you think of them."

There was a scramble for the front of the room, a multitude of hands grabbing for the Xeroxed sheets of paper, a new outburst of more pointed questions.

"Is there going to be a nuclear war?"

"Will we beat the Russians to the moon?"

"Do we find a cure for cancer?"

"Sorry," Jeff shouted. "No questions about the future. Everything we have to say is in this document."

"One last question," called a bespectacled man in a fedora that looked as if it had been sat on. "Who's going to win the Kentucky Derby this Saturday?"

Jeff grinned, relaxed for the first time since the tension-filled news conference had begun. "I'll make a single exception for this gentleman," he said. "Majestic Prince will win the Derby and the Preakness, but Arts and Letters will beat him out of the Triple Crown. And I think I just made my own bet worthless by telling you that."

Majestic Prince left the gate at 1-10 odds and paid $2.10 to win, the lowest return permissible under the laws governing parimutuel gambling. After the story on Jeff and Pamela had hit the networks and the wire services, almost no one had bet on any of the other horses in the Derby. The Kentucky State Racing Commission ordered a full investigation, and there was talk in Maryland and New York of canceling the upcoming Preakness and Belmont.

The phones in their new office in the Pan Am Building began ringing at 6:00 A.M. on the Monday after the race; by noon, they had hired two more temps from Kelly Girls to handle the calls and telegrams and the curiosity seekers who walked through the door without an appointment.

"I have the list from the past hour, sir," said the awestruck young woman in the pleated midi-dress, nervously fingering her long strands of beads.

"Can you summarize it for me?" Jeff asked wearily, setting aside the editorial in that day's *New York Times*, the one calling for "rational skepticism in the face of would-be modern Nostradamuses and their manipulation of coincidence."

"Yes, sir. There were forty-two requests for private consultations—people who are seriously ill, parents of missing children, and so on—nine stock-brokerage firms called, offering to take you on as clients at reduced commission; we've had twelve calls and eight telegrams from people willing to put up money for various gambling schemes; eleven messages from other psychics wanting to share—''

"We aren't psychics, Miss . . . Kendall, is it?"

"Yes, sir. Elaine, if you like."

"Fine. I want that clearly understood, Elaine; Pamela and I don't claim to have any psychic powers, and anyone who makes that assumption should be informed otherwise. This is something very different, and if you're going to work here you have to know how we choose to be represented."

"I understand, sir. It's just that—"

"It's a little hard for you to accept, of course. I didn't say you had to believe us yourself; just make sure the basic elements of what we've had to say don't get twisted around when you talk to the public, that's all. Now, go on with the list."

The girl smoothed her blouse, referred to her steno pad. "There were eleven . . . I suppose you'd call them hate calls, some of them obscene."

"You don't have to put up with that. Tell the other girls they can feel free to hang up on anyone who becomes abusive. Contact the police if any one caller persists."

"Thank you, sir. We've also had several calls from some futurist group in California. They want you to go out there for a conference with them."

Jeff raised an interested eyebrow. "The Rand Corporation?"

She glanced back down at her notes. "No, sir; something called the 'Outlook Group.' "

"Pass it on to my attorney. Ask him to have them checked out, see if they're legitimate."

Elaine jotted his instructions on her pad, went back to the list. As long as I'm talking to Mr. Wade, I need to tell him about all these airlines that are threatening to sue: Aeronaves de Mexico, Allegheny Airlines, Philippine Airlines, Air France, Olympic Airways . . . also both the Mississippi and Ohio State Tourist Boards, their lawyers called. They're all very angry, sir. I just thought I should warn you.''

Jeff nodded distractedly. "That's it?" he asked.

"Yes, sir, except for a few more magazines, all trying to arrange an exclusive interview with you or Miss Phillips, or both."

"Any scholarly journals among them?"

She shook her head. "The *National Enquirer, Fate* . . . I guess you could say the most serious of them was *Esquire*."

"Still no word from any of the universities? No research foundations other than this outfit in California, whatever it may be?"

"No, sir. That's the whole list."

"All right." He sighed. "Thank you, Elaine; keep me posted."

"I will, sir." She folded her pad, started to go, then paused. "Mr. Winston . . . I was just wondering . . ."

"Yes?"

"Do you think I ought to get married? I mean, I've been thinking about it, and my boyfriend's asked me twice, but I'd like to know . . . well, I'd like to know whether it would work out or not."

Jeff smiled tolerantly, saw the desperate desire for foresight in the young woman's eyes. "I wish I knew," he told her. "But that's something you're going to have to discover for yourself."

Aeronaves de Mexico dropped its lawsuit on June fifth, the day after one of its jet liners crashed into a mountainside near Monterrey, as Jeff and Pamela had predicted. Mexican political leader Carlos Madrazo and tennis star Rafael Osuna were not on board the plane in which they had died five times before; only eleven people had seen fit to take the doomed flight this time, not seventy-nine.

After that, of the remaining airlines for whom disaster had been foretold, only Air Algerie and Royal Nepal Airlines chose to ignore the warning and not cancel the flights in question. Those two companies suffered the only fatal accidents in all of the world's commercial aviation for the rest of 1969.

The U.S. Navy refused to bow to what Defense Secretary Laird called "superstition," and the destroyer *Evans* proceeded on course in the South China Sea; but the Australian government quietly ordered its aircraft carrier *Melbourne* to cut engines and drop anchor for the first week of June, and the collision that had always sliced the *Evans* in half never happened.

The death toll in the Fourth of July Lake Erie floods in northern Ohio was down from forty-one to five, as residents heeded the highly publicized alerts and sought higher ground before the storms hit. A similar situation prevailed in Mississippi; tourist bookings at the Gulf Coast resorts of Gulfport and Biloxi were down to almost nothing for mid-August, and the local populace fled inland at a rate never before achieved by mere civil-defense warnings. Hurricane Camille struck a nearly deserted coastline, and 138 of her previous 149 victims survived.

Lives changed. Lives went on, where they had never continued before. And the world took note.

"I want an injunction filed now, Mitchell! This week, if we can; the middle of next, at the latest."

The lawyer concentrated on his glasses, polishing the thick lenses with a precision befitting the care that might be taken with an expensive telescope. "I don't know, Jeff," he said. "I'm not sure that'll be possible."

"How soon can we get it, then?" asked Pamela.

"We may not be able to," Wade admitted.

"You mean not at all? These people are free to go on spewing their ridiculous fantasies about us, and there's nothing we can do about it?"

The attorney found another invisible spot on one of his lenses, wiped it away delicately with a little square of chamois. "They may well be acting within their First Amendment rights."

"They're leeching off us!" Jeff exploded, waving the pamphlet that had prompted this meeting. His photograph was prominent on the cover of the booklet, along with a slightly smaller picture of Pamela. "They're profiting from our names and our statements, with no authorization from us, and in the process they're making a mockery of everything we've tried to do."

"They are a nonprofit organization," Wade reminded him. "And they've filed for tax-exempt status as a religious institution. That kind of thing is hard to fight; it takes years, and the chances for beating them are slim."

"What about the libel laws?" Pamela insisted.

"You've made yourselves public figures; that doesn't leave you with much protection. And I'm not sure their comments about you could be construed as libelous, anyway. A jury might even see it as the opposite extreme. These people worship you. They believe you're the incarnation of God on earth. I think you're better off just ignoring them; legal action would only give them more publicity."

Jeff made a wordless exclamation of disgust, crumpled the pamphlet in one hand, and threw it toward the far corner of his office. "This is just the kind of thing we wanted to avoid," he said, fuming. "Even if we ignore it or deny it, it taints us by association. No reputable scientific organization is going to want to have anything to do with us after this."

The lawyer slipped his glasses back on, adjusted them on the bridge of his nose with one thick forefinger. "I understand your dilemma," he told them. "But I don't—"

The intercom on Jeff's desk buzzed in two short bursts followed by a single long one, the signal he had established for notification of an urgent message.

"Yes, Elaine?"

"There's a gentleman here to see you, sir. He says he's with the federal government."

"What branch? Civil defense, the National Science Foundation?"

"The State Department, sir. He insists on speaking with you personally. You and Miss Phillips both."

"Jeff?" Wade frowned. "Want me to sit in on this?"

"Maybe," Jeff told him. "Let's see what he wants." Jeff keyed the intercom again. "Show him in, Elaine."

The man she brought into the office was in his midforties, balding, with alert blue eyes and nicotine-stained fingers. He sized up Jeff with a quick, penetrating glance, did the same to Pamela, then looked at Mitchell Wade.

"I'd prefer we had this talk in private," the man said.

Wade stood, introduced himself. "I'm Mr. Winston's attorney," he said. "I also represent Miss Phillips."

The man pulled a thin billfold from his jacket pocket, handed Wade and Jeff his card. "Russell Hedges, U.S. Department of State. I'm afraid the nature of what I have to discuss here is confidential. Would you mind, Mr. Wade?"

"Yes, I would mind. My clients have a right to—"

"No legal advice is required in this situation," Hedges said. "This concerns a matter of national security."

The attorney started to protest once more, but Jeff stopped him. "It's all right, Mitchell. I'd like to hear him out. Think over what we were talking about before, and let me know if you come up with any workable alternatives; I'll give you a call tomorrow."

"Call me today if you need to," Wade said, casting a scowl at the government representative. "I'll be in my office late, probably till six or six-thirty."

"Thanks. We'll get in touch if necessary."

"Mind if I smoke?" Hedges asked, pulling out a pack of Camels as the lawyer left the room.

"Go right ahead." Jeff motioned him to one of the seats facing the desk and slid an ashtray within his reach. Hedges produced a box of wooden matches, lit his cigarette with one. He let the match burn slowly to a blackened stub, which he dropped, still smoldering, into the large glass ashtray.

"We've been aware of you, of course," Hedges said at length. "Difficult not to be, what with the media spotlight you've been in for the past four months. Though I must admit, most of my colleagues have tended to dismiss your pronouncements as parlor tricks . . . until this week."

"Libya?" Jeff asked, knowing the answer.

Hedges nodded, took a long drag from the cigarette. "Everyone at the Middle East desk is still thunderstruck; our most reliable intelligence assessments indicated King Idris had a thoroughly stable regime. You not only named the date of the coup; you specified that the junta would come from the middle echelons of the Libyan army. I want you to tell me how you knew all that.''

"I've already explained it as clearly as I'm able."

"This business about reliving your life—'' His cool gaze took in Pamela. "Your lives. You can't expect us to believe that, can you?''

"You don't have any choice,'' Jeff said matter-of-factly. "Neither do we. It's happening; that's all we know. The only reason we've made such a spectacle of ourselves this time is because we want to find out more about it. I've made all this very plain before.''

"I expected you'd say that.''

Pamela leaned forward intently. "Surely there are government researchers who could investigate this phenomenon, help us find the answers we're looking for.''

"That's not my department.''

"But you could direct us to them, let them know you're taking us seriously. There are physicists who might—''

"In exchange for what?'' Hedges asked, flicking a long ash from his cigarette.

"I beg your pardon?''

"You're talking about a commitment of funds, manpower, laboratory facilities . . . What would we get in return?''

Pamela pursed her lips, looked at Jeff. "Information,'' she said after a moment's pause. "Advance knowledge of events that will upset the world's economy and lead to the deaths of thousands of innocent people.''

Hedges crushed out the cigarette, his keen blue eyes riveted on hers. "Such as?''

She glanced at Jeff again; his face held no expression, neither approval nor admonishment. "This thing in Libya,'' Pamela told Hedges, "will have disastrous, far-reaching consequences. The man in charge of the junta, Colonel Qaddafi, will appoint himself premier early next year; he's a madman, the most truly evil figure of the next twenty years. He'll turn Libya into a breeding ground, and a haven, for terrorists. Dreadful, unimaginable things will happen because of him.''

Hedges shrugged. "That's awfully vague," he said. "It could be years before those kinds of assertions are proven or disproven. Besides, we're more interested in events in Southeast Asia, not the ups and downs of these little Arab states."

Pamela shook her head decisively. "You're wrong there. Vietnam is a lost cause; it's the Middle East that'll be the pivotal region during the next two decades."

The man looked at her thoughtfully, fished another cigarette from his crumpled pack. "There's a minority faction at State that's expressed just that opinion," he said. "But when you claim our stance in Vietnam is hopeless . . . What about the death of Ho Chi Minh day before yesterday? Won't that weaken the resolve of the NLF? Our analysts say—"

Jeff spoke up. "If anything, it'll strengthen their determination. Ho will be all but canonized, made into a martyr. They'll rename Saigon after him, in—once they've taken the city."

"You were about to name a date," Hedges said, squinting at him through a haze of smoke.

"I think we should be somewhat selective about what we tell you," Jeff said carefully, giving Pamela a cautioning look. "We don't want to add to the world's troubles, just help it avert some of the clear-cut misfortunes."

"I don't know . . . There are still a number of doubting Thomases in the department, and if all you can offer are evasive generalities—"

"Kosygin and Chou En-lai," Jeff declared forcefully. "They'll meet in Peking next week, and early next month the Soviet Union and China will agree to hold formal talks on their border disputes."

Hedges frowned in disbelief. "Kosygin would never visit China."

"He will," Jeff asserted with a tight smile. "And before too long, so will Richard Nixon."

The March wind off Chesapeake Bay stirred the light rain into a fine, chill mist, stopped the scattered droplets in their fall, and whipped them this way and that, into an atmospheric microcosm of the whitecaps that slapped across the choppy bay. Jeff's hooded slicker glistened blackly in the omnipresent moisture as the cold, clear drizzle lashed and trickled invigoratingly across his face.

"What about Allende?" Hedges asked, trying without success to light a sodden Camel. "Does he stand a chance?"

"You mean despite your people's mucking about in Chilean politics?" It had long since become obvious to Jeff and Pamela that Russell Hedges had only the most tenuous connection to the State Department. Whether he was CIA or NSA or something else entirely, they didn't know. It didn't really matter; the end results were the same.

Hedges gave one of his ambiguous half-smiles, managed to get the cigarette going. "You don't have to tell me whether he's actually going to be elected or not, just whether he stands a reasonable chance."

"And if I say he does, then what? He goes the way of Qaddafi?"

"This country had nothing to do with the Qaddafi assassination; I've told you that time and again. It was purely an internal Libyan affair. You know how those third-world power struggles go."

There was no point arguing about it with the man again; Jeff knew damned well that Qaddafi had been killed, before ever taking office, as a direct result of what he and Pamela had told Hedges of the dictator's future policies and actions. Not that Jeff mourned the death of a blood-thirsty maniac like that, but it was widely assumed that the CIA was linked to the murder, and those well-founded rumors had led to the creation of a previously nonexistent terrorist outfit called the November Squad, headed by Qaddafi's younger brother. The group had vowed a life-time of revenge in the name of its slain leader. Already, a massive petroleum fire raged out of control in the desert south of Tripoli, where three months earlier the November Squad had blown up a Mobil Oil installation, killing eleven Americans and twenty-three Libyan employees.

Chile's Allende was no Qaddafi; he was a decent, well-meaning man, the first freely elected Marxist president in history. He would die soon enough as it was, and probably at American instigation. Jeff had no intention of hurrying that shameful day.

"I have nothing to say about Allende one way or the other. He's no threat to the United States. Let's just leave it at that."

Hedges tried to draw on the soggy cigarette, but it had gone out again, and the wet paper had begun to split. He threw it off the wharf and into the restless water with dismay. "You had no such compunctions about telling us Heath will be elected prime minister in England this summer."

Jeff eyed him sardonically. "Maybe I wanted to make sure you didn't decide to have Harold Wilson shot."

"Goddamn it," Hedges spat out, "who set you up as the moral arbiter of U.S. foreign policy? It's your job to supply us with advance information, period. Let the people in charge decide what's important and what's not and how to handle it."

"I've seen the results of some of those decisions before," Jeff said. "I prefer to remain selective about what I reveal. Besides," he added, "this was supposed to be a fair trade. What about your end of the bargain—is any progress being made?"

Hedges coughed, turned his back to the wind off the bay. "Why don't we go back inside, have a warm drink?"

"I like it out here," Jeff said defiantly. "It makes me feel alive."

"Well, I'll be dead of pneumonia if we stay out here much longer. Come on, let's go in and I'll tell you what the scientists have had to say so far."

Jeff relented, and they began walking toward the old government-owned house on the western shore of Maryland, south of Annapolis. They'd been here for six weeks now, conferring on the implications of Rhodesian independence and the coming overthrow of Cambodia's Prince Sihanouk. At first, he and Pamela had regarded their stay here as something of a lark, a vacation of sorts, but Jeff was growing increasingly concerned over the detailed grillings by Hedges, who apparently had been assigned to them as a permanent liaison. They'd been careful not to say anything they felt could be put to harmful use by the Nixon administration, but it was becoming harder to know where to draw the line. Even Jeff's equivocal "no comment" about next fall's elections in Chile might be rightly interpreted by Hedges and his superiors as an indication that Allende would, in fact, win the presidency; and what sort of covert U.S. action might that assumption provoke? They were walking a dangerous tightrope here, and Jeff had begun to regret they'd ever agreed to these meetings at all.

"So?" Jeff asked as they approached the tightly shuttered house, an inviting column of smoke rising from its red brick chimney. "What's the latest word?"

"Nothing definitive from Bethesda yet," Hedges muttered beneath the upturned collar of his raincoat. "They'd like to do some more tests."

"We've had all the medical tests imaginable," Jeff said impatiently, "even before you people got involved. That's not the crux of it; it's something beyond us, something on the cosmic level, or the subatomic. What have the physicists come up with?"

Hedges stepped onto the wooden porch, shook the beads of water from his hat and coat like an overgrown dog. "They're working on it," he told Jeff vaguely. "Berget and Campagna at Cal Tech think it could have to do with pulsars, something about massive neutrino formation . . . but they need more data."

Pamela was waiting in the oak-beamed living room, curled on the sofa in front of a hearty fire. "Hot cider?" she asked, raising her mug and tilting her head with a questioning look.

"Love some," Jeff said, and Hedges nodded his assent.

"I'll get it, Miss Phillips," said one of the dark-suited young men who stood permanent watch over this secluded compound. Pamela shrugged, pulled the sleeves of her bulky sweater up over her wrists, and took a sip from the steaming cup.

"Russell says the physicists may be making some progress," Jeff told her. She brightened, her fire-flushed cheeks radiant against the bunched blue wool of her sweater and the flaxen sheen of her hair.

"What about the skew?" she asked. "Any extrapolation yet?"

Hedges twisted his mouth around a fresh, dry cigarette, lowered his eyelids in a cynical sidelong gaze. Jeff recognized the expression, knew by now that the man held little credence in the notion that they had lived before, would live again. It didn't matter. Hedges and the rest could think whatever they liked, so long as other minds, perceptive and persistent scientific minds, continued to focus on the phenomenon that Jeff knew to be all too real.

"They say the data points are too uncertain," Hedges said. "Best they can come up with is a probable range."

"And what's that range?" Pamela asked quietly, her fingers tense and white around the hot mug.

"Two to five years for Jeff; five to ten in your case. Unlikely it would be any lower than that, they tell me, but the high end could be greater if the curve continues to steepen."

"How much greater?" Jeff wanted to know.

"No way to predict."

Pamela sighed, her breath rising and falling with the wind outside. "That's no better than a guess," she said. "We could have done as well on our own."

"Maybe some of the new tests will—"

"To hell with the new tests!" Jeff barked. "They'll be just as 'inconclusive' as all the others, won't they?"

The taciturn young man in the dark suit returned to the living room with two thick mugs. Jeff took his, stirred it angrily with a fragrant cinnamon stick.

"They want some more tissue samples at Bethesda," Hedges said after a careful sip of the hot cider. "One of the teams there thinks the cellular structure may—"

"We're not going back to Bethesda," Jeff told him with finality. "They have plenty to work with at it is."

"There's no need for you to return to the hospital itself," Hedges explained. "All they need is a few simple skin scrapings. They sent a kit; we can do it right here."

"We're going back to New York. I have a month's

worth of messages I haven't even seen; there might be something useful among them. Can you get us a plane out of Andrews tonight?''

"I'm sorry . . ."

"Well, if there's no government transport available, we'll just take a commercial flight. Pamela, call Eastern Airlines. Ask them what time—"

The man who had brought the cider took a step forward, one hand poised before his open jacket. A second guard came in through the front door as if silently signaled, and a third appeared on the staircase.

"That's not what I meant," Hedges said carefully. "I'm afraid we . . . can't allow you to leave. At all."

≡17≡

". . . ATTEMPTED TO STORM the U.S. embassy in Tehran but were repulsed by units of the Eighty-second Airborne Division, who have surrounded the American diplomatic outpost since last February. At least a hundred and thirty-two Iranian revolutionaries are believed to have been killed in the fighting, and U.S. casualties stand at seventeen dead, twenty-six wounded. President Reagan has ordered new air strikes against rebel bases in the Mountains east of Tabriz, where the Ayatollah Khomeini is believed to be—"

"Turn the damned thing off," Jeff told Russell Hedges.

". . . the revolutionary high command. Here in the United States, the death toll from last week's terrorist bombing at Madison Square Garden has now reached six hundred and eighty-two, and a communique from the so-called November Squad threatens continued attacks on American soil until all U.S. forces are withdrawn from the Middle East. Soviet Foreign Minister Gromyko has declared his nation's 'sympathy with the freedom fighters of the Islamic Jihad,' and Gromyko says the presence of the U.S. Sixth Fleet in the Arabian Sea is 'tantamount to—'"

Jeff leaned forward, snapped off the television set. Hedges shrugged, popped a peppermint Life Saver in his mouth, and fiddled with a pencil, holding it the way he had always held his once-ubiquitous cigarettes.

"What about the Soviet buildup in Afghanistan?" Hedges asked. "Are they planning a confrontation with our forces in Iran?"

"I don't know," Jeff said sullenly.

"How strong are Khomeini's followers? Can we keep the shah in power, at least until next year's elections?"

"I don't fucking know!" Jeff exploded. "How could I? Reagan wasn't even president before, not in 1979; this was Jimmy Carter's mess to deal with, and we never sent troops to Iran. Everything's changed. I don't know what the hell's going to happen now."

"Surely you must have some idea whether—"

"I don't. I have no idea at all." He looked at Pamela, who sat glaring at Hedges. Her face was drawn, pale; in these few years it had lost its feminine roundness, become almost as angular as Jeff's own. He took her hand, pulled her to her feet. "We're going for a walk," he told Hedges.

"I still have some more questions."

"Stuff your questions. I'm all out of answers."

Hedges sucked at the Life Saver, regarded Jeff with those cold blue eyes. "All right," he said. "We'll talk more over dinner."

Jeff started to tell him yet again that it wouldn't do any good, that the world was off on a strange and undefined new course now, about which neither he nor Pamela could offer any advice, but he knew the protestation would be pointless. Hedges still assumed they had some sort of psychic ability, that they could predict future events based on any set of current circumstances. As their foreknowledge had begun to dissipate in the face of drastically altered world events, he'd silently but clearly blamed them for withholding information. Even the sodium pentothal and polygraph sessions they'd been subjected to yielded little useful data these days, but they'd stopped objecting to the drug interrogations; maybe, they thought, as the value of their answers declined they'd be left alone, perhaps someday even be released from this lengthy "protective custody." That was an unlikely hope, they both knew, though they still clung to it; it was better than the alternative, which was to accept the obvious truth that they were here to stay until they died again.

The water was calm and blue today, and as they walked along the dunes they could see the hump of Poplar Island off the Eastern Shore. A clutch of boats trolled among the marker buoys, working the rich Chesapeake Bay oyster beds. Jeff and Pamela took what comfort they could from the deceptive serenity of the familiar scene and did their best to ignore the pairs of dark-suited men who kept pace a steady twenty yards ahead of and behind them.

"Why don't we lie to him?" Pamela asked. "Tell him there'll be a war if we maintain our military presence in Iran. Christ, for all we know there may be one."

Jeff stooped to pick up a slender stick of driftwood. "They'd see through it, particularly when they put us on the pentothal."

"We could still try."

"But who knows what effect a lie like that would have? Reagan might even decide to launch a preemptive strike. We could end up starting a war that may still be avoided."

Pamela shuddered. "Stuart McCowan must be happy," she said bitterly, "wherever he is."

"We did what we thought was right. No one could have predicted this sort of outcome. And it hasn't been all bad; we've saved a lot of lives, too."

"You can't put human life on a balance sheet like that!"

"No, but—"

"They won't even do anything about the storms and the plane crashes anymore," she said with disgust, kicking at a clump of sand. "They want everybody, particularly the Soviets, to think we just disappeared, so they keep on letting all those people die . . . needlessly!"

"Just as they've always died before."

She spun toward him, her face full of a rage he had never seen in her. "That doesn't cut it, Jeff! We were supposed to be making the world a better, safer place this time—but all we really cared about was ourselves, finding out how much longer our own precious little lives were going to be extended; and we haven't even been able to do that.''

''It's still possible that the scientists will come up with a—''

''I don't give a shit! When I look at the news, all the death we've caused by what we've told Hedges: the terrorist attacks, the military actions, maybe even a full-scale war coming . . . When I see that, I wish—I wish I'd never made that goddamned movie, I wish you'd never come to Los Angeles and found me!''

Jeff tossed the stick of driftwood away, looked at her in pained disbelief. ''You don't mean that,'' he said.

''Yes I do! I'm sorry I ever met you!''

''Pamela, please—''

Her hands were shaking, her face was red with anger. ''I'm not talking to Hedges anymore. I don't want to talk to you anymore, either. I'm moving into one of the rooms on the third floor. You can tell them any fucking thing you like; go ahead, get us in a war, blow the whole damned planet up!''

She turned and ran, slipped awkwardly in the sand and found her footing again, dashed toward the house that was their prison. One of the teams of guards raced after her, the other closed in on either side of Jeff. He watched her go, watched the men escort her back inside the house; Hedges was at the door, and Jeff could hear her shouting at him, but a gust of summer wind from off the bay swallowed up her words, drowned out the meaning of her cries.

He awoke in a current of cold, synthetic-smelling air. Sharp, thin rays of brilliant sunlight sliced through half-closed slats of venetian blinds on the nearby window, illuminating the sparsely furnished bedroom. A portable stereo sat silent on the floor in front of the bed, and an old cassette recorder and microphone with a WIOD logo lay cushioned on a pile of clothes on the dresser.

Jeff heard a distant chime over the hum of the air conditioner, recognized it as a doorbell; whoever it was would go away if he ignored it. He glanced at the book in his hands: *The Algiers Motel Incident,* by John Hersey. Jeff tossed it aside, swung his feet off the bed, and went to the window. He lifted one of the white slats of the blinds, peered out, and saw a tall stand of royal palms; beyond them there was nothing but flat marshland, all the way to the horizon.

The doorbell rang again, and then he heard the approaching whine of a jet, saw it glide past a few hundred yards behind the palm trees. Landing at Fort Lauderdale–Hollywood International, Jeff realized. This was his apartment in Dania, a mile from the beach and too close to the airport, but it had been the first place he could really call his own, his first wholly private living quarters as an adult. He'd been working at his first full-time news job, in Miami, beginning his career.

He took a deep breath of the stale, chilled air, sat back down on the rumpled bed. He'd died on schedule, at six minutes past one on October eighteenth, 1988; there'd been no all-out war, not yet, though the world had been—

The doorbell sounded again, a long ring this time, insistent. Goddamn it, why wouldn't they just go away? It stopped, then rang immediately a fourth time. Jeff pulled on a T-shirt and a pair of denim cut-offs from the heap of clothes on the dresser, stalked angrily from the room to get rid of whoever was at the door. As he walked into the living room a motionless wall of sweltering, humid air hit him; must be something wrong with the air conditioner in here, that was why he'd been in the bedroom in the middle of the day. Even the broad-leafed fern in the corner was limp, yielding to the force of the claustrophobic heat. Jeff pulled open the door just as the bell began its urgent chime once more.

Linda stood there, smiling, the golden streaks in her waves of russet hair highlighted by the sun behind her. His wife, once-wife, his wife-not-yet: Linda, beaming with the undisguised extravagance of her fresh-born love for him, and in her outstretched hand a bunch of daisies. All the daisies in the world, it seemed, and on that sweetly unforgotten face shone all the ardent bliss and generosity of youth.

Jeff felt his eyes brim with tears, but he couldn't look away from her, couldn't even bring himself to blink for fear of losing one precious instant of this vision that had lived in his memory for so many decades and now stood recreated in all its loving radiance before him. So long, it had been so goddamned long . . .

"Aren't you gonna ask me in?" she asked, her girlish voice at once coy and inviting.

"Ahh . . . sure. Yes, I'm sorry, come on in. This is . . . wonderful. The flowers are great. Thank you. So unexpected."

"Have you got something to put them in? God, it's hotter in here than it is outside!"

"The air conditioner's broken, I—Just a minute, let me see if I can find something for the flowers." He glanced distractedly around the room, trying to remember if he'd owned a vase.

"Maybe in the kitchen?" Linda said helpfully.

"Yeah, that's a good idea, let me just check in there. You want a beer, a Coke?"

"Some ice water would be fine." She followed him to the cramped little kitchen, dug out a vase for the daisies as he poured her a tall glass of water from a pitcher he found in the refrigerator. "Thanks," she said, fanning herself with her open hand as Jeff took the flowers. "Could we open some windows or something?"

"The air conditioner's working fine in my room; why don't we go in there?"

"O.K. Better put the flowers in there, too. They'll wilt in this heat."

In the bedroom he set the daisies on a nightstand, watched her pirouette before the vents of the air conditioner, her bare skin in the backless sundress gleaming with jewels of perspiration. "Oooh, this feels nice!" she said, raising her slim arms above her head, her small, firm breasts rising beneath the thin white dress as she did so.

They'd done exactly this before, Jeff recalled: found the vase for the flowers, come into his room to stay cool, she'd twirled and posed in just that way . . . how long ago? Lifetimes gone, worlds past.

Her wide brown eyes, the liquid warmth in them as she looked at him: Jesus, no one had looked at him that way for years. Pamela had secluded herself on the top floor of the government house in Maryland as she'd threatened, had coolly averted her gaze from him on the rare occasions when she'd joined the rest of them for dinner. The eyes Jeff best remembered from the past nine years were the dangerous blue orbs of Russell Hedges, staring at him with increasing malice as the world slid into its hellish morass of terrorist attacks and border skirmishes and U.S.–Soviet confrontations of which Jeff knew nothing, could predict nothing.

What would become of that drastically altered world now, Jeff wondered, if it continued on its own divergent time line, followed the course he and Pamela had, with all good intentions, inadvertently set for it? A state of martial law had existed in the United States for three years already, in the aftermath of the November Squad's destruction of the Golden Gate Bridge and the massacre at the United Nations Building. The 1988 presidential election had been indefinitely postponed because of the newly imposed restrictions on large public gatherings, and the heads of the three major intelligence agencies were effectively in control of the country "for the duration of the emergency."

It had seemed likely that a fascist American state was in the making, which of course had been the goal of the international terrorist underground from the beginning. Its members had wanted nothing more than to bring on a genuinely oppressive regime in the United States, one that even ordinary citizens might consider fighting to overthrow. Unless, of course, the militantly anticommunist CIA/NSA/FBI troika that ran the interim government first decided to bring on the worldwide nuclear conflict that had been threatening to erupt since the late seventies.

Linda stood with her naked silken back against the cool rush of air, her eyes closed and one hand holding her hair high on her head to expose her slender neck to the soothing flow. The shafts of light from the blinds showed the stretch of her dancer's legs through the sun-sheer white dress.

Pamela had been right to turn on him, Jeff thought with anguish; right to denounce them both for what they'd set in motion, however unwittingly or altruistically. In making themselves known to the world and in dealing with the government in exchange for the paltry information they had received, they had sown the seeds of a vicious whirlwind that some other world must now reap. It remained to be seen whether she—or either of them, for that matter—would ever be able to forgive themselves for the brutal global violence they had wrought in the name of benevolence and understanding. . . . And it would be years, perhaps a decade or more, before he would even have the opportunity to try to talk to her again, to attempt some reconciliation of their personal estrangement and to come to terms with the tragic totality of their failure to improve mankind's lot. That world was lost, as surely as Pamela was now lost to him for unknown years to come, perhaps forever.

"Tickle me," Linda said in her sweet, clear voice, and for a moment Jeff didn't know what she meant. Then he remembered the delicate touch she once had relished, the slow, gentle trailing of his fingertips across her skin, so lightly it was almost not a touch at all. He took a daisy from the bunch that she had given him, used its feathery petals to trace an imaginary line from her ear along her neck and shoulder, down her right arm, and then back up her left.

"Ooh, so good," she whispered. "Here, do it here." She loosened the thin shoulder straps of her dress, let it fall away from her youthful breasts. Jeff caressed her with the flower, bent to kiss each nipple as it came erect. "Oh, I love that." Linda sighed. "I love you!"

And on this perfect, twice-lived day he took his needed solace in the unquestioning passion and affection of this woman with whom those feelings had been so long denied. In her love for him, his refound love for her, he lived again.

The citrine streaks in Linda's hair had been lightened to an even paler yellow by the days in the Moroccan sun, making it seem as if her hair were reflecting the imagined light from the great gold sunburst tapestry behind the lengthy bar. She clutched at the bar's railing, laughing, as the ship rolled gently in the North Atlantic swells. Her gin and tonic began to slide across the tilting oaken surface, and she caught it with a deft move, the ice in the glass tinkling with her laughter.

"Encore, madame?" the bartender asked.

Linda turned to Jeff. "Do you want another drink?"

He shook his head, finished his Jack Daniel's and soda. "Why don't we take a walk out on the deck? It's a warm night; I'd like to look at the ocean." He signed the bar tab with their cabin number, handed it to the bartender. *"Merci, Raymond; à demain."*

"À demain, monsieur; merci."

Jeff took Linda's arm, and they walked through the slightly swaying Riviera Bar and out onto the Veranda Deck. The striking red-and-black smokestacks of the S.S. *France* jutted above them into the night sky, their sleek horizontal fins like the immobile flippers of two gigantic whales frozen in mid-leap. The great ship rose into an oncoming swell, dipped smoothly into the trough between the immense but steady waves. The stars above were unobscured by clouds, but far to the south a line of thunderheads lit the horizon with constant bursts of lightning. The storm was moving this way, though at thirty knots they'd be clear of the tempest before its violent winds and pelting rain reached this stretch of ocean.

Heyerdahl, Jeff thought, wouldn't have the luxury of escaping such a random fury; he'd see the coming storm with different eyes, wary and concerned at the tiller of his little papyrus boat, so far from land. It was just such a storm that had stopped him last year, forced him to abandon his damaged craft in heavy seas, six hundred miles short of his goal.

"Do you really think he'll make it this time?" Linda asked, staring at the jaggedly illumined clouds in the distance. She'd been thinking the same thing, wondering about the fate of the affable bearded Norwegian with whom they'd shared the labors and accomplishments of the past three weeks in the ancient fortressed port of Safi, where he'd built—and had last week launched—his historic, purposefully primitive little boat.

"He'll make it," Jeff said with assurance.

Linda's filmy dress fluttered in the wind from the approaching storm, and she held tightly to the ship's railing. "Why does he fascinate you so?" she wanted to know.

"For the same reason Michael Collins and Richard Gordon fascinate me," he told her. And Roosa, he could have added, and Worden and Mattingly and Evans, and the POWs who'd start returning three years from now, in 1973. "The isolation, the utter apartness from the rest of humanity . . ."

"But Heyerdahl has a seven-man crew with him," she pointed out. "Collins and Gordon were completely alone in those capsules, for a while, anyway."

"Sometimes isolation can be shared," Jeff said, looking at the billowing ocean. The warm smell of the oncoming tropical disturbance made him think of the Mediterranean, of a day when that same scent had drifted through the open window of a villa in Majorca. The peppery savor of paella, the lacerating wistfulness of Laurindo Almeida's guitar, the mingled joy and grief in Pamela's eyes, her dying eyes.

Linda saw the shadow that had crossed Jeff's face, and she moved her hand to his, gripped it as firmly as she had the ship's railing. "I worry about you sometimes," she said. "All this talk about loneliness and isolation . . . I don't know if this project is such a good idea. It seems like it's getting you too depressed."

He pulled her to him, kissed the top of her head. "No," he reassured her with a smile full of affection, "it's not depressing me. Just making me thoughtful, that's all."

But that wasn't entirely true, he knew; his meditative state had brought about the undertaking that obsessed him now, not the reverse. Linda's presence, her unaccustomed loving openness, had calmed his battered senses since that day in August 1968 when he had resumed this life to find her waiting at his door with an armful of fresh-cut daisies. But not even the unexpected rebirth of all they'd shared so long ago had been enough to make him forget the torments he had indirectly inflicted on the world through Russell Hedges in that previous life, or the estrangement all of that had forced between him and Pamela. Guilt and remorse were inescapable; they formed an unremitting undercurrent that seemed to constantly erode the foundations of his resurrected love for the woman he once had married. And that ongoing diminution led to new modes of remorse, a present guilt made all the worse by his conviction that he should be able to change his feelings, let go the past and give himself as fully to Linda as she now did to him.

He'd immediately quit his reporter's job at WIOD in Miami, couldn't stomach the daily task of seeking and observing and describing human tragedy, not after all he held himself responsible for during those dead years at the government retreat in Maryland. That October, Jeff had waited until Detroit was down three games to one; then he'd put his savings on the Tigers to sweep the last three games of the Series. Mickey Lolich had brought it home for him, as Jeff had known he would.

The stake had enabled him to get a new apartment on the water at Pompano Beach, closer to where Linda still lived with her parents and attended college. He'd met her every afternoon when she was done with classes, swam with her in the gentle ocean or sat beside her by the pool at his place as she studied. She'd moved in with him that spring, told her parents she was "getting a place of my own." They endured the fiction, never visited the tenth-floor oceanfront apartment that Jeff and Linda shared, and continued to welcome him into their home for Sunday dinner every week.

It had been that summer, 1969, when he'd conceived the project that now consumed him. Linda's father had planted the seed in his mind one Sunday evening over coffee at the dinner table. Jeff's habit by then had become to ignore the news, to politely tune out any discussion of national or world events. But that week, his former father-in-law had seized on a single topic, wouldn't let it go: the just-aborted voyage of Thor Heyerdahl and the Norseman's quixotic attempt to prove that early explorers, sailing in papyrus-reed boats, could have brought Egyptian culture to the Americas more than three thousand years before Columbus.

Linda's father had ridiculed the concept, dismissing Heyerdahl's near-success as outright failure, and Jeff had kept quiet his knowledge that the adventurer-anthropologist would triumph with a second expedition one year later. Still, the conversation set him thinking, and that night he had lain awake until dawn, listening to the churning surf beneath his apartment windows and envisioning himself adrift on that dark sea in a flimsy vessel of his own making, a fragile craft that might succumb to this year's storms but would return to vanquish the ocean that had claimed it.

That same month he and Linda had driven up to the Cape, as they had before, to witness the controlled fury of the massive *Saturn V* rocket that lifted *Apollo 11* to the moon. After the launch, as they'd inched their way back down the already overdeveloped Gold Coast with a hundred thousand other cars full of spectators, Jeff's mind was filled with thoughts of insularity, of removal from the day-to-day affairs of humankind. Not the sort of seclusion and retreat that he had once sought in Montgomery Creek, but a *voyage* of isolation, an epic journey of aloneness toward a goal as yet unproven.

Heyerdahl knew that feeling, Jeff was certain, as did the crew of the mission they had just watched depart, and none among that crew more than Michael Collins. Armstrong, and to a lesser extent Aldrin, would receive the glory, take those historic first steps, speak the garbled first words, plant the flag in lunar soil. . . . But for those dramatic hours that his crewmates were on the surface of the moon, Michael Collins would be more alone than anyone had ever been: a quarter of a million miles from earth, in orbit around an alien world, the nearest humans somewhere beneath him on that hostile demi-planet. When his command module took him past the moon's far side, Collins wouldn't even have radio contact with his fellow beings, would be unable even to see the faraway blue-and-white globe of his birth. He would face the bleak infinity of space in an utter solitude and silence that only five other human beings would ever experience.

Jeff had known then, as he sat stalled in that thirty-mile traffic jam on U.S. Highway 1 near Melbourne, that he must meet these men, must understand them. Thereby, perhaps, he would come to a better understanding of himself and the solitary voyage through time that he and Pamela had been thrust upon.

The following week he'd begun the first of many trips to Houston. On the strength of his Earl Warren interview the previous year, Jeff persuaded NBC to help him obtain NASA press credentials as a freelance journalist. He interviewed and gradually befriended Stuart Roosa and, through him, Richard Gordon and Alfred Worden and the others. Even Michael Collins proved relatively accessible; the world's attention and adulation remained focused on the men who had actually set foot on the moon, not on the one who had been, and the others who would be, left behind in lunar orbit.

What had begun as a personal quest for insight into his own state of mind soon grew beyond that. For the first time in many years, Jeff was applying his talents as a journalist, delving skillfully into the thoughts and memories of his subjects, interviewing them best at moments when they had ceased to think of the conversation as an interview, when they had let down their guard in the face of his obviously genuine interest and begun to speak with him on a deeply human level. Pathos, humor, anger, fear: Jeff somehow elicited from these men the fully textured range of emotions that the astronauts had never before revealed. And he knew that their special vision of the universe was part of something he could no longer keep to himself, but had to communicate to the world at large.

He'd written to Heyerdahl that autumn, arranged the first of several meetings with the explorer in Norway, then in Morocco. As the initial impulse that had led Jeff to seek out these special individuals expanded in his mind, as the images and feelings that he gleaned from them took on a power of their own, he realized at last what he was unconsciously but determinedly developing: a book about himself, using the metaphor of these separate lonely voyagers as a means to grapple with his own unique experience, to explain the marbled tapestry of his accumulated gains and losses and regrets.

A fresh chain of lightning illuminated the far-off storm clouds, its dim white reflection playing across the contours of Linda's angelic face.

And joys, he thought, tracing his fingertips lightly across her cheek as she smiled up at him. He must communicate the joys, as well.

Jeff's writing room, like most of the other rooms in the house at Hillsboro Beach, south of Boca Raton, had a view of the ocean. He'd come to rely on the constancy of that sight and the unending sound of the surf, much as he had once been so drawn to the white-peaked vision of Mount Shasta from his place in Montgomery Creek. It soothed him, anchored him, except on the nights when the moon would rise from the ocean, reminding him of a certain film that remained unmade in this world and of a time best left forgotten.

He pressed the foot pedal of the Sony dictating machine, and the deep resonance of the heavily Russian-accented voice on the tape was evident even through the little playback unit's tinny speaker. Jeff was midway through transcribing this interview, and each time he heard the voice he could picture the man's surprisingly modest home in Zurich, the plates of *blini* and caviar, the well-chilled bottle of pepper vodka on the table between them. And the words, the outpouring of eloquent world sorrow interspersed with unexpected gems of wit and even laughter from the husky man with the unmistakable red-fringed beard. Many times during that week of intensely expressed wisdom in Switzerland, Jeff had been tempted to tell the man how fully he shared his grief, how well he understood the sense of impotent rage against the irrecoverable. But he hadn't, of course. Couldn't. He'd held his tongue, played the callow if insightful interviewer, and merely recorded the great man's thoughts; left him alone in his pain, as Jeff was alone in his.

There was a tentative knock on the door, and Linda called to him: "Honey? Want to take a break?"

"Sure," he said, turning off the typewriter and the tape machine. "Come on in."

She opened the door, came in balancing a tray with two slices of Key lime pie and two cups of Jamaica Blue Mountain coffee. "Sustenance." She grinned.

"Mmmm." Jeff inhaled the dark aroma of the coffee, the cool tang of the fresh lime pie. "More than that. *Infinitely* more than that."

"How's the Solzhenitsyn material coming?" Linda asked, sitting cross-legged on the oversized ottoman next to his desk with the tray in her lap.

"Excellent. I've got a lot to work with here, and it's all so good I don't even know where to start cutting or paraphrasing."

"It's better than the stuff you got from Thieu?"

"Much better," he said between bites of the excruciatingly delicious pie. "There are enough good quotes in the Thieu material to make it worth including, but this is going to form the backbone of the book. I'm really excited about it."

With good reason, Jeff knew; this new project had been forming in his mind ever since he'd begun writing the first book, the one about Heyerdahl and the lunar-orbit astronauts. That had been a modest critical and commercial success when it was published, two years ago, in 1973. He felt sure that this one, for which his research was almost complete now, would surpass even the best segments of his earlier work.

He would write, this time, of enforced exile, of banishment from home and country and one's fellow men. In that topic, he felt he could find and convey a core of universal empathy, a spark of understanding rising from that metaphoric exile to which all of us are subject, and that Jeff grasped more than anyone before him: our common and inevitable expulsion from the years that we have lived and put behind us, from the people we have been and known and have forever lost.

The lengthy musings Jeff had elicited from Alexander Solzhenitsyn—about his exile, not about the Gulag—were, as he'd told Linda, unquestionably the most profound of all the observations he had gathered to date. The book would also include material from his correspondence with deposed Cambodian Prince Sihanouk, and his interviews in both Madrid and Buenos Aires with Juan Perón, as well as the reflections he had garnered from Nguyen Van Thieu after the fall of Saigon. Jeff had even spoken with the Ayatollah Khomeini at his sanctuary outside Paris. To ensure that the book was fully democratized, he had sought the comments of dozens of ordinary political refugees, men and women who had fled dictatorial regimes of both the right and the left.

The notes and tapes he had amassed overflowed with powerful, deeply moving narratives and sentiments. The task Jeff now faced was to distill the essence of those millions of heartfelt words, to maximize their raw power by paring them to the bone and juxtaposing them in the most effective context. *Harps upon the Willows,* he planned to call it, from the hundred and thirty-seventh psalm:

> By the rivers of Babylon,
> there we sat down, yea, we wept,
> when we remembered Zion.
> We hung our harps upon the
> willows in the midst thereof . . .
> How shall we sing the Lord's
> song in a strange land?

Jeff finished his Key lime pie, set the plate aside, and sipped the heady richness of the fresh-brewed Jamaican coffee.

"How long do you think—" Linda began to ask, but her question was interrupted by the sharp ring of the phone on his desk.

"Hello?" he answered.

"Hello, Jeff," said the voice he'd known through three separate lifetimes.

He didn't know what to say. He'd thought of this moment so many times in the past eight years, dreaded it, longed for it, come to half-believe it might never arrive. Now that it was here, he found himself temporarily mute, all his carefully rehearsed opening words flown from his mind like vanished wisps of cloud in the wind.

"Are you free to talk?" Pamela asked.

"Not really," Jeff said, looking uncomfortably at Linda. She had seen the change in his expression, he could tell, and was regarding him curiously but without suspicion.

"I understand," Pamela told him. "Should I call back later, or could we meet somewhere?"

"That would be better."

"Which? Calling back later?"

"No. No, I think we ought to get together, sometime soon."

"Can you get to New York?" she asked.

"Yes. Any time. When and where?"

"This Thursday, is that all right?"

"No problem," he said.

"Thursday afternoon, then, at . . . the Pierre? The bar there?"

"That sounds fine. Two o'clock?"

"Three would be better for me," Pamela said. "I have an appointment on the West Side at one."

"All right. I—I'll see you Thursday."

Jeff hung up, could sense how pale and shaken he must look. "That was . . . an old friend from college, Martin Bailey," he lied, hating himself for it.

"Oh, right, your roommate. Is something wrong?" The concern in her voice, on her face, was genuine.

"He and his wife are having bad problems. It looks like they may get a divorce. He's pretty upset about it, needs somebody to talk to. I'm going up to Atlanta for a couple of days to see if I can help."

Linda smiled, sympathetically, innocently, but Jeff felt no relief that she had so readily believed the impromptu falsehood. He felt only guilt, a sharp, almost physical stab of it. And, intensifying that guilt, a rush of undeniable elation that he would be seeing Pamela again, in only three days' time.

≡18≡

JEFF TOOK THE elevator down from his room at the Pierre at 2:20, turned left, and walked past the gray Italian marble with brass inlays that marked the entrance to the Café Pierre. He found a quiet table toward the back of the long, narrow bar, ordered a drink, and waited nervously, watching the entrance. So many memories he had of this hotel: He and Sharla had watched most of that pivotal 1963 World Series from a room here, near the beginning of his first replay, and he'd stayed here frequently in the decades past, most often with Pamela.

She walked in at five minutes before three. Her straight blond hair was just as he'd remembered it, her eyes the same. Her generous lips were set in a familiar expression of seriousness, but without the bitter, downturned tightness he had seen her mouth take on during those final years in Maryland. She was wearing delicate emerald earrings to match her eyes, a white fox fur . . . and a light gray, stylishly tailored maternity dress. Pamela was five months pregnant, maybe six.

She came to the table, took Jeff's hands in hers, and held them for a long, quiet moment. He glanced down, saw the plain gold wedding ring.

"Welcome back," he said as she sat down across from him. "You . . . look lovely."

"Thank you," she said carefully, her eyes on the table-top. A waiter hovered; she ordered a glass of white wine. The silence lingered until the wine was set before her. She sipped it, then began rubbing the cocktail napkin between her fingers.

Jeff smiled, remembering. "You going to shred that?" he asked lightly.

Pamela looked up at him, smiled back. "Maybe," she said.

"When—" he began, and stopped.

"When what? When did I start replaying again, or when am I due?"

"Both, I guess. However you want to start."

"I've been back for two months, Jeff."

"I see." It was he who turned away this time, stared at one of the gold sconces against the satin drapes.

Pamela reached across the table, touched his arm. "I couldn't bring myself to call, don't you understand? Not just because of the differences we'd had last time, but . . . because of this. It was a tremendous emotional shock for me."

He softened, looked back into her eyes. "I'm sorry," he said. "I know it must have been."

"I was in a children's clothing shop in New Rochelle. Buying baby clothes. My little boy, Christopher—he's three—was with me. And then I felt my belly and I knew, and . . . I just broke down. I started sobbing, and of course that frightened Christopher. He started to cry and call out, 'Mommy, Mommy' . . ."

Pamela's voice cracked, and she dabbed at her eyes with the napkin. Jeff took her hand, stroked it until she regained her composure.

"This is Kimberly that I'm carrying," she said at last, quietly. "My daughter. She'll be born in March. March eighteenth, 1976. It'll be a beautiful day, more like late April or early May, really. Her name means 'from the royal meadow,' and I always used to say she brought the springtime with her."

"Pamela . . ."

"I never thought I'd see them again. You can't imagine—
not even you can imagine what this has been like for me,
what it still is like, and will be for the next eleven, almost
twelve, years. Because I love them more than ever, and
this time I *know* I'm going to lose them."

She started to weep again, and Jeff knew there was
nothing he could say to make it easier. He thought of what
it would be like to hold his daughter Gretchen in his arms
again, to watch her playing in the garden of the house in
Dutchess County, all the while aware of the very day and
hour when she would disappear from his life again. Impossible bliss, incalculable heartbreak, and never a hope of
separating one from the other. Pamela was right; the unbearable, ever-constant wrenching of those paired emotions was beyond even his acutely developed empathetic
powers.

After a time she excused herself from the table, went to
stanch the tears in private. When she returned her face was
dry, her light makeup newly applied and immaculate. Jeff
had ordered a fresh glass of wine for her, another drink for
himself.

"What about you?" she asked dispassionately. "When
did you come back this time?"

He hesitated, cleared his throat. "I was in Miami," he
said. "In 1968."

Pamela thought that over for a moment, gave him a
perceptive look. "With Linda," she said.

"Yes."

"And now?"

"We're still together. Not married, not yet, but . . . we
live together."

She smiled a wistful, knowing smile, ran her finger
along the rim of the wineglass. "And you're happy."

"I am," he admitted. "We both are."

"Then I'm glad for you," Pamela said. "I mean that."

"It's been different this time," he elaborated. "I had a
vasectomy, so she'll never have to go through the difficulties she once had with pregnancy. We may adopt a child. I
could handle that; I did before, when I was married to

Judy, and it wasn't the same as . . . You know what I mean.'' Jeff paused for an instant, regretting having raised the issue of children again, then went on hurriedly. ''The financial security has helped our relationship considerably,'' he said. ''I haven't bothered to go all-out with the investments, but we're quite comfortable. Very nice house on the ocean; we travel a lot. And I'm writing now, doing some very rewarding work. It's been a kind of healing process for me, even more so than the time I spent alone in Montgomery Creek.''

''I know,'' she said. ''I read your book; it was quite moving. It helped me put away so much of what went wrong between us the last time, all that bitterness.''

''You—That's right, I keep forgetting you've been replaying for two months already. Thank you; I'm glad you liked it. The one I'm working on right now is about exile; I've interviewed Solzhenitsyn, Peron. . . . I'll send you an advance copy when it's done.''

She lowered her eyes, put a hand to her chin. ''I'm not sure that would be a good idea.''

It took Jeff a moment to catch her meaning. ''Your husband?''

Pamela nodded. ''It's not that he's an overly jealous man, but . . . Oh, God, how can I say this? It would require too many explanations if you and I remained in touch, started writing and phoning and seeing each other. Don't you see how awkward that would be?''

''Do you love him?'' Jeff asked, swallowing hard.

''Not the way you obviously love Linda,'' she said, her voice steady but cool. ''Steve's a decent man; he cares for me in his own way. But mainly it's the children I'm thinking of. Christopher's only three, and Kimberly's not even born yet. I couldn't take them away from their father before they even had a chance to know him.'' A sudden fire of anger flared in her eyes, but then she dampened it. ''Even if you wanted me to,'' she added.

''Pamela . . .''

''I can't resent your feelings for Linda,'' she said. ''We've been apart too long for me to turn possessive, and I know how much it must mean to you to have that work out positively, after the problems you and she had the first time.''

"That doesn't change anything about the way I feel for you.''

"I know,'' she said gently. "It has nothing to do with us, but it's real, and right now it takes priority for you. Just as I need this time with my children, my family; I need it desperately.''

"You're not still angry about—''

"Everything that happened last time, with Russell Hedges? No. Not angry at you; we both set that in motion and did what we thought was best. There were so many times, during those last few months particularly, that I wanted to turn to you, apologize for having blamed you . . . but I was stubborn. I couldn't handle all the guilt I felt. I had to saddle someone else with it to protect my own sanity, and that should have been Hedges, not you. I'm sorry.''

"I understand,'' he told her. "I did then, too, though it was difficult.''

The longing in her eyes, the deep regret, mirrored his own emotions. "It'll be even harder now,'' she said, covering his hand with her smooth palms. "It's going to take a lot of understanding, on both our parts.''

The gallery was on Chambers Street in TriBeCa, the Triangle Below Canal Street, which had replaced Soho as Manhattan's primary artists' enclave. Since the mid-eighties, though, the same process that had led to the exodus from Soho had begun anew in TriBeCa: Trendy bars and restaurants were sprouting on the side streets off Hudson and Varick, the prices in the shops and galleries had begun to reflect the spending power of their uptown patrons, and loft space was at a premium. Soon the young painters and sculptors and performance artists whose presence had set in motion the flowering of this once-desolate corner of the city would be driven out to some new bohemia, some thoroughly undesirable, and thus affordable, sector of this congested island.

Jeff spotted the understated brass plaque that identified the Hawthorne Gallery, and led Linda through the doorway of the renovated building that had once been a tenement next to an industrial warehouse. They came into an elegantly sparse reception area, white walls and ceiling, a low black sofa facing a curved black desk. The only decoration was a surprisingly delicate piece of hanging ironwork, its elongated slender swirls like a distillation and extension of the intricate iron filigree typical of the gates and balconies of old New Orleans.

"May I help you?" asked the whippet-thin young woman behind the desk.

"We're here for the opening," Jeff said, handing her the embossed invitation.

"Certainly," she said, consulting a printed list and crossing off their names. "Go right in, won't you?"

Jeff and Linda walked past the desk, into the main gallery space. The walls were the same stark white, but devoted to the display of what might have seemed a riot of images, had their placement not been subject to such careful design. The one huge room had been subdivided here and there into intimate little alcoves suited to quiet study of the contemplative pieces they contained, while at the other extreme the full grandeur of the larger works was enhanced by the openness of the areas in which they were exhibited.

The gallery was dominated by a twenty-foot canvas of an undersea vista that could exist only in the imagination of the artist: a serene mountain peak far beneath the waves, its unmistakably distinctive symmetry undimmed, the snows upon its heights undisturbed by the waters that surrounded it. A school of dolphins swam among the crevasses of its lower slopes; looking closer, Jeff could see that two of the dolphins had ageless, clearly human eyes.

"It's . . . stunning," Linda said. "And look, look at that one over there."

Jeff turned to see where she had pointed. The smaller painting there was no less striking than the image of that drowned mountain; this one depicted the view from within a sailplane, stretched as if by a wide-angle lens to encompass a one-hundred-and-eighty-degree field of vision. In the foreground, the rudder stick and struts of the plane were visible; through the windows, another glider could be seen close by . . . and both were soaring, not through blue sky, but in the infinity of space, in orbit around a dusky-orange ringed planet.

"I'm glad you could come," Jeff heard a voice behind him say.

The years had been kind to her this time. There was none of the drawn, haggard emptiness that had haunted her face in Maryland, and in New York after they had first met Stuart McCowan. Though she was unambiguously a woman in her late thirties, her face shone with the clear light of contentment.

"Linda, I'd like you to meet Pamela Phillips. Pamela, this is my wife, Linda."

"I'm so pleased to meet you," Pamela said, taking Linda's hand. "You're even lovelier than Jeff had told me."

"Thank you. I can't tell you how impressed I am by your work; it's absolutely magnificent."

Pamela smiled graciously. "That's always nice to hear. You should look at some of the smaller pieces, too; they're not all quite so imposing or austere. Some of them are even quite humorous, I think."

"I look forward to seeing the whole show," Linda said eagerly. "It was kind of you to invite us."

"I'm happy you could make it up from Florida. I've been an admirer of your husband's books for years, even before we met last month. I thought he and you might enjoy seeing some of the things I've been doing."

Pamela turned toward a knot of people who stood nearby, sipping wine and nibbling from small plates of pasta salad with pine nuts and pesto sauce. "Steve," she called, "come on over; there are some people I'd like you to meet."

A friendly-looking man wearing glasses and a gray twill jacket detached himself from the group and moved to join them. "This is my husband, Steve Robison," Pamela said. "I use my maiden name, Phillips, for my work, and Robison for real life. Steve, this is Jeff Winston and his wife, Linda."

"A pleasure." The man beamed, gripping Jeff's hand. "A genuine pleasure. I think *Harps upon the Willows* is one of the best things I've ever read. Won the Pulitzer, didn't it?"

"Yes," Jeff said. "I was gratified that it seemed to strike a chord in so many people."

"Hell of a book," Robison said. "And your last one, the one on people returning to the places where they grew up, that runs a close second. Pamela and I have both been big fans of yours for a long time; I believe some of your thoughts have even influenced her own work. I couldn't believe it when she told me she'd met you on the plane from Boston a few weeks ago. What a wonderful coincidence!"

"You must be very proud of her," Jeff said, sidestepping the fiction he and Pamela had concocted to explain their knowing each other. She'd written him at the beginning of the summer, wanted to see him, at least briefly, before this final autumn wanted him to see this opening. Jeff hadn't even been to Boston this year. Pamela had flown there and back alone to set up their prearranged story while he spent a week in Atlanta, walking around the Emory campus and thinking of all he'd been through since that first morning when he'd awakened in the dorm room there.

"I'm extremely proud of her," Steve Robison said, putting an arm around his wife. "She hates to have me talk this way about her, says it makes it sound like she's not even in the room. But I just can't help boasting when I think of all she's accomplished, in so short a time and with two kids to raise."

"Speaking of which"—Pamela smiled—"that's them over there by the phoenix sculpture. Behaving themselves, I hope."

Jeff looked across the gallery, saw the children. The boy, Christopher, was an endearingly ungainly fourteen-year-old, on the awkward brink of manhood; and Kimberly, at eleven, was already a young facsimile of Pamela. Eleven. Just two years younger than Gretchen, when—

"Jeff," Pamela said, "there's an exhibit I especially

want to show you. Steve, why don't you get Mrs. Winston
some pasta and a glass of wine?''

Linda followed Robison toward the caterer's buffet and
bar, and Pamela led Jeff toward a small cylindrical enclo-
sure, a tiny room within a room, at the center of the
gallery. Several people stood waiting to enter the cubicle,
outside of which was mounted a small card requesting that
it be occupied by no more than four persons at a time.
Pamela turned the card around so that it read "Temporarily closed for repairs." She apologized to those in line,
told them she needed to make some adjustments to the
equipment. They nodded sympathetically, wandered off to
other areas of the show. After a few moments a quartet of
guests emerged from the booth and Pamela took Jeff inside, closing the door behind them.

The exhibit was a video display, a dozen color monitors
of various sizes set into the inner walls of the darkened
cylinder, with a round leather seat in the center. The
screens flickered from every direction, an arm's reach
away wherever the viewer turned. Jeff's eyes moved from
one to the next at random, focusing, adjusting. Then he
began to comprehend what he was seeing.

The past. *Their* past, his and Pamela's. The first thing
he noticed was the news footage: Vietnam, the Kennedy
assassinations, *Apollo 11:* Then he saw that there were
also bits and pieces of various movies, television shows,
old music videos . . . And suddenly he caught a glimpse
of his cabin in Montgomery Creek on one of the monitors,
and on another was a quick still-frame of Judy Gordon's
college yearbook picture, followed by a video tape of her
as an adult, waving at the camera along with her son,
Sean, the boy who in another life had studied dolphins
because of *Starsea.*

Jeff's eyes darted rapidly now from screen to screen,
trying to take it all in, trying not to miss anything:
Chateaugay winning the 1963 Kentucky Derby, his parents' house in Orlando, the jazz club in Paris where Sidney
Bechet's clarinet had pierced his soul, the college bar
where he'd watched Pamela begin replaying, the grounds
of his estate nearby . . . And there on one monitor was a

long shot of the hillside village in Majorca; the camera zoomed slowly in to the villa where Pamela had died, then cut abruptly to a blurry home-movie clip of her at age fourteen, with her mother and father in the house in Westport.

"My God," he said, transfixed by the ever-changing montage of all their replays. "Where did you find all this?"

"Some of it was easy," she said. "The news-file footage is readily available. As for the rest, I shot most of it myself, in Paris, California, Atlanta. . . ." She smiled, her face illuminated by the flashing screens. "I did a lot of traveling for this one. To some familiar places and to others that I only knew about through you."

One of the screens now showed the corridors and wards of a hospital, all the beds filled with children; Jeff assumed it was the clinic in Chicago where she'd been a physician her first time back. On another monitor was the boat they'd once rented in Key West, anchored off the same deserted island where they'd decided to begin their search for other replayers. On and on the surrounding images played, an incessant kinetic collage of their many lives, together and apart.

"Incredible," he whispered. "I can't tell you how grateful I am for the chance to see this."

"I did it for you. For us. No one else can understand it; you'd be amused at the interpretations some of the critics have come up with."

He tore his eyes away from the screens, looked at her. "All of this . . . the whole show . . ."

Pamela nodded, returning his gaze. "Did you think I'd forgotten? Or that I no longer cared?"

"It's been so long."

"Much too long. And a month from now, we begin all over again."

"Next time. Next time is for us, if you want it to be."

She looked away at one of the monitors, which was displaying scenes of the surfside restaurant in Malibu where they'd had their first long conversation, their first disagreement over the film she'd planned to make to convince the world of the cyclical nature of reality.

"It may be my last," she said quietly. "The skew was almost eight years for me this time; next time I won't come back until sometime in the eighties. Will you wait for me? Will you—"

He pulled her to him, silenced her fearful words with his lips, his hands, caressing, reassuring. They embraced within that silent cubicle, lit by the reflected glow of all the lives they'd lived, and warmed by the finite promise of the single, brief life that remained for them to share.

"What's the matter, can't you hear me? Turn down that damned television. Since when do you care about ice skating, anyway?"

It was Linda's voice, but not as he had grown to know it. No, this was a voice from long ago, tight with strain and sarcasm.

She strode into the room, turned off the volume of the TV set. On the silenced screen, Dorothy Hamill leaped and spun gracefully across the ice, her bobbed hair falling immaculately into place each time she came to rest.

"I said, dinner's ready. If you want it, come get it. I may be the cook around here, but I'm not a servant."

"It's all right," Jeff said, struggling to adjust, trying to identify his new surroundings. "I'm not really hungry, anyway."

Linda gave him a derisive scowl. "What you mean is, you don't want to eat what I've cooked. Maybe you'd rather have lobster, hm? And some fresh asparagus? Champagne?"

Dorothy Hamill went into a final quickened spin, her brief red skater's skirt a twirling blur above her thighs. When she'd finished her routine she smiled and blinked into the camera, and the network replayed that look in slow motion: sweet elation, the gradually spreading smile like a rising sun, the decelerated blink become an expression of both modesty and sensuality. In that one lengthened moment, the girl seemed the very emblem of fresh, vital youth.

"Just tell me," Linda snapped, "just tell me what kind of gourmet meal you'd like instead of meat loaf tomorrow. And then tell me how we're supposed to afford it—will you do that?"

The freeze-frame image of Dorothy Hamill's smile faded into blackness, was replaced by one of ABC's mini-tours of Innsbruck, Austria. The Winter Olympics, 1976. He and Linda would be in Philadelphia. Camden, New Jersey, actually; that was where they'd lived while he was working at WCAU, across the river.

"Well?" she asked. "Have you got any bright suggestions as to what we might use to buy something other than ground beef or chicken next week?"

"Linda, please . . . let's not do this."

"Not do what—Jeffrey?"

She knew how he hated the long form of his name; whenever she'd used it, she'd been openly goading him into a fight.

"Let's not argue," he said complaisantly. "There's nothing more to argue about; everything's . . . changed."

"Oh, really? Just like that, hm?" She put her hands on her hips and turned in a slow circle, making an exaggerated show of inspecting the cramped apartment, the rented furniture. "I don't see that anything's changed at all. Not unless you're about to tell me you've gotten a better-paying job, after all these years."

"Forget the job. That's irrelevant. There won't be any more worries about money."

"And what's that supposed to mean? Have you won the lottery?"

Jeff sighed, flicked off the distracting television set with the remote control box. "It doesn't matter," he told her. "There won't be any more financial problems, that's all. For the moment, you'll just have to trust me on that."

"Big talk. That comes easy to you, doesn't it? From way back when, all your talk about 'broadcast journalism,' how you were going to be such a hotshot newsman, some kind of latter-day Edward R. Murrow. God, you had me snowed! And what does it all come down to? One piddling little radio station after another, moving all over the country to live in crappy places like this. I think you're *afraid* to succeed, Jeffrey L. Winston. You're afraid to move into television or to get into the corporate end of the business, because you're scared you just don't have what it takes to make it. And I'm beginning to think you don't.''

"Stop it, Linda, right now. This isn't doing either of us any good, and it's pointless.''

"Sure, I'll stop it. I'll stop it good.''

She stormed into the kitchen. He could hear her angrily preparing dinner for herself, setting the table with a deliberate clatter, slamming the oven door shut. Reverting to one of her 'silent treatments.' Those had started around this time and had become lengthier, more frequent, as the years went on. The arguments in between had almost always been about money, but that had been only the most conspicuous source of their difficulties. The real problems had been more deeply rooted, had derived from and been severely aggravated by their inability to communicate about the things that truly troubled them, such as the ectopic pregnancy. That had happened the year before this, and they'd never openly dealt with what that disappointment had meant to each of them, how they might overcome it and move beyond it together.

Jeff glanced into the kitchen, saw Linda hunched bitterly over the table, picking at her food; she didn't bother to look up at him. He closed his eyes, remembered her at his door with a bunch of daisies, pictured her in a warm breeze on the deck of the S.S. *France*. But that had been a different person, he realized; someone with whom he had shared his innermost feelings, if not the details of his numerous lives, from the beginning. Now the patterns of silence were set; all the money in the world wouldn't help at this point, not if they couldn't even talk to each other about the things that mattered.

He found an overcoat in the tiny hall closet, pulled it on, and left the apartment. Not a word passed between them as he went.

Outside, the snow was grimy, patchy, as unlike the pristine sheets of white the television had shown from

Innsbruck as the woman in that kitchen was from the
Linda he had loved these past nineteen years.

He'd make the money fast this time, he decided, and see
to it that she had enough to keep her comfortable for the rest
of her life, but there was no way he could bring himself to
stay, not now. The only question was what to do with
himself until Pamela arrived, whenever that might be.

≡19≡

THE BLUE JAY, darting and flitting outside the kitchen window as it built its nest in the backyard elm tree, was the first thing Pamela saw. She watched the bird's colorful aerial dance, took several long, deep breaths to calm herself before she looked around or moved.

She was in the process of making a cup of coffee, had been just about to insert the filter in the machine. The kitchen was cozy, familiar. Different than it had been last time, but she remembered it well from her first life, before the replaying had begun. Last replay she hadn't spent much time in here, had been too busy in her studio, painting and sculpting; the room had taken on the character of the maid they'd hired more than of herself. This kitchen, now, bore the stamp of her own personality, or at least the personality she'd had that first time around.

There was a Barbara Cartland novel lying open on the table, and next to it a copy of *Better Homes and Gardens*. Various clippings and notes to herself were stuck to the refrigerator door with little magnets shaped and painted like tiny ears of corn or stalks of celery. A drawing she'd done of the children—well executed, but without the finer skills of lighting and composition she'd acquired through years of practice in other lives—was taped to one of the cabinets. A large kitchen calendar hung above the table. It was open to March 1984, and the dates were neatly crossed off almost to the end of the month. Pamela was thirty-four. Her daughter, Kimberly, would have just turned eight; Christopher would be eleven.

She set the coffee filter aside, started to leave the kitchen, but then stopped and smiled as she recalled something. She opened one of the lower drawers beneath the counter, rummaged behind the boxes of flour and rice . . . And sure enough, there it was, right were she'd always kept it hidden: a Zip-Loc plastic bag containing most of an ounce of grass and a packet of E-Z Wider rolling papers. Her lone vice in those days, her one real escape from the tedium of housework and "parenting," as it had come to be called.

Pamela put the marijuana back where she'd found it, walked into the living room. The family photographs were hung there, along with two of her paintings from college. The promise that they showed had never been developed in this lifetime. Why had she ever let her talent go to waste for so long?

She could hear muffled music from upstairs: Cyndi Lauper's cartoonishly bouncy voice singing "Girls Just Want to Have Fun." Kimberly must be home from school; Christopher would probably be in his own room, playing with the Apple II computer they'd bought him that Christmas.

She sat on the chair in the foyer, took a pencil and a pad of paper from the telephone table, and dialed information for New York City. There was no listing for a Jeff or Jeffrey Winston in Manhattan or Queens. No Linda or L. Winston, either. It had been a long shot, anyway; there was no reason to think he might be back in New York. Pamela tried information again, this time in Orlando. His parents were listed. She called, and Jeff's mother answered the phone.

"Hello, my name is Pamela Phillips, and—"

"Oh, my goodness! Jeff told us you'd be trying to get in touch with him, but Lord, that was ages ago. Three *years* ago, I think, or maybe even four.'' The woman's voice faded as she apparently turned away from the mouthpiece, called in an aside: ''Honey! It's that Phillips girl that Jeff said might call, remember? Could you find me that envelope he sent?'' She came back to the phone. ''Pamela? Hold on just a minute, dear; there's a message for you here from Jeff. My husband's getting it.''

''Thank you. Could you tell me where Jeff is, where he's living now?''

''He's out in California, in a little town—well, right outside it, he says—called Montgomery Creek, up close to Oregon.''

''Yes,'' Pamela said. ''I know where it is.''

''He said you would. You know, he doesn't even have a phone out there, can you imagine? It worries me sick, thinking what could happen to him in an emergency, but he says he's got a shortwave radio for that kind of thing. I just don't know what came over him, a grown man quitting his job and leaving his wife and—Oh, I'm so sorry. I hope I wasn't speaking out of turn, to—''

''It's quite all right, Mrs. Winston. Honestly.''

''Well, it was just the strangest thing, anyhow. You might expect that kind of foolishness from a college boy, but for a man his age—he'll be forty before too very long, you know—Oh, thank you, honey. Pamela? I've got that envelope he sent us for when you called. He said we ought to just open it up and read it to you. Do you want to get a pencil or something?''

''I'm all set.''

''O.K., then, let me see . . . Hmmph. You'd think after all this time and so much mystery, there'd be more to it than this.''

''What does it say?''

''It's just one line. It says, 'If you're coming, be sure to bring the children. I love you. Jeff.' That's all there is to it. Did you get that? Do you want me to read it again?''

''No,'' Pamela said, a grin spreading wide on her suddenly flushed face. ''Thank you so much, but I understood it perfectly.''

She set the phone down, looked toward the staircase.

Christopher and Kimberly were old enough now. They wouldn't like the idea of leaving home at first, but she knew they'd soon grow to love Montgomery Creek and Jeff.

Besides, Pamela thought, biting her lip, it wouldn't be for long. They'd be back here in New Rochelle, back with their father, before they started high school.

Three and a half years. Her final replay; the last months and days of her phenomenally protracted life.

She planned to enjoy them all, to the fullest.

It was one of those rains that will neither cease nor get on with it and be done, but simply keeps on falling with a dull and intermittent insistence.

They'd been stuck inside the cabin like this for two days now; it was getting musty, the air dank with the smell of mildew from a leather vest that Christopher had left hanging on the porch railing overnight and had brought inside the next morning to dry by the stove.

"Kimberly!" Pamela said with exasperated dismay. "Will you please stop drumming on that plate!"

"She can't hear you," Christopher said, and leaned across the table to lift the miniature foam headphone away from his sister's left ear. "Mom says to cut it out," he yelled over the tinny sounds of Madonna's "Like a Virgin."

"As a matter of fact, just turn that off," Pamela said. "It's rude to listen to music by yourself while we're all having lunch."

The girl put on her most aggrieved grimace and pout but took the headphones off and put the Walkman away, as she'd been told. "I want another glass of milk," she said in a petulant tone.

"We're out of milk," Jeff reminded her. "I'm going into town tomorrow morning; I'll bring some back then. You can ride in with me, if you'd like; it may have stopped raining, and we could walk down by the falls."

"I've already seen the falls," Kimberly whined. "I want to watch MTV."

Jeff smiled tolerantly. "Out of luck there, kiddo," he

said. "We could listen to the shortwave, though; see what they're saying in China, or Africa."

"I don't care about China or Africa! I'm bored!"

"Why don't we just talk, then," Pamela suggested. "That's what people used to do, you know."

"Yeah, sure," Christopher muttered. "What'd they ever find to talk about so much?"

"Sometimes they told each other stories," Jeff put in.

"That's an idea," Pamela said, brightening. "Would you like me to tell you a story?"

"Oh, jeez, Mom, come on!" Christopher protested. "What do you think we are, in kindergarten or something?"

"I don't know," Kimberly said, turning thoughtful. "Maybe it would be fun to hear a story. We haven't done that in a long time."

"You willing to at least give it a try?" Pamela asked her son. He shrugged, didn't answer.

"Well," she began, "thousands and thousands of years ago, there was a dolphin named Cetacea. One day a strange new awareness suddenly came into her head, as if it had come from the sky above her ocean and beyond. Now, this was in the days when dolphins and people sometimes spoke to one another, but . . ."

And with the gentle summer rain in the background, she told them the story of *Starsea,* of the common bond of loving hope that linked the intelligent creatures of the earth, the sea, the stars . . . and of the catastrophic loss that ultimately brought humanity to the sorrowfully exalted moment of first full contact with its ocean kin.

The children fidgeted a bit at first, but as the tale wore on they listened with increasing fascination while their mother verbally recreated the film that had once won her worldwide acclaim and had brought her together with Jeff. When she had finished, Kimberly was weeping openly, but with a glow of otherworldly rapture in her young eyes; Christopher had turned his face away to the window and didn't speak for a long time.

Just before dusk, a single shaft of sunlight broke through the overcast sky, and Jeff and Pamela stood outside on the porch to watch it slowly fade. The children chose to stay inside; Kimberly had borrowed some of Pamela's water-colors, and was painting images of stars and dolphins, while Christopher was absorbed in one of John Lilly's books.

The shifting light played vividly across the rain-soaked meadow, the billion droplets beaded on the fresh-cut grass shimmering like unearthly jewels in a field of green fire. Jeff stood quietly behind Pamela, his arms around her waist, her hair against his cheek. Just before the light failed, he whispered something in her ear, a line from Blake: " 'To see a world in a Grain of Sand,' " he murmured, " 'and a Heaven in a Wild flower.' "

She pressed her hands to his, softly completed the quote: " 'Hold Infinity in the palm of your hand,' " she said, " 'and Eternity in an hour.' "

The towplane taxied into position, and when it had come to a stop, engine still turning, the line boy ran out to attach the two-hundred-foot nylon rope from the sailplane to the hook at the tail of the idling Cessna up ahead.

"Christopher, you want to check out the controls for me?" Jeff said to the boy who sat in the student's seat in front of him.

"Sure thing," Pamela's son answered, his tone serious with pride at being part of the preparations, not just some-one who was along for the ride. The boy wiggled the glider's stick left and right, and the ailerons at each wing tip responded; then he pushed back and forth on the stick, and Jeff turned back to see the elevator at the tail of the craft flap up and down, as it should, followed by the shimmy of the rudder as Christopher moved his feet on the pedals. All the controls seemed to be in good working order, and Jeff smiled his approval.

The towplane ahead of them began to inch forward, slowly taking up the slack in the rope. Its rudder waggled the pilot's "Ready?" query, and Jeff answered with a matching right-and-left movement of his own rudder. The Cessna moved down the runway, pulling the sailplane behind it. The wing boy ran alongside, holding the craft level and keeping it headed into the wind. Jeff kept his

eyes on the tow plane, judging the level of his wings by
the horizon line ahead. They picked up speed, the ground
crew boy dropped back, and Jeff eased back slightly on the
stick; they were airborne.

Out of the corner of his eye Jeff noted low swirls of
puffy white clouds near the base of the mountain ahead.
Good sign; that meant unstable moist air and thermals
already developing. No time to look for them now, though;
he stared intently at the towplane and the line, kept the
nylon rope rigidly straight, and turned smoothly as the
Cessna turned.

They reached altitude, three thousand feet above the
lower slopes of the mountain. Jeff pulled the release knob,
waited a moment to see the undone tow line snap forward
like a rubber band, then went into a climbing turn to the
right as the tow plane veered off and downward to the left.
The Cessna's engine faded away as it returned to the little
airport they had left, and soon there was no sound at all
but the smooth rushing of the air against the Plexiglas
canopy. They were in steady, powerless flight.

"God, Jeff! This is great!"

Jeff smiled, nodded as Christopher turned in his seat to
look back at him, the boy's eyes wide and gleaming. He
held the sailplane in a long, looping turn, using the leftover energy of their tow speed to gain as much working
altitude as possible. The unearthly white cone of Mount
Shasta slid by on their left, then reappeared in front of
them, a sun-bright beacon urging them ever upward.

Jeff looked back toward the southwest, where the town
named after the mountain lay nestled in the great surrounding forest of ponderosa pines. A second single-engine
Cessna, towing another white-and-blue sailplane, was approaching. Jeff circled lazily, his speed beginning to drop
to the normal cruising range of forty to fifty miles per
hour, as he waited for the other craft to join him.

When it was a mile or so away, the second glider broke
free of its umbilical and swept up and away from the
powered tug in a maneuver exactly like the one Jeff had
just performed. Christopher pressed his face to the side of

the clear canopy, watching the new arrival as it swooped toward them and drew alongside in smooth formation.

Pamela smiled and gave a thumbs up from the rear control seat of the other sailplane, and in the front seat Kimberly beamed ecstatically, waving at Jeff and her brother.

Jeff gently touched his left rudder pedal as he banked the wings leftward with the stick, breaking the loop they were in and turning toward the great symmetrical bulk of the mountain. Pamela followed suit, staying just behind and to the right of him.

The snowy treetops on the mountainside seemed to reach for them as they drew nearer and the angle of the slopes beneath them steepened. A lone deer chanced to look up and gave a startled shiver, then stood transfixed, staring at the great soundless birds not far above. Farther on, a quarter of the way around the mountain, Christopher pointed excitedly at a lumbering black bear, oblivious to the strange metal creatures sweeping low through his sky.

They found a bit of ridge lift, a swirling updraft of reflected wind, in front of and above the crest of a jutting cliff on the more rugged backside of the mountain. Jeff and Pamela glided along the ridge for several minutes, back and forth, looking at the silent, untouched snow that seemed so close they might have reached out to scoop up a powdery handful. Then Jeff spotted a thin wisp of cloud just forming against the blue sky slightly east of the mountain. He broke formation, headed for the newborn puff of condensation.

As he reached it, his right wing tip lifted slightly, and he immediately veered in that direction. When he did, the whole plane began to lift, and he slowed into a tight, controlled turn. The sailplane rose dramatically, kept on rising.

Below him, it was clear that Pamela saw what he had found. She turned abruptly away from the gentle upcurrents off the cliff, headed in his direction. Her glider seemed to diminish in size with every second as Jeff and Christopher rode the lifting mass of air higher and higher, locked into a steeply banked turn to stay within the narrow confines of the thermal's center.

Pamela flew in looping circles downwind of his position, searching. At last she caught the nebulous warm updraft, and the distance between them closed as her plane lifted swiftly and silently toward his . . . until, wing tip to wing tip, they soared together in the crisp, clean skies above Mount Shasta's ageless and enigmatic peak.

Kimberly had stopped crying, was outside picking a bunch of September wild flowers to take with her on the trip east. Christopher was being a man about it. He was fifteen, after all, and had long since begun to emulate Jeff's attitudes of acceptance in the face of adversity and unrestrained joy where joy—as it so frequently had these past few years—became appropriate.

"My hiking boots won't fit in the suitcase, Mom."

"You won't really need them in New Rochelle, honey," Pamela said.

"I guess not. Except maybe if Dad takes us up camping in the Berkshires, like he said he would, I could wear them then."

"How about if I send them to you?"

"Well . . . You don't have to do that. It's O.K. We'll be back before Christmas, anyway, and I'd just have to mail them back here again."

Pamela nodded, turned her head away so her son wouldn't see her eyes.

"I know you'd like to have them with you," Jeff put in. "Why don't we go ahead and send them along, and we'll . . . get you another pair to keep here. We can do that with all your stuff, if you'd like."

"Hey, that'd be great!" Christopher exclaimed with a grin.

"It makes sense," Jeff said.

"Sure, if I'm gonna be spending half the year with Dad and the other half here with you and Mom . . . You sure that'd be O.K.? Mom, is that all right with you?"

"It sounds like a very good idea," Pamela said, forcing

a smile. "Why don't you go make a list of all the things you'd like us to send?"

"O.K.," Christopher said, heading toward the two-bedroom annex Jeff had built on to the cabin for the boy and his sister. Then he stopped and turned. "Can I tell Kimberly? I bet there's a lot of things she'd like to have back east, too."

"Of course," Pamela told him, "but don't you two take too long about it. We have to leave for Redding in an hour, or you'll miss your flight."

"We'll hurry, Mom," he said, running outside to fetch his sister.

Pamela turned to Jeff, let flow the tears she'd been holding back. "I don't want them to go. It's still another month before . . . before . . ."

He embraced her, smoothed her hair. "We've been through all this before," he told her gently. "It's best for them to have a few weeks to adjust to being with their father again, to make new friends . . . That may help them absorb the shock a little."

"Jeff," she said, sobbing, "I'm scared! I don't want to die! Not . . . *die* forever, and—"

He hugged her tightly, rocked her in his arms and felt his own tears trickle down his face. "Just think of how we've lived. Think of all we've done, and let's try to be grateful for that."

"But we could have done so much more. We could have—"

"Hush," he whispered. "We did all we could. More than either of us ever dreamed when we were first starting out."

She leaned back, searched his eyes as if seeing them for the first time, or the last. "I know," she sighed. "It's just . . . I got so used to the endless possibilities, the *time*. . . never being bound by our mistakes, always knowing we could go back and change things, make them better. But we didn't, did we? We only made things different."

A voice droned on interminably in the dim background of

Jeff's consciousness. It didn't matter who the voice belonged to, or what it might be saying.

Pamela was dead, never to return. The realization washed over him like seawater against an open wound, filled his mind with an all-encompassing grief he had not felt since the loss of his daughter Gretchen. He clenched his fists, lowered his head beneath the weight of the undeniable, the intolerable . . . and still the voice babbled forth its senseless litany:

". . . see if Charlie can get a reaction from Mayor Koch on Reagan's Bitburg trip. Looks like this one could really whip up into a firestorm; we've got the American Legion coming down on him about it, and Congress is starting to buzz. That's—Jeff? You O.K.?"

"Yeah." He glanced up briefly. "I'm fine. Go ahead."

He was in the conference room of WFYI in New York, the all-news radio station where he'd been news director when first he died. He was seated at one end of a long oval table; the morning and midday editors were on either side of him, and the reporters occupied the other chairs. He hadn't seen these people for decades, but Jeff recognized the place, the situation, instantly. He'd had this same meeting every weekday morning for years: the daily assignment conference, where the structure of the day's news coverage was planned as best it could be in advance. Gene Collins, the ongoing midday editor, was frowning at him with concern.

"You sure you're feeling all right? We could cut this short; there's not much else to discuss."

"Just go ahead, Gene. I'll be fine."

"Well . . . O.K. Anyway, that's about it for metro stories and local angles. On the national front, we've got the shuttle going up this morning, and—"

"Which one?" Jeff rasped out.

"What?" Gene asked, puzzled.

"Which shuttle?"

"*Discovery*. You know, the one with the senator on board."

Thank God for that at least; so immediately after Pamela's final death, Jeff wasn't sure he could have handled a repeat of the chaos and depression in the newsroom on the day of the *Challenger* disaster. He should have known better, anyway, if he'd been thinking clearly; Reagan had gone to Bitburg in the spring of 1985. That would make this sometime around April of that year, nine or ten months before the shuttle would explode.

Everyone at the table was looking at him strangely, wondering why he seemed so distraught, so disoriented. To hell with it. Let them think whatever they wanted.

"Let's wrap it up, all right, Gene?"

The editor nodded, began gathering the scattered papers he had brought to the meeting. "Only other good story developing is this rape-recant thing in Illinois. Dotson's going back to prison today while his lawyer prepares an appeal. That's it. Questions, anybody?"

"The school-board meeting looks like it might run long today," one of the reporters said. "I don't know if I'll be able to make this 2:00 P.M. Fire Department awards thing. You want me to dump out of the school board early, or would you rather put somebody else on the awards?"

"Jeff?" Collins asked, deferring to him.

"I don't care. You decide."

Gene frowned again, started to say something but didn't. He turned back to the reporters, who had begun to mumble among themselves. "Bill, stick with the school board as long as you need to. Charlie, you hit the Fire Department ceremony after you talk to the mayor. Give us a live shot on Koch and Bitburg at one. Then you can hold off filing until after the awards are over. Oh, and Jim, Mobile Four is in the shop; you'll be taking Mobile Seven."

The meeting broke up quietly, with none of the usual wisecracks and raucous laughter. The reporters and the offgoing early-morning editor filed out of the conference room, casting quick, covert glances at Jeff. Gene Collins hung behind, stacking and restacking his sheaf of papers.

"You want to talk about it?" he finally said.

Jeff shook his head. "Nothing to talk about. I told you, I'll be all right."

"Look, if it's problems with Linda . . . I mean, I understand. You know what a rough go of it Carol and I had a couple of years back. You helped me through a lot of that—God knows I bent your ear enough—so anytime you want to sit down over a beer, just let me know."

"Thanks, Gene. I appreciate your concern, I really do. But it's something I have to work out for myself."

Collins shrugged, stood from the table. "That's up to you," he said. "But if you ever do feel like unloading your problems, feel free to dump a few in my direction. I owe you."

Jeff nodded briefly, then Collins left the room, and he was alone again.

≡20≡

JEFF QUIT WORK, made enough bets and short-term-yield investments to enable Linda to get by on her own for the next three years. There was no time to build a major inheritance for her; he increased his life-insurance coverage tenfold and let it go at that.

He moved into a small apartment on the Upper West Side, spent his days and evenings wandering the streets of Manhattan, taking in all the sights and smells and sounds of humanity from which he had so long isolated himself. The old people fascinated him most, their eyes full of distant memories and lost hope, their bodies slumped in anticipation of the end of time.

Now that Pamela was gone, the fears and regrets she had expressed came back to trouble him as deeply as they'd disturbed her toward the end. He'd done what he could to reassure her, to ease the grief and terror of her final days, but she'd been right: For all that they had struggled, all they'd once achieved, the end result was null. Even the happiness they had managed to find together had been frustratingly brief; a few years stolen here and there, transient moments of love and contentment like vanishing specks of foam in a sea of lonely, needless separation.

It had seemed as if they would have forever, an infinity of choices and second chances. They had squandered far too much of the priceless time that had been granted them, wasted it on bitterness and guilt and futile quests for nonexistent answers—when they themselves, their love for each other, had been all the answer either of them should have ever needed. Now even the opportunity to tell her that, to hold her in his arms and let her know how much he had revered and cherished her, was eternally denied him. Pamela was dead, and in three years' time Jeff, too, would die, never knowing why he'd lived.

He roamed his city streets, watching, listening: tough-eyed bands of punks, furious at the world . . . men and women in corporate attire, hurrying to accomplish whatever goals they had established for themselves . . . giggling swarms of children, exuberant at the newness of their lives. Jeff envied them all, coveted their innocence, their ignorance, their expectations.

Several weeks after he'd quit his job at WFYI, he got a call from one of the news writers who worked there, a woman—girl, really—named Lydia Randall. Everyone at the station was concerned about him, she said, had been shocked when he'd resigned, and worried further when they'd heard his marriage had broken up. Jeff told her, as he had told Gene Collins, that he was all right. But she pressed the issue, insisted that he meet her for a drink so she could talk to him in person.

They met the next afternoon at the Sign of the Dove on Third Avenue at Sixty-fifth, took a table by one of the windows that was open to a gloriously sunny New York June. Lydia was wearing a shoulder-baring white cotton dress and a matching wide-brimmed hat from which a pink satin ribbon trailed. She was an exceptionally pretty young woman, with a mass of wavy blond hair and wide, liquid-green eyes.

Jeff recited the story he'd concocted to explain his sudden retirement, a standard tale of journalist's burn-out combined with some half-truths about the recent "luck"

he'd had with his investments. Lydia nodded understandingly, seemed to accept his explanations at face value. As
far as his marriage went, he told her, it had effectively
been over for a long time; no specific problems worth
belaboring, just a case of two people who had gradually
grown apart.

Lydia listened solicitously. She had another drink, then
began to talk about her own life. She was twenty-three,
had come to New York right after she'd graduated from
the University of Illinois, was living with the boyfriend
she had met in college. He—his name was Matthew—was
eager to get married, but she was no longer so sure. She
felt "trapped," needed "space," wanted to meet new
friends and have all the adventurous experiences she'd
missed growing up in a small town in the Midwest. She
and Matthew were no longer the same people they used to
be, Lydia said; she felt she had outgrown him.

Jeff let her talk it out, all the commonplace woes and
longings of youth that to her were freshly overwhelming
and of unprecedented import in her life. She hadn't the
perspective to recognize how utterly ordinary her story
was, though perhaps she did have some glimmering of that
awareness, since she had at least expressed her urgent
desire to break free of the cliche her life had become.

He commiserated, talked with her for an hour or more
about life and love and independence . . . told her she had
to make her own decisions, said she had to learn to take
risks, said all the obvious and necessary things that one
must say to someone who is facing a universal human
crisis for the first time in her life.

A gusting breeze from the open window stirred her hair,
wafted the ribbon from her hat against her face. Lydia
brushed it away, and Jeff found something inexplicably
touching about the gesture, the girlish way her hand moved.
In her prettily animated face he suddenly saw a reflection
of Judy Gordon, and of Linda on that day she'd brought
him the daisies: bright promise, unshaped dreams aborning.

They finished their drinks, and he saw her to a taxi. As
she got into the cab she looked up at him and said, with all
the optimism and presumed infinity of youth, "I guess it'll

be O.K.; I mean, we've got plenty of time to work it out. We have so *much* time."

Jeff knew that illusion, far too well. He gave the young woman a halfhearted smile, shook her hand, and watched her ride away toward life, her long pink ribbon blowing free.

The Metro North commuter train pulled to a stop precisely on time, Jeff noted from his vantage point a hundred feet farther down the platform. At this time of day it was something of a misnomer to call it a commuter train, he thought; not many businessmen would have taken the 11:00 A.M. run into the city.

Jeff began walking briskly toward the ramp to the Terminal, as if he'd just gotten off a different line. He slowed his pace a bit as he passed the train from New Rochelle, and saw that he'd been right: There were a number of women dressed for shopping trips, a smattering of college students, but almost no one with a suit and tie and briefcase among the disembarking passengers.

She was one of the last to leave the train. He almost missed her, and had begun to worry that the information he'd been given might be incorrect. She was nicely dressed, but without the fanatical attention to detail that marked the women headed for Bendel's or Bergdorf's. Her low-heeled shoes were designed for walking, and her pale blue linen dress and light wool sweater had an appealing air of practicality about them.

Jeff fell into step twenty or thirty paces behind her as she walked up the ramp and into Grand Central's huge Main Concourse. He was afraid he might lose her in the crowd, but her height and distinctive straight blonde hair helped him keep her in view as they weaved their separate ways through the swarms of people.

She went up the broad stairs that led to the Pan Am Building, and Jeff dropped back a bit as he followed her through the less-crowded lobby and out onto East Forty-fifth Street. She strode across Park Avenue, past the Roosevelt Hotel and across Madison to Fifth, where she turned north. The window displays at Saks and Cartier caused her only the briefest of pauses, during which Jeff slowed to feign interest in a Korean Airlines' package tour or the matched sets of Mark Cross luggage.

She turned west again at Fifty-third Street, and entered the Museum of Modern Art. The detective agency Jeff had hired six weeks ago was right, at least as far as today went: Every other Thursday, they'd told him, Pamela Phillips Robison took a train into Manhattan for an afternoon of visiting galleries and museums.

He paid his admission fee, and noticed as he went through the turnstile that his palms were damp with perspiration. Now he had lost track of her for the moment.

Jeff still wasn't sure just why he'd gone to such lengths to arrange to see her, if only from a distance; he was fully aware that this woman was not the Pamela he had known and loved, and that she never would be. Her replays had reached their end. He could never hope for that sudden look of awareness and intimate recognition he'd seen on her face that night in the college bar when she'd understood who she was, who he was, who and what they'd been together over the decades.

No, this version of Pamela would remain forever ignorant of all that; yet he longed to look once more into her eyes, perhaps even to briefly hear her voice. The temptation had finally proven irresistible, and he felt no shame for harboring that desire, no guilt for having followed her.

Jeff looked for her in the Museum Shop off the lobby first, on the unlikely chance that she might have stopped in only to purchase a book or a poster, but Pamela wasn't among the browsers. He walked back through the lobby, into the glass-walled Garden Hall and over to the first-floor galleries before coming back to take the escalators to the upper levels. There were two main exhibits under way, in addition to the familiar displays from the permanent collection: One was a show in commemoration of Mies van der Rohe's centennial year; the other was a retrospective of the sculptor Richard Serra. Jeff gave the exhibits only the most cursory of appraisals; he had yet to catch a glimpse of Pamela again.

On the fourth floor he saw something that made him smile despite his growing impatience: As part of the van der Rohe exhibit, the museum had installed numerous examples of the architect's furniture designs—including a Barcelona chair exactly like the one Frank Maddock had chosen for Jeff's office at Future, Inc., so long ago.

Still no sign of Pamela. He might have to wait two weeks before she came into the city again, trail her to another museum or perhaps devise some kind of momentary, seemingly accidental encounter in the train station itself . . . just long enough to look her full in the face one time, maybe to hear her say "Excuse me," or "It's twenty minutes to noon."

Back on the third-floor level of the Garden Hall Jeff stopped to rest, leaned against a railing, stared out the great glass wall . . . and saw, in the Sculpture Garden below, the soft blonde helmet of her hair and the sky-blue linen of her dress.

She was still outside when he got down to the garden. She was standing with her arms crossed, looking at one of the Serra sculptures. Jeff stopped ten feet away from her, felt a thousand conflicting emotions and memories go through his mind. Then Pamela unexpectedly turned toward him, said "What do you think of it?"

He hadn't prepared himself for what he might do or say if she initiated a conversation with him, hadn't even thought beyond the moment of being confronted once again, however briefly, with those piercing green eyes he knew so well—No, he forcefully reminded himself, he didn't know these eyes at all, they hid a soul that had been and forever would be closed to him. This woman in the garden would know only a single lifetime—soon to end, with no reprise—in which he played no part at all.

"I said, what do you think of the Serra?"

As forthright as ever; it was part of her basic nature, he realized, not something that had been instilled in her by the experience of the replays.

"A little too abrasive for my taste," he finally answered, his thoughts on anything but the artist's work.

She nodded pensively. "There seems to be a sort of implied threat in most of his stuff," she said. "Like that one piece, *Delineator, II?* The one with the big steel plate flat on the floor and the other one bolted to the ceiling above it? All I could think about was what would happen if the top one tore loose and fell. Anybody standing under it would be crushed to death.''

He couldn't stand here and make museum small-talk with her; his mind was leaping from image to image of their lives together: Her smiling from the canopy of a nearby sailplane, her in the kitchen on Majorca, her in the many beds they had shared through the years . . . it was as if, through memory alone, he had created an inner replica of the video exhibit of their lives that she'd once put together as a gallery piece of her own.

''And that other one,'' she went on, ''the one called *Circuit, II* . . . I know the effect was supposed to be an interesting division of the room's space, but all those sharp steel rectangles coming out of the corners made me feel like I was surrounded by guillotine blades.'' She gave an easy, self-mocking laugh. ''Or maybe I've just got a particularly morbid imagination, I don't know.''

''No,'' Jeff said, regaining his composure. ''I know what you mean. I felt the same way. He has a very aggressive style.''

''Too much so, I think. It interferes with my ability to appreciate the forms on an objective level.''

''This one looks like it might topple over any second,'' Jeff said.

''Right. And in this direction, too.''

He laughed in spite of himself, felt a rush of the same easy self-confidence with her that he had felt when—he willfully stopped his thoughts again. It would do no good to recall those other times, times spent with someone this woman only outwardly resembled. And yet, and yet: She still had the same dry wit, the same aura of warmth beneath a coolly analytical sensibility . . . it was a pleasure to talk to her, even though she would never have the slightest recollection of all they'd been through together.

''Listen,'' he said, ''do you want to get out from under this thing before it crashes on us, and maybe have some lunch?''

*   *   *

They ate in the cafe overlooking the Sculpture Garden, laughed some more about the blatantly menacing nature of the Serra pieces, bemoaned the museum's increasing reluctance to showcase newer artists. Jeff helped her on with her sweater as the shadow of the condominium tower above the museum fell across the garden; his hand brushed her hair as he did so, and it was difficult to restrain himself from caressing that familiar, long-lost face.

She talked about her abandoned art career, about the frustrations and joys of raising her family. He could see the restlessness in her eyes, the gnawing sense of a life not fully lived; a life, Jeff knew, which soon would end. He ached to tell her of all she'd once achieved.

There came a moment when the lunch was finished, the conversation at an awkward lull.

"So," he said, wanting to prolong the encounter but not certain how. "This has been very pleasant."

"Yes, it has," she agreed, fumbling uncomfortably with her coffee spoon.

"Do you get into the city very often?"

"A couple of times a month."

"Maybe we could . . ." his voice trailed off; he wasn't sure what he was proposing, was even less sure whether he should propose anything at all between them.

"Could what?" she asked, into the silence.

"I don't know. Go to another museum. Have lunch again."

She fidgeted with the spoon. "I'm married, you know."

"I know."

"I don't just—I mean, I'm not—"

He smiled, handed her a paper napkin.

"What's this for?" she said, startled.

"For tearing into very tiny pieces."

Pamela laughed abruptly, then stared back at him with a quizzical look. "How did you know I . . ." She shook her head slowly from side to side. "Sometimes I feel like you can read my mind. Like when you asked if I'd ever painted dolphins. I never told you how much I love whales and dolphins."

"I just thought you might."

She ripped the napkin straight down the middle with an exaggerated flourish, and looked up at him with curious merriment and an air of sudden resolve.

"There's a Jack Youngerman show at the Guggenheim," she said. "I might come down for that next week."

The musk-warm scent of their lovemaking clung to him, permeated the bedroom with its aromatic catalogue of memories. That sweetly pungent essence brought back vivid recollections of nights beneath thick blankets at the cabin in Montgomery Creek, hot bright days on the foredeck of a yacht off the Florida Keys, Sunday mornings wrapped in the sheets of their suite at the Pierre . . . and finally the afternoons, one year's worth of stolen afternoons, here in this apartment.

Jeff looked down at her face against his chest, her eyes closed, her lips parted like a sleeping child's. His mind brought forth, unbidden, the lines from the *Bhagavad-Gita* that she'd once spoken with such passionate intensity on that long-ago evening in her Topanga Canyon retreat:

"You and I, Arujna, have lived many lives.
I remember them all. You do not remember."

Pamela stirred in his arms, uttered a wordless sound of contentment as she stretched, her body sliding against his like an affectionate kitten.

"What time is it?" she asked, yawning.

"Twenty after six."

"Damn," she said, sitting up in bed. "I have to get going."

"Will you be down again on Tuesday?"

"My class was canceled, but . . . I haven't mentioned anything about that at home. We can spend the whole day together."

Jeff smiled, tried to look pleased. Next Tuesday. The whole day together. Faint, bittersweet echoes of what once had been; but of course she had no way of knowing that.

"Maybe I can finish the painting then," she said, slipping out of bed and gathering up her scattered clothes.

"When do I get to look at it?"

"Not till it's done; you promised."

He nodded, feeling slightly guilty that he'd sneaked a look at the covered canvas the day before. Her talent had progressed in the past year, since she'd started painting regularly again and taking graduate courses in advanced composition at NYU; but she'd never again reach the level of ability, the bold flights of imaginative brilliance she had displayed in other, unremembered lives.

The painting she had almost completed was a nude study of the two of them, hands joined, laughing and running through a sun-dappled tunnel of white, vine-covered trellises. Jeff was touched by its simplicity, by the naivete of the free-spirited joy it portrayed; it was a painting by an artist who had only begun to love, who had not yet had the chance to test the limits of that love, or of life itself.

The time they'd spent together since that first unplanned meeting at the museum had been inescapably circumscribed: An afternoon once or twice a week here at his apartment, a rare overnight when she'd told her husband she wanted to stay in the city for a concert or a play . . . and once, once only, they'd gone away for a long weekend together to Cape Cod. She'd told her family she was in Boston, visiting a woman she had known in college.

The possibility of divorce had been raised once, briefly; but Jeff knew she wasn't ready for such a drastic break. There were more limitations on what they could share than she would ever know, a piercing line of demarcation between their awareness of each other. Pamela seemed to sense it sometimes, vaguely: In a faraway look on Jeff's face, in a suddenly halted conversation.

He loved her, genuinely loved her for the self she was today, not merely as a reflection of all those other Pamelas, in other existences . . . and yet the constant reminder, in her unknowing eyes, of all that had been put behind them tinged everything they did with an unremitting melancholy.

She had finished dressing and was brushing the bed-tangles from her fine, straight hair. How many times had he watched her do that, in how many mirrors? More than she could imagine, or than he could now bear to recall.

"See you next week," Pamela said, bending to kiss him as she scooped her purse from the night stand. "I'll try to get an early train."

He returned her kiss, held her shining face between his open hands for a lingering moment, thinking of the years, the decades, the hopes and plans of their lifetimes fulfilled and thwarted . . .

But next week they'd have all day together; a day of warmth, of early spring. It was something to look forward to.

The first breath of winter blew in from off the lake, stirring the red and yellow leaves of the trees on Cherry Hill. The fountain in the Concourse burbled its chill waters as Jeff and Pamela walked past it toward the graceful cast-iron sweep of Central Park's Bow Bridge.

On the other side of the bridge they wandered north along the wooded pathways of the Ramble, skirting the lake to their left. Birds by the hundreds twittered excitedly all around them, getting ready for the long voyage south.

"Wouldn't it be nice if we could join them?" Pamela said, huddling close to Jeff as they strolled. "Fly away to some island, or to South America . . ."

He didn't answer her, simply held her tighter, his arm protectively around her waist. But he knew with bitter certainty that he could offer no protection from what was soon to happen to them both.

At the north end of the lake they stopped on Balcony Bridge, and stood gazing at the woods below, the water reflecting the surrounding towers of Manhattan.

"Guess what?" Pamela whispered, her face close to his.

"What?" he said.

"I've told Steve I'm going to visit my old roommate in Boston again next weekend. Friday through Monday. We *can* fly away somewhere, if you want to."

"That's . . . great." There was nothing he could say; it would be the height of cruelty to tell her what he knew: That this was the last day they would ever see each other. This coming Tuesday, five days from now, the world would cease forever for both of them.

"You don't sound all that thrilled about it," she said, frowning.

Jeff put on a grin, tried to mask his grief and fear. Let her cling to her innocent trust in the years she assumed would be there to be lived; now, at the end, the greatest gift that he could give her was a lie.

"It's wonderful," he told her with pretended enthusiasm. "I'm just surprised, that's all. We can go anywhere you'd like to go. Anywhere at all. Barbados, Acapulco, the Bahamas . . . you name it."

"I don't care," she said, snuggling to him. "Just as long as it's warm, and quiet, and I'm with you."

If he spoke again, he knew, his voice would give away too much. Instead, he kissed her, willed all his heartsick sorrow into a final, tangible expression of all that he had ever felt for her, all they'd ever—

She gave a sudden moan, fell limply against him. He gripped her shoulders, kept her from collapsing to the ground.

"Pamela? God, no, what—"

She regained her footing, pulled her face back and looked at him in shock. "Jeff? Oh, Jesus, *Jeff?*"

It was there, all of it, in her widened eyes: comprehension, recognition, memory. The accumulated knowledge and anguish of eight varied lifetimes spilled across her face, twisted her mouth with sudden confusion.

She looked around her, saw the park, the New York skyline. Her eyes filled with tears, sought Jeff's again.

"I was—it was supposed to be over!"

"Pamela—"

"What year is it? How long do we have?"

He couldn't keep it from her; she had to know. "It's 1988."

She looked back at the trees, the coppery leaves drifting and swirling everywhere about them. "It's already fall!"

He smoothed her wind-mussed hair, wished that he could stave off the truth for one more moment; but it would not be denied. "October," he told her gently. "The thirteenth."

"That's—that's only five days!"

''Yes.''

''It's not fair,'' she wept, ''I'd prepared myself last time, I'd almost accepted—'' She broke off, looked at him with new bewilderment. ''What are we doing here together?'' she asked. ''Why aren't I at home?''

''I . . . I had to see you.''

''You were kissing me,'' she said accusingly. ''You were kissing *her,* the person I used to be, before!''

''Pamela, I thought—''

''I don't care what you thought,'' she snapped, jerking herself away from him. ''You knew that wasn't really me, how could you have done something so . . . so perverse as that?''

''But it was you,'' he insisted. ''Not with all the memories, no, but it was still you, we still—''

''I can't believe you're saying this! How long has this been happening, when did you start this?''

''It's been almost two years.''

''Two years! You've been . . . *using* me, like I was some kind of inanimate object, like—''

''It wasn't like that, not at all! We loved each other, you started painting again, went back to school . . .''

''I don't care what I did! You seduced me away from my family, you tricked me . . . and you knew exactly what you were doing, what strings to pull to influence me, to . . . control me!''

''Pamela, please.'' He reached for her arm, trying to calm her, make her understand. ''You're twisting everything, you're—''

''Don't touch me!'' she shouted, backing off the bridge where they'd embraced just moments before. ''Just leave me alone and let me die! Let us both die, and get it done with!''

Jeff tried to stop her as she fled, but she was gone. The last hope of his last life was gone, lost on the path that led to Seventy-seventh Street, into the anonymous, devouring city . . . to death, immutable and certain death.

≡21≡

JEFF WINSTON DIED, alone; yet still his dying wasn't done. He awoke in his office at WFYI, where the first of his many lives had so abruptly ended: Reporters' schedules posted on the wall, framed picture of Linda on his desk, the glass paperweight that had cracked when he had clutched his chest and dropped the phone so long ago. He looked at the digital clock on his bookshelf:

12:57 PM OCT 18 88

Nine minutes to live. No time to contemplate anything but the looming pain and nothingness.

His hands began to shake, tears welled in his eyes.

"Hey, Jeff, about this new campaign—" Promotions director Ron Sweeney stood in his open office door, staring at him. "Jesus, you look white as a sheet! What's the matter?"

Jeff looked back at the clock:

1:02 PM OCT 18 88

"Get out of here, Ron."

"Can I get you an Alka-Seltzer or something? Want me to call a doctor?"

"Get the hell out of here!"

"Hey, I'm sorry, I just . . ." Sweeney shrugged, closed the door behind him.

The tremors in Jeff's hands spread to his shoulders, then to his back. He closed his eyes, bit his upper lip and tasted blood.

The phone rang. He picked it up in his shaking hand, completed the vast cycle that had begun so many lifetimes ago.

"Jeff," Linda said, "We need—"

The invisible hammer slammed into his chest, killing him again.

He woke again, looked in panic at the glowing red numbers across the room:

1:05 PM OCT 18 88

He threw the paperweight at the clock, smashed its rectangular plastic face. The phone rang and kept on ringing. Jeff blotted out the sound of it with a scream, a wordless animal bellow, and then he died, and woke with the telephone already in his hand, heard Linda's words and died again, again, again: waking and dying, awareness and void, alternating almost faster than he could perceive, centered always on the moment of that first heavy agony within his chest.

Jeff's ravaged mind cried out for some release, but none was granted; it sought escape, whether in madness or oblivion no longer mattered . . . Yet still he saw and heard and felt, remained alert to all his torment, suspended without surcease in the awful darkness of not-life, not-death: the eternal, paralyzing instant of his dying.

"We need . . ." he heard Linda say, " . . . to talk."

There was a pain somewhere. It took him a moment to identify the source of it: his hand, rigid as a claw where he clutched the telephone. Jeff relaxed his grip, and the ache in his sweaty hand eased.

"Jeff? Did you hear what I said?"

He tried to speak, could issue nothing but a guttural sound that was half-moan, half-grunt.

"I said we need to talk," Linda repeated. "We need to sit down together and have an honest discussion about our marriage. I don't know if it can be salvaged at this point, but I think it's worth trying."

Jeff opened his eyes, looked at the clock on his bookshelf:

1:07 PM OCT 18 88

"Are you going to answer me? Do you understand how important this is for us?"

The numbers on the clock changed silently, advanced to 1:08.

"Yes," he said, forcing the words to form. "I understand. We'll talk."

She let out a long, slow breath. "It's overdue, but maybe there's still time."

"We'll see."

"Do you think you could get home early today?"

"I'll try," Jeff told her, his throat dry and constricted.

"See you when you get here," Linda said. "We have a lot to talk about."

Jeff hung up the phone, still staring at the clock. It moved to 1:09.

He touched his chest, felt the steady heartbeat. Alive. He was alive, and time had resumed its natural flow.

Or had it ever ceased? Maybe he had suffered a heart attack, but only a mild one, just bad enough to push him over the edge into hallucination. It wasn't unheard of; he himself had made the analogy of a drowning man seeing the events of his life played back, had half-expected something like that to happen when the pain first hit him. The brain was capable of prodigious feats of fantasy and time compression or expansion, particularly at a moment of apparent mortal crisis.

Of course, he thought, and mopped his sweating brow with relief. That made perfect sense, much more than believing he'd actually been through all those lives, experienced all those—

Jeff looked back at the phone. There was only one way to know for certain. Feeling slightly foolish, he dialed information for Westchester County.

"What city, please?" the operator asked.

"New Rochelle. A listing for . . . Robison, Steve or Steven Robison."

There was a pause, a click on the line, and then a computer-synthesized voice read out the number in a dull monotone.

Maybe he'd heard the man's name someplace, Jeff thought, perhaps in some minor news story. It could have gotten lodged in his mind, to be subtly woven into his delusion weeks or months later.

He dialed the number the computer had given him. A young girl's voice, thick with sinus congestion, answered.

"Is, ah, your mother home?" Jeff asked the child.

"Just a minute. Mommy! Telephone!"

A woman's voice came on the line, muffled and distorted, out of breath. "Hello?" she said.

It was hard to tell one way or the other, she was breathing in such quick, shallow gasps. "Is this . . . Pamela Robison? Pamela Phillips?"

Silence. Even the breathing halted.

"Kimberly," the woman said, "You can hang up the phone now. It's time for you to take another Contac and some cough medicine."

"Pamela?" Jeff said when the girl had put down her receiver. "This is—"

"I know. Hello, Jeff."

He closed his eyes, took a deep lungful of air, and let it out slowly. "It . . . happened, then? All of it? *Starsea*, and Montgomery Creek, and Russell Hedges? You know what I'm talking about?"

"Yes. I wasn't sure myself that it was real, until I heard your voice just now. God, Jeff, I started dying over and over, so fast, it was—"

"I know. The same thing happened to me. But before that, you really do remember all the things we went through, all those lives?"

"Every one of them. I was a doctor, and an artist . . . you wrote books, we—"

"We soared."

"That, too." He heard her sigh, a long, empty sound full of regret, and weariness, and more. "About that last day, in Central Park—"

"I thought it would be my last time, I thought that you—were gone. Forever. I had to be with you toward the end, even if it was only . . . a part of you, that didn't really know me."

She didn't say anything, and after several seconds the silence hung between them as the lost years once had.

"What do we do now?" Pamela finally asked.

"I don't know," Jeff said. "I can't think straight yet, can you?"

"No," she admitted. "I don't know what would be best, for either of us, right now." She paused, hesitated. "You know . . . Kimberly's home sick from school today—that's why she answered the phone—but it's not just that she has a cold, this is the day after she got her first period. I died just as she began to become a woman. And now . . ."

"I understand," he told her.

"I've never seen her grow up. Neither has her father. And Christopher, he'll just be starting high school . . . These years are so important for them."

"It's too soon for either of us to try to make any definite plans right now," Jeff said. "There's too much we need to absorb, to come to terms with."

"I'm just so glad to know . . . that I didn't imagine it all."

"Pamela . . ." He struggled for the words with which to express all that he felt. "If you only knew how much—"

"I know. You don't have to say any more."

He set the phone down gently, stared at it for a long time. It was possible they'd been through *too* much together, had seen and known and shared more than they

could ever measure up to in this world. Gaining and
losing, taking hold and letting go . . .

Pamela had once said that they had "only made things
different, not better." That wasn't wholly true. Sometimes
their actions had had positive results for them and the
world at large, sometimes they'd been negative, most
often they'd been neither. Each lifetime had been different, as each choice is always different, unpredictable in its
outcome or effect. Yet those choices had to be made, Jeff
thought. He'd learned to accept the potential losses, in the
hope that they would be outweighed by the gains. The
only certain failure, he knew, and the most grievous,
would be never to risk at all.

Jeff looked up and saw his own reflection in the dark
smoked glass of his bookshelves: flecks of gray in his hair,
faint puffy bags beneath his eyes, thin lines beginning to
crease his forehead. They'd never be smoothed out again,
those marks of age; they would only deepen and prolifer-
ate, new hieroglyphs of lost youth written ineradicably
across his face and body with each passing year.

And yet, he mused, the years themselves would all be
fresh and new, an ever-changing panoply of unforeseen
events and sensations that had been denied him until now.
New films and plays, new technological developments,
new music—Christ, how he yearned to hear a song, any
song, that he had never heard before!

The unfathomable cycle in which he and Pamela had
been caught had proved to be a form of confinement, not
release. They had let themselves be trapped in the deceptive luxury of focusing always on future options; just as
Lydia Randall, in the blind hopefulness of her youth, had
assumed life's choices would forever be available to her.
"We have so *much* time," Jeff heard her say, and then his
own repeated words to Pamela echoed anew in his brain:
"Next time . . . next time."

Now everything was different. This wasn't "next time,"
and there would be no more of that; there was only *this*
time, this sole finite time of whose direction and outcome
Jeff knew absolutely nothing. He would not waste, or take
for granted, a single moment of it.

Jeff stood up and walked out of his office into the busy newsroom. There was a large, U-shaped central desk at which Gene Collins, the midday editor, sat surrounded by computer terminals flashing the moment-by-moment output of AP, UPI, and Reuters, television monitors tuned to CNN and all three networks, a communications console linked to the station's reporters in the field and their own network's correspondents in Los Angeles, Beirut, Tokyo. . . .

Jeff felt it flow through him, the electric freshness of the once more unpredictable world out there. One of the news writers hurried past, rushing a green bulletin sheet into the air booth. Something important had happened—perhaps something disastrous, perhaps some discovery of surpassing wonder and benefit to humankind. Whatever it was, Jeff knew that it would be as new to him as it would be to everyone else.

He'd talk to Linda tonight. Though he wasn't sure what he might say, he owed her, and himself, at least that much. He wasn't sure of anything anymore, and that realization thrilled him with anticipation. He might try again with Linda, might someday rejoin Pamela, might change careers. The only thing that mattered was that the quarter century or so he had remaining would be *his* life, to live out as he chose and in his own best interests. Nothing took precedence over that: not work, not friendships, not relationships with women. Those were all components of his life, and valuable ones, but they did not define it or control it. That was up to him, and him alone.

The possibilities, Jeff knew, were endless.

≡EPILOGUE≡

PETER SKJØREN WOKE, a memory of shock and excruciating pain fresh in his mind. He had been in the Bantu Republic on business, was having lunch with a Deputy Trade Minister in Mandela City, when—when he had *died*. Keeled forward right at the table, spilling his drink on the government official's trousers—he had noticed that, was embarrassed by it, even through the crushing pressure in his chest . . . and then the red-rimmed darkness, then nothing.

Until now. Here in the shop in Karl Johansgate, back home in Oslo, where he'd first learned his mercantile skills, where he'd first found his calling in the world of commerce.

The shop that had been razed for an apartment block, twenty years ago.

Peter opened the ledger on his desk, saw the date, looked at his hands and saw young, smooth hands, no wedding band.

None of it had happened yet. Not the avalanche in Switzerland that had taken his son Edvard from him, not the nights of brooding melancholy that had driven his wife Signe into her hopeless downward spiral of alcoholism. He

312

had no son, no wife; he had only a bright new future, whose pitfalls and opportunities he knew intimately, and could avoid or seize as the occasion demanded.

Those years, those familiar and long-past years from 1988 to 2017, were his to live again, knowing the mistakes he'd made before. This time, Peter Skjøren vowed, he would do it right.

New York Times bestsellers—
Berkley Books at their best!